WHEN WE STILL LAUGHED

LAUGHED

CANADA'S HISTORY BY THOSE WHO LIVED AND DREAMT IT

ESTHER SUPERNAULT

Order this book online at **www.trafford.com**
or email orders@trafford.com

Most Trafford titles are also available at major online book retailers.

This is a fictional tale with fictional characters that may or may not exist on some other plain . . .
and so it was . . . .

Printed in the United States of America.

ISBN: 978-1-4669-0494-1 (sc)
ISBN: 978-1-4669-0493-4 (hc)
ISBN: 978-1-4669-0492-7 (e)

Library of Congress Control Number: 2011961820

Trafford rev. 10/09/2013

 www.trafford.com

North America & International
toll-free: 1 888 232 4444 (USA & Canada)
fax: 812 355 4082

OTHER BOOKS WRITTEN BY ESTHER SUPERNAULT

Blue Diamond Journey
The Healing of a Reluctant Seer

ISBN: 978-1-4269-4115-3 $17.49   Non-Fiction 2011

A descendant of Native American/Aboriginal and Celtic seers, who have visions and premonitions, Esther cautiously shares her intuitive gift, offering natural alternatives for her breast cancer without chemotherapy or radiation. She would dream, 'see' or 'hear' what foods to eat, what therapies to take or avoid, then find solid medical research to back up her spiritual messages. Discover her amazing information about the real antidotes to cancer, beyond the fear, all the way back to health.

ForeWord Clarion Book Reviews gives her book **four stars out five**, a story "relentlessly honest . . . warm, sincere and informative . . . a message of courage and hope and a welcome companion for those who have chosen an alternative path to treating their cancer."

* Now available online through local bookstores, Trafford Publishing or Amazon.com

The following two books are used as University texts in Social Work classes across Canada. Hobbema First Nations in Alberta also purchased them for their social work program. The Nishnawbe Aski Nation from Thunder Bay, Ontario, rated them as number one in all of the family violence healing texts they had researched from across Canada. American healing centres claim the lengthy bibliography and easy to read text offers assistance to students, staff and clients alike.

A Family Affair

1. **Published by: Native Counseling Services of Alberta (NCSA), Edmonton, Non-Fiction**
   ISBN: 1-895963-00-1   **Price: $15.00**

This book addresses the historical and cultural reasons for family violence in Canada's Native communities. Seven traditional Native principles about relationships are documented then tracked through drastic changes under European influence. These seven principles thus outline the solutions for healing violence in a community-based treatment program.

A Warrior's Heart (for our men)

2. **Published by: Native Counseling Services of Alberta, Edmonton, Non-Fiction**
   ISBN: 1-895963-01-X   **Price: $20.00**

<u>This book offers a personal pathway for our men and women's healing from the violence in their lives</u>. No distinction is made between victim and perpetrator. Using Native traditional ways, the book introduces the warrior within, helping people find their own answers in a good way that harms no one. Personal quotes, poems, laughing memories and heart-felt humility from people who have already completed their healing journey are added for encouragement. Using the medicine wheel of healing, a pathway of understanding is opened through teachings about spiritual, physical, emotional and intellectual development. One Aboriginal man said, "This is the first book I have read that makes sense to me."

Books Co-written or Edited by Esther Supernault

Heartbeat Angels

Published by Pauline Newman of Newman Publishing, Non-Fiction
Edited by Esther Supernault ISBN: 9688594-0-2 Price: $20.00

This collection of seventy short stories is written by people who encountered or experienced the uplifting presence of angels or spiritual messages at crucial times in their lives. These honest, heartwarming testimonials offer comfort and inspiration to all. The threads of similar incidents woven through these stories, from people who have never met, prove there is something more than their imaginations at work. Esther included her own story called, "Voices".

Many Faces—One Heart

**Published by: Stony Plain Heritage Agricultural Society,
©1997—Non-Fiction**
Edited and partially written by Esther Supernault Price: $10.00

Esther wrote seven of the seventeen well researched, hilarious and tragic stories tracking the early history of Stony Plain's pioneers plus the Cree and Stony (Sioux) First Nations. The visionary heritage of the now world famous Lac Ste Anne Pilgrimage is also included. Another story describes Esther's fiery Ojibwa/Anishnabeg family who helped build the early railroad through Stony Plain.

**All of the above books will be available from Esther Supernault's
website in 2012 or through her e-mail: <u>kesther@xplornet.ca</u>**

Multiple orders receive discounts.

Acknowledgements

Many thanks to: my late Grandpa Charlie Sewell for the inspiration; my late parents Evelyn and George Sewell, for giving me the faith I could accomplish anything I set my mind to; my husband Cliff, for always believing in me; my children Jay and Lara, for keeping me honest and broad-minded; my granddaughters, Fawn and Kistin, for teaching the true meaning of unconditional love; my grandsons Coner, Spencer and Sam for enriching my life with love and laughter; and to my writing mentor, the late Al Vanberg, for showing me truth beyond the fear. Most of all, I thank Creator for the gift of writing.

CONTENTS

Introduction

A Seer's Way to Tell a Tale

My inspiration for this book started from a dream about my Irish grandfather, a seventh son of a seventh son. I too am the seventh child in my family (if you include one miscarriage before my birth). In Celtic belief, this magical birth position offers unlimited spiritual knowledge and visions. Though he had passed away thirty years earlier, my grandfather visited me in this dream, for the first time ever. He handed me what looked like a cartoon section of a newspaper, a storyline in squares of coloured scenes marching across the page. He showed me if I rubbed each square with my fingertips, the characters started to move and I could actually hear Mac and Broken Arrow talking. What I remembered most was their laughter. Pieces of fur, feathers, dirt and leaves flew off the page whenever they argued about man's greed and its consequences for the land.

I would spend the next ten years in research (while I wrote other books) filling in my questions about what Canada's Aboriginal people and pioneers actually wore, ate, the medicines they used, how they made a living, survived the harsh climate, why they fought and most of all, what they laughed about. Nothing defines the strength and depth of people like their humour—something sadly missing from our dour history books.

Often I would sit in my favourite reclining chair, cover myself with a warm Native blanket and just hang out with these two men around their campfire. I didn't participate, just observed. The chapters unfolded one by one. Broken Arrow came in a later dream, telling me his background, his relationship with Melissande, how he got his name and how he met Mac. Though he spoke with a heavy Cree accent I could never duplicate, he told me not to portray him so, especially in *my* world of political correctness. Instead, I gave Mac the accent, utilizing my Irish father's words, music, actions and personality quirks. Dad never backed from a fight either. Mitsue and Moya, my cherished 'M & M's are a mix of the many wonderful Cree and Ojibwa ladies I have sat and drank tea with. We would share stories, tease one another and laugh like dogs. When they show up in the story, brace yourself!

When I 'saw' Alorah picking flowers on the hillside, I got up from my chair and walked away. I was *not* writing a romance tale! Still, every morning, there she was . . . waiting. Finally I gave in and what unfolded offered startling new insights into both men.

The Wolf and Mud Woman dreams were mine. Other stories I gathered as the daughter of pioneers in northern British Columbia and the wife of a Cree Metis raised in Northern Alberta. I grew up in a world of trappers and hunters; log cabins and wood stoves; racing our horses bareback; horse-drawn plows and wagons and strong, eccentric people with wild, funny tales of life in the bush of Northern Canada. My father-in-law survived the actual bear fight without a limp, much to the awe of his doctors when they saw the damage to his leg. My son and I lived through a tornado in Saskatchewan where the house we were in took a direct hit. Those reversed waterfalls and spinning water ropes were real! Tall Man's mischievous tale came from my husband's Cree/French Grandfather who stood 6'6".

A Seer(ess) is a visionary, someone who foresees or foretells future events; a person who 'sees' and observes; a person endowed with profound moral and spiritual insights or knowledge; a wise person or sage with intuitive powers. In my case, the messages come in my dreams and lately in daytime visions that I am compelled to write about and share. My work is to portray them as honestly as I can, blocking my ego from adding its not so lovely two cents worth.

This book's powerful ending took me years to write. Mud Woman's wisdom raged in my dreams, unforgettably powerful because I am Celtic and Ojibwa or Salteaux:

> "**This is not a time to sit back on your haunches and contemplate your hands! Your people have entered a period of great stress and it cannot be taken lightly as something that will pass into oblivion. This is your heritage! This is your soul journey to find your own answers. You have been chosen for your wisdom and the ancient heritage you carry in the memories passed down to you from your ancestors and the thunderbirds. Do not think it will pass lightly onto someone else's shoulders! This is what comes from drinking freely of the waters of history. You become charged with the responsibility of owning the task yet to come. You have not been forsaken, you have been foretold. This is part of your heritage and when the time comes, you will know how to end it. Remember, you have not been forsaken. We are with you. You will see the way soon enough.**"

I had to develop my own spirituality and find my own crystal soul before I could wrap my story around the story's final haunting image from my grandfather. This book represents the very best of me, my Ojibwa/Celtic heritage and my faith in God, the Creator. **It is my prayer for society.**

1.

THE BLOW-IN

Early spring, 1863

Northwest Territories in what would one day become the Province of Manitoba, Canada,

Mac couldn't believe his horse had been stolen—neither could his feet. Not here, not on this endless parched prairie, miles from the backside of nowhere, with nothing but his gun and his hat between the blistering hell surrounding him. He surveyed his badly wrinkled white shirt, hitched up his corduroy trousers and sighed over the tattered remnants of his bluchers. Back east, these half-boots were bang-up to the nines. Heavier and shorter than Wellingtons with an open front tied over a tongue, their higher heels were top-notch for riding but nay so good for wading prairie creeks and swamps. The leather had dried, cracked and kindled. In disgust, he kicked a boot off, yanked at his sock then sucked air through his teeth when skin ripped away too. With a weary sigh he surveyed the blisters rimming his foot, like warts on a toad's back. Standing on one aching foot, he yearned for the promising shade offered by distant trees. Should he turn around and just go home?

He shifted his saddlebags to his other sore shoulder. At least the thieving badach had left him clothes and food, heavy though they were. Squinting into the burning sun, he swore. For all the good it did. Twas was hotter than the devil's breath and twice as dry. If not for the hum of grasshoppers, the silence would have deafened him. Last year's grass, grey and withered, fanned away from his feet, mangled into tortured clumps by the endless winds and long gone snow. Inquisitive tiny shoots peeked between the dead strands of their ancestors. Through the shimmering haze, he glimpsed a distant mirage of 'water' floating upon the scorching land. A few scraggly poplars and willows pierced the silvery mist, outlining the sluggish Assiniboine River meandering away from him towards purple hills on the horizon. His back slumped in exhaustion.

A horse snorted in his ear.

Mac spun so fast his neck cricked. He slammed into a black and white spotted horse, bounced off and hopped backwards struggling to regain his balance on one leg. In desperation, he dropped his bare foot—right onto prickly-pear cactus. Howling in agony, he grabbed his abused foot and hopped about like a *daft culchie* (crazy country boy) on a pogo stick.

On the paint's back rode an Indian wearing only a breechcloth and a choker necklace, his long hair tied down with a white cloth around his forehead. His stillness made him part of the silent, broiling land. Only his hair lifted in the wind. He wore no paint – a good sign Mac decided, especially when the man reached neither for the brass studded gun in a sheath at his knee nor the knife strapped to his waist. A quiver of arrows and a red willow bow backed his right shoulder; a beaded fire bag rode his hip. His face held no expression whatsoever. Only his dark eyes burned, hot as the winds that wrapped him.

The man stared down at Mac, his high wide cheekbones, smoothly rounded features and straight nose marked him Cree, like so many others Mac had seen back east in Fort Garry. The man's nostril's flared suddenly. His face never changed but now a bright spark lit those tilted black eyes. If Mac didn't know better, he'd swear the man was laughing at him. Well here he was weavin' and stumblin' about like a *sally* (willow) tree in the wind.

Mac hopped back to his empty boot and casually stuck his bare foot on top, ignoring the cactus biting deeper. Call it stubborn, call it embarrassment but Mac found himself setting aside his university cant and hauling out his roughest brogue. "Top o' the mornin' to ye sar!" He swept his black hat off with an elegant bow and then squinted sideways at the man's face. A sudden intake of air above him made him think his ploy worked. Few people had seen the likes of the fiery flames in John MacArthay's Irish red curls, probably fewer Indians in this West Country. But confusion rode him hard as he watched fury quickly masked to bleak darkness in the man's eyes.

Silence drifted between the two. Wary eyes met and held, measured and challenged. Just when Mac found it unbearable and opened his mouth to speak, the man swung a leg over his horse's neck and dropped lightly to the ground, towering a good five inches above Mac's sturdy five foot ten. The Cree Indians were usually taller and bigger boned than the bandy-legged Europeans but this one was exceptionally so. Mac guessed him close to his own age, somewhere in his mid-twenties. He stuck out his hand. After a brief hesitation the man accepted with a cool grip. Mac shook it while the stranger merely held it as he studied Mac's green eyes.

"John MacArthay or Mac for short. In Gaelic '*Mac*' means son." He found himself babbling foolishly to fill the awkward silence. "So I'm really the son of Arthay or Arthur, one of me Irish great-great grandfathers."

"Broken Arrow." The big man continued to search Mac's face relentlessly, his eyes narrowed and angry again. Despite his coppery skin, his face seemed to pale suddenly. And still his gaze burned, like the sun overhead.

What did the man search for? Mac felt like he'd been scratched, scraped and rendered up with all his foibles and sins in that long, piercing examination. "Hell, ye want me ancestral lineage trotted out too, like a regular Blow-in?" he growled defensively.

"Blow-in?"

"Aye, tis what we call any man in Ireland who can no' trace his ancestors back at least two hundred years on Irish soil."

The man's face never changed, but his eyes definitely sparked this time, "Then most white men are blow-ins to this land."

Mac sighed and brushed dust from his coat, "Aye. We all be blow-ins in this fair land. But isn't it the devil's own luck you'd be findin' me here." He detected very little accent in the Cree's words and wondered where he learned such good English.

"Why would I look for you?"

Something in the man's incredible stillness bothered Mac. Had the Indian followed him? He chose to prattle on, "I'm headin' west to Fort Edmonton. I hired an Assiniboine scout in Portage La Prairie but he stole me horse three days ago, leavin' me high and dry. I figured walking forward might be closer to someone than walking back. I hoped to meet some of the Metis Cart brigades along this Carleton Trail." He indicated the heavy lines of cart tracks, sixteen ruts wide, that he followed across the prairie.

The man looked about, "The *Assinipwotak* live south of here. He probably went to visit his family."

"The Assini—what??

"*Assini-pwo-tak*", he drew it out slowly, "our Cree word for 'Stone People'. They add red hot stones to their hide pots to boil the water and cook their food. The French call them Assiniboine but they call themselves Sioux."

"D'ye think he'll come back?"

The Indian studied the prairie around them but remained silent, his face partially hidden by thick flowing hair. Two large eagle feathers, tied in a topknot at the back of his head, swung gently in the wind.

"Aye," Mac sighed replacing his hat, "Probably not. I truly wanted to see this land. I thought I covered all possible emergencies but never did I consider losing old Jim. Best hoss I ever owned. We've been through a lot, him and me." He searched the flat horizon, wondering where the Sam Hill the man had come from, and why he never saw or heard him coming. Mac ducked his head. "I miss the ole sawbones."

When the silent Indian continued staring into wavering heat waves, Mac went on, "Tis strange how I felt I had to come out West. I had to see this land. Maybe because I'm the seventh son of a seventh son . . . I don't know . . . but I'm here and I'll not be turning back." His vehemence surprised him but he felt its truth echo through him. He recalled his mother's tears when he'd announced his decision to go west. After finishing University, restlessness dug at him. When he packed his gear, she'd slammed lids on her wood stove, muttered about losing her baby forever then wept into her tea towels when he refused to reconsider.

But his father understood. The night before Mac left, he'd clapped his son on the shoulder and sighed, "Do what ye must son. Then come back to us if ye can. There are reasons ye be knowing things ye don't understand. Mayhap yer answers lie in the west winds. Aye and ye'll no' settle 'til ye find 'em."

Why Mac felt compelled to explain this now, he had no idea. "Ye see, in our Celtic ways, the seventh son of a seventh son has the ability to see and know things, without knowing why. Mayhap tis a tradition from our learned ones and priests, the druids, forgotten in our history now. My grandparents were descendants of the druids. I even have an aunt called Dryadia, which means 'Druidess'."

After another wearing silence, the Indian dug in the beaded bag at his side and pulled out a small smoked hide drawstring pouch. He opened it and offered it to Mac who rummaged with a curious finger, hauling out a chunk of sweet smelling salve.

The Cree explained, "It is made from the sticky red buds of black poplar. Rub it on your blisters." A tiny smile worked its way across his mouth, "and the cactus holes."

Mac leaned a hand against the horse's shoulder and ground his teeth as he plucked several cactus spines from his arch, "Jaysus! Nobody told me about the cactus, sagebrush and sand out here. Even the wily grass has barbs. Back east all I heard was how this land be like "the Glory Hills of Connemara in Ireland," he mimicked the eastern newspaper with heavy Irish scorn. "Oh aye, 'a treeless landscape of lakes, waterfalls and crystal creeks flowing through rocks and golden turfs trimmed with flowers'." He snorted as he rubbed the salve on his feet, "No' that I've seen Ireland. I was born in Griffintown, Lower Canada, but tis what me Da remembers. Here, the land is grey and green, already dry and burning from the sun. And the creeks are far and away from anything, with nary a waterfall in sight on this flat land." Bending to pull his sock on, he groaned.

An aromatic whiff of smoke drifted from a pair of moccasins thrust under Mac's nose. "These won't rub your feet. They're buffalo hide." In comparison to the plain, scuffed ones the Indian wore, these were new, decorated across the top in colourful beads and porcupine quills.

"Thank you." Mac accepted them gratefully, wishing he'd thought to bring an extra set of boots. But really, how much could one carry in a saddlebag? He slid his abused foot into the roomy moccasin lined with shaggy buffalo hair and sighed in relief. It was too long but it would stay on. He tugged his other boot off but when he bent to toss them away, the Indian stilled his arm, damned easily too.

"Save the leather. We may need it."

'We?' Sure'n Mac was tired of his own company so he simply tied his laces together and slung them over a shoulder.

In one motion, the Cree swung a leg over his horse and landed firmly on its back, his long breechcloth flying out to display a flash of much whiter butt. Mac noted the warrior wore a snug leather undergarment beneath his breechclout, no' like the brawny Scots and Irish in their swinging kilts.

Broken Arrow straightened and pointed behind him with his chin, "We'll ride to my camp over there. He dipped his head to his paint horse, "Blackfoot can carry us both." He lifted Mac's saddle to his thigh, "Jump on behind."

Mac leapt upwards and swung a leg to mimic the man's spring and damn near castrated himself on the horse's rump. He slid off while several blisters happily squished in unison as he landed. "Jaysus, Mary and Joseph! I'm near tuh loosin' muh whole family tree." Bent double in agony, he hobbled knock-kneed in a circle back to the horse's side. He warily accepted the Indian's out thrust foot hooked upward as a makeshift stirrup. Mac clasped the man's hand, ignoring his flashing grin as he hauled him up behind him.

Once aboard, Mac retrieved his saddle then realized he had nothing to hang onto, his free hand hastily backing away from the man's lean naked waist. Cautiously he dropped his hand upon his own thigh, adjusting his body to the horse's movements.

They trotted over a knoll and down into a small dip. Broken Arrow pointed out a large circle where the ground lay bare, beaten and exposed, all plant life dug out. "Buffalo rolled here. The dirt protects them from mosquito, bull fly and sand fly bites."

"Too bad we can't do the same." Mac groused swatting lazy flies around them.

What looked like flat prairie, Mac realized, actually hid a series of small dips filled with sloughs and short bushes. At least the Cree hadn't come out of thin air. He'd probably followed these low areas for some time. Wisps of his long hair occasionally stung Mac's face. But it wasn't unpleasant. The man had no smell, none what so ever, other than wind and prairie. Mac, on the other hand, stank of damp wool, swamp and sweat.

His embarrassment, close-up to a stranger, made him chatty. He eyed the strip of leather tucked into the man's belt, "So ye find the breechcloth comfortable?"

The man glanced over his shoulder, "You want one?"

"Nay," Mac hastily declined, "I prefar to protect me ballocks a wee bit more."

"You think some cloth would protect you from my knife, White Man?"

Mac glanced down at the wicked looking blade strapped to the man's waist.

"Nay, but my tongue might."

The Indian froze then spun sideways with a fierce frown to look him up and down.

Mac's face heated up, "Nay! I mean . . . Jaysus Mon! Don't be takin' me for one of those backstreet Nancy boys! I just meant me mouth often gets me out of more situations than me fists . . . talkin' that is . . . no' that I don't prefar me fists sometimes." His brogue deepened with his embarrassment.

The Cree's intent gaze moved away. "In our clan, these people are honoured. We call them 'two-spirited', because they live in two worlds, seeing and living life from both the male and female sides. They use their gift to find good names for our babies."

Mac watched the Indian's eyes slide to the bump on his nose, a reminder of the days before he'd learned the greater subtlety of pugilism. "Your nose is turning pink." The Indian relaxed enough to twist forward again, the plume of eagle feathers swinging in his hair.

"Oh aye," Mac sighed, relaxing too. "'Tis the curse of the Celts. We like tae burn our faces in summer and freeze our arses in winter. No' like you, who revel in the rays." The Indian's skin was so brown it looked blue in the shade of Mac's shoulders.

The man's answer drifted back over a golden shoulder, "If those spots on your nose all burned together, your skin would look like mine."

"Never insult an Irishman's freckles, why tis said they're made from the very kisses of the fairies themselves." Mac was enjoying himself, his aching feet easing with the ride.

"My paint has prettier spots; he didn't need your fairies."

Mac grinned in delight at the stranger's back. Now humour he understood.

"Ah ye strike to the very soul of an Irishman when ye insult our fairies, the little people who flit about our emerald Ireland, bringing gold or mischief to the unwary or foolish."

Mac zeroed in on the man's short bow inside the quiver of arrows hanging from his right shoulder. Mac guessed the Cree could easily clear both bow and arrow with one swift grab. They sparked a memory from Mac's classical literature classes. "Ye know the ancient Greeks saw three arrows tied together as a sign of male virility. They represented male bonding for hunting or fighting."

"Virility?"

Mac's smile deepened. "Aye, ye know the male power we pack between our legs."

The man turned sideways once again, one side of his mouth lifting, "You speak of our *mitakisiy*."

Mac strove to look wise, "Ah, that be your name for it. In ours, we liken it to the cock, the rooster."

"A chicken?" The question held deepening scorn.

"Well, the Romans often carried totems of a rooster with its beak shaped like a . . . mitakisiy or pizzle." Mac cleared his throat sternly, striving for intellectual freedom. "In our Gaelic language, tis called a *bod*. So when the ladies are after our bod, they are no' talkin' about our bodies!" His sun-burnt cheeks reddened but he persevered—in the name of wisdom. "The Romans carved them with wings or legs of a cock." He leaned closer, lowering his voice, "They say that hidden deep within the Vatican, the holiest place of the Roman Catholic Church, is a bronze sculpture. Tis a rooster's head with a beak of a giant *bod* attached to the shoulders of a man. At its base are some words written in Latin." He paused dramatically.

Finally the Indian asked, "What words?"

"Saviour of the World!"

*   *   *

The next morning, pounding hooves woke Mac from a deep sleep. He opened his eyes and rolled with a bellow towards the campfire. Racing horses missed him by inches. He leapt to his feet in fury, only to recognize Broken Arrow on the back of the farthest horse and leading a tall grey horse.

Mac rubbed sleep from his eyes as the Indian held the new horse's reins out to him, "We ride now."

Mac cautiously took the braided lines wrapping the grey horse's muzzle, "What is this?"

"Shaganappi, raw buffalo hide with the hair removed. Our women work it until it is soft but strong."

Broken Arrow subdued his labouring horse, its lathered legs dancing sideways and back, still wanting to run.

"Where did you get such a fine beastie so quickly?" Mac patted the tall grey horse's sweaty neck as it lowered its magnificent head and whickered softly. A beautifully beaded fringe crossed the brow band of its bridle. Mac slid a curious hand down a well muscled foreleg. "This one has Irish bloodlines, I can tell by his long legs and deep chest—certainly no simple prairie mustang!" He dug in his pocket, "How much do I owe ye for him?"

"He is yours. I took him from some sleepy Sioux warriors this morning." The tall Indian held his pony with one hand, tugging casually at his leggings. They, along with his moccasins were covered in dew, mud and fresh grass stains.

"Took?" Mac stared stupidly, his brain still fogged with sleep, "You stole him? Jaysus! And from Sioux warriors! D'ye be havin' a death wish Mon?"

Broken Arrow glanced over his shoulder to the prairie, his eyes bright sparks of laughter as he reined in his dancing horse. He bent and jerked the reins of his packhorse free from the small tree it had been tied to. Mac noted the brown paint was fully loaded, its pack tied down and ready for travel. "We have about two hours of running on them before they find the rest of their horses."

Cursing silently, Mac rolled up his bedroll and yanked it together with a fast knot. He scrambled around for his cup, plate, tea kettle and wooden handled cutlery, jangling them into his packsack willy nilly. When he slammed his saddle over the big grey, it snorted and rolled its eyes to the white but stood sound, flanks quivering. Mac quickly cinched the saddle, tied on his gear and leapt aboard.

"Sure'n guess who'll be coyote bait if they find us!" Mac glared at his companion. "Or, watch me swing for horse stealin' if word gets to the forts!" He shook his head. "How could ye do this? Stealin' yet!" He lifted a palm in helpless frustration even as he kicked his horse into motion.

Broken Arrow grinned openly, his horses easily keeping pace, "They can always try to steal him back."

In spite of himself, Mac guffawed, "Let's ride Hoss Thief!" They galloped across the open land; prairie chickens' exploding from the tall buffalo grass beneath their horses' racing hooves.

2.

SILENCE

Broken Arrow rode quietly, irritated beyond measure. He listened to Mac drone on and on—about the weather of all things—a humming bee that never stopped. The man arose in the morning and talked. He spent all day talking. When he rolled into his bed at night, he was still talking: talk, talk, talk, talk. And when he wasn't talking, he sang or whistled. Did he ever listen to the voice inside? How could he hear it with all the noise? Did the man ever stop and just think?

Broken Arrow wasn't used to this. Did Mac fear silence? What did he think would happen if he stopped talking? He should have left the noisy *Moniyaw*, (White Man) on the prairie with his blisters. Thank Creator there were no Sioux nearby or they would have attacked long ago just to stop all the noise. The tall Indian drew a deep breathe and released it slowly. He longed for silence.

What forced these white men to constantly speak? Broken Arrow often sat amongst them amazed at their rudeness to one another. He grew up with people who spoke softly, politely waiting for a speaker to finish. They listened carefully and spent time in silence, thinking deeply about the speaker's words and ideas. These white men yelled in ordinary conversation. The more excited they became, the louder their voices grew, grating and hard, worse than an angry magpie. Yet they weren't angry; the opposite most times. Sometimes they all spoke at the same time and nobody listened. Sometimes they joined conversations around them, rudely jumping in without permission or forethought. It made Broken Arrow feel off-balance and tongue-tied. Then they stared at him waiting for his reply. Before he could gather his thoughts to respond, they'd be off on another story or idea. They seemed to speak without thinking, to rush into words immediately. Only their words seemed important without any wisdom behind them.

He wasn't used to this, couldn't understand the need for haste. These white men were always in a rush, in constant motion. They barely listened to the speaker at all. They were too busy preparing their answer, speaking as soon as the other stopped.

Sometimes he would get up and leave, frustrated beyond belief, isolated and alone. If he stayed and tried to join in, he found his anger rising when others interrupted him, eager to push their ideas forward before he had finished his. If he paused at all, they took it as a signal to express their opinions and arguments. It made him so angry, he wanted to knock heads together, take his knife and cut a few throats, just to find some silence. They were like yapping puppies, nipping at his heels. He had no way to defend himself beyond kicking them away and his self-discipline would never allow that.

He snorted to himself, remembering a time his grandfather, Tall Man, found him kicking the leg of a yapping puppy, a gift from his grandmother, Mitsue. For his cruelty, Broken Arrow was ordered to carry the puppy all day around the village, never allowing its injured leg to bear weight. He had to feed and water the puppy, before he could eat or drink. He even held the little dog while it relieved itself. Throughout the long day, his arms grew weary and his back ached, for the puppy was half-grown and heavy. It humbled him in front of everyone who knew he carried the dog for a lesson. Before the day was out, the frustrated whelp had bitten him several times for his confinement. Broken Arrow discovered many ways to make peace with the young dog so it agreed to being carried. By that evening, Broken Arrow wearily sought his bed, his back muscles cramping, his arms and cheeks smarting from the many scratches and nips. He had learned a new respect for the puppy's strength to carry himself, to live his life as he chose, unhampered and free.

The next morning Tall Man quietly reminded him, "It is important to remember our lives depend on how we treat our fellow creatures. Animals like your dog will help and protect you when you are alone. Your dog could save your life one day. He deserves your respect and kindness in return." Broken Arrow had hung his head in shame, silently vowing to never harm another living creature, unless he meant to eat it.

What made the *Nehiyawewin* (Cree people) so different from the White Man? He remembered Tall Man sitting down, smoking his pipe and staring into the fire, unmoving, unspeaking for hours. Nobody bothered him; nobody spoke to him or interrupted him in any way. Sometimes, as a child, Broken Arrow would sit by him, also in silence, waiting for his grandfather to stir and speak first. Elders always spoke first, that was The Way. Giving your silence to an elder was a sign of respect for the teacher before you.

He remembered a lesson Moya, a friend of his Grandmother Mitsue, had taught him about being a warrior. "Silence," she swung her arm across the prairie where the two sat alone, some distance from camp, "is what this land represents, our greatest lesson from it. When we walk into the silence, spend time in it, we hear the wisdom in the wind, learn the endurance of the Stone People, the rocks and feel the timeless cycles of the Standing People, the trees. We understand self-control from the rivers who find their own path, adjusting to new curves but still moving in the same direction, year after year. Find your path and follow it, never turning away. When you can walk through the storms of your life, calm and unshakable, you are walking the good Red Path of our people. And you will walk it in silence. Silence is the perfect balance of body, mind, heart and spirit. The longer you can hold that balance, the more peace you will find in your spirit."

Mac turned to him, "Are you listening? Have you heard a word I said?"

"No."

"Well and now." Nonplussed, Mac looked away then back, his eyes narrowing, fed up with this taciturn Indian. "And why not?"

"I was thinking."

"And?" It carried surly weight.

"I'm not finished."

Mac threw his arms in the air, making his horse snort and dance sideways, "Faith and Begorra! That's all ye do is think! Think! Think! Why don't ye say something? Talk to me! Tell me some of yer thoughts. Tis very hard travelling with a Stoic." Mac had had enough. Maybe if they talked this thing through he could get beyond the irritation he felt for this mute Indian. The burden of constantly carrying the conversation had become very heavy.

"Stoic?" Broken Arrow had never heard the word before.

"Aye, tis a philosophy, a way of thinking for a group of people who lived over two thousand years ago. They followed a Greek leader called Zeno. He believed virtue is the highest good: being kind, just and pure of heart. Man should be free from passion and unmoved by life's happenings, expressing neither joy nor grief. Whatever happened in his life, he was to remain calm, stern, unexcited, cool, controlling all emotion, ignoring pleasure or pain."

Broken Arrow nodded; pleased that some white men had ideas like his people.

Mac turned on his friend, "And you! Tis very hard to know what you're thinking or feeling, if anything. You sit there, like a bump on a log, with no expression on your face. I look at you and I wonder if you're in there or off dreamin' about some other land. They say eyes are mirrors to the soul but yours hold their secrets well—probably because ye never look at me anyway. I tell ye, tis like talking to a damned wall!"

Broken Arrow stared at him in amazement. This is how the white man saw him? An unfeeling, unthinking wall? He seethed with feelings! They boiled through him in never ending waves of patterns and thoughts. Some were deadly enough to kill. Yet they were his, not to be thrown at other people on a whim, without thought. It might interfere with their life. It was The Way—being careful, cautious, polite around others, lest one offend. That was proper behaviour. Besides, it was rude to stare into people's eyes, peeking into their soul. Some took it as a direct challenge. By watching other people's movements, he understood exactly what they thought and felt anyway. Words weren't necessary to understand them. Everyone knew that. Except this noisy White Man. He wanted words! Did he not trust his eyes? Was he blind to what his heart told him? Could only words make him believe? *Mah!* No wonder they were so loud, these talkative, white men.

Did Mac think so little of him because he saw only a wall of nothing? The Cree felt offended, cornered and uncertain how to defend himself on a front he had never encountered before. So he attacked.

"Why must you talk all the time? Most of your talk this morning could have been said in a few moments if you had thought it through first. You waste words and say nothing!"

"Nothing! 'Tis important to carry the conversation. You, on the other hand, never say anything!" Mac yanked his horse to a standstill, glaring at the bull-headed Indian," I'm forced to do all the talkin'. 'Tis very wearing."

"Then be silent."

"Sure'n look like an *idjit culchie*, the country fool stuck for an answer, too stupid to carry on a normal conversation!" He kicked his horse in his ribs, riding ahead of Broken Arrow.

Broken Arrow followed more slowly, allowing his horse to meander like his thoughts. He was disgusted with this rude, pushy White Man who never listened because he was too busy thinking of a reply before he, Broken Arrow had finished explaining.

Mac turned on him, his face reddening. "See! Ye're doing it again! Ye never answer! How am I to know what ye're thinkin' if ye never reply?"

"I'm thinking about an answer."

Mac threw his hands up in despair. "Why can you no' think and talk at the same time? At least it keeps the flow going in a normal way."

"Flow? You think of talking as a flow? Like a river? For every word or speech from one, the other must respond, then the other?" Broken Arrow struggled with this, knowing it was somehow important, but not sure how to fit it into The Way he knew. He thought of his many conversations with Tall Man. He would listen carefully to Tall Man's words. Then he'd think about his answer before he spoke, so he didn't look like a fool. Yet this Irish Man claimed to *not* speak was to look the fool! Did other white men see him the same way? Had they judged his silence as stupidity? Simply because he paused before responding? He shook his head in confusion. To speak without thinking was to surely look a fool!! He opened his mouth, speaking slowly, struggling to find his way through his words, "Then it is important to speak or look foolish?"

"Aye, only the daftest canno' speak and think at the same time."

"Why the haste? Why must you hurry into each conversation? Why not take time to think it through, and then reply with some wisdom behind your words? Why waste another's time with silly words?" The Cree was amazed at the need to rush into words without thought.

Mac scratched his head now, "Is that what you do? You think it through in silence, so you don't look the fool when you speak?"

Broken Arrow nodded slowly, watching Mac's stillness, the sincerity in his eyes and his small frown of deep thought. The White Man truly did not understand. He realized he could read Mac's motions and facial expressions much easier than Mac could his. The *Nehiyawewin* practiced a calm face to retain their privacy in a community of close living. They guarded their thoughts and actions in the same manner, ever aware of how others read them constantly. White men, however, seemed too busy talking to see the unspoken language of the body. Not all answers from the soul came through the eyes or words.

Mac held up a palm, struggling through this new way of communicating. "Then what about the long silences? I grew up believing it impolite to have long stretches of silence in a conversation. People grow uncomfortable in long gaps with no words. They feel awkward, thinking the silence is an unspoken message to leave. They no longer feel welcome when nobody talks to them."

This time Broken Arrow frowned. "Silence to the White Man means he is unwelcome? That the conversation is over? *Mah!*" His mouth fell open in wonder, "No wonder you get angry with me! To my people, silence means we are pausing to think for a while. To sit and smoke in silence together is a sign of deep friendship. We show our respect by politely waiting until the other person feels like saying something. If he chooses not to speak that too is acceptable. Often Tall Man and his friends will sit in a circle for hours and nobody talks. They find comfort in each other's presence, sharing the silence. To speak is to . . . interfere with the peace from Mother Earth."

Mac grinned in delight then shook his head, "I understand what ye're saying. But I can no' see my family comfortable with that much silence. They'd have to fill it with words or music or insult their company. My relatives would leave in a huff if nobody talked to them for any length of time. The grossest insult is to *not* speak to your visitors. It means judgement; dislike . . . even anger or disgust. A wife's way to show displeasure with her husband is to refuse to talk to him. We call it the 'Cold Shoulder' or 'Silent Treatment'."

Broken Arrow chuckled, "Not in our camps. Our men appreciate their silence too much. If a women grew angry with her partner, she might stitch his clothes shut or throw a bitter herb in his soup to make him use the bushes often. If she was really angry, she could add a root to make him roll on the ground in agony."

Mac chuckled, easing back into his saddle, comforted by this new way of looking at conversation. "Aye, back home they say 'hell hath no fury like a women scorned'. Some things stay the same in any culture."

Broken Arrow joined his laughter and the two rode on . . . in peaceful silence.

3.

TALES

The old men gathered for their early morning plunge into the river. They honored the connection between their spirit and body so they bathed every day. Cleansing one cleansed the other. They taught their children the same. "You want to be a respected person, you must learn this. If you want to be strong, face the cold waters. Scrub your body clean—every day." Boys were taught to get up early, before any female in the family. Male children must be good hunters, good fisherman and good providers. "Follow nature," the elders advised. "Get up and watch the birds sing before daylight. This is a new dawn of your life. Honour it awakened and refreshed."

After their bath, the old men sat about playing their favourite game of tall tales, a wicked mix of creative truth stretched long and lean. It tested their will power because if they laughed, they paid a forfeit to the storyteller.

Tall Man sat under the quiet sky with the early morning sun heating his back. His face was a leaner, more rugged version of his grandson's, Broken Arrow. Dark skin over high cheekbones, a thin nose and full lips created a face carved into ancient lines of thought and life. Like his old companions, Tall Man's arms and legs bore the scars of many encounters with the enemy, evidence of his devotion to his tribe and its safety. Now it was his turn to rest and be protected by the younger warriors.

Radiating folds deepened the shadows around his amused jet black eyes, hiding them from his old friends. They knew him too well. He leaned forward, picked up a flaming sliver of wood, lit his pipe, tossed the wood into the flames and puffed quietly as he studied the area around him. Tall spruce trees surrounded the meadow the band camped in. Soon they would pack up their tipis and move out of the sheltering parkland of their winter homes and back onto the prairies to hunt buffalo for the summer.

For now, silence filled the area. A good peacefulness, the old chief thought. Made a man comfortable, able to think his thoughts without interruption. Why speak? Who could improve on silence? Beside him, his old friend, Pipestem, wriggled back on his haunches, peering at Tall Man to see if he had something to say.

Kamistatim, another scarred old warrior who refused to bend to age bestirred himself, projecting his quiet voice into the air. In a language over thirty thousand years old, his eloquent, descriptive words flowed like an endless array of images through his listeners' minds.

"This dog wandered into our camp during the season of Blueberries and the Flying Moon, when ducks and geese teach their babies how to fly. The dog was a ragged looking thing, not very big; of no particular colour, a little gold of the coyote, maybe some grey of a wolf and the brown of a camp dog. But she wanted to live with me. I was only seven summers, not too smart. But she must have known a good man when she saw one."

Several eyes glittered at his sly bragging, but nobody smiled.

"So I shared my deer bones with her and she slept beside me every night. Never let anyone near me unless I told her it was alright. She really liked the water. Cold or warm weather, she would swim out and bring back anything I hit with my arrows: beaver, muskrat, duck or big goose. So I called her Water Dog. Nothing stopped her. If the bird fought her, she'd wrestle it until it gave up or died. Then she'd carry it to shore and drop it at my feet. Never once did she take a bite for herself. She'd just sit and watch me with her shining brown eyes. Wishing. Women do that around me a lot."

Pipestem's head jerked but he continued cooling himself with a fan made from hawk wing feathers wrapped in birch bark that had been soaked, wrapped around the wing and allowed to dry permanently to the shape of the wing.

"One day, I went hunting ducks. I came to this small creek with several deep ponds where it turned under the willows. A family of ducks swam across from me in and out of the shade. Nice big mallards, their green feathers catching flickers of sunlight. They floated easily, fattened up for the flight south. Most of them had their heads under the water, straining bugs through their bills. Only one big male kept watch. Water Dog and I slowly crawled up on them. We'd wait for that male duck to look the other way then we'd move. Soon as the duck looked back we froze. Water Dog could stop in any position, one foot in the air and her tongue half out; wouldn't blink an eye until the duck looked away.

"Finally I got close enough for a good shot. I notched my arrow, waiting until they lined up in a row. Then I shot. My arrow sank through three of them. The ducks flapped and kicked but the shaft held."

Pipestem smoked on, his eyelids drooping in the warm sunshine. Kamistatim cleared his throat loudly to wake him. Pipestem lazily opened one eye then pretended to doze on.

Kamistatim closed a wizened eye against his smoking pipe. "I sent Water Dog to get them. When she got close, she dove then surfaced right under them, grabbing the arrow shaft between the ducks. She scared them so badly they flapped hard; lifting right off the water. Her weight pulled them down but those ducks were scared and they fought back. Water Dog hung on, whining and twisting her body until she had them pointed towards me. Then she tucked her legs in and let them fly.

"There they were!" Kamistatim swung a stringy arm up over his forehead, "Coming right for me! I was so surprised I fell over backwards. Poor old Water Dog, she wouldn't let go. As she flew over my head, she looked down at me with her big sad eyes and moaned."

Kamistatim rubbed his face, eyes glittering. "Those wishing eyes. Never will I forget her big brown eyes, begging me like women still do. It makes me so weak I have to give in and let them have their way with me."

Several of his companions blinked slowly, the lines in their faces unmoving.

"I could have let the ducks fly away but her eyes . . . ." He shook his head, his narrow shoulders slumping in defeat. "I think this is when my woman problems all started. I was just too weak. I had to save Water Dog. So I ran after them, climbed a stump and jumped as high as I could. I managed to grab the arrow.

"Now the ducks were really scared and they flew away with me too!"

Greying heads leaned around the circle to look at the storyteller, who continued. "I didn't know what to do. Then I started plucking feathers and we dropped a little. I pulled out some wing feathers and we dropped some more. Next thing I knew we landed in camp. But the ducks still drug us around, beating our faces with their wings but neither Water Dog nor I would let go.

My mother chased us yelling 'Break it!'

I thought she meant their legs so they couldn't run away. I wasn't too smart so I did—every leg I could reach!"

Some bent shoulders rocked forward. Everyone stared at the ground.

"No!" My mother yelled, "Break the arrow!" So I did. Now I had wounded ducks limping and flopping all over camp, knocking over pots and fire poles with kids and people yelling and chasing them in every direction. Only one flew away."

Kamistatim's eyes grew wily, "So, if you ever see a half-naked duck with broken legs. It's mine."

A couple of the men grunted and smoked on, enjoying their pipes and watching the crackling fire before them. Some eased aching joints by shifting a leg or rearranging their woven willow backrests.

Pipestem cleared his throat, knocked out his pipe, refilled and lit it. The rest waited, knowing he had something to say. The old man took his time, enjoying several puffs before removing the stem from timeworn lips.

"We had a cold winter one year with lots of heavy snowfall. Our families were hungry, needing meat. Animals were scarce; many had died of starvation or were killed by wolves. My brother-in-law, Ayamsis, (the big burly one with bad jokes) and I set out on our snowshoes to hunt.

"We walked all day. Found nothing! Finally, just at dusk, we caught the trail of a deer. From the size of the tracks and how deep they sank, we knew it was a big buck. We tracked him until we couldn't see the trail. No moonlight that night so we made camp. It was so cold we built two fires and slept between them. Makes for a long night."

Grey heads nodded. Keeping two fires burning all night needed lots of wood and getting up every hour to replenish the fire. And still the head and feet stayed cold.

Pipestem went on, "We arose at dawn, ate some pemmican and continued tracking. That buck was on the move and strong enough to fight his way through the deepest snowdrifts. He must have known we tracked him because we followed all day without ever catching a glimpse of him. That night, we made camp and heated up our pot of rabbit stew."

Again, heads nodded. Out of respect for the hunted animal, one never took its meat on the trail. Why hunt for meat you already had? It proved greed more than need.

"We were both enjoying our stew after the long walk. Across the fire, Ayamsis looks at me, stops chewing and peers closer. 'Ahhh!'

He points at my face and falls backward off his log, laughing. In the firelight, all I can see are his knees and his moccasins shaking.

"I look down at myself, but I see nothing wrong. I feel my face and something dangles from my mouth. I pull it out. It's a mouse tail."

Wrinkles in wizened faced immediately bunch into deep crevices. Several men snort. Stillness eventually descends on the waiting group.

Pipestem slid a peek at his old friends then took up his tale once again. "Around noon, the next day, we crested a big hill and there was the buck, caught fast in a deep snowdrift—right to his shoulders. He must have ran up the hill and tried to jump over the drift but got hung up.

"Before I can aim, Ayamsis runs at the deer, drops his gun across the antlers, grabs the horns with both hands and jumps on its back, snowshoes and all. 'Ah-ha!' he shouts, 'You've been acting smart for three days! Now I have you!' and he shakes the antlers."

"Suddenly, the drift falls away and the buck breaks loose. Instead of letting go, that crazy Cree hangs on! He's bellowing and still shaking the horns, 'No! You're not getting away! You're mine!' He's fighting the horns, twisting the buck's head, trying to tip him over. 'Shoot him!' He yells at me while the buck lunges away, gathering speed.

"But I'm on my knees, laughing too hard.

"Then the buck starts jumping high in the air, with poor old Ayamsis stretched out across the back, his big belly bouncing and his snowshoes flapping and banging out behind him like rags in the wind. And he still won't let go!"

Silence reigned over the circle of ancient warriors. Not one man moved or reached for his pipe. Pipestem took great delight in out-waiting them. Akapow, the small man beside him, thrust out his jaw, scratched solemnly and pursed his bottom lip in contemplation.

Eventually, Tall Man drew a long breath, released it and slowly returned his pipe to his mouth for a few puffs.

After a lengthy wait, Pipestem sighed. "That wasn't the worst part."

Several sets of eye widened.

He nodded sagely, "At the bottom of the hill, the deer had enough. With a few stiff legged jumps he threw Ayamsis head first into a drift. But I had to dive into a snow bank too. The trigger on the gun in his horns must have hooked on an antler point. When that buck turned and jumped, the gun went off. Now he's shooting at me!

"My-brother-in-law gets mad and yells at me. He thinks I'm shooting at him!" Now we're both hiding in a snow bank and the buck runs away."

He sighed, "When I dug Ayamsis out he had two cracked ribs and a broken snowshoe. Now *we* both were afraid. We still had one gun but the deer . . . had the other."

Several listeners slowly turned their heads, lips turning down as they contemplated the storyteller. A few gnawed the inside of their jaw while irregular breathing filled the quiet circle.

Tall Man puffed slowly on his pipe, surrounding his head with a blue cloud of swirling kinnikinik. He savoured the smell of the dried and ground willow bark. It reminded him of a walk through the trees in the summertime.

"I went hunting not long ago," his quiet voice finally broke the stillness, "But I was deeply disappointed with my gun. It was a Thomas Barnett trade gun with the silver dragon carved on the side plate. Best gun I ever had.'

His ancient friends nodded in understanding. A good gun was rare. The barrel often rusted or twisted from travel; sights fell off or bent; powder went damp or lead balls wouldn't fire properly, sometimes damaging the firing mechanism. The well-crafted Barnett was worth a lot of beaver pelts at the trading posts.

The men waited peacefully, puffing on their long stemmed pipes, soaking up the warm summer sunshine. No clouds marred the blue perfection above them. Thick, warm grass cradled bony thighs. Its crushed green spikes lifted a fresh tang into the soft breeze as it played with greying braids. A Blue Jay imitated a red-tailed hawk's scream from a nearby tree. Smaller birds and animals instantly abandoned their food and fled to the trees, leaving more food for the sly bird.

Tall Man continued, "That morning, I tracked a bull moose, his trail fresh in the early morning dew. His hooves were wide open, pacing full stride, pushing his hind legs until they overstepped his front hoof prints. They looked like a young spiker's, probably one or two years old. I walked quickly, tracking him for some time. Finally, I spotted him across two valleys and up a far hill, just a black speck in the distance. He'd stopped and looked back. Probably caught my scent. I didn't want to waste my shot. It was just too far for my gun. It's not supposed to shoot that far."

He shifted to his other hip, puffed again. "But then I thought about fresh young meat . . . roasting over hot coals . . . smoking a little as the fat dripped." He spread his hand, palm downward, smoothing the air in front of him for emphasis.

Wrinkled throats swallowed with rich tasting memories.

"So I braced the gun against a good strong tree root and waited for the spiker's ear to twitch so I could sight him in for a good neck shot. I checked the wind and calculated how much drift the bullet might need. For the drop of the bullet at such a long distance I aimed high as the tree tops. My gun has a kick so I stayed well back so the sight wouldn't catch me between the eyes. Then I held my breath to freeze the sights, matched my heartbeat to the sway of the barrel and squeezed when it swung into place."

He puffed a few times while his friends waited patiently. Some lazily drew in the aroma rising from a copper kettle on a tripod before them. Small chunks of deer meat simmered in a golden broth of wild onions, carrots and ground turnip with sage leaves. Soon Mitsue would add a few Saskatoon leaves for flavouring and bulrush roots for thickening.

Tall Man coughed politely, "It was such a long shot." He shook his head, "I gathered some twigs to make tea while I waited to see if the bullet would hit the moose. Then I lit my pipe. Finally, just when I finished my tea, the moose fell over."

Pipestem removed his pipe and inspected his old friend. Muscles around his mouth shifted slightly, giving his mouth a crinkled contortion.

Tall Man ignored him, knocked out his cold pipe, refilled it, tamped it and relit it from a burning stick on the fire.

"So I packed up my pot, picked up my gun and set off down the first valley. It was a burned out area with a few summers of regrowth; lots of deadwood, thick red willows and big trunks to climb over. Occasionally I'd climb a high deadfall to make sure I kept the tall spruce tree behind the moose in sight. In the second valley I ran into a *muskek* (swamp) full of water. I had to wade through deep water, holding my gun over my head.

"When I finally climbed the hill where the moose lay, it was too late."

His friends eyed him in silence.

Tall Man sighed, "The moose was already bloated with maggots crawling out. When I checked my gun, the barrel was huge. It's not supposed to shoot that far."

Pipestem stared into the fire, but his eyes rounded. Across from him, Lone Man, a lean rangy Blackfoot, coughed a couple of times and rubbed his mouth. Akapow scratched a wrinkled jowl and looked thoughtful. Kamistatim bent his head, digging diligently at the ground with a small stick. Pipestem's mouth pulled down.

All the old warriors removed their pipes, waiting.

Tall Man focused gleaming eyes upon his pipe, his face shifting into heavy lines of sadness. "Yes, a sad day indeed. I had to throw away both my rotten moose *and* my stretched gun."

The old men slapped their knees and rolled back on their haunches, howling in glee. They tossed Tall Man a twist of tobacco or specially carved sticks used for forfeits in their bowl game. "You win!" they crowed.

4.

THINGS THAT WERE AND YET WERE NOT

Mac breathed through his mouth but his throat dried and froze. Frost had already pinched his nostrils shut. He swallowed and blinked rapidly, struggling to see through a late May blizzard—not that unusual for the land, according to Broken Arrow. They had travelled north towards Fort Ellice, following the Assiniboine River. The storm's snowflakes, laden with water, pelted them, weighing them down, soaking their feet and legs. They had left their horses behind at camp to stalk elk. But the elusive animals remained out of sight. Broken Arrow reluctantly turned back towards camp as the snow increased its fury.

The constant marching steps, lifting his feet high to clear the heavy drifts, exhausted Mac. Wind howled in his face, snatching his breath away. He grabbed it back in hasty, panicky gulps. Ahead of him, Broken Arrow shouldered aside a snow laden branch then disappeared completely into a stand of grey and white birch trees. As Mac followed, the trees enclosed him, their white paper bark the same hue as the surrounding snow and sky. He struggled to see where snow ended and trees began. Their dots of black bark swam together in his frozen tears created by the harsh winds. Giant flakes wrapped him in white loneliness, silent, merciless and wild. As he walked on, he felt his isolation, far from family and home, his body the only dark shape in this world of white. He curled his fists, his one source of power midst the elements surrounding him in the deepening gloom. And still the snow came at him, seemingly from every direction, until he no longer knew what was up or down or sideways. He found himself floating, dizzy with confusion, lost in a terrifying vision of white liquid, fighting to remain upright.

Despite the freezing temperatures, cold sweat pored down his back and trickled down his forehead, stinging his eyes. He swiped at it angrily, leaving icy streaks down his cheeks. Knotting the scarf tighter around his neck, he struggled to block the icy draught blowing down his chest. Yet he felt hot, so damn hot! When his foot hooked on a hidden root, he tumbled headlong into a snowdrift.

He fought to his knees, flinging the snow away in fury. "Jaysus Christ on a flamin' crutch! Is there no end to this god-forsaken ice hole?"

Broken Arrow appeared like a great shadow out of the white mist, bending to pull his partner to his feet. He took one look at Mac's ice-coated face and shoved him back into the drift. "You fool! You stupid *Moniyaw*! Why didn't you say something?"

Mac came up sputtering, "What the hell is wrong now? I was keepin' up!"

The tall Cree grasped for patience, swinging about in tight lipped fury. "You're sweating! You can not allow yourself to sweat! You have to let the air move around your body, to keep it dry. You have bundled yourself too tightly. Now you'll freeze as soon as you stop! Your wet clothes offer no protection from the cold. We make camp! Now!"

"But you said we are only a few miles from our camp!"

"You'll never make it." The big man yanked a small hatchet from his belt and began slashing at spruce tree boughs. He turned to glare at the stunned man. "Gather firewood and start a fire before you freeze on the spot."

Mac doubled his fists, wanting to punch the bossy bugger, but already he felt the trickles dripping down his back turn to jagged painful shards. Wind poked icy fingers through the seams in his coat and tracked frozen trails down his trembling legs. Mac bent and broke dry branches off dead trees, pulling birch bark paper off for fire starter.

Broken Arrow worked furiously, cutting down small trees and tying them together, creating a windbreak for the man who was already struggling not to shiver. He sighed. Foolish *Moniyaw*. Didn't know enough to respect the cold! He dug dry hide pants from his backpack, his last pair but they would do until they reached camp. Pulling off his thick moosehide jacket, he held the clothes out to Mac. "They will warm you. Remove all your wet clothes. We'll hang them near the fire to dry."

"What about you?" Mac's entire body vibrated in bone-chilling shivers as he struggled with his sticky garments. Broken Arrow now wore only a thin deerskin shirt and vest with his heavier moose hide pants.

"I am warm and will keep busy until the fire is hot." He bent to his work, tight-lipped and silent.

Mac was wet clear through to his skin. He pulled the warm buffalo hide coat around him, yanked on the long pants and spread his shaking hands towards the growing fire. It was a lesson he would not forget. At least the Indian was polite enough to not rub it in with endless recriminations and criticism. A lesson well learned needed no further reproof.

*   *   *

That evening, heat from the fire filled their triangular shelter. Broken Arrow had built a framework of saplings then covered them with layers of heavy spruce boughs. He'd sealed the back with snow and more boughs, creating a tiny, very snug, three-sided shelter open on the fourth side to the blazing fire. It became a golden haven of warmth and comfort with its window on the blustering, white-flaked night beyond the dancing flames.

Once Mac's teeth stopped chattering, he told the Cree about his strange feeling of floating amongst the snow and birch trees. "Jaysus twas strange. I could no' be tellin' up from down, land from sky. Like the twilight Otherworld, it was."

He squinted through the smoke at Broken Arrow. "Ye know, we Celts were often called, 'The Twilight People,' because we honoured the in-between states, thinking them a direct doorway from this world to the ghostly realm of spirit we called the Otherworld."

Mac cupped his hot tea, staring into the fire. "My ancestors were fascinated by things that were and yet were not. They worshipped their sacred Mistletoe, a vine which never touched the land but grew upon the oak tree. Twas a plant yet not a plant because it drew its life-force from the king of trees. The Celts adored things like crystal and glass—seen, yet seen through—like the Tor of Glastonbury at Avalon, a glass-like place, whose name was *Ynys Wytrin* or Glass Isle. It has long been known as an entrance point to the Otherworld. The Celts were also fascinated with fog, dew and mist: waters which were and yet were not. And they honoured the twilight times of Dawn, Dusk, Midnight and Eclipse—those moments of in-between light and dark which belonged to neither. Their most reverent time was the sixth day after the full moon, the phase in-between the dark side of the moon and its first visible sickle of new moon. They considered it the most powerful time for working magic."

Mac gazed into the deep blue night, realizing he and Broken Arrow also existed between two worlds: dark and light; cold and hot; wet and dry . . . and yes, death and life. He shuddered inwardly, wondering if he would have survived this storm had he still been alone. Yet, here they sat, safe and sound: an Irishman and a Cree. Could they bridge their differences to an in-between they could share?

Amongst the crackling flames before them, dry spruce bark exploded merrily, raining the men's moccasins with small sparks. Broken Arrow absently kicked the larger ones away. He didn't know this White Man well enough to share inner thoughts, but he was deeply interested in these Celts and their ways.

"My people also believe in the two worlds, one of this life and one of Spirit. Our elders know what it takes to move freely between these two worlds. My grandfather, Tall Man, taught me to pay attention during the brief moments between waking and sleeping, another in-between time, when we are aware of both worlds. Powerful spiritual messages may come at that time."

5.

TREES

The next day broke warm and peaceful. Snow fell in great wet clumps from tree branches heavily burdened from snow and new green leaves. Some branches had split in two from the weight while weaker tree tops remained bowed to the ground. Water ran everywhere. Mac donned his own dried clothes and felt in good charity with the world once more.

"Broken Arrow is a bit of a mouthful. Back east, we often call people by their initials, the first letters in their names. Would ye be mindin' if I just called ye 'B.A.'?"

The Cree's eyes crinkled as his head tilted sideways in agreement, offering no comment as he ate his breakfast.

"Why do ye eat in complete silence? Ye never speak until ye're finished." This silence habit of Broken Arrow's still bothered Mac who grew up with lengthy, wonderful conversations during mealtime.

"It is our way of giving thanks to *Kisemanito*, The Great Mystery, for our food." The Cree continued peeling a baked duck egg he had pulled from the edge of campfire coals, tossing the smoking egg from hand to hand to cool his hot fingers.

"Beggin' your pardon but why don't you just say a prayer at the beginning and be done with it? Then we can at least visit and enjoy our food together." Mac reached for another egg and began peeling, hoping it contained only white and yellow, none of that bloody stuff with bones attached. He quelled his shuddering gut.

BA's eyes narrowed. "You think you know the only truth? That your way is the only way? We take time to sit in silence with this land, to honour its gifts and to give thanks for what it gives us. It is one way of giving something back."

"Ah, ye make this land sound alive instead of just dirt, rocks, trees and water." Mac popped the delicious yellow yoke into his mouth and chewed in delight. He washed it down with a sip of warm wild mint tea, a dried staple from the swampy lands around them. Broken Arrow called it *Lebom*. Mac never knew if it was a Cree or French word. The Indian didn't care.

B.A. grunted, his dark eyes expressing an amused tolerance. "I know the Black Robes say we are heathens who see spirits in every rock and tree but we feel just one Great Spirit, *Kisemanito*, around us."

Mac's jaw dropped. "Great Spirit? The Celts called him that too!"

B.A. nodded, "He is one energy we are all part of, connected to. And we honour this connection. The elders teach us to sit quietly, respectfully and humbly then we can reconnect and learn the wisdom taught by the land and the rocks and the trees that are also part of him. They are not always what they seem. Any one of them could have a special power. So we treat everything with respect. There are many teachings in this land the White Man does not hear or see yet. Some he will find only in his dreams or visions."

"Haw!" Mac scoffed. "Sure'n you'll soon be tellin' me ye talk to the trees too!" Mac dipped his cup in the nearby creek, refusing to search its contents for any squiggly characters. But he wanted to. Instead, he swallowed and leered at his friend in a stubborn bravado.

B.A. leapt upon him, his knife to his throat.

"Alright! Alright! Jaysus Mon I'm jokin'!" Mac struggled to straighten his face, shoving his laughter down, knowing how sharp the bloody knife was. He'd watched B.A. gut too many prairie chickens and rabbits with a few deft strokes.

Eyes narrowed in fury, B.A. backed away, his knife still poised. "I will not accept your scorn for something you know so little about, White Man!"

Mac rubbed his jaw slowly, sorry he had truly offended his new friend. "So you say we are all connected? Prove it." He threw the rest of his water away. Next time he'd copy B.A. and whack the water with his fist to scare the wee beasties away before dipping or drinking.

Broken Arrow squatted, adding more wood to the fire, letting the muscles in his shoulders ease. It was time to teach this blind, bossy White Man a lesson. "Do you believe you have a soul?"

"Well Father O'Reilly used to damn it so I guess I do . . . never thought much about it." Mac dug in his pack for some dried apples and tossed a few to B.A.

"And do you think you are the only thing on this earth with a soul?"

"I dunno." Mac scratched a stiff curl. He really wanted a bath, to wash some of the dried sweat off his body and stiffened clothes but they had not camped near a stream. He sighed, wiping dirty fingers on his trousers and settled down near the campfire once again. "Old Jim, my horse, sure had a heart; maybe he had a soul too."

"And is that all? What about other animals? Or trees?"

"Trees have no soul. They have no brain or heart, they're just wood." Mac snorted at such a notion. He wanted to roll his eyes but didn't dare.

B.A. leaned back against a big white poplar. "Prove it, White Man."

Mac scratched his ear, "Well, sure'n they grow leaves, they move in the wind and when they're dead, they fall down and rot away. So yes, they live and they die. But 'tis no' like they can hear, see, think, feel or remember like we do."

B.A. watched him intently. "Grab that willow beside you with your left hand and close your eyes."

Mac reached back for the slim red willow reed beside him, crushing the soft silvery green leaves beneath his big fingers. He shut his eyes and wondered where the Sam Hill this was all going.

Silence. Nothing.

Mac felt like an idjit. Sure'n B.A. was probably laughin' at him for the fool he was. He peeked with one eye but the tall Indian sat quietly watching him, leaning against a tree, unmoving and solemn.

The willow in Mac's hand began to move, so slightly, so gently he never noticed at first. Slowly it gained momentum, moving in stronger and stronger surges until it whipped wildly in his hand, up and down, into bigger and bigger swirls until his entire arm was caught up in the motion. Mac snatched his hand back, shoved it beneath his other arm and hugged it to his side. The slender willow swung on its own then slowly ceased, drooping silently into its former position.

"Sweet Jesus! How the Sam Hill did ye do that?" Mac sensed a trick but how?

Broken Arrow smiled slowly, "I did nothing. You just connected with a dumb tree."

Mac glared at the unmoving willow and felt a clutch of fear as he eyed the dark canopy of trees looming above him. "That never happened before. I've been around trees all my life!"

"Why would it happen? To you, they are unfeeling, unknowing. Nothing they can do will prove otherwise."

"But it moved . . . like it had a mind of its own. It felt . . . Jaysus, it felt like a heartbeat!" Mac wriggled his fingers to rid himself of the lingering sensation, not liking the prickling hair shuddering up the back of his neck.

B.A. relaxed against the big poplar, resting his arms atop his splayed knees, pitying this man's ignorance. "My grandfather, Tall Man, talks to the trees. He calls them his old friends. They tell him stories of the land, of incidents that happened near them, like a cow moose defending her calf from wolves. They show him visions to explain their tales. He says they will sometimes tell him their name; sometimes not. Some are too solemn. We call them the 'Standing People'.

"We have stories about how the Creator made the trees. Then one day, he had to go away. So he asked the trees, the Standing People, to stand guard, to watch over the land while he was gone. The trees agreed. He was gone for a long time. He was gone so long; the trees grew weary of watching over the land. Some became so tired, they fell asleep. But the spruce and the pines refused to sleep. They kept their watch until the Creator returned. When he saw the other trees sleeping, he grew angry with them. To punish them, he told them from that day forward, they would lose all their leaves, every year just before winter. And that is why evergreens never lose their leaves. When we look at them, we are reminded never to break a promise."

Mac's eyes narrowed. He knew B.A. well enough by now that his stories always had a purpose, a lesson behind them. "So . . . what promise are ye keeping here?"

B.A. grinned, "I promised *Ohkomimaw* my grandmother, Mitsue, to teach the dumb White Men whenever I could." He chuckled, easily ducking a small stick Mac heaved towards him.

For the rest of the day, Mac tried to get more answers but Broken Arrow ignored him, unwilling to share any more. That night, Mac rolled into his bedding and turned his back on the Cree in disgust. It was a long night. Rustling leaves bothered him now though he couldn't bring himself to consider why.

Twas foolish nonsense . . . .

In the morning, he couldn't leave it alone. Like a man with a bad toothache, he couldn't quit poking no matter how much it hurt. He joined B.A. for their daily ablutions, a quick dip in the sluggish creek they stopped beside. Both gathered a small handful of the leaves from the creeping clematis vine tumbling over nearby bushes and rocks. As they worked the leaves into a soft lather for their hair, Mac had to ask, "Have you actually talked to the trees?" Last night was just too odd and he hated the uncertainty it generated in his gut.

B.A. rinsed his long hair and wrung out the ends, "What do you want to ask them?"

Mac sank beneath the water, lost his breath completely and lunged for the freezing air. Well, he'd wanted a bath! He tried not to shiver at the chunks of snow still floating by. Though he considered it a wee bit much to bathe everyday like B.A., bedamned if he'd be the one that stank! He'd get used to this if it killed him. As he waded into shore, shaking water from his curls, he still wanted to believe the Indian tricked him but last night was too real.

B.A. pulled on his leather thong and pointed to a thick black poplar, "Put your left hand on that tall tree beside you. Close your eyes and stand still."

"Aw! Why do I always have to close my eyes?" Mac groused as he yanked on his pants and dug around for clean socks. He sighed gratefully for the warm sweater he slipped over his shivering back.

"Do you want to do this? Or just complain?" Broken Arrow yanked up his moose hide pants and tied them at his waist.

"Alright! Alright! I'll do it. Why my left hand when I'm right handed?" Mac wanted to fight this, deny any reason for following through even though he'd started it.

"Because your left hand is closely connected to your heart, which is also on the left side of your body. You connect to your soul through your heart. You also connect with the spirit of the earth through your heart and body. Shut off your mind. It thinks too much and it blocks your heart's feelings. You must think with your heart, feel it in your body and soul. Don't expect words White Man. It might come in waves of feelings, distant ripples of ideas or perhaps in a vision planted behind your closed eyes. Now . . . tell your mind to be silent. Focus on your heart. Can you feel a tiny pain there?"

Mac surprised himself by nodding. He did feel a slight energy around his heart and it hurt with a tiny yet sharp pain. Odd, surely he was too young for a heart attack . . . .

"Shut your mind down. Keep your eyes closed. Walk yourself from your head down to where your heart dwells."

Mac squeezed his eyes shut; feeling equally stupid and relieved nobody could see him besides the Cree.

"Now . . . walk from your heart, down your left hand, to the tree you touch."

Mac shoved the scepticism away and slammed the door on an image of his university friends howling with laughter. He squeezed his eyes shut and focused on the journey . . . from his head . . . to his heart, down his arm . . . to the cool rough bark of the tree . . . and waited . . . in the silence.

He felt his arm then his body sway not at his bidding because he kept a rigid stance. No, it belonged to something else, like a gentle swing in a breeze, something like the surge he had felt in the small willow. Yet no wind stirred. His skin sensed the calm air around him. Still he swayed, gently, softly, peacefully. It soothed him enough that he stayed with it; kept the connection. Then, ever so softly . . . he felt it: a heartbeat. Was it his own? No . . . there was his own steady beat. This vibration came through his palm. *From the tree?* It felt like a movement, a wave, a sensation of motion, steadily waxing and waning, a gentle rhythm that touched him, moved up his arm in a warm, rich flow, like a bloodline, not foreign . . . but something . . .

always there . . . just forgotten . . . beneath the surface, like a quiet memory from long, long ago . . . .

A stark image suddenly loomed in front of his closed eyes: the inside of a tree, cut with a thousand tunnels, crawling with a thousand black, glistening ants. It was so vivid, so horrifying after the peaceful sensations that Mac jumped back, yanked his hand away and opened his eyes, staring in startled wonder at the huge trunk before him.

"I saw the inside of a tree! It had ants crawling all over it! Killing it from the inside! Jaysus!"

"Look up." B.A.'s voice held a depth of quiet sorrow.

Mac stared at the majestic tree above him, studying the wrinkled and split bark. Then he saw them, scurrying in and out of their holes and burrows, a million tiny soldiers, penetrating the tree's final defence. He looked higher, past the green rippling leaves to the grey and blackened branches, barren and empty at the top.

"It's dying!" He swallowed painfully. The reality of his vision hit him hard. "It was real! Saints preserve me! The tree showed me its insides. It's dying!" He reached a shaking hand out to the tree and gently touched the dark trunk that now felt like rough skin. Through his palms he *felt* the tree's sorrow and quiet acceptance. "It knows! Ah Sweet Mary! *It knows!*" He placed both hands on the tree, leaning his forehead against the cool trunk, allowing sensations to flow through him, barely breathing with the heavy weight upon his chest.

Eventually he turned and slid down the tree onto one of its protruding roots, lost in thought and whirling emotions. He slumped against the weathered trunk, still unwilling to break the profound rightness of this incredible connection.

B.A. sat, quietly amazed at how quickly this man had moved into this new moment of truth—almost quick as his people. Perhaps, all men had this ability. Had they simply forgotten their stories that taught them so?

In quiet patience, he combed his long hair, parted it and began braiding, one braid over each ear like all Woodland Cree, unlike the Plains Cree who made a third braid down the middle of their back. He secured the ends with rawhide strung with tiny brass ornaments. As he worked, he relaxed into the ground, folding his legs in a cross-legged seat, feeling the heartbeat from Mother flow up through his legs, through his heart, off the top of his head and back down into the ground. She never failed him in her comfort.

After a long period, Mac sighed, tipping his head towards his silent friend. "Did ye know our philosophers say humans around the world have an instinctive deep yearning for the security of the forest in which their ancestors lived for so long? When humans stray too far from this forest or when they destroy it, they try to recreate it, even if they have to make trees of stone. In ancient Mesopotamia, in the city of Babylon, King Nebuchadnezzar built his famous Hanging Gardens and filled them with exotic trees to remind his Meidan wife, Amytis, of her wooded home.

"The Greeks and Arabs continued this trend with their small parks and courtyards. The word 'Park' comes from an ancient Persian word *paridaeza*, Latin *paradisus* and English *paradise*. Perhaps our ancestors knew about this mystical connection ye talk about and I just felt."

He thought for a while. "Ye know, mayhap the druids understood it too. The word Druid is *'Dru'* means 'oak knowledge' and *'wid'* means 'to know' or 'to see'. Maybe they saw the trees like I just did. One of their sayings was: 'To have knowledge of the trees was nature's gift of survival instincts and therefore wisdom'. They honoured the oak tree with its many branches of wisdom. Often they carved tree trunks with an old man's face in the bark. They called him the 'Green Man'. Why would they do so unless the tree carried some powerful significance?" He unconsciously echoed his partner's thoughts, "Maybe deeper meanings were lost through time."

Mac pulled a knee to his chest, his mind searching back through his University courses. "I learned many ancient churches were built on the site of Druidic oak stands. Our druids believed the oak is the best emblem of the chief God. They called it the '*crann bethadh* or Tree of Life'. It symbolized the 'Father of the gods'.

B.A. nodded, "We also have a Tree of Life in our legends. A tree links heaven and earth; the leaves and branches catch the energy of the Sun, grand ruler of the sky and move it down through the trunk into the earthly roots of this world. It reminds us we too are rooted on this Earth with our bodies in the sky, standing on the land connected to both, part of both."

Mac expanded it, sitting upright in excitement, sharing another piece, "Leaves were often carved into the column clusters of the Greek and Roman temples and the cathedrals of Europe. Notre Dame Cathedral at Chartres in France, finished four hundred years ago, has two large spires rising over the community like giant trees." Mac paused, frowning, "Ye know, the forests don't look like cathedrals; instead, the cathedrals look like the forest!" Recognizing these truths filled Mac with awe. "Where did we lose sight of our connections with nature and her trees?"

B.A. stood, brushing twigs and dirt from his leggings, "Some part of us will always need the forest. Trees heal us, soothe us and help us understand our relation with Earth Mother. They are like us and we need them. The White Man refuses to accept this connection. He calls trees dumb and soulless. Then he can kill and use them without conscience. He does not understand the land's cycles. With death comes rebirth. When we kill a tree, we honour the tree's gift and rebirth coming from its seeds. We are responsible for caring for the trees and honouring their cycles.

"In each of our clans, one chosen family was responsible for the management of the land. Its teachings were handed down from father to son. This family watched over the land and all that lived in their clan's territory. They studied the ways of the trees and the animals so their people could live in harmony with the land. They understood each animal's seven year cycles of slow growth to abundant numbers, followed by diseases, which killed them back to only a few again.

Every creature was counted and if certain animals or fish became too scarce, they stopped all hunting or fishing in that area until the numbers returned. The family knew which trees grew at what stage of a forest's lifetime. And they knew what areas needed to be burned each year for an older forest's renewal. Only this family could give permission for other tribes to hunt in our territory. Such decisions were always based on what was best for the next seven generations. This is how our people take care of the land and keep harmony with its cycles. This is why we are still willing to share this land with the White Man. It is not ours to own, only to care for."

Broken Arrow packed his belongings and rolled them into his buffalo robe, "When Creator made my people; he also created the tobacco plant and trees. When we must kill a tree or plant or animal for our use, we thank it and the Creator for offering its life so we may live. We place tobacco beside it to honour its gift. Whatever we take, we must give back in some way. This is balance. Does the White Man really believe he can kill the trees without any reaction from Creator and Earth Mother? This land is not free! If we kill all the trees, how soon until we die too?"

Mac sat up, his face darkening. "Killing? Dying? Faith Mon, we're just beginning to survive in this land! I'm a son of Irish immigrants tis true but this be my homeland too! I was born here, same as the Indians! Sure'n I hear the drums beating for your people but I've also heard our old melodies of the famines back in Ireland. We can no' leave so we stay and we build and we grow into this industrial world we're entering."

Mac's ire rose. Didn't this Indian know how advanced they were back East? "In this year of 1863, we have gas lights in Ottawa now. The Ontario, Simcoe & Huron railroad, which some call the Oats, Straw and Hay Railway, extends from Toronto to near Barrie and soon on to Collingwood. Telegraphs already stretch from Quebec and Montreal to Toronto and Hamilton. Everything is coming west! Factories are springin' up all over, building plows and hoes for the farmers. Two years ago, our farmers grew 25,000,000 bushels of grain. The government is already building its parliament buildings in Ottawa. Upper and Lower Canada's population reached one million twenty years ago! Lord knows what it is now!"

Mac flung his hands wide, "Ye can no' stop progress! The future always rips apart the old ways. The coming trains need many trees for tracks. And God help those who fall behind and refuse to change! My people have suffered for centuries and we learned the hard way to make the best of what we had. What this Territory and the Canadas offer is a lot better than anything left in Ireland. Sometimes it's hard to stand back and watch it happen, but civilizations rise and they fall. Such is the history of the world. Some say we are poorer for every lost culture. But others argue tis the price of progress."

He stood, dusting his pants, the tree forgotten in his defensive anger, "I am an opportunist. I'll take what I can and leave the philosophers to their armchairs and empty smoke."

Broken Arrow stubbornly clung to his belief, "Tall Man used to say, 'How can we own the land? How can man own something he is a part of? Can the hummingbird own the tree it sits upon? Can the tree own the land it grows upon? How can we sell something given to us as a gift from Kisemanito? We can give thanks, be grateful and ask permission for its use. But own it? It's like owning the wind!"

Mac truly wanted his friend to understand the situation. "Well back East they're dividing this land into little squares and selling it off—every day. People say it's no' fair to the Indians. Jaysus, Mary and Joseph! Life was never fair to the Irish either else they'd never have left Ireland. I once saw a man leave his wife and children to come out West and never did he return. Where's the fairness for that penniless woman with a houseful of mouths to feed I ask ye! As for this so-called 'free land for the taking', ye need a strong back and a good mind to survive it! Tis a test of wills I tell ye! And God help those who weaken because nature sure as hell doesn't! The snowstorm reminded me of that lesson! Aye, we use the land. We need it to survive! Sure'n we can give thanks for its use. But who will dig the potatoes? Plow the fields and feed the hungry mouths? If you think a knee-full of prayers and talking to the trees will help, ye're crazy!" Mac gathered up his belongings and strode to his horse.

"It's the difference between honour and greed White Man!" B.A. slammed the bundled pack onto his startled paint who warily danced sideways. "All you see in the land is the money it brings you. Our people take only what we need, nothing more. We accept the responsibility of managing the forests, replacing and reseeding what we take. You puny White souls see not the majesty or constant need for balance in giving and taking. Instead, you keep more than you should or could ever use. 'Save it' you say, 'Keep it hidden away and no' be sharin' it in case there be famine and suffering ahead'." B.A. sneered in rough imitation of Mac's Irish accent. "Yet the White Man will suffer anyway, for such is man's lot. Suffering is a part of life, like birth and death. And all the hoarding in the world will not stop it from happening!"

He tied his gear on with angry jerks. "Your people take and take and take! You give nothing back! No honour! No gratitude! No management! You steal from the land because you fear you might have less than you need. You have no faith in the Creator's ability to provide so you dishonour his gifts and you take and you hoard and you waste. Soon there will *not* be enough for everyone. I see how many trees are falling under your axes and how many buffalo are wasted by your guns. What then? You bring your worst fears to life! Your greed and your fear will have us all starving! What foolish people you are!" In disgust B.A. swung to the back of his paint and rode away.

Mac yanked his grey up beside him, sneering, "Sure'n we'll be seein' who dies and who survives through it all too!"

6.

WHY THE WHITE MAN CAME

After a cold lunch, they rode out from a silent camp. Broken Arrow, his face hard and grim, rounded on Mac. "Do you know why you are here?"

Taken aback Mac swept his palm out. "Here? Me? Because I wanted to come."

An exasperated B.A. shook his head, "I mean all White Men! Do you know why you are here in this land?"

"For the land, furs, wood, farm, family . . . a better life?" Mac shrugged. Now what?

Broken Arrow spun forward, his dark face set and determined. "I will share with you what *Ohkomimaw*, my grandma Mitsue told me:"

"Why did the White Man come here?" demanded a very young and angry Broken Arrow as he plunked himself down beside his great aunt, sister to his grandfather Tall Man. Mitsue had raised her own family then lost her husband in a Sioux raid. She had willingly accepted the care of her aging brother and his tiny grandson after both the boy's parents died in a smallpox epidemic. Broken Arrow had been with his grandparents at another camp when the disease wiped out his entire family including two older brothers and a sister.

Tall Man's wife, Listens to the Wind, had died soon afterwards, her heart broken from age and too many losses. In Native tradition, Mitsue automatically became a grandmother to all her sibling's grandchildren as well as her own. This was the root of the care, love and respect given to all elderly people in their tightly knit tribes.

Mitsue sat quietly sewing her moccasins outside Tall Man's tipi, her weathered hands big-knuckled and thick fingered from a lifetime of scraping and curing hides. Her intricately designed beadwork was prized throughout their many clans. Men traded dearly for a pair of her beautifully crafted, sturdy moccasins, hide shirts, vests or leggings. Other women sought her advice on how to improve their sewing. Many strove to copy Mitsue's handiwork but few succeeded.

She settled her heavy legs into a more comfortable position beneath her navy broadcloth skirt decorated with rows of colourful ribbon. She accepted these White Man clothes only because they were cooler in summer than her hide skirts. Her agile fingers retained a swift rhythm with a bone needle threaded with dried white sinew removed from a buffalo leg. Once dried, the strong sinew was split into many long strands. Earlier, she had used a small charred stick to draw a pattern of graceful leaves and rose petals on the smoked and cured moosehide. Tougher and thicker than deer, the moosehide made better moccasins and winter clothing than the lighter deer and elk hides were used for summer coats, vests, dresses and leggings. After carefully tacking a strand of raw cut pink beads—another concession to the White Man—into the pattern, she tacked small, almost invisible stitches across the strand between each bead to secure it to the hide. Bead by tiny bead, she created a masterpiece of curving vines, graceful leaves and life-size roses, replicas of the fragrant pink roses dotting her heavily treed landscape. Her pattern was a Woodland or Northern Cree design. They, along with the Metis, sewed large flowers on their clothing, using silk as often as beads, earning them the name, 'Big Flower People', by other tribes. The Plains Cree preferred smaller flowers, like those spread across the prairies. Blackfoot women created small, geometrical triangles and squares while the Slavey or Chipewyan to the north copied the dainty curling vines, tiny bluebells and brilliant fireweed petals of their land. With one glance at the floral designs on a stranger's garb, Native people could easily identify which tribe the individual came from.

As she worked, Mitsue thought about what the ancients had told her.

"*Ekosesa,* (And so it was) . . . the White Man came from a land of all white people. He had to come here. His isolation in that faraway land bred a pride in him he needed to fix.

"White people are very cruel to one another. They constantly fight one another, trying to be better, stronger and more powerful than their neighbours instead of accepting themselves as equals. Such fierce competition forces them to constantly criticize and judge. The White Man developed two faces, one for those he judged higher or better than himself and one for those he judged lower or worse than himself. Neither face is his own so he feels bad inside. White people learned to feel bad about themselves, unequal, lesser and unworthy. When people feel bad about themselves, they see others and the world in a bad way too. The White Man had to come here to learn how to value himself in a good way. Because only a person and a race self-confident in the best sense of the word is able to listen to the voices of other races and accept them as equals. This is true within all four races of the Earth.

"To teach them confidence in themselves, Creator gave each race a special gift to develop. We gain confidence and self-worth by being good at something, a gift we can offer the world. Each person must feel important enough to make a difference with his or her gift. When that person is honoured and respected for developing his special gift and sharing it, he learns to feel good about himself.

"The White Man's special gift from Creator was Motion, constantly doing and moving. Unfortunately, the White Man, in his isolation, began to think he was the best. When he travelled about, his swiftness made him see others as lesser than himself. He felt it his duty to teach them his superior ways. He gave no honour or respect to other races' special gifts."

"But we are not to interfere in anyone's life. It shows no honour or respect for that person, right *Nohkom* (loving form of 'my Grandma')?" Broken Arrow's young face twisted in thought as he struggled to understand.

"*Tapwe*, (True). So the White Man needs to come here and learn to live with all the races. He needs to learn and honour the special gifts given to each race by Creator. Each race's gift is equal to the White Man's, just different. He needs to learn this."

Mitsue took her charcoal stick and drew a small circle in the dirt between them. She divided the circle into four. "We are like this circle. There are four parts to each one of us. Each part represents a part of our selves: our mind, body, heart and spirit. We must develop all four equally and at the same time, in order to grow and learn in balance and harmony." She looked up at Broken Arrow who nodded in full understanding so she continued.

"The circle of life teaches we are all children of the Earth, that we all share an equal place in the circle. Creator made four colours of man: yellow, white, black and red." Again she pointed to the four parts of the circle. "When mixed together, the four colours of races create brown, the colour of Mother Earth. And to each of these races, Creator gave a task of developing one part of this circle so that others in the circle might learn from one another.

"To the White Man, he gave the task of learning about Motion, to understand and develop the human body, its motion and speed. White Man's fascination with motion made him create all kinds of tools to make himself go faster and farther. As a result, the White Man has learned to travel the Earth using wheels, engines, boats and trains. It's his task, his gift to the other races. The Creator cautioned him, however, about moving so fast he fails to stop and learn from the other races and their gifts in the circle."

She moved her stick to the next quarter, "The human body is connected to the mind. Creator gave the Yellow Man the task of developing the mind. His job was to discipline the mind so it does not overpower the body, heart or spirit but finds harmony with all parts."

B.A. leaned forward excitedly, "In mission school they talked about these yellow people and their great wise men, one called Buddha and his monks. They also spoke of the wise sayings of a man called Confucius. Their warriors were taught how to use their minds in balance with their body. Nohkom, they are developing their gift very wisely indeed!"

She smiled at his enthusiasm. "Creator cautioned the Yellow Man about spending too much time in his mind, forgetting to listen to his body, heart and spirit."

"And what of the black people my Grandma? What is their gift?"

Mitsue tapped the third quarter of the circle. "Theirs was more difficult, *Nosisim* (loving form of 'my Grandson'). Creator asked the black people to develop the heart. And since the heart has no words, they had to find other ways for expressing feelings. So they used music, rhythm, song and dance to speak of love and anger, fear, sorrow and joy." Mitsue's eyes filled with sorrow. "Grandson, sometimes I think Creator asked too much of them when he allowed them to become slaves to the White Man. Their situation forced them to find ways to express their broken hearts. Perhaps they needed to have their hearts broken in order to find them." She sighed, shaking her head.

The young boy felt her sorrow, his eyes darkening also. As a child he remembered seeing five black-skinned people chained together like animals, led about a fort by a posturing white man. "What were they cautioned about?"

"Never to lose sight of their mind, body and spirit, or they would stay lost in the bitterness of their broken hearts."

"And our Red People, Grandma. What is our task?" Broken Arrow leaned anxiously over the circle.

Mitsue considered her grandson of twelve summers, growing tall and handsome, soon to go on his first hunt. Was he ready to understand? Perhaps it was time to add to his journey into manhood. "Our task was to develop our spirit, connected through the heart from the mind and body. For only when we know our body, mind, heart and spirit, can we find our soul, the total of all four parts." She tapped the centre of the circle. "Then we can hear our soul, understand it, speak with it and make it a part of our daily life." When her grandson would have asked more, she quelled him with a quiet look in her eyes. "All the races were to develop their gift then come together and share it. They were to help each other find their souls. When the wisdom learned from developing these four gifts is shared equally between the races, harmony will abound."

She lifted a heavy arm and swung it wide, "This land is sacred land set aside by the Creator. *Canata* or Canada means 'Clean Land'. It is held in trust by the Red People, a place where all the races will come together one day and live together peacefully, without anger or war. No bloodshed can be spilled between the races on this sacred land. Our elders cautioned our warriors about this for hundreds of years. We are to share this land with the White, Black and Yellow Men so they can share their wisdom with each other—as equals. That is why in our sweats, we pray for all four races and tie up the flags of their four colours."

Mitsue tucked a thin strand of grey hair behind one ear before bending to her work once more. She tied a swift knot, cutting the sinew with her strong white teeth. Her people's well-balanced diet without the White Man's sugar ensured their teeth and bodies remained healthy. Using her sharp animal bone needle, she pierced the tiny holes in twenty-five emerald cut glass beads, sliding them onto her uneven, sinewy white thread. Then she added brilliant yellow beads, silently counting their number before tacking the entire strand into the outer shape of a green leaf, the yellow becoming the inner stem.

She took up her teaching once again for the young boy who had waited politely for her to continue. "The White Man needs to learn the truth of the four races and their gifts of equal worth. Instead of his pride and wish for leadership, he needs to learn compassion and reverence, for himself, true, but also for the gifts of the four races. Then and only then, can the Yellow Man teach him to control his mind in a good way, the Black Man how to use his heart with compassion and the Red Man how to find his spirit."

"And the *Nehiyawewin,* Cree people? What is our caution?"

She drew a deep breath, her eyes distant and filled with concern. "Sometimes I think we have the hardest path of all. We must lose our spirit in order to find it and develop it fully."

To join the decorated toe piece to the already gathered front sole of the moccasin, Mitsue lined up the two pieces facing each other and punched needle holes through both with an awl, a small, sharpened piece of steel, thinner than a nail. The round wooden handle protected her palm. She began sewing the two pieces together using a double strand of sinew for extra strength. The beaded piece would become the decorative upper part of the moccasin; the gathered piece would become the toe.

"How do we do that?" Broken Arrow crossed his legs and settled more comfortably at Mitsue's knee.

"Ah! My fine grandson, our people also learned too much pride in their isolation from the other races. And where there is pride, there can be no spirit, no truthful growth. Only through humility, the burning of our pride, beyond the loud voice of our selfish demands, can we hear the softer voice of our inner spirit, our connection to our soul." She shook her head, her eyes filling with tears as she looked away to the distant hills. "And how hard our people will struggle with this lesson."

B.A. frowned at the heavy lines in his beloved grandmother's face. She had been his teacher and mother all his life. It hurt him inside to watch tears slide into the heavy crevices of her cheeks.

"Our elders already know what will happen. They saw it long ago in their visions and dreams. They know we will become prisoners in our own land. Yet our greatest battle won't be with the White Man, but within ourselves. We must lose our pride to regain our spirit. When we fall on our knees in despair, we will remember bended knees offer the greatest lessons in forgiveness and humility. Forgiveness is the purest form of love we can give ourselves and one another—the true pathway to spirit. But we shall lie in the dust for many generations before we learn once again to stand on our hind legs and reach into our forgiveness, for the memories of spirit, then teach them to the other races."

*   *   *

Mac rubbed his jaw, his eyes upon the distant hills. "Well and now, I do believe the White Man has done a lot with his gift of Motion. Who else has built the strongest ships and sailed the seven seas with them? They've built wagons, carriages, steamboats, paddle wheelers and trains. One of our Italian artists, Michelangelo, created designs for flying machines over ten thousand years ago. Who knows where we'll go next. Maybe to the moon!"

He mused on, "And tis true the Romans were a cruel breed. They brought their levels of power through their emperors, senators, generals, soldiers and hangers-on. Everyone wanted to be the leader, rich and powerful. They've passed their class systems onto the British who added dukes, earls, barons and such. To be sure the Celts never had a class system. Their family heads were the only leaders they followed. The British ton certainly uses their levels of power to make the rest of the people feel badly, particularly the Irish. We were pushed to the bottom of their pyramid of power. They tried to convince us our value depended upon blind obedience to their standards." He snorted. "Aye, the Irish see only one face from the British and tis never kind. Rather than accept their authority, we have rebelled for centuries. You're no' the only ones considered heathens and pagans, filthy savages and drunks ready to fight at a moment's notice."

When B.A. turned his head and frowned at him, Mac nodded, "Aye, ye be standing in line for those grand titles. Tis what the Romans called the Celts and what the British called the Irish and Scots, before they took their land away. Now they call your people the same. Tis nothing new, this cruel prejudice. I faced it every day at University with the English students. Never did they let me forget me Irish red hair and temper. Aye and I was foolish enough to prove them right." He glumly surveyed his scarred fist.

"Why do they do it?" B.A. never understood this need for cruelty, to constantly put another down, to criticize, to judge with no wisdom or understanding behind it. It stunted people's growth. His aunts and grandmothers had taught him how to say good things, honourable and respectful words to people to keep them growing and advancing their soul.

Mac shrugged, "They try to convince ye they are better, more civilized. Aye, grand Christians they be, savin' yer soul. If ye be savin' some poor fool from hell and damnation, I guess ye can justify taking his land and not be callin' yerself a thief. Tis what they did to the Irish too. Did y'know a Spanish theologian, someone who studies religion, created a grand theory that Indians were not far removed from the state of wild animals so they needed religion to be controlled before they could become useful labourers for the Spaniards."

B.A. grunted, "Our ceremonies to Creator are far less cruel than the Turtle People's who whipped people in the name of God until their backs bled."

"Turtle people?"

"Named from the helmets the Spaniards wore. They looked like turtles. An old Navajo told me the gentle Anastazi left their stone houses in the mountains further south and went with the Sky People before the cruel Spaniards could capture them."

Mac's eyes widened, "Sky people? Where do they live?"

B.A. pointed to the clear blue canopy above them. "In a group of stars you call Orion's belt."

Mac stared upwards in awe, trying to remember his studies about flying machines and their images carved into South American temples. Could they actually be real? He settled for compromise, "The Anastazi was right. The Spanish were cruel. They tortured and killed many Indians trying to find their source of gold. The British are no better. Preacher Gray, a scholar of St. John's College at Cambridge, England lectured how the Englishman had a solemn duty to seek out fresh land to relieve the overcrowding at home. He said, "If the land be inhabited by savages, then the Englishman must take the land from the idolatrous heathen.""

B.A. frowned, "Idolatrous heathen?"

Mac grinned, "Aye. They think ye love your coupling overmuch."

B.A.'s lip curled, "Maybe they're jealous."

Mac shook his head, "Not those stalwart Christian souls. Their university professors actually created so-called 'scientific theories' that Indians are mentally and morally inferior to Europeans and therefore not able to look after themselves."

"*Mah!*" Broken Arrow growled, "Our people have survived in this land for thousands of generations, long before the White Man came. We do not need his iron or his diseases!"

Mac cried, "'Tis a colonial way of thinking! They force the natives to depend on the raiders. If the British view Indians as children, then they can become the superior parents! If they view Indians as brutal, they can enforce brutal laws to control them! If they view them as stupid, they can justify stealing their land from beneath them! But God help any White Man who marries into the heathens. They keep the races apart to protect their true lineage and power. Marriage is therefore taboo between races according to the British."

B.A. chuckled, "Tell that to the Metis. They say their nation started nine months after the first White Man arrived!"

Mac briefly wondered how willing the Native women had been for such an early coupling. Not likely! He rubbed his face, eyes darkening with worry. "Professor Gray only summed up the British plan: convert the heathen, make them servile and obedient to God and therefore to their English masters who could then create a peaceful takeover of this land." Mac moved into an orator's stance, one arm aloft, the other placed over his heart 'For the Land must be claimed at any cost for the Children of God'."

"And what are we?" snapped B.A. his eyes narrowing to furious slits.

"The Puritans called you, 'Children of the Devil'. Those pious Christian soldiers sent letters back to England stating the Indians they encountered might profitably be wiped out and their lands appropriated. White Traders gave the Mic Mac Indians of the Eastern seaboard blankets from people with smallpox! It destroyed entire camps in no time. Today, very few Mic Mac are alive." Mac blew out his breath, eyes to the distance. "Stand in line Indian Man or stand aside. Tis the land they want and the land they'll get even if they have kill you to get it!"

"And what of our prophecies about *Canata*?" B.A. growled.

Mac's eyebrow lifted, his lips turning down in thought. "Tis a grand vision of the four races' gifts. I'd not heard it before. It makes sense, in the larger picture. But who is teaching the rest of the world this? Not too many seem to know it."

B.A. recalled Mitsue's final words when his youthful shoulders had slumped and his head dropped. She touched his knee with gentle fingers. "It will play out, Nosism. The lessons must be learned by all four races, ours included. The children of the next seven generations, children from all the races of the world who come to this land will suffer this lesson before they understand one another. Always it is seven generations. Always! Perhaps mankind must have a time of darkness before we can all learn what a blessing the light is. But in that darkness, lies one glimmer of hope. Their lessons will be painful but their capacity for pain will smooth the way for their capacity to love one another. That is the path until Spirit comes fully to all four races. For we must all be with Spirit, balanced and whole before we can find harmony on this Earth once again."

B.A. contemplated her words for some time before one corner of his mouth kicked up and he grinned at Mac. "When you are wiser in the ways of the land, Irish Man, I will tell you about Mud Woman, the spirit of Mother Earth and her answer." Dodging Mac's flicking rein, he picked up the pace and rode into a land darkened by a gathering storm.

7.

THE BLUFF

The two men rode west now, towards Fort Ellice after breaking camp. Both craved bigger game than the prairie chickens and ducks they'd stuffed with wild onions and prairie sage before roasting in campfire coals. Suddenly Broken Arrow dismounted. "See these?" he pointed to animal tracks in the mud.

Mac slid from his horse and bent for a closer view, "Looks like cow tracks."

"Bull moose. See the narrow slit in his hooves? That means he's walking, it's wider when he runs. A bull always walks a straight line, dragging his feet. A cow moose lifts her feet and zig zags through willows to confuse any wolves tracking her and her calf. Besides, willows make so much noise she can hear them coming." B.A. stuck his fist into the indentation, noting wet mud pushed up around the track. "It's fresh, some time this morning. He's a big one, still in his prime but getting old . . . tougher chewing."

"Sure'n d'ye know his pedigree too?" Mac groused, not fully believing the big Cree who often pulled his leg with some wild story.

A shot rang out.

The men heard a solid 'Thwack!' followed by a guttural rumble up ahead. They froze as twigs snapped and heavy footsteps stumbled towards them. Out of the trembling, crackling bush, a huge bull moose staggered down the path towards them, his ears laying back in fury as he spotted them. Broken Arrow lifted his gun into position while Mac scrabbled for his. But the moose's forelegs suddenly buckled, ramming his gigantic nose into the dirt. His massive horns hooked birch saplings with a hollow clattering of heavy palms. With a hoarse groan, he toppled sideways, kicked a few times and lay still.

Mac moved towards the animal, but B.A's arm held him back. "If he can get up, he will."

The moose lay still and silent, a tiny zephyr ruffling the long stiff hair across his humped shoulders. Dark blood spread from beneath the moose into a widening pool. B.A. drew his knife and cautiously crept to the animal's head. The tall Cree seemed dwarfed by the huge wrack of horns. When no sound or motion disturbed the animal, B.A. swiftly sliced the animal's throat. He backed away as blood gushed out in a slow pulsating stream, sinking into the soil from whence it came.

Broken Arrow studied the black carcass glistening in the morning sunshine while its lifeblood ebbed away. "Somebody shot him right through the heart. A good shot."

From up the path, a young man, probably late teens, strode into the clearing, followed by two shorter men, carrying guns and leading three horses.

"I say Ol' chap, I do believe that is my animal," the youth spoke up. His overcoat, a dark fashionable bang-up, revealed a stark white shirt and neck cloth complete with gold breast pin beneath a tight-bodied vest. Its brass buttons with engraved initials—probably his own, Mac sneered silently—his stark white stockings and tri-corn hat cried 'gentry'. The scrawny Toff made an elegant bow towards Mac and B.A. "Sir Henry Grenfell, at your service." He lifted his chin, surveyed them with negligent contempt and tucked his hands beneath his greatcoat.

"I do believe it is, 'Ol' Chap!'" Mac tipped his head in sarcastic echo. Sweet Jesus, he'd left the East to get away from these piss proud devils and here they were again. They'd made his life at University a living hell. To them he was the 'Tipperary Irishman, ready to fight at the drop of a hat'. Aye and he'd cleaned the clocks of quite a few of them before they'd learned to keep their distance. This one walked like he had a frozen carrot stuck up his arse. Mac's brogue deepened out of sheer stubbornness. "Me friend here was good enough to bleed 'im for ye so ye'd be savourin' excellent meat."

The Englishman's hooded eyes stared down his nose, albeit tilted upwards, to the tall Indian. "Yes, well, in our country, only the Quality is allowed to hunt game. Any peasant daring to touch a lord's meat was shot or hanged. I do believe it an excellent ruling. It would certainly keep this sport a 'Gentlemanly Diversion' without heathen involvement." He rudely turned his back to address the two men bringing up the horses. "James, you may commence dressing the animal. And Harold, build a fire to make some tea whilst I wait."

Mac's lip curled in disgust at how quickly the older men responded to the arrogant little bugger. "Ye know, in this country, people do for themselves. It's called 'Equality', not Quality. Why don't ye make yer own damned tea if ye want it so bad."

The slender young man pursed his lips and glared coldly at the sturdy Irishman. He removed a tiny, elegantly carved pewter box from an inner pocket, snapped its lid open, pinched off a small piece of snuff with forefinger and thumb, raised it to his upturned nostril and delicately sniffed it.

The bastard probably had the ingredients mixed just for him Mac fumed sourly, recognizing the tactic for what it was.

The fair Englishman drawled, "You have been amongst these savages too long sir. Perhaps it is time to return to civilization; else you forget your manners entirely."

B.A. brushed past the posturing fool and bent to the smaller man, James, leaning over the moose. He'd made an odd slit across the chest, from foreleg to foreleg. "Have you skinned a moose before?"

James glanced up and then back to his work, shaking his head. His short stature and thin arms made the Cree hunter wonder how this slight man ever hoped to hang a massive animal weighing over a thousand pounds. But the man gamely grinned up at him, "Nay, but it can't be much harder than skinning a hare."

Harold, his equally short but stockier companion trundled over with a small armload of wood. He too bent to examine the carcass, confusion and awe carved into his beefy face. "Gor 'e's a big un ain't 'e?"

B.A.'s eyes sparked, "Would you like some help?"

"Cart'inly! Be pleased!" The two chorused in relief.

Squatting on his heels, Broken Arrow quickly slit the animal from sternum to scrotum, careful to cut the masculine paraphernalia away before it tainted the meat. He then sliced off the bell, the long thin chunk of hide and hair that hung beneath the animal's chin. Standing, he lifted it and carefully draped it over the branches of a willow above them, his lips moving in a prayer of gratitude.

At the two men's questioning looks, he explained, "This sets the animal's spirit free and honours his gift of food."

Overhearing them, the young Englishman sneered, "Heathen nonsense! It is nothing but a silly animal without the brains to run away like a fox would have." He sighed, "But, what else can one expect in this provincial backwoods with its equally backward inhabitants. Get on with it James and do stop wasting time Harold. I promised Mother I'd be back in time for high tea."

"Look Boyo! Who the hell are you to come waltzing into this country and insult people! If ye'd shut yer yap once in a while ye might learn a thing or two. Ye damned milksop! Ye were likely booted out of England fer yer devilish ways and sent here to find some manners. And I know a few to start ye off with!" Mac leapt forward his fists up and ready.

B.A. turned back and grabbed his arm, halting him in mid-stride. Mac shook his arm free, his green eyes glittering with rage. The Englishman lifted one eyebrow in distain but when the glowering Mac took another step, the younger man cautiously pulled his head and upper body back.

The Cree bent once more to the carcass. After pulling the steaming entrails out, he reached inside all the way to the spine between the rib cage and hip bones. He hooked his fingers onto two long strips of meat lying on either side of the backbone and ripped them free. "I think my friend and I will leave you to your work. I'll just take these two scraps for my dog. Good day!"

As the two rode away, Brownfoot snorted, sidling sideways from the iron taint of fresh blood. When they were some distance from the trio, the Cree's lips lifted in mischief as he regarded the fuming Irishman who was still muttering.

"Damned Limey's, always lordin' it over everyone. I left the East to be rid of their arrogant hides. The *badach*, bastard probably won't lower himself to even eat the meat—too wild for his delicate taste buds. He'll just stuff the head and hang the horns so he can brag to his cronies from England. To him, large game is just another status symbol for the rich—another way to lord it over everyone. Even the English fur traders think only the big game animals are worth hunting!"

B.A. frowned, "These English, they hunt just to brag? They don't eat the meat? Mah! What a waste of a good animal. The bull chose to reveal himself, sacrificed his life so man can live from his flesh. So we thank him and release his spirit. We never kill anything we don't eat."

"Stupid greedy buggars." Mac stormed on, "They used up their own land then came to Ireland and stole ours. When the potato famine hit, the English lords could have stopped it. They knew how. But no! Instead, they let the Irish starve and die, just for the land." He turned to B.A. "Never let them herd you onto reservations. That's what they did to me grandparents and their families. Promised they'd take care of the Irish and keep them from starvin'. The close quarters made the disease easier to spread, easier to kill our families. Once my relatives had died off from the potato plague, the English bastards bought their land for a few measly pounds in back taxes."

B.A. searched the vast forest about him, saddened by such greed, wondering what it would do to this land. Then his black eyes sparkled, "The English Man, he talks a good bluff."

Mac turned to him in surprise, his fists still clenched in fury. "Ye admire the badach? He insulted ye!"

B.A. rode on unconcerned. "You saw a lord trying to bully you. I saw a boy suffering from 'buck fever'. Young hunters get it after their first kill. Some are so afraid they'll drop their guns without a shot. The Englishman's knee caps were still bouncing in fear. He hid his hands behind his back because they shook. So he bluffed his way through. But it is your choice to accept his bluff or not. What matters is . . . who has the greatest bluff."

To Mac's jaundiced eyes the Cree appeared to be in unusually high spirits, his shoulders easy and relaxed.

"What the Sam Hill does that mean? And what were ye blatherin' about back there?" Mac groused, "Ye don't have a dog!"

B.A. turned merry eyes towards the angry man. "We feast tonight my friend." He swung the two strips of bloody meat towards Mac's face.

"Pah!" Mac swiped the meat away, "What the hell are these scraps anyway?"

B.A. grinned in mischievous delight, "The best part of a big animal. I believe in your language, you call it tenderloin. The French call it Filet Mignon."

8.

MEDICINE WHEEL

"What is this?" Mac and B.A. stood on a high hill, golden prairie grassland stretched out from them in all directions. At their feet lay long radiating lines of stones, like a gigantic wheel with spokes hundreds of feet long. The centre of the wheel topped the crest of the hill.

"We call them medicine wheels." Broken Arrow's hair lifted in the breeze, partially obscuring his face. "We use them as a place to pray, to fast and to think. Grandmother Grizzly Bear, one of the wise women I once met who held Medicine Wheel ceremonies, taught how medicine wheels are a sacred, magical circle. She claimed we have the right to be here, to sit in this circle because the Creator knows us. She encouraged us to speak to the stones here because they all know us, because we are ALL ONE. Here is a place to ask for help and guidance, to let our intent be known. The Medicine Wheel is handed down for thousands of years. It is about movement, change and understanding, encouraging us to be open to life."

He stood swinging his arm wide, "See the spokes? The wheels are placed upon the earth, beneath the sky, in recognition of Mother Earth below and Father Sky above. Together they represent the six powers of direction in the circle: north, east, south, west, above and below. The seventh power is within us, where our soul dwells. Some lines in this stone circle follow the sun's rays on the first day of spring, summer, fall and winter.

"The old people saw life as a circle . . . from birth to death . . . and we journey around the wheel many times throughout our lives because we always have new beginnings and endings; new things to learn and do; new things to consider which eventually adds to our wisdom, ending another cycle. Each direction helps us understand ourselves a little bit more." He pointed to the four spokes which marked the four directions. "Each of the four directions offers many teachings."

He pointed in the direction of the rising sun. "East is about new beginnings, light, morning, innocence, birth, rebirth, childhood, new understandings, guidance, the time in spring when day and night share equal time and the part of the circle representing our spirit."

Broken Arrow's long arm pointed to the south spoke of the wheel. "In the south we find the qualities of noon, the day of summer when the sun reaches its highest point, youth, nurturing, generosity, compassion, anger at injustice, balanced development of the physical body and the part of the circle representing our emotions."

His arm swung to the west spoke of the wheel. "In the west, we find ourselves at sunset, the time of leaves falling and equal night and day, adulthood, introspection, letting go, the unknown, dreams, meditation, ceremony and the part of the circle representing our physical body."

When Broken Arrow turned north, Mac turned with him, struggling with the information from this fascinating culture. "North," the Cree continued, "is where we find midnight, the time of the longest night and shortest day, when winter comes, the white haired elders, wisdom, understanding, fulfilment, completion from growing the spirit and the part of the circle representing our minds."

His dark eyes searched the green of his companion's, "You may start anywhere on this circle, at any time, because you will move around it many times, discovering different parts to yourself, gaining understanding and growing your soul throughout your life. To live according to the Medicine Wheel, one must be balanced in the physical, mental, emotional and spiritual parts of this circle—always—a child of the Creator." He turned back to the circle, his eyes narrowing, "Traditionally, people would do whatever was necessary for survival in the proper manner."

Mac scratched his head, awed by the powerful symbolism this circle represented, like a handbook on life. His bible suddenly seemed rambling and vague.

The Cree moved to the centre of the circle and knelt. "Our elders often say Mother Earth yearns to communicate, and that all of nature is in fact language. Often there are special stones, clear like the White Man's glass beneath the ground here, stones like no other in this land. But to disturb them is to anger the spirits of the ancient ones who guard these places.

"Tall Man said all the stones in the wheel are like warriors, lined and waiting, protecting this place, holding its life force, creating a place for man to enter the Silence, in respect and prayer. A sacred circle for us to think about and listen to the messages from Spirit we find in our dreams and visions."

Kneeling beside him, Mac stared upward then around the site. "Reminds me of our fairy circles in Ireland. In Britain alone they have over nine hundred of these stone circles, the most famous being Stonehenge. They also have spokes which mark the seasons. We call the spokes dragon lines of energy which connect through energy lines to other circles all over the land. The ancient religions used them for some sort of ceremonies to the Earth Mother Goddess. But the Christians called them pagan, based on witchcraft and evil. They covered such pagan sites with their churches and built their alters right over the centre of these circles."

"If they were such evil places, why would they bring their people there to worship the Christ?"

Mac looked up in surprise, "I dunno. Mayhap they thought they could chase the evil away with their holy water and prayers."

"And mayhap they forced people to come to their Christian churches by putting them in the same space." B.A. scorned as he sat down.

"Same space . . . ." Mac narrowed his eyes in thought as he joined his friend between the stone lines. "My people believed this world and the spiritual Otherworld occupy the same space anyway. To them there was no soul journey after death; the eternal is at home, within each of us. The Irish say, 'The land of eternal youth is behind the house, a beautiful land fluent within itself.' It is not parallel, but fused with our mortal, physical world. Behind the curtain or veil of the familiar, strange things await us."

B.A's lips pursed as he leaned his elbows on his bent knees, "Our people call it the Spirit World and it also takes up the same space as we do. But we cannot see it. Only through our dreams, visions, prayers and ceremonies may we enter it but only for a short time because we may wish to stay."

Mac shoved his hat back on his head, squirmed to a comfortable seating position and squinted into the grey clouds above. "I heard about some great stones they found on Mystery Hill, New Hampshire that were lined up with the summer and winter solstices and star and moon patterns. Another was found near Woodstock in Vermont. Our Celtic people used religious writings called *Ogham* over 2,500 years ago. Yet those stones here in North America had writings in Ogham." He grinned over at B.A., "Mayhap we have mutual cousins."

He suddenly looked about him in dawning wonder, "The Druids also used the Spirit of the Stone Circle." In a quiet awe, he continued, "Like your people, the Celts lived together in a fenced circle of homes. They too were all related families, some as far as ninth removed. Several families such as these became a *tuath*, like your band or tribe! Each leader was elected by the community. Each *tuath* lived independently, making everything it needed to survive as a community. Everything was owned by the entire group. It had its own rules, even its own gods."

Mac back leaned on his hands, seeing more similarities, "Like your elders, the Celts believed writing anything down was to lose memory. So their training to be a Druid, an educated person, was long with difficult memorizations. Students studied twenty years to pass one test. Both men and women entered Druid training. They learned Latin, Greek, mathematics, art, literature and the healing arts. Druids ran hospitals and surgery, law courts, held morality judgements, while others like the bard masters sang, played instruments and quoted poetry and music. In those days, if anyone spoke Latin, it was a Druid or someone taught by a Druid. For centuries, to be a scholar and an Irishman was the same thing. When a young man in Europe wanted the best education, he went to an Irish monastery. In fact, the Celtic education centres and those who went out from them, kept wisdom alive during the Dark Ages of Europe in the fifteenth and sixteenth centuries.

"The Celts were the fair-haired, fair-skinned people who lived all over Europe and as far south as the Mediterranean Sea at one time. Our history claims they even farmed the English Channel before the ice melted from the glaciers and filled it. It certainly explains their close relationship with the people of Britain and France. Mayhap Ireland was also once connected to Britain. The Celts even sacked Rome in a bid for their riches. The Roman Empire grew as the Romans fought back, defeating the Celts all the way to Britain." Mac chuckled, "but they never defeated the black-haired Scottish Picts or the Irish."

"How did the Celts lose to the Romans?"

Mac plucked a blade of grass, stuck the soft sweet end closest to the root into his mouth and sucked contemplatively, "In the end, our family divisions made it hard for anyone to agree on anything and put up a united front. Men fought for their families, not the land. Their personal quarrelling couldn't maintain a large united force against the organized Roman soldier troops. Aye, the Roman soldiers never defeated the Irish, but their priests did in the end. Through the last centuries, Ireland eventually became Roman Catholic. Some people held out, remained Protestant in defence against the Church. But eventually Christianity overruled the Celtic values and religion." He turned to his dark-skinned friend, "And now they do the same to you and yours."

B.A. felt the impact down to his nauseated gut. "What did your people do about it?"

Mac blinked rapidly, "They fought, for centuries, and still do, uselessly, endlessly. Anger keeps them violent, revenge their only power, their final weapon. My family fled the wars and potato famine to find a more peaceful, freer life here." He snorted in disgust, "Yet the British were already here, along with their priests, well established and wantin' more, just as destructive and blindly uncaring as ever. Even my family converted to Catholicism. Ah Jesus, Mary and Joseph! How could it come to this?" He dropped his head, his shoulders slumped and weary.

B.A. squinted in the sunlight, "Are not these Romans the ancestors of the British?"

Mac nodded, "Aye, they probably still hold a bit of their blood and definitely a lot of Roman values. Theirs was a cruel soldier society, based on whippings, brutality and power."

B.A. thought for a while, choosing his words carefully, "Then they have learned nothing from our peoples' generosity and wisdom. Tall Man used to trade with an old Iroquois named Angus Callihoo. He said it was his ancestors who foolishly kept the Pilgrims alive when they landed on their shores. They actually allowed those strange white people to steal food from their storage buildings after they came ashore. The Iroquois elders decided they must really be starving to do such a terrible thing. It was the Iroquois who taught the Pilgrims their Thanksgiving Ceremonies, giving thanks to the Creator for the abundant harvest each fall. And each spring, they taught these black and white people how to care for the soil and plant their crops the right way. Now I hear talk this Thanksgiving is a holiday brought here by the Pilgrims!

"Old Callihoo claimed it was the Iroquois League of Five Nation's method of democracy which the American White Man used to write his Declaration of Independence. The White Man took these ideas and now calls them his own!" B.A. grunted in disgust.

Mac's laugh was rusty with scorn. "Considerin' the Europeans came from a feudal society of kings and peasants, I'd be hard pressed to see any of them comin' up with an idea of equality among men, let alone women!" He snorted, "And so begins the flood my friend."

B.A. shook his head. "Callihoo said the White Man forgets how their White House is shaped like the Iroquois tipi. Now they call it the Pentagon. The old Iroquois talked about his people's thanksgiving designs of corn and squash being carved right into the White House's limestone walls to honour the Iroquois. They were rubbed out after the Cherokee Trail of Tears and the Indian wars. Now nobody talks about what the Iroquois did for the Pilgrims or the American Government." B.A. studied the land around them, a land created for a purpose it struggled to fulfil.

Mac took out his penny whistle flute and began to play an old Irish melody. No words accompanied it, only the haunting sorrow of ancient people whose warrior clans fought and died, who struggled to survive, who passed on their lineage and their legacy of grief and loss. A culture destined to die, not because of its evil but because of its goodness. Aye, he thought, the Irish were Masters of the Sorrows. The song both pained and soothed his heart. It filled him with a sweet melancholy, a yearning for something more. His people called it a longing for *Tir-nan-Og,* the mystical place beyond the setting sun, a place of the Otherworld, filled with unsurpassed beauty, peace and abundance. A place for things that were and yet were not—lost now in the blue mists. Mac played on, his mind filled with graven images of times passed, his childhood, his family and the bleak world of power that had destroyed his family's dreams, forcing them to seek new ones in a new world.

Another sound entered his ears, resonating in tune with his melody, only deeper, softer, a blooming richness of rhythm adding dimension to his tin whistle. In surprise, he looked up to see B.A. walking back from his horses, blowing into a long wooden flute, its end a carved and painted loon's head. B.A. followed the melody effortlessly, his sparking eyes laughing down into Mac's before seating himself nearby. Mac closed his own and gave himself up to the folk music, letting it fill him, soothe him, then empty him of all thought. Together the men's flutes blended and rippled, calling out to one another, joining in partnership until they flowed in endless symmetry down through the silent countryside.

As the song ended, B.A. took up another, this one of his land. With his eyes still closed, Mac allowed the sound to vibrate through him, fill his mind and heart and beyond. Instead of sorrow and tragedy, he heard the wind as it slipped down rocky crevices, flowed over rippling waves and danced through emerald leaves. Instead of legacy, he heard presence. Instead of history, he heard the sound of the moment, this moment in time, suspended, filled and fulfilling, pure and clean and soft—a lilting prelude only hope can create.

Behind closed lids, Mac considered this 'Now', this 'Moment' B.A. had tried to explain to him over a campfire a few nights ago. He said it was not attached to the past which cannot change anyway, nor was it attached to the future which cannot be reached. But this moment, this clear crystal moment, is all man really has, full total, this 'Now'. Could life remain this simple? This minute awareness of life, passion and the clean cut presence of a single second held up for perception, cherished for its experience and lived to its fullest capacity? The music wrapped him in joy, comforting his lonely soul. He found himself moving his head, swaying to the rhythm and simply experiencing life to the fullest in this moment. . . . Ahh!!!

Maybe B.A. was right. Dwelling on the past made one sad because it blocked living in the Moment. Dwelling on the future meant a lack of faith in the Creator's plan. Only simple faith allowed it to unfold, as it should, as it would, with or without man's insistence. Was there a bigger plan to the British greed, ignorance and selfish pride? Was life a place of learning for all men as B.A.'s elders taught? For them every Moment was sacred, to be honoured with an open mind and a closed mouth. Yet the past was respected as greatly as the future when making decisions because they affected the seven generations gone before and seven generations yet to be born. To do so, meant living in the Moment and the privilege of life it brought.

Now he understood B.A.'s earnest words. "When you give yourself to the Moment, you are not living in it, nor living for it like a duty.

You are just **living it**, with passion, honour and great, great love. Each Moment deserves everything you have to give." Mac lifted his whistle to his lips and poured everything he had, everything he had ever been and hoped to become into the melody. It cried out through him and into the wind flowing across the land.

And his soul danced free—in the moment.

9.

SILKIES

Mac lay dreaming in his bedroll. From out of the blue mists before him, pure sound came to him, clear and soft; an undulating lilt of melody without words, a sweet, pure rhapsody from the throat of a young woman. He reached out, saw his hand part a veil in the vapour, disappearing ahead of him then reappearing as he moved between the veils. Into the soft haze he drifted. It swirled around him, until he saw nothing but mist yet he continued moving ahead. He felt a sense of trust, unafraid of the force gently compelled him onward. Uncertain of the terrain and totally unaware of his surroundings, he still moved towards the singer, wanting to see, to touch and to find the heart rendering sweetness that drew him. He felt encumbered by the very heaviness of his body and wanted to free himself, lift above it, into the song, until he was a part of it, inside it. For the first time, he would be one, whole, not fragmented like he had felt for so long. A vague shape appeared in the distant vapours. He drifted closer, flowing into rippling waves of sound until his fingers touched something solid. Now the song vibrated through him. Throwing his head back in ecstasy, he let it slide within him, become part of him, and he part of it until it filled him, satiated him like never before. He blinked rapidly. If only he could see her. His yearning heart reached deeper into the sound, wanting more . . . .

Then something pulled him back. He fought furiously, struggled with all his might to stay and couldn't. Back, back he flew through the veils.

He flinched at the agony of severance, her voice fading into the blue mists while he, a mere mortal . . . awoke . . . opened his eyes and groaned at his loss. *"Tha m'anam a' sn'mh an ce'o,* my soul swims in mist!"

Across the fire, B.A. awoke, rose to an elbow and sleepily regarded him. "You are in pain?"

Mac lifted his head, moved his fingers and found them wrapped around a small birch sapling, so tight, his knuckles were white. He unfurled his fingers, painfully stretching their tension and stiffness. "Jaysus . . . that was some dream."

Broken Arrow studied the Irishman who checked the quiet night with uneasy eyes, as if searching for something. They were camped along the Pheasant Plains, not far from Cut Arm Creek. He waited.

Mac rubbed a shaky hand over his bristling face. "I heard music, the most beautiful, incredible melody from a young woman's singing. Her song had no words, didn't need it. Twas a soft, lilting sound, the way our Irish women sing the old Celtic songs of haunting melodies." He shook his head to clear it. "Yet this song was deeper, with a richer resonance, so magical I didn't want to come back. I wanted to stay with her, find her in the mists. I fought the awakening, but something drew me back and away from the mists."

He sat up and leaned against a tree; the remnants of the aria still wafted through his mind, truly a siren's song. "Ye know, in Irish legends we have silkies, the seal women, who can change to female form. They sit amongst the rocks along the ocean and lure the sailors to their deaths, simply by singing their siren songs." He closed his eyes, not wanting to lose the memory of the melody and still it faded, distant already. "But, ye know, if those sailors heard what I just heard, I think they chose to die, to free their spirit and just remain with the song and the spirits who sang it. I wanted to stay, as crazy as that sounds, I wanted to stay with her too."

He glanced at B.A. to see if he laughed at such fanciful words, but the man studied him solemnly.

"You may have heard one of Mud Woman's daughters. They are the souls of trees. I noticed your hand wrapped around that birch as you slept. You may have heard its song."

Mac whipped his head around and frowned at the slim birch sapling. A young female? In a tree? This tree stuff was really beginning to spook him yet curiosity drove him to ask, "Your grandfather, Tall Man, you said he talked to the trees?"

"Many of our elders could."

"Are trees really male or female?"

"Everything else is."

Mac frowned, reached a tentative hand out and wrapped his fingers around the birch sapling. Nothing. Neither sound nor song reached back. All he felt was the tree's movement in a quiet breeze. The beauty of the earlier melody drifted away forgotten in the mists of his dream. A stark loneliness echoed through the emptiness left inside him.

"Who *is* Mud Woman?" Mac rubbed the sapling with gentle finger tips, smoothing over the flakes of loosened bark, unwilling to break the connection, his heart yearning still.

B.A. settled back against a tall black poplar, "She is made of leaves and mud, roots and seeds. Her hair is grass and vines, both dead and alive. Her eyes are two golden leaves; her hands the gnarled roots of ancient trees. Like an old mound of muskeg hummocks, she rises out of the swamp and connects with all of Mother Earth's creatures for she is the Nurturer, the Grower of all things."

Bemused, Mac stroked the birch's visible roots, "She sounds like what we call Mother Nature—the spirit of this earth. In ancient times, she was worshipped, a feminine goddess, if you believe the tales of Avalon and King Arthur of the Round Table."

B.A. gave up on further sleep and made himself comfortable, "Tell me your legend White Man."

Mac tilted his head back to survey the heavens, "Don't be thinking' I'm a *seanachie*, a Gaelic storyteller, but I'll do my best. They say the purpose of myth or legend is to let us experience our soul here, not somewhere else long ago."

Broken Arrow nodded, "My elders say the same. The purpose of vision, dreams, meditation and ceremony is for us to experience our spirit here and now. Their messages offer us truth far beyond what we see, hear or touch."

Mac gazed drifted to the distant hills. "There is a Holy Island in the Summer Sea, off England's coast. Twas was once called Avalon. And if a traveller had the will and knew only a few of the secrets, he could set sail through the mists and arrive in Avalon, the gate to the world of Earth Mother, a gate where the world of reality, or this life, opened to Otherworld of the goddess. All the traveller had to do was to think and believe. This was our religion, the Celtic faith. We had celebrations at different times of the year in honour of Ishtar, our goddess of fertility and growth.

"The high priestess of Avalon was called 'Lady of the Lake', from the Summer Sea and she followed the druid beliefs of the Goddess, a powerful female creator, the feminine version of life, with her intuition, her dreams and visions along with her ability to accept new ideas, using her gift with compassion, nourishing all life around her."

Broken Arrow raised his eyebrows, "In our beliefs too, the female is the Idea Maker; the male, the Doer."

Mac nodded, still focused on his tale, "In an attempt to find harmony between the very masculine Catholic religion and the ancient female Goddess faith, the Lady of the Lake gave a young man called Arthur, the sword, Excalibur, and a leather sheath formed by druid prayers and rites. Arthur was a nephew to the Lady of the Lake and raised with the ancient religion of the druid priests. But he accepted the baptism of Christianity under the insistence of his very Christian wife, Guinevere.

"The joining of the masculine and the feminine religions never worked. Arthur as king became more Christian than druid. His faith allowed the monks to set the people against the Lady of the Lake. They condemned her priestesses as witches and all her holiday celebrations as evil, the Devil's work. Arthur died at the hand of his own son along the shores of Avalon. When his knight, Lancelot threw Excalibur back into the Summer Sea, a hand rose out of the lake, caught it, brandished it three times then drew it beneath the waves."

Mac kicked a few more logs closer into the centre of the smouldering embers. "The Christian monks, believing Avalon infringed upon the power of their masculine God, built a monastery on the island of Avalon and called it Glastonbury. They safeguarded it with the sound of their church bells, to drive away all thoughts from a traveller about the Otherworld that still existed in the same space. Avalon gradually receded into the mists. People lost the faith to believe in Avalon; therefore they could neither find it nor Our Lady of the Lake in the mists."

Mac shook his head, "If she was anything like the lady in the mists of my dream, mayhap we should not have let her go so easily . . . ."

He grinned suddenly, "Aye, we exiled her, but mayhap she lives on. The Goddess had many names, including Isis and Ishtar. Did ye know that as much as the Catholics and Protestants wish to claim Easter celebrations for Christ, Ishtar's original symbols for this holiday remain? Easter is a twisted version of her name. The Easter bunny symbolizes her totem, the hare or rabbit. Easter eggs represent her eternal fertility, Goddess of Mother Earth." Mac chuckled, "And nothing breeds faster than rabbits! They say the female gets pregnant again the day her litter is born."

Broken Arrow smiled and nodded.

Mac squinted into the fire, "People say the Holy Thorn from Avalon grew itself in the Chapel of Mary, the nuns' convent on Glastonbury. Eventually this thorny plant moved into the abbeys and churches of all Christendom. And in the days that followed, as long as the land shall last, every queen of England is given this Holy Thorn at Christmas in token of 'She' who is Queen in Heaven, as in Avalon.

Some call it the Christmas cactus and I have seen many women growing them in their homes in the Canadas. So they are spreading across this land too. In Ireland, we still have statues of our old saint Brigid. She is not Christian though the priests would have us believe so, but from the ancient Goddess herself." He chuckled, "Aye, she has not gone away, only shrouded herself in the mists. Perhaps she still sings to those who would believe.

"The druids taught what man believes, he creates in the world around us, daily anew. As man saw reality, so it became. While the ancient Goddesses were seen as benevolent or life-giving, so indeed was Mother Nature to man. When the priests taught men to think of Nature as evil, alien and hostile so she became. And when they insisted the old Gods and Goddesses were demons, even so they became, surging up from within a part of man which he fears the most."

B.A. rolled to his side on his buffalo robe, resting his chin on a raised forearm. "So they made for themselves the kind of God they thought they wanted. Or . . . perhaps the kind of God they deserved."

10.

SPENSE

Mac struggled with his saddlebags and extra gear he had purchased at different places since Fort Ellice. They kept falling out of his makeshift pack and generally rattling about behind him. In total exasperation, he swore to find a packhorse. One day, they came upon a herd of horses grazing in a shallow valley. Some bore various brands, most did not. Their frenzied run from the men marked them as a wild roving band—maybe. With no one nearby to claim them, Mac decided to cut out a big unmarked grey. He justified the 'taking' as recompense for his stolen horse, Jim. They returned to camp with Mac bragging incessantly about his matched greys. He didn't seem to mind that his 'new' horse was much larger than his saddle horse, Willy (named after the willy nilly way B.A. stole him).

Something bothered B.A. Mac noted the deepening creases around the Cree's eyes and the way his mouth turned down at the corners, looking rumpled and uneven. Right away his back stiffened, "What are ye laughin' at?"

With a very sober expression, B.A. glanced into Mac's accusing face then looked quickly away.

Mac glared at him, "I know yer 'blander than bread-pudding' look, like ye got no face muscles whot move. I also know yer damned eyes and ye're laughin'. What's so funny?"

"Your horse."

Mac spun to look at his Irish saddle horse grabbing grass clumps and switching his tail peacefully. "Willy? What's so funny about him? He looks the same as he does every day."

"The new one." B.A. turned his back no longer able to keep a straight face.

Mac shoved his hat back in bewilderment. "Why? Tis a fine stallion he is. Lots of stayin' power in those big legs."

Broken Arrow's ancestors had traded horses for over a hundred years. "Ehe! Yes, he's big. He's Percheron, a draft horse from France, the strongest of horses. For their size, they can pull more than any other horse; more than the weak backed, hairy-footed Clydesdales from Scotland. The only ones to out-pull them are the bigger-boned gold and red horses from Belgium."

"Well and now," Mac felt somewhat mollified, until he realized his friend visibly struggled to contain his mirth. "And?" he challenged, "Whot's so funny about that?"

Broken Arrow strode to the stallion and opened the horse's mouth, "His teeth are worn." When Mac's puzzled face remained the same, B.A. coughed unable to hide his grin, "Percherons are . . . always black or bay. As they get older, they slowly . . . turn . . . completely white."

Mac tilted his hat back and stared at his new prize with dawning horror, "Jaysus! All that work and I stole a hoss whot's grey because he's old?"

The grey in question chose that moment to turn and snort loudly in Mac's direction.

B.A. doubled in half, collapsing upon a rock as his knees gave way.

Mac kicked a clump of dirt, "Well hell and damnation." His Irish brogue deepened with his disgust. "Tis a foin mornin's work I've accomplished. D'ye think we should give 'im back?" He watched his partner fall off the rock, his hair picking up leaves as he rolled about on the ground, holding his stomach and howling with laughter.

"Aye, and didn't the good Lord pay me back for me thievin' ways!" Mac sniggers turn to belly-deep guffaws.

When they finally sobered, Mac walked to his new acquisition, "I think I'll call him Spence. Seeing as he's dis-spensed with a lot of years."

B.A. grinned at him. "At least he's kind hearted. Some of those big horses will step on a man's foot and when he screams, they'll bite him. This one is a *cayuse,* meaning he has enough prairie mustang in him he can eat the grasses. Some of the full blood horses from across the water kick their bellies and die screaming in pain, unable to survive on the barbed buffalo grass—too used to barn oats and fresh hay."

"So he won't kick the bucket right away."

Broken Arrow started chuckling all over again, "He's grey . . . not white." And he was off again. Mac's snorts soon joined in.

11.

FORT QU'APPELLE BRAWL

"Damned badach! I don't trust him as far as I could kick his arse on a wet Sunday." Mac held out a cup of whiskey to Broken Arrow at Fort Qu'Appelle. The fort lay in the bottom of a rich vista of purple, green and gold rolling slopes, their backs coated with prairie grass and cacti; their deep gorges filled with short trees and shrubs sheltered from the wild prairie winds. Below the hills meandered a placid river gouging this panoramic scene deep into the prairie floor. The fort's name came from the river: *Kab-tep-was* in Cree meant 'River that Calls'. According to B.A.'s legend, a Cree man paddling to his wedding heard his name called out. He recognized the voice of his bride, who was still many days distant. He answered, "Who calls?" A spirit echoed him, "Who calls? Who calls? Who calls?" The man rushed home to find his bride had died, uttering his name with her last breath. When the Metis arrived in the area, they called the river *'Qu'Appelle'*, French for 'Who calls?'

On this day, Mac and Broken Arrow had watched the arrogant Hudson Bay factor buy furs from a couple of young warriors. Their hair bangs, topped by a single strand of beads down each cheek marked them as Ojibwa or *Ocipwe* as B.A. called them, a Cree word for their very distinctly pointed toe moccasins in comparison to most tribes' round toe moccasins. The slick trader slowly but surely robbed the two young men blind with his underpriced purchase of their furs and his overpriced goods. Finally, Broken Arrow quietly warned them in their own language. The two immediately brought out their knives, forcing the trader to a better price.

Born a trader, Broken Arrow knew the worth of his purchases and refused to pay extra. Together, he and Mac bargained a good price for food supplies and a sturdy pair of boots to replace Mac's cracked bluchers. The trader appeared reluctant to accept Mac's old boots in trade but the Cree knew they would quickly be sold to patch harnesses, halters and leather aprons. The lanky factor recognized Broken Arrow from previous trips and grudgingly respected the big Cree's firm stand. Pushing lies awarded him nothing but a dark, slant-eyed glare.

"How many languages do ye speak anyway?" Mac marvelled at how easily Broken Arrow switched from one language to another.

"Cree is my family's language. It is very close to the *Ocipwe*, like your Irish is close to the Scots." He looked away, uncomfortable with bragging. It bred a pride the elders always warned against. "I also know some Blackfoot, *Assinipwat* or Assiniboine, Sioux and French." His face tightened, his eyes darkening, "I learned English from a white captive who lived with us."

Mac noted the bleakness in B.A.'s eyes and left it alone. "I barely know me own Celtic language, along with English and a smattering of French thrown in. How did ye learn them all?"

"Most Indians know several languages. My people are traders; have been for many generations. They learned the languages to trade with people without insulting or angering them."

Mac nodded, tipped his mug. "*Slainte!* To your Health," and drank deeply. He spewed its contents, gagging and struggling to breathe too. "Jumpin' Jehosephant! Whot the Sam Hill is this!!?"

Broken Arrow took a cautious sip, "Some Perry's Painkiller, Bitters," he licked his lips thoughtfully, "Tea, Castile soap, Blackstrap chewing tobacco and alcohol." He swirled the contents, peering inside, "red ink for colour, ginger, cayenne pepper and some water to weaken the taste." He grinned at Mac's dawning horror, "Firewater."

"Jaysus! That factor be truly a vengeful fellow! He swore one mug was worth the cost of a buffalo hide. Hell, twould probably burn a hole through it! Back home, me Da stirred up *poitin*, a vicious drink. He claimed it warmed a man's insides like a peat fire on a cold December day. Me uncles swore twas more like a torchlight procession down the throat! But it tasted grand beside this god-awful swill. Ye truly drink it?"

Broken Arrow sighed, shook his head and poured his drink onto the ground. "I used to. Until I saw what happened to my older relatives who drank it. My grandfather was a trader all his life. He warned me of the powers hidden in the firewater. Once in a while, the Hudson Bay factors will offer me good whiskey. This is not one of them."

"Aye," Mac dumped the stuff too, half expecting the grass to disintegrate in a puff of smoke. "We'll go find us some good whiskey and have a wee tot to friendship."

They went in search of the head *Engage´*, a French name for the men employed by the fort as wilderness guides, hunters, fishermen, freighters, blacksmiths, carpenters, farmers and cattlemen. The foreman Engage´, a wiry, soft spoken Missouri man sold them a bottle of his Old Captain Jim's Whiskey. Carrying their prize to the shady side of the post, the two found a spot of cool grass to sit upon and poured their cups full.

Mac took a swig and sighed in delight, "Now this be Scotch Whiskey whot's old enough to vote!"

Several '*Slainte´*'s later', both felt in good charity with each other and the world.

Mac squinted through the fine vapours of whiskey at his big companion. "Where did ye get such a name as Broken Arrow anyway? I know yer names often have a story behind them."

Broken Arrow leaned against the logs of the trading centre, stretching his legs out in front of him. "When I was but three summers, I wanted a bow and arrow like Tall Man's. He made me one, but a child's size. They told me I threw the tiny bow down in contempt. I walked to Tall Man's bow, notched an arrow like I had watched him do and fired it at a tree. I missed but hit a rock with such force, it broke the arrow. My grandfather was amazed at the strength in my hands. From that day, he called me Broken Arrow."

A crafty light appeared in Mac's eyes. "And do ye still have strong hands?"

Broken Arrow looked up in surprise. "Why?"

Mac rolled to his stomach on the grass, propping himself on his elbows. "Come here me wee laddy. Let's see just how strong ye be. Put up yer duke."

Broken Arrow set his cup down, wiped his mouth and rolled to his stomach facing Mac, watching every move. Cautiously he extended his hand, leaning on his other elbow.

Mac guided their elbows into position and clasped their hands.

B.A. immediately snatched his back, eyes narrowing.

"No! No!" Mac rushed to explain, "Tis a wee contest of strength called 'Twistin'." He demonstrated in slow motion, clasping their hands then flipping B.A.'s down to the grass.

B.A. frowned in concentration, testing the motion, trying to see the conflict.

"Tis all in the wrist motion," Mac explained, wanting his friend to have a fair advantage. "Ye lock your wrists . . . so . . . then pull yer opponent towards ye until ye got him. Once he gets past the point of the weakest angle, he's yours."

Broken Arrow experimented a few rounds while Mac instructed on finer points of angle and positioning. "Never let yer opponent take up too much elbow room. He'll get ye by increasin' the angle. And don't let him twist yer wrist or ye lose all your power to pull." Mac demonstrated then licked his lips in anticipation. Back East, his boxing workouts made him more powerful than most of his opponents. Couple that with Irish stubbornness and he'd seldom lost.

But when he locked in with B.A. he recognized another realm of power.

Their fingers gripped and held. When their eyes met they laughed in delight, in challenge and in friendship. Knuckles whitened and muscles pinged. Through a long drawn out silence, neither man budged. Both quietly released their breaths, pulled them in and held. A faint quiver appeared in their fists. Neither opponent accepted ownership. Mac worked the fists towards him a fraction of an inch only to see it move back to centre then cant away. He dug deeper, felt the solid anchor of his elbow and gritted his teeth, his eyes never leaving the twisted fists. He felt them give a tiny bit towards him. He wanted to howl in glee then groaned instead as it moved away once again. How long . . . . ? He didn't know but he wasn't there yet. The knotted muscles in his arm burned now. Sweat prickled on his forehead and down his back. He made himself breathe and lost a bit more advantage. But the extra oxygen moved the fists in his favour as B.A. released his breath and dug in, holding the movement. Now their fists quivered, shivered and slipped on sweaty palms.

B.A. made no sound. His head dropped down, long hair all but covering his face. His shoulder joint cracked quietly but his big bicep never moved. He drew another breath, released and breathed again, deeply, slowly. A small smile darted around his mouth and disappeared.

A rough voice came at them out of the gloomy interior of the worker's barracks. "What the bloody hell is an Irishman doing wastin' himself on a goddamn Indian?" As the two looked up, a mountain of a man rolled through the doorway, followed by a slightly smaller, also unshaven, also filthy replica in similar grey shirt and moose hide pants. Identical dark eyes, matted black hair and crooked noses made them brothers, if not twins. The bigger man thrust his jaw forward and hiked up low hanging trousers with a dirty paw, his suspenders still dangling past his hips. He kicked lazily at the friend's clasped hands, "Indians don't know squat about twistin'."

Mac and B.A. immediately let go and rolled to their feet.

To Mac, the men's greasy blackened pants and oily hair indicated a true lack of interest in water.

"Obviously more'n ye know about soap." He deliberately turned his back on the duo and stepped away. Only B.A. saw his shoulders tense, before he turned, spreading his legs into an easy stance. The tall Cree eased away from his cup, never taking his eyes from the two hunters as they swaggered forward.

The shorter one, by a couple of inches, stuck beefy hands into the button loops of suspenders worn grey and frayed. He tilted back on his heels, looking these two newcomers over. A sneer curled his lip, "And what do we have here? You run out of friends, Irishman that you gotta consort with the savages?"

His bigger brother guffawed, dark gaps like holes in a cave showing up between tobacco stained teeth. "That's a good un Greyson, 'consort'. I swan you come up with new words ever day." He spat a gob of chewing tobacco on the ground, missing Broken Arrow's moccasin by inches.

Mac felt more than saw his companion's fury. B.A. wouldn't have moved a muscle but his eyes would burn. Macs hands curled to fists, though he kept them at his sides. "So that brings your impressive vocabulary up to what? Ten words now?"

Men gathered around them, appearing from all directions, drawn by the tension between the four.

"Now Earl and Grayson, you two stop looking' for trouble. There's work to done." The American Engage' rounded a corner with two ninety pound packs of pemmican on his shoulders. "We have plenty more in the carts to unload before nightfall."

The dirty duo ignored him, their narrowing eyes fastened on the two strangers who stood alone before them.

Earl spat again, meaty hands like hambones riding his hips. "Did he just insult you Grayson?"

Mac shrugged, "Take as many days as you need to figure it out. Don't be hurtin' yerself in the tryin'."

"Why you scrawny little buggar!" Earl threw a wild haymaker.

Mac dodged easily. Fists lifting, he rolled his shoulders into the forward tuck of a boxer. Rising on the balls of his feet, he danced sideways, watching his opponent recover his balance, his feet heavily planted. The man might be a bully, but he was no boxer. Gentleman rules aside, Mac felt the excitement rise within him. It felt good to be in position again. Aye, indeed it did!

The giant turned ponderously, swinging about to keep Mac in his vision. Mac couldn't resist a quick pop to Earl's jutting chin then danced away before the man's head finished its backward snap. He knew old Earl's lips just went numb.

With an angry bellow the man lunged, both arms like giant stovepipes swinging wide to yank Mac into a rib-crushing grip. Mac slipped away but not before delivering a quick flurry to the man's stomach. When Earl doubled forward, Mac snapped a powerful right to his bent face.

Blood spurted. The man sprayed snot and blood into Mac's eyes, making him blink. He never saw Grayson rising up behind him ready to slam a double fist into the back of Mac's head.

Broken Arrow lunged for Grayson. Wrapping a greasy neck with a heavy forearm, he yanked the stinking weasel backwards, pulling him off balance. With a kick to the back of Grayson's knees, the man's legs buckled as B.A. rolled down tossing the man head first over his body. With a snap of his shoulder, B.A. flipped to his feet.

Grayson scrambled to his knees, lifting his hand to a groggy head that had found a rock in the heavy grass. He opened his eyes just in time to see two moccasin feet slam into the soft spot below his rib cage. It stopped his breath and nearly his heart. He never felt the ground as it rushed up to meet his back.

B.A. rolled to his feet, looking for Mac. A bloodied and battered Earl threw his ponderous weight at the slighter man, slamming him to the ground. Earl immediately straddled him, his massive hands wrapping Mac's throat. Face turning blue, Mac struggled with the giant sitting on his chest. Broken Arrow rammed two fingers into the corner of the Earl's mouth and yanked sideways and down.

Forced to follow his face, Earl howled in fury. His hands released Mac's throat and went for Broken Arrow's. But the backward motion twisted his body into an awkward angle, forcing him to grab land for anchor. His frantically wind milling arms couldn't lever his body into position. Mouth agape; his horrified eyes watched a vicious bolo wrap his neck. One end, attached to a smaller rock slammed across his windpipe, squeezing it flat. In slow motion, his stunned eyes followed the other longer end wrapped with a fist-sized rock. It wound his head with an angry whistle, spinning closer and closer until the heavy rock smashed his temple with a bone-crunching thud. He collapsed into the grass.

Grayson crawled forward, his fist aiming for Broken Arrow's head. Mac hooked a hard right, bracing himself on both knees. It snapped the man's jaw with a crack that made the onlookers wince. Grayson folded in a silent heap next to his unconscious brother.

"Anybody else want a try?" Mac glared at the clump of silent men, his fists still clenched.

"Hell no!" A cheerful voice answered from the midst of the group, "You two were all over them like a bad case of measles. A man'd be dumber than a barrelful of deer horns to take you on."

"Ja!" Agreed a tall blonde Norwegian, who hooked his fingers in his combinations and rocked onto his heels studying the downed men before he drawled, "But I tink you bedder go before dey vakes oop!"

Mac crawled to the fallen Earl, "Filthy badach! Why is it these colossal mountains never have the good sense to be leaving well enough alone?"

The American Engage's blue eyes crinkled with laughter as he leaned over to pull Mac to his feet. "Well ole Earl here, never knew 'cum here' from 'sic 'em'. And Grayson's only a half a step ahead of him. The two of them shoulda been tossed down a gopher hole at birth with a skunk thrown in afterwards. And that would be a sorry sight indeed, even fer a polecat. The two had it comin'."

He shook Mac's hand, "It's a pleasure to see you in action. If you entered some boxing matches around here, you'd probably make a fair amount of money."

Mac shook his hand, "Nay, I'm off to see the West. Mayhap I'll come back this way eventually. I'll think on it." The Engage´ nodded, stepping back with a brief respectful dip of his head to Broken Arrow.

B.A. unwrapped his sling of shaganappi from around Earl's head and returned it to his beaded fire bag. "I think he's coming around."

"Next time, use a bigger rock," Mac rasped. He coughed, rubbing his bruised neck.

B.A. tilted his head, taking a second look at Earl's bloody face, "You broke his nose."

Mac sucked a bloody knuckle, "Well it won't hurt his looks! Ye know, me grandmother had the right of it. She used to say these ugly ones are the luckiest."

B.A. looked at him, his eyes curious.

"They get to live behind their ugly mugs. Tis the rest of us out front whot get the jolt." Grabbing up his almost empty bottle and cups,

Mac threw an enthusiastic arm across B.A.'s shoulders, staggering along beside him. The crowd parted for the two now zig zagging along like a Virginia fence line.

"Teach me those punches." B.A. demanded.

"Sure'n I'll share, if ye teach me how to wrestle like that."

"On horseback or on foot?"

Mac swaggered sideways, pulling his partner with him then whacked B.A.'s broad shoulders hard enough to loosen dust. "Now there be a useful art. Both!"

They untied their horses, taking up the reins of their packhorses before crawling onto their mounts. Mac continued, "Ye know, I could have taken both of 'em. After those first few punches I had old Earl weavin' like a sally tree in the wind."

"You boast too much Irish Man. You should stick to your mouth like you said and let me take the scalps. His brother had a big fist coming at the back of your head when I took him down." Broken Arrow guided his horse out the fort gates and onto the darkening prairie once again.

"Well, tis said to be the least sensitive part of an Irishman. Y'know the Celts were head-hunters. They cut off the heads of their enemies and preserved them in cedar oil. The heads were passed down through the generations as trophies. Families kept them in special sanctuaries, the spoils of war. Nobody parted with them for any amount of money. They believed the spirit of a man dwelled in his head. So ye see, you're no' the only one whot likes to brag."

Broken Arrow chuckled, "Scalps are easier to carry!' He joined Mac's hoot of laughter as they rode across a darkened prairie lit with the blue and black brilliance of a full moon.

Mac ranted on, loquacious with his heady victory, "Celts used war paint too. In battle, they wore their hair long, shavin' their entire body except the head and upper lip. They stained themselves with a blue dye made from a wode plant and their piss. Frightful lot in battle they were: runnin' full tilt at their enemies, roaring their heads off, naked as the day they were born. First time the Romans saw them; they turned tail and ran like hell."

B.A. grinned enjoying his friend's rambling, "We paint our faces in battle too so the Creator can find us easier if we die."

Mac waved his arms expansively, "Some of me own ancestors were warriors of Royal Branches who guarded kings. They were the *Naisc Niadh*, knights of the Eoghanacht kings of Cashel. Their descendants were called the MacCarthay Mor, one of Europe's oldest pedigrees stretching back in unbroken male descent from King Eeoghan Mor, born 192 years after Christ died. These warriors wore a golden collar or torque, an award of recognition of service. The *Niadh nask* is still presented—one of the oldest known honour systems in Europe."

B.A. nodded, impressed. "We give an eagle feather to our warriors for their courage in battle or other honourable deeds. Our wisest most worthy men earn a full headdress over a lifetime."

Mac considered it for a moment, "Honour among men. We're no' so different Cree Man!" He began singing an old Irish ditty about warriors and their chalices.

12.

BLACKFOOT

From that time on, B.A. attacked Mac from behind trees, wrestled him off his horse and jumped him as he washed in a creek, throwing them both into the oozing mud. Once B.A leapt off a cliff, knocking Mac from his horse with such force he almost broke his arm. But Mac learned the moves, crouching down, using the Cree's momentum to flip him off, trip him up or knock his wind from him with a wild haymaker of clasped fists. It became a contest to see who could flatten the other when he least expected it.

It was harder for Broken Arrow to learn the foreign boxing steps.

"What the Sam Hill is that?" Mac bent down for a better look.

Broken Arrow accommodated him, stepping out a graceful toe-heel shuffle, spinning backwards in a dancing s-curve. "Grass dance. Our dancers use it to flatten the grass before a Sun Dance or summer gathering."

"Do it again!" When B.A. complied, Mac howled with laughter, "Damnedest footwork I ever seen. But use it, even if you can't hit 'em, your steps will baffle the hell out of 'em." He lifted his fists and moved into a fighter stance, "Now pay attention. Keep one fist up to protect your chin."

"Why." Broken Arrow drew a fist, copying his stance, his broad shoulders hunching awkwardly.

Mac popped one by him and an astonished Broken Arrow swiped a bloody lip. "That's why. A man's chin is his weakest point. You can knock a man out if you clip him right."

Infuriated, B.A. ploughed up with a left which Mac blocked easily only to measure his weight on his back when B.A. kicked his feet out from under him with one furious swipe.

When he got his breath back, Mac groaned to his feet, "Here and now, 'tis about boxing; none of that."

"You draw blood, I will too."

Mac guffawed, "And how'll I be teachin' to hit if you can't take a few punches."

"Draw blood again and I'll use my knife."

Mac sighed gustily, "Aye, tis a barbarian I'm teachin' the Gentleman's rules."

One morning, Mac strolled lazily into camp from the river, wearing nothing but his boots and his hat, his freshly washed clothes still over his arm. He was bellowing an off-key, "Tura-lura-ra-lura, Tura-lura-ley!" when the Indian jumped him.

Mac automatically rolled to a bare shoulder and flipped the man over his head, summersaulting to his feet with a shout of triumph.

The warrior scrambling to his feet flung long unbraded hair away from his face. A flurry of feathers swirled on the back of his head. His thick animal-skin shirt, decorated with quill work, had a painted circle in the middle of his chest. He wasn't smiling and his raised knife was no toy.

"Jaysus Christ on a Flamin' . . . ! Mac kicked up with a heavy heel, smashing the man's hand and sending the knife skittering into the bush. As the man grabbed for his neck, Mac brought up a left hook, a real sockdologer right from his toes. It snapped a tooth when it connected with the man's chin. With a look of total surprise, the warrior's eyes rolled up and he crumpled in a silent heap at Mac's feet.

Mac cussed a blue streak wondering if he had just busted a knuckle. A hand on his shoulder had him spinning and swinging again. B.A. blocked his fist with a forearm, tossed a string of partridges aside and bent over the fallen man. "He's Blackfoot." Cautiously, he nudged him with a toe. When there was no response, he went to his horse, uncoiled a strip of rawhide and quickly looped it around the waking man's wrists. As the warrior groaned, B.A. yanked him to a sitting position then peered into his face, frowning.

The warrior finally got his eyes focused enough to glare through narrow bangs hanging to the bridge of his nose. He scowled at his tied hands. His head dropped, long hair forward sliding over hunched shoulders.

B.A. grabbed a handful of dusty bangs, exposing the man's throat and wild eyes. This was a young warrior, probably in his late teens but big enough to do some damage, judging from his broad shoulders and thick arms.

B.A.'s eyes narrowed as he searched the young man's features, finally addressing him in Blackfoot, "Are you from Black Hawk's tribe?"

Now the younger man grew wary. He nodded, a deep pride filling his eyes as he tensed for the blow.

It never came.

"Are you related to old Blue Thunder?"

The youth's eyes widened but again he nodded, "Grandson."

B.A.'s eyes sparked, "Yellowbird?"

The youth could not completely hide his astonishment, "You know me? But you are Cree! Enemy to the Blackfoot!"

B.A. spoke in English for Mac's sake. "I am Broken Arrow, grandson of Tall Man."

The young warrior searched his face, frowning. "Broken . . . Arrow?" He too switched to English. Suddenly his eyes rounded. "Tall Man was a Cree who used to trade at my grandfather's camp. He had a grandson called Broken Arrow." He squinted up at B.A. in amazement then flashed strong white teeth, "We were young boys together! You traded me a good knife for my colt and called him Blackfoot!"

B.A. gestured to his older packhorse horse and the brown paint. "And his son, Brownfoot."

The warrior chuckled deep in his throat, "So we never stole him back. I always looked for him in our raids! I still have your knife too," he reached for it, remembered his tied hands then glanced at the bushes where it had fallen. His features immediately switched to polite indifference as he warily glanced up at the still naked Mac.

"Sure'n I'll just go fetch the wee stick for ye me lad," Mac growled, his hands still fisted in fury, "I'll no' soon ferget ye damned near sliced me gullet in two."

"Will you have tea with us?" B.A. crouched before the warrior.

The Blackfoot searched the two faces before him, straightened his back and nodded, "I will."

"And is that also a promise not to be slittin' our throats in the near future, me lad?" Mac sneered, unwilling to accept the promise, still streaked enough to want further damage.

The warrior looked offended, sending Mac a scathing look of pure disgust.

B.A. untied the ropes and helped the young man to his feet. He staggered slightly then righted himself, his face fierce with determination and pride. B.A. knew that by accepting the tea, this man agreed not to harm them, at least not at this meeting. To break the vow would destroy all honour.

Mac retrieved the knife and held it out to the man, point first, his face still grim. The Blackfoot hesitated, retrieved it cautiously and sheathed it slowly, never losing sight of the red-haired man's hands.

Mac felt somewhat better when the Indian turned aside to jiggle his chipped tooth with a cautious fingertip. Turning his back on the Blackfoot, Mac stomped away. Retrieving his hat, he whacked the dust from it against his thigh. He leaned against a big tree trunk and pulled on clean clothes, hanging his damp ones on a branch to dry. Hunkering down he glared at the Blackfoot and B.A. crouched around the campfire now, visiting like a couple of old grannies over their tea kettle, their hands creating animated yet oddly flowing motions.

"So how is Blue Thunder?" B.A. queried, recalling a tall gaunt man who laughed uproariously at Tall Man's stories and teasing. The two elders had been friends since their grandparents had peacefully traded together. Each year as a child, Broken Arrow had travelled west with Tall Man to trade with Blue Thunder's tribe. He remembered Tall Man once presenting Blue Thunder with a highly prized German silver bracelet pounded into beautiful images of racing horses. He had recognized it on Yellowbird's wrist.

The eastern Cree along with the Assiniboin or Sioux traded the land-bound western Blackfoot for their handmade antelope and buffalo skin garments plus their pelts of wolf, mink, marten, ermine, otter, beaver and muskrat furs. In exchange, the entrepreneurial Cree offered Hudson Bay guns, hatchets, kettles, knives, powder and shot, arrowshods (flint arrowheads), long knives and bayonets. Tall Man's group also received horses stolen by the Blackfoot from their enemies the southern Snakes or Shoshone. Mitsue along with the other Cree women traded their cowrie shells, basket beads, hawk bells and thimbles in exchange for the Blackfoot women's' highly prized dentalium shells. B.A. wore a choker of the three inch-long slender white sea shells, raided by the Blackfoot from the westerly

Kootenay and Flatheads who in turn got them in trade, or raid, from the west coast tribes.

After a good summer of trading, Tall Man and their Assiniboine/ Sioux allies, bundled the furs into forty-foot birch canoes and paddled back east on the South Saskatchewan (Derived from the Cree word, *Suskutchiwan,* meaning 'Smooth Running Water'). By late summer they were shooting wild rapids on the North Saskatchewan near Cumberland House. Hitting forty strokes a minute, they faced the massive waves on the great lake, Winnipeg before reaching Norway House and the Churchill River, which connected them to York Factory on the Hudson Bay. After bartering their furs for more of the White Man's goods, the Cree returned to the forks of the two Saskatchewan Rivers just as fall ice lined the river systems and lakes. They wintered south of Fort Carleton (near what is now Prince Albert, Saskatchewan), then headed west again in the spring.

Over the years, the Hudson Bay Company traders had moved inland, setting up their forts, and gradually cutting out the Cree middlemen. By the early 1800's, the HBC had set up posts from the mouth of the Saskatchewan River where it emptied into Lake Winnipeg to its source on the North Branch in the Rockies. The Cree and Assiniboine slowly lost their status as traders and lost their economic standard of living. Having to hunt and trap the animals, in direct competition with the Blackfoot, was a bitter blow to their business acumen. Many of the clans, like Tall Man's, quit the trade business and turned to a more relaxed lifestyle of hunting the buffalo in the summer and moving north into the sheltered parklands for winter. They became part of the Downstream Cree of the South Saskatchewan, the House people, from around Fort Carleton. Later, when Broken Arrow had reached manhood, Tall Man moved his band to the Portage La Prairie area, south of Lake Winnipeg.

The ones who stayed in the trades became more and more dependent on White Man goods like the powder and shot to protect them and provide food. Some found a lucrative business in supplying fish and buffalo meat to the growing trading posts. But they needed horses to hunt the buffalo and to haul the meat back to the forts for the employees and families. And they also needed women to dry the meat and fish. In an attempt to gain more horses, the Cree formed an alliance with the Crow, the hated enemy of the Blackfoot. Seeing this as a betrayal, the Blackfoot angrily attacked bands of roving Crees. In the mid 1800's the two once peaceful tribes furiously raided one another's camps for horses, supplies and women. The raids happened so often, the horses knew the trails between the warring camps better than the warriors! Unfortunately the rift between the tribes created endless violent battles across the prairies and destroyed long held ties of family, friendship and brotherhood. B.A. had lost many friends in the Blackfoot Cree wars, from both sides. But he remembered the good times, when the two tribes and their families still laughed together.

Yellowbird absently fiddled with his tooth, "Blue Thunder died from smallpox. The American settlers on the Boseman Trail, south of the U.S. border brought it with them." On seeing the instant grief in the Cree's face, he felt something ease inside. This man remembered his family, had shared meals, laughed with them and now mourned their loss. Yellowbird felt his anger fade, replaced by a deep sorrow for all that had passed between the families since they last met. He drew a deep breath then sipped his tea. "And Tall Man? I remember he was a real joker."

B.A. chuckled. "He was still telling tall tales and teasing the old ladies when I left him this spring."

Yellowbird slapped his thigh, grinning "I always remember him telling us the story about why dogs smell each other's hind ends."

To politely draw Mac into the conversation, B.A. slanted a smile towards his surly friend, "Do you want to hear it?"

Mac shrugged noncommittally, tying his version of a fichu around his neck. He thought the scarf lent him a westerly air.

B.A. settled himself comfortably and took a slow sip. "All the dogs gathered for a council meeting, trying to decide what to do with

Wesakechak, the Trickster. He was always pulling tricks on them and making them mad. So the females brought food for everyone at the meeting. Out of politeness to their hosts, all the dogs hung their tails up outside the tipi before entering.

"Wesakechak, of course, wasn't invited, but he heard about it and came anyway. When he got there, he was very hungry and smelled the tasty food inside the tipi. He decided if he crawled up close to the tipi and scared the dogs away, he could have all the food for himself.

So he yelled, 'Fire!!!'"

All the dogs ran outside in a panic. In the confusion, they got their tails mixed up. Some grabbed the closest one just to get away from the fire. Wesakechak crawled in and stuffed himself with food before the dogs realized there was no fire. That's why to this day; the dogs smell each other's butt whenever they meet. They're still looking for the right tail."

The Blackfoot chuckled, "Do you know it was years before I realized the other meaning for 'the right tail'?" B.A. grinned and glanced at Mac, "Our Wesakechak or Coyote stories have many meanings. A child could enjoy them but an adult would hear much deeper meanings. It is up to the listener to figure them out."

Mac managed little more than a grunt. He couldn't get over how the Cree and Blackfoot seemed mortal enemies one minute and then happy as hell they knew each other's families. They were so damn forgiving, these Indians.

He wasn't used to that. "Why is he called a Blackfoot?"

B.A. laughed mischievously. "A long time ago, a lone warrior dressed much like this one walked into a camp of the Cree people. He was a brave man to walk alone into a strange camp. Out of respect for his courage, the Cree never bothered him. They had no name for this stranger but they noticed he must have walked through a prairie fire because the bottoms of his moccasins were black. So they called him 'Blackfoot'.'

The Blackfoot warrior chuckled, "Do not believe too many stories the Cree tell. Most are lies. They dried up many of our prairie rivers and streams by sitting around drinking too much tea and telling lies."

B.A. grinned in good humour, "What are you doing so far from home?" Blackfoot territory ranged from the South Saskatchewan to the foothills of the Rocky Mountains. This man was deep in Cree territory.

The young Blackfoot's head dipped, his cheeks reddening, "I stole a girl from Chief Piapot's band near Fort Qu'Appelle. She ran away and I'm trying to track her down."

B.A. noted the young man's high rugged cheekbones, long nose and thin face – a face easily forgotten because a woman's loyalty must be earned. The Cree's eyes lit up, "Need some lessons on how to keep a woman?"

Yellowbird shyly rubbed his inflamed cheeks, "*Hukay*, (okay) . . . she *was* a good cook!"

Broken Arrow snickered.

The restless Blackfoot changed the subject, "Is Tall Man still bragging about women?"

B.A. snorted, "But Moya . . . do you remember her?"

Yellowbird frowned then nodded, "A tall thin woman. Sat in Council Meetings and our women's' circles whenever our tribes met. Doesn't *Nemoya* mean 'No' in Cree?"

"Ehe!" B.A. bobbed his head, his big shoulders moving in rhythm, "She was a warrior when she was younger, but never married. She likes men well enough and loves children, just never wanted to get married."

The Blackfoot caught on, "So the men called her 'No'?" He smirked when B.A. nodded, broad cheeks lifting into a wide grin.

"But Moya got Tall Man back." B.A. continued. "He was bragging about chasing women last spring. He's about eighty-three summers now. His wife, Listens to the Wind, died many summers ago. On this day, Tall Man dressed himself in his best beaded hides and new moccasins. He announced that he was going 'hunting'. He claimed he was feeling so good, his root was just constantly pointing into the air." B.A. held up his hand, his index finger pointed skyward, walking his hand along through the air in small bobbing steps.

The cross-legged Blackfoot chortled.

"But Moya said, '*Mah*! You're pitiful old man!'"

'Why?' asked Tall Man in surprise.

'Because it probably just shrivelled up and dried that way!'"

This time Mac's guffaw joined the two men's as they rocked back and forth, pounding a thigh with big fists. He marvelled how Natives accepted no bounds when it came to sexual stories. The earthier the tale, the more it delighted them – a far cry from the rigid Victorian view where sex was a sinful, dirty word.

When the Blackfoot could talk, he asked, "And Mitsue? I remember her because her name means 'Eat!' She looked like she enjoyed doing a lot of it."

B.A. nodded, still smiling, "She is still ordering people to eat. She's my grandmother too, Tall Man's sister. She and Moya are always getting into trouble."

Mac sipped his tea, waiting for another story. He was learning more about B.A.'s family than he had in all the weeks they'd travelled together.

B.A. leaned forward, "I used to follow them when they went out gathering roots and berries. They would say the craziest things to each other then they'd laugh and laugh. Some of it I never understood until I grew older. But I'd practice my stalking skills on them. Mitsue never noticed, but looking back, I think Moya knew. She had a way of talking louder than necessary sometimes. Probably so I could hear her.

"This one time, they went out to their favourite patch of Saskatoons." For Mac's benefit he explained, "They are deep purple berries found on bushes. We dry them and add them to our pemmican."

He turned back to the Blackfoot and continued his story. "This time, they saw two white women picking in their favourite patch. Before the women could see them, Mitsue plunks herself down behind the roots of a huge Tamarac tree that had uprooted in a strong wind. You know how high they are."

The Blackfoot nodded, "They look big and black like a moose from a distance. I've stalked a few before I knew what they were." The two warriors grinned at one other.

"That day," B.A. continued, "Mitsue started howling like a wolf. Moya bent over and looked into her face to see if she'd gone crazy. Then 'Boom! The whole top of the tree root above Mitsue's head exploded into a shower of dirt, roots and grass. Moya dropped to her stomach, face to the ground. Mitsue just sat there, her legs spread out in front of her, her eyes so big they had white all around them. When Moya raised her head, her eyes were as big as Mitsue's. Moya clapped a hand over her mouth and started to giggle.

'D'ye think ye got him Charmaine?' a white woman called out.

'I dunno,' the other one answered, 'I don't hear anything movin.'

Mitsue and Moya heard the metallic click of a gun reloading.

Suddenly Mitsue leans over Moya, 'Yip! Yip?' she says, motioning with her hands for Moya to join her. Moya frowns at her bug-eyed friend.

'Yip! Yip! AOOOOOhhhhh!' Mitsue howls, gesturing frantically at Moya to join her.

Moya catches on, rolls onto her back and moans eery enough to scare away the spirits. Then she claps her hands over her mouth to smother her giggles. Mitsue slaps her friend on the arm while her own big body shakes and bounces in mischief.

"Then Mitsue's, 'Ahooooo! Yip! Yip!' is again joined by Moya's 'Owwwwwwwoooooooh!"

"I decided to join them with my own," B.A. threw his head back and howled "AAAAAh oooooooooooohhhhhhh!" Yellowbird joined him with his own rendition and the two leaned back snickering like daft culchies. Mac rolled his eyes and refused to join the idjits.

B.A. continued his story, relaxing against a big rock. 'Run Emily!' a woman yelled, 'He's got his whole bloody pack with him!' Two loud wails rose to howling screams. "We heard crashing and crackling, loud as a bull moose!" B.A. sniggered.

"When Mitsue and Moya stretched up to see over the roots, the women were running for their lives, clearing stumps and short bushes with their little short legs, their skirts flapping in the wind and berries flying everywhere."

B.A. scratched his head, "So, we got our patch back. Mitsue made me fill all her birch bark baskets for sneaking around and following them."

*   *   *

That evening after a shared meal, the two watched the Blackfoot ride westward to a far ridge. Mac turned to study B.A.'s pensive features. "What would you have done if you hadn't known him?"

"Killed him, just as he would have killed us. He would have hacked us to pieces and drank the blood from our hearts, to steal our strength." B.A. said quietly, his face remaining impassive as he watched the silhouette of the Indian crossing the dark skyline before riding out of sight.

13.

WARRIOR WOMEN

The next day, after a breakfast of boiled wild rice and dried blueberries from B.A.'s pack, they rode out. Mac kept a wary eye on their tail while B.A. scanned the horizon with his usual, unflappable demeanour.

Mac leaned over his pommel, "So your women are warriors too?"

"If they want to be."

Mac rubbed his growing stubble. Uneasy about the Blackfoot, he'd chosen not to dally with his daily shaving. Now they were on the move, he relaxed enough to visit once more. "Our Celtic women were also warriors. One Roman leader, Ammianus Marcellus, complained it was difficult enough to deal with the wild Celts. But twas far worse if they brought their women to fight; their blows cracked bones."

"Tell me about your women warriors. What were they like?" Broken Arrow enjoyed Mac's stories about the white men and the women.

"I studied my Celtic ancestors in University. What surprised me the most was how our knights and heroes were always taught by women warriors. Sir Lancelot, King Arthur's best knight was taught by his aunt, the Lady of the Lake, the high priestess of Avalon. So was Arthur who received his magical sword, Excalibur from her as well.

In our legends, the women taught young men the mystery of the sword, the sense of its responsibility and its power. They also taught honour, dignity, obedience to the life forces, integrity and peace loving truth. The warrior's show of power and strength must always be tempered with a compassion called chivalry. Women taught a warrior to destroy the enemies of truth. He was to protect against what causes despair or injustice, oppression or abuse. His destruction cleared a space for renewal and a better, renewed order."

Something about the renewal niggled at the back of Broken Arrows mind but he chose to ignore it—for now. Rather than rudely interrupt, he listened silently.

Mac went on, "In Ireland, one of our heroes, Cu Chulainn, received his training in weapons and battle from Scathach-Buanand on the Island of Skye which still bears her name. She was a fierce warrior-woman who could also foretell a warrior's future. She taught many young men the skill of arms. I've seen paintings of this fierce woman, her arms and face covered with sword scars. Other men trained under the Irish warrior-woman Morrigan. In our legends she was associated with death and battle, sexuality and birth. She could be a screaming bloodthirsty hag, the *banshee* fey who warned of a coming death, or a beautiful maiden. Her totem bird was the crow. She carried off the spirits of warriors killed on the battlefields, but she also supervised their rebirth." Mac scratched his head, "Funny how these stories of our powerful women warriors got changed to them being evil witches.

"Who had the most to gain by changing the stories?"

Mac's eyebrows rose. Who had gained? Certainly not the women. He shrugged, "After the Dark Ages, the church and kings branded them as witches with crows as their familiars."

"Familiars?" Something shivered down Broken Arrow's neck.

"Aye, ye know, spirit animals that guide and protect. Now, the call of a raven has become an omen of death instead of just a messenger."

B.A. nodded, "In our ways, the call of an owl warns of death. In our stories, the crow and raven are connected to the Thunderbirds, the most powerful spirit animals on Earth Mother. Thunderbirds have feathers of many shades of brown, gold and white. Some say they were made from the feathers of every bird on Mother Earth. Thunderbird's giant wing beats create thunder. Lightening flashes when they blink their eyes. They were once eagles who flew higher than the clouds and changed to thunderbirds, the closest birds to Creator or to heaven as you call it."

Mac listened in awe. "Ye know, I read the top druid bard, the best storyteller in the land, wore a cape of many coloured feathers. The upper part of the cape held the green sheen of mallard heads. Below the belt, the cape was made from the feathers of every bird in the land."

The two considered this similarity. It teased their memories, an ancient calling from deep within their bones.

B.A. frowned, "The power of the thunderbird is like the earth shaking, the mountain crumbling. His fire brings change, the burning of the old to make room for the new growth." A renewal, he realized in surprise but refused to share his thoughts for now.

After a few moments, Mac went on, "The Celtic heaven was like the earthly world, only far better, a land without sickness, misfortune or old age. People were beautiful, especially the women. The sun always shone, birds always sang and no one wanted for food or drink, which appeared in abundance as if by magic. In the ancient Irish legends, the gods often invited heroes to join them there, calling it *Tir inna m Beo*, the Land of the Living. By describing such a heaven, the Druids made the Celts powerful warriors because death became a seductive, fascinating temptation.

"Our Druids were the intellectuals, or learned class of the Celts. They were not only priests but philosophers, judges, teachers, historians, poets, musicians, physicians, astronomers, prophets, and political advisers – the elite class. They believed in life after death. The great Roman emperor Julius Caesar wrote how the Celts believed souls passed from one body to another after death. The Keltoi or Celts leant money believing it could be repaid in the next life or reincarnation! Such faith made the Celts fearless, almost unbeatable on the battlefields because they believed they never really died, just moved on to the next life."

B.A nodded, "*Tapwe*, truly. We believe the same."

Mac continued, caught up in his revelations. "And our women were just as fearless. I remember reading about our black-robed druidesses, called the Dar Abba, who cursed the invading Roman soldiers when they attacked Anglesey Britain in A.D. 61. At the same time, the British Queen, Boudicca, raised a revolt in the east of Britain. She impaled her prisoners upon stakes in sacrifice to the goddess Andraste which means 'Victory.' No shrinking violets, our Celtic women! They were as hardy and fierce as their men.

"These women taught their men, inspired them, advised and trained with them. It wasn't until A.D. 697, twelve hundred years ago, that a group of clergymen at Tara, Ireland passed the *Cain Adamnan*, the Law of the Innocents. It forbade women, children and clergy from being harmed in war. But it also forbade women to be warriors or leaders in war. I still think it was for the benefit of the clergy not the women because it took away women's right to rule or command."

"And the women agreed to this?" B.A.'s eyes widened.

Mac scratched his head, "Under Celtic law, women could own land, be queens and pass it onto their daughters. The Celts also had many female saints. Our female church leaders were equal to their male counterparts when preforming the 'Divine Sacrifice of Mass'. This infuriated the Roman Catholic priests when they brought Christianity to the Celts in 500 AD.

"What did the priests do?"

"Just as the Israelites overthrew the gods of the Canaanites, the Christian priests created the idea of a God who would reinforce and encourage their new patriarchal consciousness, the power of the male over the female." He tilted his chin, "According to them men ruled; women obeyed." He silently wondered if this was also when the women's stories changed from warriors to witches.

B.A. looked totally astonished. "In our clans, the women agree only if they want to. They obey nobody. Though they respect their elders' counsel, they would fight if forced to be lesser than their men in their community."

Mac sighed, "I dunno. Somehow the Christian priests persuaded the Celtic women or maybe just controlled them through their men. Maybe women couldn't fight the clerics and their husbands and fathers too. Eventually, women warriors were sent back to their hearths to 'keep the home fires burning'."

"How did the Romans treat their women?"

"Their women bore children and were mere objects of pleasure for their men. That was their only purpose. When the Romans invaded Britain, they brought their laws with them. All land was now owned by men, the heads of families. Men and their sons as household leaders therefore gained total control over their women."

B.A. was shocked. "The women allowed this? Mah! Ours would beat us about our heads for even thinking such a thing! In our Cree language, we have the same word for him or her: *wiya*, because they were the same, equal. In many tribes, women sit on council, sit on council with the men but have their own councils too. Moya, Mitsue's friend, sits on a council of leaders with other men and women. They use their wisdom and life experiences to consider their people's problems about hunting, war, clan gatherings even family quarrels. They decide the punishments for wrong-doing. Together this council has the power to gather the forces for spiritual practices, tribal relations or war in a manner which would benefit their people.

"Our women decide who travels with our group each winter. They own the tipis and are very involved in teaching children and upholding

'The Way' of living in a good way, just as much as their husbands. Never would our women agree to have such controls placed upon them. They would refuse to marry any man under such conditions."

Mac shook his head, readjusting his hat. "All I know is things changed under the Roman Christian faith. Women lost their role as warriors and trainers of warriors. They lost their right to own land, make decisions, vote, sit on council or have any say in anything outside their homes. Afterwards, they were practically owned by their fathers and husbands. From this era sprang the knights of chivalry, honouring and protecting the shrinking, weak women, who sat in the corner and cried helplessly."

"*Hiyee!*" B.A. growled in disgust, "Maybe they cried because they could not take up a weapon and kill their men! Our women would never allow such a ruling."

Mac gave a heavy sigh, "They may not have a choice, any more than our women did. For the clerics and the priests deemed it otherwise. The laws they made were never broken, even today. And they bring the same laws to this land now."

14.

COUNTING COUP

Broken Arrow pondered what Mac had told him about his women warriors and what they taught the young men. The next morning, he turned to Mac across the campfire from him. "I have a story about Mitsue and Moya. They taught a young Blackfoot warrior a good lesson.

"One morning, the two old ladies were gathering all kinds of flowers to dry in their birch bark baskets. They began in early spring, adding a few of each type of flower as they blossomed. In the season of the falling leaves, they pulverized and dried them. One spoonful of the mash was steeped in a cup of boiling water for a healthy drink during winter.

"On this day, they were in a small meadow, teasing each other as usual while I sat behind a big tree listening:

Mitsue bent her wide, sturdy body to study a ripening bud, 'There was something I wanted to tell you but I forgot what it was.'

'Probably a lie.' The slender Moya knelt to dig around the roots of a wild raspberry plant, a good medicine for diarrhoea. She carefully removed only a couple smaller roots and placed a small pinch of tobacco in the hole, thanking the plant and Creator for its use before carefully repacking the dirt.

'Mah! How can you say such a thing! I always tell you truth.' Mitsue scolded with good nature.

'Ehe! Like the time you bragged about Muskwa the bear sniffing around you. How you had to chase him away with a stick because you weren't in a good mood?' Moya stood up rubbing her lean back.

Mitsue chuckled as she packed wild rose petals into the woven basket on her hip.

Suddenly, a painted Blackfoot warrior on horseback tore out of the trees straight for them, his war lance raised and his war cry piercing their ears.

Moya saw him first. She looked at a surprised Mitsue and the two howled with laughter, collapsing against one another like two old tipi poles. Moya put an arm around Mitsue who leaned forward, hands on her heavy knees, her entire body shaking with mirth. The warrior's fury moved from surprise to suspicion as he yanked his wild mount back on his haunches, showering grass and sand onto the giggling women.

'Ah Hu! Hu! Hu!' Mitsue chuckled, talking to Moya in perfect Blackfoot, 'I think he wants to count coup on us.'

Moya casually waved her muddy hand, also speaking in Blackfoot, 'So, my boy.'

The strong warrior scowled. Nobody called him, 'Boy'.

'You ready to count coup by sneaking up to touch a couple of old ladies?' Moya shaded her face, ancient lines folding into a wide grin, 'Perhaps you need some help. Your arm does not look strong enough for such a swing.'

The furious warrior tried to force his horse on top of the two women but the wild-eyed animal danced away, snorting and plunging in little leaps and bounds, his mouth fighting the bit. The heavily painted young man frowned in confusion, slicing his eyes back and forth between the chuckling women. The big round flower beads on their clothes indicated they were Cree. Yet they spoke his language with ease.

Mitsue, still smiling, turned and cocked a heavy hip in his direction, patting her backside with a muddy hand. 'Touch me . . . right . . . here. It's been so long since I've been touched by a male; I can't remember what it feels like.'

'Mah!' scoffed Moya, 'You wouldn't remember what to do with him anyway old woman.' The two sniggered some more, covering their mouths with grimy palms.

'I'm not wasting a coup on you,' the warrior growled, 'I'll kill you instead!' He raised his lance.

'I'll do! I'll do it for you! Let me! Let me!' Mitsue rushed forward, startling the horse that backed away in fright, blowing and stomping. 'I've always wanted to kill this stubborn old woman anyway. But her head is so hard; it might hurt your arm. Let me do it for you!' She held up her hands for the toss of his war lance.

The warrior clutched it tighter and raising it higher, his eye furious slits.

'Mah!' Moya growled, 'You couldn't show this brave warrior anything new. I'm sure he has spent many days preparing to be so courageous today.'

The warrior glowered at her, struggling to control his white-eyed mount, trying again to push it against the tall woman who stood unflinching.

Moya turned and pointed at Mitsue's groin. 'Put your war lance right . . . there. It won't hit anything she's used in the past twenty summers.'

Mitsue whacked Moya's shoulder with her open palm, 'Such jealousy! And lies! All lies! I told you about old Muskwa the bear sniffing around me ten summers ago.'

'Eehe!' grunted Moya, 'And how you chased him away with a stick!

'But he came back!' Mitsue protested. 'This time I was in a better mood! I needed a new fur coat.' She slapped her knee and guffawed, 'Haw! Haw! Haw!' Her laughter revealed narrow gaps in her strong white teeth. Moya joined her and they cackled like two ancient hens who'd abandoned their nests for wide open spaces.

Red and white spots appeared on the warrior's cheeks, his lips curling in disgust. Glaring down at the giggling women, he ground his teeth, pivoted his horse on two legs and fled the clearing, leaving the two old bawds still laughing like dogs."

*   *   *

Mac leans forward, staring into the fire. "So they shamed him into leaving them alone. Brave ladies."

B.A. smiled, "Moya reminded him of a warrior's duty to protect women, children and elders. Counting coup is about stalking your enemy until you can touch him either with your hand or a coup stick *without* his awareness. Such quiet stalking, patience and courage are honoured by the Warrior Clan. But a warrior can never be part of taking advantage of the weak. It takes no courage; therefore there is no honour in killing two defenceless old ladies."

15.

ISKWESIS

"Help Momma! Help!" A child's screams pierced the afternoon's peaceful tranquillity.

Mac and B.A. spurred their horses towards the cries coming over a hill to their left. At a dead run, they broke the crest to find a small log cabin nestled by a creek below them. Nearby, stood a small weathered cattle barn and corral. A little girl with blond hair ran towards the cabin, her long braids flying out behind her. A red-haired woman rushed outside, lifting her cotton skirts as she flew to the child and bent towards her.

"It's Hamish!" the child shrieked, pointing to the creek, "He's bleeding again Momma!"

As one, the two riders and the woman raced to the embankment. The woman's fear had her reaching it before the dismounting riders. She plunged down the bank to the small boy kneeling by the water. Intent as she was on the child, the woman whirled at the heavy footsteps crashing behind her. She backed frantically towards her son, eyes never leaving B.A.'s headlong flight. Mac leapt down behind him, skidded to a halt at his side and hastily yanked his hat off. The women turned to him and paused.

"It's O.K. ma'am! We just want to help. We mean no harm to ye or yer children!"

The woman's eyes darted frantically between the two rigid men. Fear for her child won out. "My son, Hamish, is a bleeder. When he gets a nose bleed, he bleeds for hours. I canna . . . I canna stop it once it gets goin'!" She knelt beside a dark-haired little boy, about five years old, who cupped both hands over his nose. Blood ran freely between his fingers, down his arms onto his faded cotton shirt and leather short pants.

"Did ye try pinching his nostrils?" Mac fell on his knees and peered into the child's face while B.A. turned away, searching for something in the grass. "Sometimes cold water on his forehead helps," Mac whipped off his neckcloth, dipped it in the water and handed it to the mother who quickly placed it on the child's forehead. The tiny boy, pale and thin, made no sound. His wide blue eyes rolled back and forth between the men and his mother.

"Here!" B.A. knelt on one knee, holding out a handful of crushed tiny fern-like leaves, green and fresh, "Push these into his nose. They will stop the bleeding."

The woman held her small son tighter, visibly unnerved by this big man. She looked at Mac, a question in her panic-stricken eyes.

He nodded, "He's my good friend Ma'am. And he knows the plants and medicines of this land far better than we do."

The woman reached out a shaking hand and gathered the leaves in tentative fingers. "They're Yarrow leaves!" Her face puckered in confusion.

Broken Arrow nodded when she queried, "Up his nose?" but he remained quiet and still. He was glad it was cooler that day so he'd worn his buckskin shirt. These white women seemed terrified by too much unclothed skin.

The women gently stuffed the leaves into the little boy's nostrils, packing them carefully but firmly. He wrinkled his face, twitching his nose against the unfamiliar heaviness, opening his mouth to breathe, but he didn't complain. The blood slowed, dripped and eventually stopped.

With a cry, the woman hugged her child then reached out a trembling bloody hand to grasp B.A.'s arm and squeeze. Tears filled her eyes as they searched his, her voice rolling out a soft Scottish burr, "Ooch, thank ye, sarrh. I thank ye so verra, verra much." With a ragged sob, she buried her face in her child's neck and rocked him gently.

The two men watched, awkward on their knees, relieved and silent. Finally they stood; waiting until the woman rose too, still carrying her son. She moved to B.A. and placed her small son in his arms. "Would ye mind carryin' him awa'doon tae th' house?" He searched her eyes for a moment, recognizing both her apology and trust. Finally, he turned with his small burden and climbed the path to the cabin. Behind him, Mac bounded a few steps up the embankment then held out an open hand to the woman who had bent to the little girl still clinging to her skirt. He lifted them as one up the embankment.

Back at the cabin, the woman directed B.A. into a small lean-to where the beds were. When he'd returned to the greater room, both men stood about awkwardly until she called to them. "Please find a seat, gentlemen. I'll no' be tae long. I'll just get Hamish washed up and settled."

Mac, remembering his manners, snatched his hat off as he lowered himself to a roughly hewn wooden chair, its light cream surface stripped of bark. The seat was covered in smoked deer hide, its hair intact and cushy. A nearby table had a well tanned antelope skin spread upon it, white as paper and velvety to the touch. A huge bear skin with head and claws lay at the entrance to the lean-to. Mac imagined its warm mat was a welcome comfort to cold toes. B.A. carefully seated himself on another chair and the two crouched in ungainly discomfort, bent to the shape of the stiff chairs. An open fireplace stood kitty-corner to the doorway, its rocks plastered in place by mud and hay then whitewashed with white clay which was also spread part way across the floor's rough logs, ready to catch stray sparks. An old gun barrel protruding from the plastered wall held a heavy copper kettle over smouldering embers.

The little girl, about four years of age, hung back at the doorway, watching them silently. A decision made, she picked up a small wooden box in the corner and placed it on the table. Next, she dragged a small stool over to a wooden keg filled with water in the corner. Climbing upon the stool, she reached with tiny fingers, struggling to unhook a small tin dipper above her head. Mac raised to help her but a slight headshake from B.A. settled him back down. Eventually, standing on her toes and stretching as far as she could, the tot pulled the dipper down. She filled it with water from the keg, lifting it carefully over the steel rim, spilling a great portion before bringing it step-by-splashing step to the table. Dragging her little stool to the cupboard, she climbed up once again, this time reaching for a small biscuit tin. She struggled to open the tight lid. This time Mac did not move, watching her as silently and intently as B.A. Eventually, she sprung the lid, splaying biscuits in every direction. With a sigh of disgust, she carefully gathered them up, dusting with her skirt the ones that had bounced to the floor. Reaching up to the bottom shelf of the high cupboard, she located a tin plate upon which she carefully arranged the somewhat battered treats. These she brought to the table. With careful politeness, she offered her treasures to the waiting men who chose one and just as politely thanked her. Opening her little wooden box, she removed a miniature tea set, cups, saucers, plates and teapot. Lifting the lid of her minute teapot, she slowly poured in the dipperful of water, ignoring, to the amusement of her silent audience, when half of it missed. She filled each diminutive cup, placed it carefully upon a tiny saucer and gravely presented one set to B.A. and another to Mac.

"I only have tea, but you're welcome to it." She looked way up to the tall Indian, who carefully slid the cup and saucer onto one big palm. Large fingers pinched the dainty handle as he lifted it to his lips and cautiously sipped. His sparkling eyes and gentle smile enveloped her.

"Thank you, *Iskwesis.*" he said very softly.

She placed her hands behind her back. "What's that? Isk-sqeezes?" she cocked her head, small braids swinging over her shoulders.

"It means, 'little girl'."

She looked him over, "You have braids like me. But you're not a girl!"

His eyes gleamed, a small smile playing about his dark features, "In my family, we all wear braids."

She came closer, pointing to his deerskin leggings, "You have funny pants. I bet I can't poke a needle through them, like papa's."

He grinned openly, "And did you poke a needle through your papa's trousers?"

She stuck a finger in her mouth, then spoke around her finger, her other hand now on his knee as she leaned against his leg. "I wanted to fix his pants, he had a hole in them, but he yelled when I poked his knee." Her eyes got big, "He sweared, he said 'God Damn!' and Momma said it was blas . . . feeme." She whispered up at him, "It means not to call God if you're mad."

Mac fought a grin. B.A. looked quite serious, as he reached out to smooth a tiny blonde braid wrapped in yellow ribbon.

"And where is God, Little One?"

She never hesitated, "He's in the sky and in the ground. Sometimes I see him in the clouds. I miss him. I want to go see him.

B.A. nodded solemnly, "I would like to see him too. Thank you for reminding me. Sometimes I forget where he is." She nodded and hugged his knee with tiny arms.

The woman stepped into the room, smoothing a loose strand of russet hair into place. She paused, noting where her daughter was, then smiled gently at B.A. "Well, now, my daughter is a verra good judge of character. Us'ally she doesna take tae strangers. I see Heather has taken good care of ye." She glanced at her daughter's tea set, "More tea gentlemen?"

B.A. leaned to the little girl and whispered, "Will you join me Iskwesis? I'll share." She climbed to his lap and settled herself quite comfortably, rearranging her skirts in careful order, thus bringing a smile to Mac's and her mother's faces.

"You have a beautiful wee girleen, Mrs . . . ?"

"Mackenzie," she quickly supplied. "Aye, she's a guud lassie."

"Ah," Mac slowly remembered his manners, "I am John MacArthay and this is my good friend, Broken Arrow. But he answers to B.A. and I am just plain old Mac." He grinned in delight. "And 'tis grand to be findin' a Scottish sister so far and away from home!"

She offered a relieved smile. Now the crisis had passed, she noted his red hair for the first time, "Ooch! I havna seen hair tha' bright since we left Loch Eilean in Scotland nine years ago. Aye, straight onto a death boat we went. Whin we arrived in the Maritimes, they stoock us intae an Immigrant Shed for a month tae make sure we dinna brang a plague with us. Then they herded us ontae railway cars with nothing but benches for seats and beds. When we got off . . . we had only a shovel, hayfork and hoe for tools and a description from the Government of our homestead here.

What a daft pair we were, Dugall and I, our heads full of Butler's book, the *'Great Lone Land'*. Wide open prairie and free land for the takin' we were promised." She shook her head, "We dinna ha' the brains to be mindful o' what all this space and emptiness meant. My husband toils from morn 'til night and still we barely get by. Most years he hauls freight around Fort Qu'Appelle just tae buy our staples.

"I'm no' goin' tae tell ye tis an easy life. Ye've never seen boogs like they have here. The small black flies are a trial all their own. They hang around th' eyes of our poor cattle, burrowing in like woodworms, they do. In nae time, th' horse's withers ha' nae hair left from scratching. Th' poor beasts will run awa' cross th' land, trying tae outdistance the wee mites. Then ye ken those bull-dog flies? They do nae bite, they give ye bleedin' blisters!" She flapped her tea towel at a stray house fly. "It's no' natural, these vast beasties. They invade in legions from first thaw 'til freeze up. Dugall swears the mosquitoes are sae thick in th' evening, if ye swing a knife through the air, ye'll draw blood!"

She fed the fireplace a few more sticks and swung her kettle over the increasing blaze. "And the other wee beasties are no' so wee. Ooch! I had a fright t'other day when I walked outside and came face tae face with a great black bear. I wailed loud enough tae wake th' dead whin I ran inside. Probably scared him out o' a week's growth fer I've no' seen hide nor hair o' him since.

Mac frowned, "So you regret coming ma'am?"

She smoothed her apron over a faded cotton dress, "Tell ye the truth, I wouldna do it again. Some days, tis hard to remember why we came but I canna gae haeme, no' across that frightful ocean." She shuddered, "Ne'er will I forget th' rollin' waves and wild storms. Twenty, thirty feet high mountains of black hell, our boat tossed round like a cork, ready tae break apart any minute." Her brogue intensified, "Aye, tis hard to hold a full thought in yer head in tha' kind of endless terror. People screaming and smashin' against the boards, their bones crackin'. Others heavin' their guts oot and prayin' tae die. Tis like a bad dream, one ye wish ye could fly out of or jost wake op from. When ye gae on like that for many an hour, e'en days, it does somethin' tae yer soul. After a while, ye be numb inside, blanked oot, e'en find peace with it. Tis the acceptance of it all, I think. Ye e'en accept yer oon death." She sighed, "But when the storm ends and tis all quiet agi'n, there ye are, jost floatin' around in the sun, you feel tired . . . sad . . . empty inside, e'en disappointed that ye must gae on livin' after all."

She reached for tin cups from her rough hewn cupboard and dug out a sugar bowl, "Aye, after facin' yer own death like tha', there is no' too much tha' can scare a person.

"I decided I can face whatever the dear Lord decides tae hand me after that. And Sweet Mary he's handed it too. Soomtimes I dinna see a blessed soul other than me husband for six months on in the winter time. Nobody moves about when the white blizzards come callin'. She smiled at B.A. "Thank the Lord, Chief Piapot's band lives nearby. Their women hae taught me sae mooch about drying meat, tanning hides and making clothes. And we ha' a lot o' fun doing it. I taught them how to make these wee bannocks." She indicated the plate of slightly battered biscuits then chuckled "Those bonnie women know how tae tease and make life fun again. And I thank the Guid Lord they were there for the birthin' o' our wee bairns too" Her eyes moved to the tanned hides about the room. "I did these myself wi' their help. Sometimes, their men will bring half a deer or antelope for us." Her grin widened, "Aye, and don't they love our Irish potatoes for trade!"

Then she frowned, "I ne'er asked them about Hamish's bleedin'. Scares the devil oot o' me. I felt so helpless no' knowin' what tae do. So I thank ye sarrh!" She held out a hand, red and rough from the heavy lye soap she used. B.A. held it gently. She looked surprised at the lack of movement or pressure in his fingers.

"In our ways," he explained softly, "when we meet and touch hands, we touch each other's spirit for the first time. So we wait and just feel it happen. No motion is necessary."

She searched the sincerity in his face and finally nodded. "'Tis a guid way tae say hello."

He reached behind his head and untied one of his eagle feathers, holding it out to her, palm up. "We also honour our warriors when they show courage. Your boat trip took great courage; so do the lonely blizzards. In honouring the strength needed to survive a frightening situation, we present our warriors with an eagle feather. The eagle is Creator's messenger who flies so high he sees all our actions."

She frowned, "But I'm a woman."

B.A.'s mouth quirked, "Our woman can also be warriors. In truth, some are the bravest of all."

She thoughtfully picked up the feather, turning it over in her fingers, noting the beaded leather thong wrapping the end of the shaft.

She looked up, blue eyes meeting brown, held the feather out and turned around. He took it from her, tying it carefully onto a thick strand near the top of her head. When he stepped back, she grinned at him and touched the feather, smoothing it into place. "I'll ne'er forget ye." Going to her cupboard, she pulled out a small jar of butter and a package of ham. "My thanks for your help."

Broken Arrow accepted the gift with a nod of gratitude. "I will show you where to gather the Yarrow for your son. You can dry it for winter use as well. And there are other plants and roots nearby which will strengthen his blood."

That evening as they rode away, B.A. searched the quiet sunset, brilliant with pink and magenta. He vented his anger on the silent Mac, "Why are you white men so selfish? You abandon your women to face the land alone and unprotected. It is too hard for them! Our people understand loneliness. That is why we live and travel together, helping one another and sharing the workload. How can there be laughter in a person's life if they must constantly work and live alone?"

Mac considered this view in surprise. He rubbed a bristly chin, "Well now . . . tis truly a harsh land for a woman alone. I never thought about it before . . . or why your people lived together." He ducked a tree branch, "Now I see why you gave her a feather. You, more than any white man would see the courage she shows facing this great land. Us, we take our women's courage for granted and scorn their tears for weakness."

They rode on in silence, finally Mac broke it. "Why did you not want me to help the little girl?"

B.A. rode for a while, "It would have robbed her pride in doing it herself."

Mac thought about it and nodded. "You meant it when you asked her about God didn't you."

B.A. looked at the dark shadow of his friend in the moonlight, "Children are our gift from the Creator. Some of our clans believe a child never gets its spirit until six moons old. Until then, it doesn't know whether it will stay or if the Creator will take it back. So we give thanks for each child in case the Creator decides he wants the child back. We cherish and respect all our children. They are closest to him, just a few years from sitting at his knee. Their wisdom comes from him and they have not forgotten."

16.

SOUL JOURNEY

"The little girl and her mother reminded me what I'm searching for. I lost a piece of my soul some time ago, when I left my people. I remember what it was like as a child. I remember the brightness, like a light that has now gone out inside me." B.A. sipped his hot tea and contemplated the flickering firelight.

Mac scowled over his own pewter cup, "A soul? Well and isn't that up to God? We were taught we just have one. What more d'ye need?"

"Yes . . . but do you know your soul's purpose or power?" B.A. picked up a stick and prodded the burning branches to increase the heat. It was a cool evening with a bitter wind that drove the men closer to the flames.

Mac swirled his muskeg tea, watching the tiny leaves whirl. He'd learned to appreciate its minty flavour and soothing warmth after a day's ride. "Well, that may take us a lifetime to figure it out. It's no' like it'll just come to ye like a flash of revelation in the night. Ye could spend your whole lifetime searching and what would ye have? Probably something that travelled with you from the beginning."

B.A. stubbornly shook his head, "I know my soul is somehow tied up in the White Man's life. That's all I know yet. So I'll search his world until I find it. Or see it. I want to see it, my soul. I want to feel it return here, whole and sound once more!" His fist slammed his chest over his diaphragm. "I want to touch it. Then, and only then, can I talk to it and finally understand it."

Mac shrugged, "See yer soul? I dunno what you mean. Father O'Reilly claimed you people worship pagan gods. Who knows the truth? Your ways may be as good as mine but don't be askin' me to change my faith and follow yours. I will not any more than you will follow mine. So we break even on that score."

Broken Arrow shook his head, trying to make this thick headed White Man see. "Soul is unknown. When we search for it, we find our inner wisdom. It takes courage to face this unknown and recognize its treasures, to balance the suffering with the joy we find along the way. Our journey is to find information and experience life. What we learn from life becomes our wisdom: the truths we discover and learn to understand moves deeply through us until it becomes part of who we are.

"Wisdom links our hearts, minds, body and spirit together in a newer, deeper unity and understanding of the total of all four parts—our soul. Wisdom is the art of living in rhythm with your soul, your life and the Creator. Wisdom is how you learn to understand the unknown, our closest companion." He remembered the long winter talks he had with Mitsue and Tall Man on this.

"The elders say spirit is our inner voice, our inner sense of knowing. If we follow it, we can never go wrong. It is the only truth in our life that will destroy all the lies and barriers blocking us from becoming what we were meant to be. When we pay attention to this voice, see its truth, it will teach us the strength, courage and self-discipline to be our true self, the soul we work to develop our entire life. Our inner voice is the source of all our wisdom so far. That voice is our connection to our soul. We just have to find it, listen to it and see its truth."

Mac suddenly felt uneasy, like a black shadow had just crossed his gut. "*See it?* And just how d'ye see something invisible as the wind?

We can no' see inside ourselves. We just have to believe it's there, like the wind around us." He wanted to stop this nonsense; it made his shoulder blades itch.

B.A.'s mouth tightened, "Can you not feel it now? Feel the blackness, the empty gaping hole, the boundless pit in a dark cave, so wide, so deep inside that if you take one false step, it would swallow you whole and you'd fall, endlessly, into darkness with no bottom?"

Mac was suddenly afraid of the black night around him. He knew that pit, had fallen into it backwards, sucked in headfirst, right off the doctor's table the night they gave him ether before they'd set his broken leg. He'd never hit bottom and felt eternally grateful when he awoke to bright sunlight hours later. Ever since, he'd seen the pit in his darkest dreams, ran from it in daylight, poured excuses, food, laughter and whiskey into it. But it remained bottomless, never filling, just waiting until the fear rose up once again and overwhelmed him in a dark horror of despair, emptiness and loneliness. He'd thought he was going crazy. Now someone else had just reached into his mind and found it again – waiting.

He leapt to his feet, restlessly pacing the length of the campfire light and back, his hands clenching into fists. "Hell! 'Tis whot hell is! 'Tis a burning fire pit of hell taking us to our deaths in endless agony if we sin without repentance. That's why we need religion – to confess our sins. Then we avoid the pit! Religion teaches us how to prevent its hold over us so we don't fall into it from sin but we live instead! We live in everlasting serenity – the eternal life versus eternal damnation. That's all we have! That's our soul's purpose!"

B.A. slammed a fist against his thigh, "Never will I believe that! Any religion is just man-made ceremonies and prayer. They teach us how to connect with the Creator. But it is not about *my* soul or *my* experience with my soul, or *my* purpose. No religion can give me that! I must listen for it and find it myself!

"Religion is just a belief system giving us direction to live by. Your Catholics base everything on fear and failure if you do not heed their messages – like a threat! You cannot question. You must follow blindly or fear punishment. Yet fear will always stop us from finding our own power, from experiencing it! All who struggle beyond the fear reach a stage where obedience is tempered with their own judgement. We have choices! We can choose our own path! And no religion or ritual or prayer or teacher can do it for us. We have to find it ourselves, inside, right inside that black pit."

Mac was sweating now; it dripped down his back in icy trickles. He felt alone; suddenly frightened of this raw, empty land that echoed a similar resonance within him. Like the dark night around him, blackness rolled down inside him, moving like a shadowed menace through his gut. Was it just the fate of the Irish? This heavy melancholy which often threatened to smother him? Or was it the brink of insanity? Whatever its root, he wanted no part of it. He reeled in his wild thoughts and shoved the bleakness back under rigid control.

His nails dug into his palms as he fought back, "Ye don't understand! We have no power! Only God has. Tis not by men but by God and the law that we are governed! You! What do you know about faith with your heathen ways?" He winced inside but his fury overran his compassion, "You've never been part of the Catholic faith! You never learned the prayers and teachings about our place in this world. You've never sang the songs and chants giving us commitment to God and his strength. You know nothing of the Mass rituals which give us peace and purpose in life: to be law-abiding citizens, to remain within the rules of the Ten Commandments in our daily lives. What more is there? What more d'ye need? By living this way we avoid the pit, the eternal fires of damnation. We live! And then we die! That's it! That's all there is!"

B.A. surged to his feet, his face a rigid mask of fury, "As a child, I heard your prayers, was forced to learn your chants on my knees or feel the loving edge of your priest's rod across my shoulders. And they called us savage! Beating a small child takes no courage. There is no honour in such cruelty and certainly no loving faith! Never will I believe so!

"The Black Robes tried to convince us our worth depended on obedience and measuring up to their requirements. You think they know the only way to live? That your religion holds all the answers? How can you follow it so blindly? Guilt . . . shame . . . fear of God . . . terrors of eternal damnation, are these good ways to live? It just creates more fear. And it controls you through your fear. Have you ever tried to get beyond the fear?

"What of the people who are not Catholic? What about other races? What about my people? What about their souls? Do you really think the Creator forgot them? Did he create all their generations just to set them adrift into nothing? Are they eternally damned because they don't sing your Catholic songs and rituals from the Black Robes? What foolish pride! Can you not see beyond the Catholic ways? You blindly accept the words of the Black Robes who are twisted by their own fears! You give away your power to their authority and you do not even question their leadership! You are afraid to possess your own truth!

"Fall into your pit White Man! I dare you! I doubt you have the stomach to face what you find!" B.A. swung away, his long furious strides pushing him into the undergrowth and out of sight.

Mac was left in the empty silence of a glade offering no comfort, only shades of darkness, filtered by occasional glimpses of moonlight on silvery leaves.

"Hell and Damnation!" He kicked at a stone which promptly buried itself in the fire with a shower of sparks.

17.

LEAVING UNSPOKEN

"Why d'ye always leave?"

Mac's owly question from out of nowhere had B.A. turning to him in surprise. "Ah?"

They had spent the early morning in total silence: B.A. unwilling and Mac unable to talk. Now close to mid-day according the sun's high position, they'd stopped for a quick lunch along a quiet stream.

Mac watched him, his eyes sober and angry, "Why do you always leave? Just when we are in the middle of a good discussion or argument, you get up and leave. I tell ye, tis hard to have a good fight with ye. Before I can get me two penny's worth in, ye're high-tailin' it away. Tis no way to settle a dispute."

When B.A. looked away, his face thoughtful, Mac ground his teeth. He'd not be gettin' another word from the damned Indian until he'd thought it through. Twas enough to make a man howl in rage, all this silence and thinkin'! Why not settle it with the fists and be done with it. To pass the time, he continued unpacking his gear, ignoring the silent man who sat unmoving, staring into the growing flames heating their tea. It wasn't until Mac poured the steeped dandelion tea and passed him some dried apples and pemmican that B.A. spoke.

"Our people spend their entire lives together. Their homes are thin, buffalo-skinned tipis, very close together. It was important, above all else, to keep harmony between us so we could live and survive together in peace. We were taught from a young age to speak quietly, never raising our voices to one another. Angry words and fighting destroy the harmony. So we kept ourselves out of other people's space and did not interfere with their lives. We never made eye contact as part of our respect for each other." He looked across to Mac who sat quietly, his eyes on the horizon. "We were taught to leave with our anger rather than speak cruel words without thought. Such words are carried on the wind to others and can never be taken back."

Mac frowned, "Well and how d'ye you finally solve your differences?" He bit into a tart dried apple then sipped his dandelion tea. He enjoyed the full-bodied flavour of the dried roots B.A. occasionally dug up. The Cree was amazed when Mac told him the bright yellow flowers had been imported by European settlers. How quickly the plant had spread its seeds on the wind across the land. The settlers enjoyed the healing powers of dandelion roots for flushing poisons out of the body and ate the new leaves as salad greens. They also made a potent wine.

"We leave until we have time to think the problem through and find its truth. It may take days or weeks. When we are ready, we will return and talk about it quietly to restore the harmony between us."

Mac huffed through his nose, "Sure'n that's well and good, but what d'ye do if ye see someone doing something ye don't like. Leaving solves nothing!"

The Cree swung a casual leg over the other, lying half sideways to give his butt a rest. He chewed a crispy leg of cold prairie chicken thoughtfully, swallowing before continuing. "We are not like you White Men. We are not our brother's keeper. It is not our duty to stop him from making mistakes. We honour his right to choose and learn in his own way. Life is about gaining wisdom – often from our mistakes. It is not our place to tell anyone when they do something wrong."

"And if it could kill him? Or somebody else? Surely ye interfere then?"

"*Tapwe*, it is true. We would stop the harm to another. We may also sit with him; tell him a story about another time when someone else did a foolish thing like he is about to. Or, we may call him by the name of that foolish person if he knows the story already. It is his choice to heed the message, or not." B.A raised himself to pack away his cup.

"Or not?" In astonishment, Mac stopped packing his empty cup in his saddlebags and spun to his relaxed companion. "Jaysus, ye'd let him kill himself? Never could I live with myself for standing back and doing nothing to stop him. Tis a great sin to commit suicide in our Catholic beliefs"

"If that was his choice and his risk to take, so it shall be."

The calm finality left Mac speechless for a moment. Finally, he managed, "Why?"

"Honour. We honour his choices by not interfering. Who are we to know what is best for our brother? We do not walk in his moccasins, nor see his path as clearly as he. It is his life to lead and we must respect his choices, even though we disagree. Anything less dishonours his purpose to walk his path his way, to think his thoughts and learn his lessons. We would appear bossy and too proud of our own ways." He could have added, but didn't, how foolish he considered this Irish man for travelling alone into a strange land he seemed unprepared to survive in. Did he seek a different form of suicide?

"So . . ." Mac worked his way through it all as he repacked his gear and tied it on behind his saddle. "If ye decide to die, I have no right to stop ye?"

"None." Broken Arrow briefly wondered, had he interfered too much by helping this White man?

"Hell and damnation man, ye make it very hard to be your friend!" Mac lifted his hat, ran a hand through his wild curls then replaced his hat with a decided plop.

B.A.'s lips quirked, deciding the topic was too serious for this sunlit day, "You could always join me."

Mac hooted, swinging a sturdy leg up and over his horse. B.A. leapt atop Brownfoot and lifted him into a cheerful canter through the belly-deep slough grass. In the distance, a hawk screamed and a mouse hid.

18.

POWAKAN

Two days later, Broken Arrow picked up their soul argument as they sat fishing beside a meandering creek with occasional groups of cattails lining its muddy banks. The men cast their hooks towards the edge of the reeds where the jackfish or Northern Pike searched for unwary minnows.

"And so Mac, have you thought any more of that pit?"

Lying on his stomach, a sweet grass stem stuck between his teeth, Mac lazily yearned for a meal of juicy flaked fish, stuffed with wild onions, wrapped in mud and baked slowly in hot coals at the edge of a campfire. Then B.A. would make a broth of the leftovers, seasoning it with some of that white pine moss. His mouth watered. The last thing on his mind was soul. His slack-jawed, "Whaaa?" ended as he rolled over to peer at his companion who had just called him 'Mac' for the very first time.

"The pit we have in our dreams and visions. Have you been in it?"

Mac's spine tightened instantly. He sighed, "Jaysus, why d'ye want to be talkin' about such a gloomy subject on a soft day like this?" A light mist overhead slowly burned away under the warm morning sunshine. Meadowlarks called in the distance. Grey and gold grasshoppers clacked and hopped around them while tiny ants struggled through the green grass.

"I'm talking about life," B.A. continued stubbornly, "and there is no better time to discuss it than the bright sunshine of this moment. There are fewer shadows to deal with." He idly flicked his line in tiny surges, imitating the dance of a curious minnow.

Mac settled himself against a black poplar that now felt like an old friend. It comforted him and drew his unease away while he watched the gentle bob of his fishing line. "I fell into that pit once. Scared the bejaysus out of me." He shuddered, remembering his infinite relief to awaken, out and away from it. "Never had any desire to go back into it. Avoid it like the plague."

B.A. searched the quiet horizon of grey haze, his eyes slipping peacefully over the occasional clumps of red willows and cattails outlining the creek's progress across the plains. "When I reached thirteen summers, I went on a three-day fast called a Vision Quest. I went off by myself, with no food, no water and no weapons. It was a time to pray, to think, to overcome the fear of hunger, of being alone, the fear of wild animals, the dark and most of all, the fear of spirit world, the world of the pit."

Mac contemplated such a feat with awe. "Where I grew up, our biggest test was 'Swingin' Trees'. We'd swing from tree to tree through the branches, seein' how far we could go without touching the ground. Sometimes we'd fall flat on our backs and lose our voices for a couple of hours. It came back as a squeak at first." Mac surveyed him with a new respect. "Helluva lot for a young boy to deal with, that Vision Quest. I know grown men who still fear the dark, let alone wild animals."

B.A. nodded, "Fear is a strange thing. It has many faces. It catches and chokes you, makes you feel helpless, sick, and alone. There is a terrible sadness in feeling alone when you are surrounded by people. It is ten times worse when you really are alone, off by yourself. You want to fight the despair, pretend it doesn't exist. Yet the more you fight it, the stronger you make it.

"I remember Tall Man telling me:

'Your power ends when your fear begins. Let the power in, let it become your own so you wield it in a gentle way, taking one thing and turning it into another. Give in to your fear. Turn and face it, see it for what it is. Often it is just a lesson. Sometimes facing the fear makes it fade into nothing'."

Broken Arrow leaned back, soaking up the sunshine and aroma of crushed grass beneath him, "Vision quest taught me to move beyond fear, to be still and quiet and wait for the words of the voice within me. It was a time to pull all the pieces of my life together and begin to find some purpose in it."

He turned to Mac, his tanned face earnest and animated, "In this stillness, you can talk with your soul. You finally have the silence to hear it. It is a time to become acquainted with yourself without interruption, duty or guilt. Solitude is also form of loneliness, so heavy you can feel it. When you move into it, experience it, express it, befriend it and know it, eventually you enjoy it. When you can weep at the pain of this loneliness, something changes inside. You find yourself accepting it, knowing it is true, that we all feel alone. It is a common thing for people, animals and plants. When you accept it as truth, it no longer requires a fight. The fear is gone. Loneliness . . . just . . . is. Once you move beyond its fear, peace comes; allowing you to enjoy all that is, as . . . is. I found I could just enjoy the peace of my aloneness in that moment."

"*Cuinas gan uagineas.*" At B.A.'s silent query Mac explained, "Tis Gaelic for 'Quietness without loneliness.'"

B.A. beamed, "So your people understood it too."

Mac sighed, "Sure'n maybe our bards and druids did. But don't be thinkin' I grasp it all." He squinted with curiosity, "What about the fear of animals? How did ye overcome that?"

"Our elders talk of a time long ago when humans and animals lived and talked together. Medicine men amongst our people are initiated into their lives as healers and prophets by animal guides who come to them in visions and dreams. Tall Man told me whatever animals appear during my Vision Quest will be my totem spirits, guardian spirits, *Powakan*. They choose to present themselves to me. They will show me how to use my body and abilities to survive and earn a long, good life. Their habits and strengths help me understand my own similar ones. They would be my assistants for the rest of my life if I did not fear them. If I showed any fear, they would disappear, waiting until I dealt with my fear. For some people, it takes years before they return."

Mac jiggled his fishing line, experimenting with motions similar to B.A.'s, "Fear is a powerful emotion so overcoming it is a true test of courage?"

B.A. shook his head. "Not just courage, faith."

"What? Now how does religion enter this?"

"Not religion but having faith, *believing* what you need to grow and learn will come to you. It's Creator's way of teaching. It may not be what you want but always what you need. That is faith. And facing any fear requires a leap of faith, like jumping off a cliff into the clear waters below. Everything happens for a reason." He grinned at his companion, "Even meeting you."

"Our meeting was just a coincidence, mere chance." Mac waved the thought away, intently watching his fishing line for movement.

"How can you prove it was not Creator's way?"

"Well, how can you prove it was? Mac groused irritably.

"Remember I said finding my spirit was tangled up in learning the White Man's ways? It's one of the reasons I left my people and searched for white men. That was one message I received during my Vision Quest." Broken Arrow was also told to teach white men about Spirit, if they would listen.

Mac tipped his hat to the back of his head, "Well, I tell ye, if you're seeking to find real White Man ways, I doubt you'll be finding them from the sorry excuses for white people we've come across since I left home. Most don't amount to a hill of beans, excepting a few like the Scots family! The rest were never part of the civilized world back east, not the society I grew up in anyway."

B.A. grinned at his friend's brilliant curls sparkling in the sunshine, "That's why Spirit sent me you."

Mac's sunburnt skin reddened further, "Ah Jaysus man, don't be thinkin' I'm any great angel sent for the salvation of yerself. I'm just a young fool full of ideals, ambitions and mistakes."

B.A. chuckled outright, "Like me. So we learn from each other as we go along. As it was meant to be."

Mac shook his head then grinned slyly, "Sure'n I can set ye straight on a couple things about fightin' and drinkin' but I don't get all your talk about Spirit."

B.A. rolled back on his side, crossing one leg over, propping his fishing stick up between a couple of his bare toes. "You will, White Man. You will."

A few lazy minutes later, Mac asked idly, "So what animals came to you?"

"I cannot answer that. It is not good to boast. Powakan are like secret friends. They will help when you need them but to brag about them is to lose their gifts. They can leave as quickly as they come if you do not honour their aide. Besides, it may make others feel less worthy of the gifts from their animal helpers. Every creature, large or small, whether it flies, runs, crawls or swims has something of value to offer and to teach. There is a reason for its life, one of Mother Earth's creatures, who help balance all life. Each has much wisdom we can learn from. The smallest ant can teach you about Earth Mother's seasons and vibrations because the whole mound lives with her heartbeat. Ants are skilled builders, creating homes of a thousand connected tunnels. They can teach how to build your life, changing your dreams into reality with the help of your family and community. They show how the greatest success comes from working together with persistence. Creatures who walk upon Mother's skin can teach you the practical ways to be strong and survive grounded always in her wisdom. The winged ones teach you a higher viewpoint, beyond your short-distanced, earth-bound vision. Every person has to find his own helpers to teach him what he needs to learn and grow in wisdom."

"And that is the purpose of life to you? To become wise?" Mac turned to look into B.A.'s eyes. Back East, purpose seemed to be about how much money one had. He'd soon realized living off the land like they did here, required very little money or the means to make it.

The Cree nodded, "Our soul's purpose is to learn. That is how we grow through our entire life. But we have to find our soul first, hear it, see it and speak with it. So we need our spirit helpers the *Powakan.* They teach us about ourselves, about our strengths and weaknesses. Your Black Robes say weakness is bad, sinful. For us, it just is. Like nature, we have many sides, both storms and sunshine. When we accept this about ourselves, then we can choose how we want to live our lives. There are some people who love the storms more than the peace."

Mac fished on, "Can anyone have these spirit helpers? Even white people?"

"We are taught anyone can talk with Spirit though your Catholics say only your pope can talk to your God. We just find a quiet place to be alone, to sit in the silence and wait. When we listen, we become aware of the Powakan when they come. It takes time to know them. It helps to study the strengths and wisdom they possess. They reflect a part of who you are and what you can become."

Mac glanced over at his reclining companion, "Jaysus, you'll have me talkin' to the animals yet."

"And mayhap you'll learn something beyond your White Man ignorance."

The warm sun and sleepy afternoon eased Mac's prick of irritation. "So how d'ye go about discovering which animals are kindred to you?"

"Has certain creatures of the water, land or air approached you when you sat alone in the woods? Did they show you a special gift or look into your eyes? When you see certain animals, do you feel your heart's pain? Like a deep ache or yearning within you? Do people call you by an animal name? All might be connections to your Powakan. Only you know if they are important. Have you ever dreamed of an animal spirit or the spirit world they live in? Stories of the spirit world have great power. Telling people of your dreams is a way of everyone staying in contact with spirit beings."

Mac lay back on the grass, tipping his hat over his face. "Well and now . . . I remember reading how the ancient Egyptians believed their thoughts and dreams were gods speaking to them."

He lay so quietly B.A. wondered if he slept, then Mac lifted the brim of his hat to spear him with one brilliant green eye. "I dreamt of a wolf once, two nights before I met you. I thought I was awake only to find the biggest, blackest wolf I'd ever seen standing over me. The hair on its head and shoulders shone in the moonlight like a white halo. The rest of it was so black, it looked half shadow. I couldn't move, just stared into its yellow eyes for the longest time. He bared his fangs and snarled and I thought for sure'n I was dead. But it backed away and disappeared. I sat up and threw more wood on the fire but it was gone without a whisper of sound. I couldn't sleep the rest of the night, just sat by the fire and threw more logs on it until I had a regular bonne fire goin'. Near cooked me knees from the heat."

He cleared his throat and swallowed convulsively. "The next night, I dreamed of a wolf again only this one was grey and female. She attacked me. Ripped me arms to bloody shreds she did when I tried to defend myself. Twas all I could do to block her from ripping out me throat. I managed to throw her off somehow and run to me house." Mac's brogue thickened, "Right behind me she was, slashing at me heels until I thought she'd be hamstringin' me for sure. I reached the door and slammed it in her face. When I raced to close the windows, there he was, the black one, anticipating my every move; tearing at my fingers with his teeth until they were so slippery with blood I could barely push the damn sills down. Then they were at the back door, scraping and scratching, pulling big chunks of wood away with their teeth. I knew they'd be getting' in soon so I ran for me gun. Had to fight like hell to load it. The barrel and shot kept slippin' away in all the blood. I timed myself to open the door and pull the trigger at the same time. When I threw it open, an old woman in a long skirt and shawl stood there grinning at me. I almost dropped me gun in shock, terrified I *might* pull the trigger. Bedamnedest thing I'd ever seen! When I finally woke up, I couldn't believe I never had a single scratch on me."

Mac looked over to see B.A. convulsed with laughter, holding his stomach. "Here and now! Tis no laughin' matter. Scared the Bejaysus out of me!"

Broken Arrow sat up, still grinning and punched Mac on the shoulder with enough force to lay him on the ground if he hadn't been there already. "Wolf clan is a powerful clan. Elders say they don't take initiates easily. They'll test you first. Your fear the first night made them back away. But your fight the next night proved your courage. Your choice to protect your home and fight back proved you worthy. They love their families and homes. Wolves live as a pack, but they have clan ways based on strength and wisdom like few other animals. They know how to hunt, but they also know how to play. They are the true spirit of this free and unspoiled land. They will stalk and gather what they need yet they seem to have a sense of what will happen in the end—like an inner knowing." His eyebrows rose as something occurred to him, "Maybe they are part of your seventh son gift to know without knowing how you know."

Mac frowned, considering this new idea while the Cree continued, his face now serious. "Wolf is a very strong power guide, Mac; it is the teacher and the pathfinder—the spirit that shows the way. Wolf teaches you to know who you are and to develop strength and confidence so you do not have to constantly prove yourself to everyone."

Mac smirked, remembering all the fights with the bloody English badachs. Aye, he'd had something to prove. He focused back on his friend's face, grave and still in the warm sunlight.

"Wolf medicine teaches you to trust your inner truth and guard against wrong actions. You had a pair come to you, male and female, which means you are being given both male and female power – a very deep gift of balance from the Powakan. Sometimes animal spirits will change to human form to talk with you. They are always old, wise spirits so we call them the 'Grandmothers' and 'Grandfathers'. And they'll have a lot of fun with you too. You'll see. Those wolves will be back."

B.A. chuckled at Mac's infinite disgust at being bested by an old grandmother. "Maybe we are here to help each other learn. For the Powakan, Wolf has the teachings of Earth wisdom. They have the ability to create new paths for learning but true freedom requires discipline—maybe something beyond your Irish temper."

B.A. rolled to his back howling in glee. "Ah oooooooohhhhh!! And you say Spirit had no hand in sending you to me?" He went into gales of laughter until Mac whacked him with his hat.

19.

THE DREAM

That night Mac dreamed. He found himself beside the pit, poised on its rim staring into the vast darkness of empty space, he felt so alone, lost in fear and a deepening sense of despair. Twas his hell he stared into with all the things that terrorized him and tantalized him. B.A.'s words echoed through him in hollow vibration, "I dare you White Man."

With an angry roar, Mac took a running leap and dove headlong into the hole, falling, falling endlessly. He fell in anger, then in terror, headfirst, straight down. His only redemption: he smelled no brimstone, saw no flames. Still he fell, deeper into darkness until the falling became an adjustment, a phase of living fiercely in the moment by moment rush of his life, commitment with no return. Then he smelled . . . moistness in the dark rush, a fertile richness of earth. Warm and gentle, it wrapped him with invisible arms of comfort. His bemusement gave him grace, loosening the bonds of fear . . . into the sheer freedom of falling, like flying.

He flung out his arms and let the warm winds filter through his clothes, under his arms, between his legs and past his ears, until he smiled, laughed and shouted at the vast quantities of air filling his mouth, gusting up his nose and slipping through his fingers. He flipped into summersaults and back flips. Still he fell—but no longer cared. The flight encompassed him. He closed his eyes, feeling made of air himself . . . existing in the moment and peaceful with the heady flight. And still, he fell deeper, endlessly into the night . . . .

With a gentle thud he landed on his hands and knees, abruptly losing all sensation of flight and ecstasy. So much for the old wives' tale of dying if a person fell and hit bottom in a dream. Earthbound and heavy once more, he yearned for the free fall, the wild heady freedom of flight, something he'd never felt before. Cautiously, he lifted his head. A high cavern surrounded him, softly lit with golden hues of shadow and light, candlelight soft without the flickering. He turned his head and drew a jagged breath.

Over him towered a gigantic crystal, a great dark, carefully hewn ball of hundreds of exquisite crystals. They extended in every direction, like a wild explosion of rock, their many elongated sides cut to pristine points. He vaguely remembered his folklore about crystal containing a universe unto itself. A powerful, natural healer, it absorbs, releases and regulates energy. Was this crystal within him, at the bottom of the pit? Or was it a crystal within the earth? He stayed on his haunches overwhelmed by the sheer magnitude of the mass looming above him, reaching for the vaulted ceiling of the glowing circular cave. He remembered rock crystal received its name from the Greek word, *krystallos,* meaning, 'ice' because they thought the crystal was water frozen forever hard by the gods. The ancients claimed the sun and the light universe were housed within a perfect crystal like a ball of crystals within a ball of the earth, within a ball of the universe. Then why the Sam Hill was he here? Made a man rethink reality as he knew it!

So be it! Mac threw himself backward upon the ground, pillowing his head with both arms, bemused by the silent mass in this empty, peaceful labyrinth. Who would have guessed it? Instead of eternal hell and damnation, he'd found eternal beauty, glowing in the soft light emanating from the crystals. He felt no fear, only curiosity and a deep sense of rightness for being there—at last. He saw no light source, neither a beginning nor end of light in this crystal filled with subtle nuances of colour, elusive sensations rather than bands of hue. The cave lay empty though its floor of smooth, loosely packed dirt looked trampled by a thousand and more feet. Arched openings around the cave revealed tunnels entering from every direction. He wondered about the ones who had made the prints. Were they seekers like him?

As he lay there, gentle radiant warmth enclosed him. Quiet pulsations, subtle at first, grew stronger until energy surged sensually through him like the willow he'd grasped. It felt so comforting, so familiar, he closed his eyes in quiet enjoyment while a part of him wondered at his fearlessness in this strange place. Still the energy pulsed through him, permeating every part of his body, surging through his fingertips, hands, chest, face, even his lips. It buoyed around him, eventually lifting him and floating him back up, towards the top of the cavern and beyond, back the way he had come and he revelled in its comforting presence. Like a babe in arms he rose as moist air gently warmed his face, filtered through his hair and cradled his body so lovingly, so carefully. Never in his entire life had he felt so warm, so comfortable and so safe. Up, up he wafted, helpless and uncaring, letting his head fall back, his arms outstretched, revelling in the gentle pulses of movement, delighted to simply be alive . . . .

By degrees of refusal, he returned to himself, clinging to the pulsations surging through him, feeling an ecstatic joy when his heart beat in rhythm, in cadence, like a melody. Tom . . . tom . . . tom.

His lip swelled with the sensual beat, his fingers filled with the urge to follow the rhythm: Tom . . . tom . . . tom . . . .

Finally, he arrived, just behind his eyelids, caught in the vibrations, melted into them, buoyed up by them, warm, cosy, comforted and connected . . . like never before. For the very first time, he felt part of something, welcomed into something missing all his life, like a vague memory of long ago. Earth, he thought drowsily. It was Her all along that he'd dove into, encountered and was resurrected by. Now, the Great Mother rocked him, comforted and enclosed him, like a new-born babe. He fully expected to open his eyes and see her great countenance above him. Danu, Mother Goddess Danu, Goddess of the earth, nurturer, protector, teacher, and healer. She was creation, birth, life and death. He felt the justice of Her approval, felt delivered up out of the mud, into the naked truth of all he was.

Sunlight filtered into sparkling auras behind his lids, tantalizing him with its crystalline fires, until he opened his eyes to warm sunshine upon his face. B.A. slept on across from him. Mac never wanted to move, for the surges still filled him, pulsed through him as he gazed up at the canopy of emerald trees above him, enthralled by their brilliant colours, fanning leaves and rhythmic swaying branches. Like him, they pulsed to the same rhythm and he cherished the music they made in unison. Never had he had seen such brilliant hues of green and wanted to remember their magnificence forever.

'Tom . . . tom . . . tom.' He felt his face split into a silly grin, a childish glee at the resonance from the lush earthy glade around him, reflecting, *living* Her heartbeat, like he did.

'Tom . . . tom . . . tom . . . tom.' A part of him wanted to leap and dance in sensual agreement with the swaying grass blades nearby while another part feared his movement would make it all collapse back into his dreams. And so he laid there, silent yet more relaxed than ever before—captivated by the in-between time of two worlds.

"*Peace.*"

Startled, he grasped the word slipping through his mind before dissolving back inside. Was this the first connection of consciousness—*from his soul?* Was this what B.A. talked about? Never had Mac encountered such elemental joy from within. It emptied him of all thought, leaving him enthralled with all his senses.

Still, as he lay there, he felt the sensations easing, disappearing gradually, so effortlessly he knew he could neither hold nor keep them. Never had he felt so aware of himself and his body, so awakened, so in tune with something so loving . . . so forgiving and enduring. It slowly faded away and he was left with only a whisper of memory, perched upon this earth once more, gazing into the ashes of a cold campfire, staring at his sleeping companion and wondering how he could even pretend to be the same again.

Broken Arrow opened his eyes to find Mac staring at him intently from across a small fire. The man's very stillness froze B.A. for a moment. Then he quickly sat up, rubbed his eyes and flung wild hair over his shoulders, wary now but unsure why.

Mac never moved. "Tell me about Mud Woman." It was more demand than request.

B.A. blinked at his companion and struggled to awaken his thoughts. He spoke slowly. "The Sioux call her Ina, other tribes call her Xumucane . . . or Sky Woman . . . or Thinking Woman . . . Changing Woman . . . or Selu. But she is still The Earth Mother of all and part of the Great Mystery we call Kisemanitou, what you call God."

Mac stared into the fire, "The early Celts had a mother goddess belief before Christianity came. She was Danu, meaning 'water from heaven'. In Celtic myth, Danu and her children were the Tuatha De' Danaan meaning 'Clan of The Immortals'. The Danube River is named after her—the heartland of the original Celts. All the ancient religions had different names for her too. Christianity has none. Egyptians called her Isis; the Greeks, Aphrodite. To the Middle East of Babylonia and Assyria she is Ishtar."

Mac dug at the fire with a dry stick, "The Hindu believe the Earth is alive and filled with different qualities of feminine energy. The Goddess of India existed both within and beyond the Universe. She was the very heartbeat and soil of the Earth. She rules not only the depths and surfaces of the Earth, but also its mountains. The world's greatest peaks, the Himalayas, are known as the 'Primal Mothers'. Mount Everest is called *Chomo-lung-ma* or Goddess Mother of the Universe. Hindus call melting snow the milk of the Goddess."

B.A. studied his friend's troubled features, wondering what he searched for.

Mac cleared his throat, "Gaia, the Greek Earth Goddess was the Great Mother of all life and Mother of the gods. She was the earth, the foundation. She supposedly gave birth to the starry heavens, the mountains and the seas. In earlier times, she was the Goddess of all plant life, wild animals and the dark, deep mystery of the underworld, the dwelling place of ancestral ghosts. She was said to be the source of all dreams which rose like vapours from her depths.

"Dreams dreamed in sacred caves, beside sacred wells and within a temple's underground grotto allowed the dreamers to find their innermost spiritual world. For the Greeks and Egyptians, there was no rigid line between imagination and reality. The human soul was part of the greater soul of nature. Nature helps people find their lives in this unseen dimension, to keep in touch with it, gain knowledge from it and apply this knowledge to the development of their soul."

B.A. nodded slowly, pulling the information into his mind and heart. "We also place great importance on our dreams. They are messages from our soul. When we lie upon Earth Mother, she takes us there in our dreams."

Mac gazed into his friend's quiet eyes, "Could I do that? Could I go to her in my dreams?"

"Did you?"

Mac rubbed frazzled hair, "Well I took your dare and dove into the pit last night. I thought it the pit of hell but I think I found . . . Her, your Mud Woman or Danu." He couldn't, wouldn't say he also thought he'd found his soul. He glanced uneasily at B.A. bracing for his laughter. None came. He felt foolish, frustrated and awed, unwilling to admit the extent of his dream, hoisted on the petard of his arrogant disbelief. It left him tongue-tied and confused. He searched his mind for his far-away books on mythology and religion.

He frowned, tried to speak and had to clear his throat, "Do you believe we are part of the Earth? Part of this Earth Mother? Could she live and breathe like us?"

"There are many deep caves throughout this country. I have noticed they breathe in for a time then out for a time, in the same pattern each day. I believe all plants and animals breathe so why not rocks?"

Mac's face became a study of worry and awe, "Hippocrates, one of our wise men, once said there is one common flow, one common breathing and all things are in sympathy. Each one of the parts is working together for the same purpose. Is this the One you talk about?"

B.A. nodded slowly, "Our elders say life is one power, one force. All things are related to everything else in a web covering the entire creation. Everything done to one part of the web is done to all. So in our sweats we pray for "All Our Relations in the air, land, fire and water of Earth Mother."

Mac scratched a straggly jaw and struggled on. "The Celts believe all breath comes in pairs, except our first and our last." His uneasy eyes drifted about the green circle of trees beyond the campfire. Another thought tightened his gut, "Hippocrates was a healer too. He noticed how some places helped people heal, while other places made them sick." Mac frowned searching the clearing. Was this a magical spot?

Again Broken Arrow nodded. "A Hopi elder once told me the earth is like a spotted fawn. Each special spot has certain powers and purpose. We have sacred places where the water wells out of the ground in a liquid green mud. Animals gather to lick the mud because it holds medicines and special foods they need to be healthy. Some animals will seek out special birthing places to have their young. Our people go to sacred spots to pray and be healed, such as little meadows or beside lakes.

"There is a special lake out of Fort Edmonton found over a hundred years ago by an Assiniboine or Stony Chief's vision about a Sacred Land set aside by the Creator for his people. It had three lakes with a big river running through them. He sent out scouts to find them but many never returned. Those that did never found the lakes and river. So the chief gradually moved his tribe north and west towards the Rockies. One night, some of his scouts camped beside a lake. That night, they heard drumming coming from a nearby island. Yet in the morning, when they paddled out to it, they found no evidence of any camp. Yet again the next night they heard drumming coming from the same island. The scouts decided it must be the little people, *the Makohde*, who drummed. The men wondered if this was one of the lakes of their chief's vision. When they brought him to the lake, he fell on his knees. It had taken him eight years to find his vision. The Stony called it *Wakamna*, God's Lake and they gathered there every summer to give thanks to Creator. Eventually their allies, the Cree, joined them. When the Black Robes came, they didn't want our people praying to a lake so they called it Devil's Lake. When our people continued to pray there anyway, the Black Robes took it over in 1842, moved the Stony Indians out and called it Lac Ste. Anne, after the grandmother of Christ. Different tribes still travel there for prayer and healing every summer."

Mac tossed small sticks to the glowing embers until a tiny flame flickered. "In Ireland, people still believe spirits of the little people inhabit the land. Danu and her children came to Ireland from four fabulous cities: Falias, Gorias, Finias and Murias. In each city they were taught by the Druids Morias, Urias, Arias and Senias. When the De Danaan, the Immortals were defeated by the Milesians, the Christians, each god was given a hill in Ireland by the Dagda, father of the gods, before he gave up his leadership of the gods. The Gaelic word *si_dhe* means 'mound or hill'. So the ancient gods driven underground became the *aes s_idhe*, the 'People of the Hills'. In later folklore we called them fairies. The most famous is the banshee, the *bean s_idhe,* the woman of the fairies whose wail and shriek warns of a coming death. Me Da said a lone bush in the middle of a field is never cut down. It could be a secret gathering place, or fairy fort, for these spirits. Local people would never intrude or build on such sacred ground."

He stoked the growing flames, adding bigger chunks of dead wood and branches, "I remember reading about the Hindu who had sacred sites called *tirthas,* meaning a 'crossing over'. These tirthas had the power to shift people out of their ordinary states of thinking and seeing. There, people remembered to remember. It awakened them to their own life force, a connection not only with the earth but with the entire universe, like a double remembering."

He squinted through the smoke, screwing up his courage, "D'ye know anything about crystals? Those clear stones with many flat surfaces, so smooth they look like they've been cut? I saw some in my dream, a great big ball of them. And I wondered what they were for. I remember reading how many stone circles in the British Isles had these crystals or quartzite in them. I believe twas at Callanist, a group of stone circles on an isle off the coast of Scotland which had pieces of hornblende, quartz or feldspar in almost every stone. They look like glass."

B.A. whipped his head up. "Remember the medicine wheel we found? At the centre of the wheel, buried deep in the ground, are strangely cut glass-like stones. Some of our people are afraid of them; others feel comforted by their presence saying the stones link us not only to Mother Earth but also to the Star People who live on a stone land in the stars."

Finally, Mac climbed out on a limb of belief, "Our earliest stories tell of our ancestors who spoke with the Gods and knew they took many forms like shape-shifters, sometimes humans, or animals, sometimes like snakes, serpents, dragons and reptiles. The ancient legends are full of the tales of dragons and their ability to merge with the mineral kingdom and their preference for crystalline structures. They flew in the heavens, swam in the oceans and walked the Earth."

Broken Arrow nodded. "We are all given a different inner vibration designed to connect with the Great Spirit, to help find our purpose, our way of offering support to Earth Mother."

Mac froze, "Vibrations, you mean like pulses? Surges, like heartbeats?" When B.A. nodded, Mac started to shake, deep in his gut, "We have spots like that all over Ireland and Great Britain. Ancient people went there to pray, to hold ceremonies, to give thanks, to dance and chant and drum. The Hindus also used rituals of music, dance, food, song, prayer and meditation to help them remember. Really, they are all just different forms of vibrations!"

B.A.'s eyebrows rose in amazement, "Then perhaps we are not so different after all White Man. Our people also believe drumming, dancing, singing, and prayer brings us closer to Spirit. We seek those sacred sites to sit and sometimes be lifted up in quite pleasure and appreciation of the Great Mystery. We experience being part of a whole, part of the Great Mother, part of the Great Mystery, part of all the relations possible."

"Hallelujah!" Mac threw himself on his back, grinning foolishly at the blue sky overhead. He wasn't going crazy, wasn't hallucinating. His dream was real! He'd just experienced such a relationship in wonderful detail—a powerful, magical, wonderful connection between his soul and Mother Earth. At last! Thank God! He felt an incredible satisfaction with himself and the world around him.

B.A. laughed at his friend's exuberance, "My people believe we must respect the plant, animal, stone and humans as part of the Great Spirit's Creation. So we pray in our sweats to 'All Our Relations'. How we treat this relationship with all living things is how we lift up and advance our souls."

"Lift up huh?" Mac felt a deep sense of satisfaction for experiencing the elevation first hand but was not about to share it. He hugged it to himself in selfish glee.

20.

Buffalo Hunt

They heard them long before they saw them. The two men rode towards Child's Mountain, a spur of the Little Touchwood Hills. It started as a faint whine in the distant. Mac turned his head, trying to make out such an unusual sound in this quiet land. B.A. noticed and pointed east with his head and stretched lips puckered like a kiss, "Metis Traders."

Mac stifled a smile, tickled at the way this Indian could point without lifting a finger. "How can you tell? You haven't seen them yet."

"Their carts." Broken Arrow turned Brownfoot towards the sound and lifted his horse to an easy canter.

"And?" Mac picked up the pace too, caught by the Cree's excitement.

"Their wagons are made totally of wood. With no grease, they squeal, very loud, very hard on the ears. Tall Man said that's why the buffalo were leaving the prairies. They hate the sound too."

By this time, the whine was louder, sharper, like a raucous cry of an angry magpie. As they drew closer, it multiplied ten fold to a hellish, unearthly wail. Mac winced, wanting to cover his ears, reminded of a thousand fingernails drawn across a thousand panes of glass. The piercing screech scraped down his spine, rendering his ears deaf and his mind shattered of all thought. How could anyone stand such a racket?

Through the cloud of dust, high, single-axled carts, pulled by a horse or oxen, appeared in a long, swaying line. Occasionally a figure materialized walking beside the carts or riding atop. A faint hum became a song, a lively version of 'Les Adieu' rose above the din by a chorus of deep male voices.

The carts wove their way across the prairies in ragged single file. At the back of each cart, tied to its right corner, walked the next horse or oxen with its cart. The dusty cavalcade thus spread out in a staggered line, angling away to the right for five carts, then zig zagging back with the next group of five carts whose animals were tied to the left corners. The wooden wheels looked like the sawed ends of giant trees, three feet in diameter. They were 'dished' or built in the shape of a saucer which also stopped the broad wheel brim from cutting too deeply into the mud. The four sides of the wooden carts were tied together with strips of dried rawhide.

B.A. called to him over the noise and swirling dust, "They stagger the carts so the ruts aren't so deep. By tying the carts together, they need fewer drivers. Each cart carries up to a thousand pounds, if the oxen pull them. Horses pull much less. They can travel about fifty miles a day on flat prairie'; not so fast on hills and swampy land."

Mac whistled in amazement. On a fast day, he estimated B.A. and he made about twenty-five or thirty miles. These people must get up with the sun and go to bed with it too. And with the long summer days, night was merely a gentle twilight for a few hours after midnight before the sun rose again.

B.A. watched the cavalcade closely then crowed in excitement, "They are from Lebret! I know them!" He touched his heels to Brownfoot, his face brightening eagerly. Several riders on horseback waved and galloped towards him.

As they rode closer, Mac noted their brightly coloured cotton shirts with a fichu or cravat around the neck. Many sported beautifully beaded hide vests. Woven or crocheted sashes in bright red, white and blue wrapped their waists and gaily flapped in the wind of their arrival. To a man, they wore black felt caps decorated with feathers and ribbons. Their black hair, luxuriantly curly or straight was not braided but cropped to the jawline and parted on the side like the popular 'Dutch cut' back east. Most sported moustaches of varying shapes and sizes. All had the dark swarthy skin and high cheeks of their Cree ancestors mixed with the finer aquiline features of their French forefathers. Here at last were the *Metis*, the French word for 'mixed', the very travellers Mac had hoped to meet up with.

Up close, he noticed the outside seams of their leggings were also decorated with beads or tufts of dyed feathers or soft down. Some of the men wore buckskin or moleskin trousers tied at the knee and ankle with colourful narrow bands of cloth called ferrets. On their feet, high sided Cree moccasin wrap-arounds protected their legs and ankles, their tops made of beaded blanket duffel. Some of the men wore coats over their colourful clothes. Mac recognized the Hudson Bay blanket *capot*, a belted, hooded coat in plain navy or the standard white with its inevitable green and red strip. Cheerfully coloured shirts peeked from beneath coats. These people obviously loved bright colours. Even their horses had gaily decorated harnesses of embroidery, fringes, bells and ribbons.

With the white flash of a wide smile beneath his thick moustache one of the men rode directly to Broken Arrow. His arm held out in welcome, the handsome older man cried, "*Nistes*, my first cousin!"

Mac looked closely between the two, seeing no family resemblance between the older, shorter man with his thick curling hair and startling grey eyes. Perhaps it was merely a greeting of tribal brotherhood.

Broken Arrow grinned in delight, reaching out and clasping the man's hand in a firm grip, almost hauling him from his saddle "Alexis! *Tan'si!* (How are you?) *Kuya's*, (old/long time since we've met!)"

"*Nemoya—nanitaw*, (not too bad!) Mah!" the swarthy man growled, "You are broader than ever! When will you stop growing?"

Lines around Broken Arrow's eyes deepened and his mouth quirked, "When the rest of me catch up to my *mitakisiy*."

The surrounding group howled with laughter, rolling their eyes dramatically like their French ancestors. They crowded closer. "Cha!" They growled, "Dat happen when you were twelve!"

Ignoring them, Broken Arrow bent to grasp the hand of another man whose moustache was liberally sprinkled with grey, "Tan'si, Narcisse! I see you have gained weight! You must have had a good winter!"

This man, taller in the saddle than the rest, sucked in his protruding paunch, "Oui, Chillay, I'm saving up for de fall rut, jus' like de ole bull moose!"

His companions hooted with scorn. "*Pahki kawi num!*" they teased, poking fun at his belly, ("he lets it fall, drop by drop!")

Broken Arrow swung his lips to his companion, pointing in Cree fashion, "Alexis Cardinal, Narcisse Goulet, this is my good friend John MacArthay." His Cree accent changed it to 'Macardi'.

Alexis dipped his head and added a French twist, "Monsieur Mecredi!"

Broken Arrow nodded to one of the grey haired men whose lined face displayed a permanent mask of laughter and joy. "Unh Baptist!" He gave it the Cree version, 'Butcheese'. You are looking stronger than ever!"

The old man grinned slyly, "Tapwe, truly. I *am* stronger. When I was a young man like you it take me two hands to bend my mitakisiy." He paused, "Now dat I am older, *moi*, me, I can bend it wit' only one hand!"

Mac joined the laughter, broadsided by the old man's earthy wit on himself.

Alexis continued chuckling, "So, do you join us for de hunt in de morning? Our scouts, dey spot a big herd up ahead." He pointed in the general direction with his lips, "We camp soon so de buffalo are not scared away by our carts." He dipped his head in old-world politeness towards Mac, "You will join us Monsieur Mecredi? *Oui*, (yes)? A pleasure, *pour moi* (for me)."

"Just call me Mac." He stalled, glancing towards B.A. for his opinion.

The Cree grinned with pleasure. "Tomorrow we hunt! If you are not afraid we will kill all your buffalo."

"Cha!" The group laughed in disgust, "You have to hit dem firs'!" Some whacked Broken Arrow's shoulder as they rode side by side back to the screeching wagons. A couple young men offered him shooting lessons so he wouldn't starve that winter. Mac got a kick out of the laughing insults. Even he had heard of the legendary Metis marksmanship.

At Alexis's hand signal, the driver's began wheeling their wagons into a large circle. As they rode closer Mac spotted some women jumping down from the wagons to gather sticks and dried buffalo dung for firewood. The older ladies wore their long braided hair pinned high in a crown around their heads like his mother's, but with gaily decorated horn combs and ribbons. All the women wore dark dresses trimmed with equally cheerful rows of multicoloured ribbons. Tartans or bright shawls wrapped their shoulders. Dressed in a similar manner but with long braids hanging down, teenage girls clumped in giggling groups behind the wagons, shyly peeking out at the newcomers. As he rode closer he noted the Metis women's large, wide eyes, smoothly rounded features and golden skin created a stunning symmetry of beauty, uniquely different on every face. Never had he seen so many beautiful women at one time. His lips curved, no wonder their men bragged so much!

While the men unloaded the carts, the women pitched their buffalo skin tipis and rolled out their bedding. They used flint and steel to start a fire and heat the Boulet, a moose hamburger stew they had brought with them. He knew by now nobody would bring buffalo meat to a hunt; it would dishonour the buffalo who were about to give their lives to feed the people.

That evening, after a filling meal of stew and bannock, the Metis men gathered in a traditional circle around their '*bonne*, (good) fire', a great, crackling one, to talk about the hunt. From pockets and beaded pouches they drew pipes of all sizes and shapes, as full of character as their owners. Some had long, thin stemmed twists of chokecherry roots which when carefully burned, left the centre hollow. The men had fitted the charred stems into various drooping bowls of carved wood and iron. Others had shorter stemmed pipes of a squat, practical nature. But each was lovingly polished and painstakingly filled, tamped, lit and drawn in the age old ritual of after-dinner contentment. A bemused Mac watched some of the older women join the group with their own pipes which they proceeded to smoke with equal enjoyment.

Many of the Metis filled their pipes with tobacco. But others like Alexis and Broken Arrow preferred the traditional kinnikinnick, a dried and ground willow bark or bearberry leaves pulverized and mixed with a little tobacco. B.A. called the willow bark mix 'a good smoke'. Seated between them, Mac inhaled the wispy blue tendrils from B.A's pipe and Alexis' big Peterson. The rich aroma reminded him of a walk through a forest of damp, shaded trees in the summertime. One of the women handed him a mug of hot water with maple sugar dissolved in it. Mac closed his eyes and savoured the rare treat. Others sipped a bittersweet tea steeped with small twigs from the chokecherry and pin cherry bushes.

After a casual discussion, the men chose Alexis as their hunt leader before voting in several captains. They were the older men, Narcisse and Baptist included, battle-scarred and well respected by the group. Each captain then chose his men, usually close friends and relatives, who would follow him. To mark his whereabouts, each captain was presented with a Metis flag to fly above his cart. Against the flag's red background lay a horizontal figure eight in white, the sign of eternity, symbol of the Metis forever.

Alexis then called out the traditional rules for the hunt. If an inexperienced hunter stampeded the herd before everyone was ready, it might take days or weeks to get near the spooked herd—or, never. The entire community could starve. For a first offence, the culprit was brought before the group, his crime called out, and his saddle and bridle cut up as punishment. For a second offence, his much prized and needed coat was cut up. On a third offence, he was whipped. The men nodded in agreement, their heads surrounded in smoky blue clouds. When Alexis finished, the group's total silence indicated their understanding and respect for such rules.

The group then fell into their favourite pastime on the prairies, telling stories and swapping lies. Mac knew some of the tales were tall ones but they were so masterfully crafted, he couldn't tell where truth ended. What he would remember most about that evening was the laughter, the belly-deep guffaws and continual cheeky side comments from others around the fire. It kept the entire group in stitches. Mac's cheeks finally ached from smiling, his throat raw from laughter. These Metis appreciated quick wit, especially from their elders. Their stories, usually told on themselves with a great deal of dry humour, drew the loudest, deepest laughter from the crowd. Yet the jokes were never cruel. The group's genuine pleasure in his company, especially when he told them about finding his grey hoss, Spence, and his snowstorm blunder, created warmth in Mac's chest, a sense of camaraderie and belonging he had never achieved with his University chums.

One of the men slapped a thin wiry man on the back, "Tell Mac about your fight with the bear Pasqually!"

Pasqually lifted his hat, scratched his pate and looked embarrassed at being the centre of attention. Mac later found out his name was a Metisse version of the Cree '*pasqwaw*', meaning 'big meadow', a teasing reference to the man's extremely bald head! Pasqually's skin, lighter than his swarthy companions, was freckled and speckled, above a heavy brush of frazzled, pale auburn beard. He stood out from the smoother-faced, moustached Metis yet he was obviously a welcome member of their group as they continued to plead for the tale. After much encouragement, he settled down and nodded briefly, looking at the ground in deep thought. A hush settled over the expectant crowd.

"My friend, Polou, and I were out checking our beaver traps one day during Frog's Return Moon when the beaver pelts are at their best, thick, long and dark." He turned to Mac, "Frog moon is the month when the frogs dig out of their winter mud and start singing. It's when the bears come out from their long winter sleep too. They are usually very skinny, and very hungry." The rest of the group nodded vigorously enough for Mac to believe him.

Pasqually continued, "Polou had already crossed the beaver dam to another dam further downstream. He had taken his rifle with him in case he spotted a moose drinking in the lower marshes. I was hauling out a trapped beaver, gutting him and tying him to a string on my backpack before resetting the trap. Head down, on my knees, I never saw him coming. The blood probably attracted him. With all those pelts on my back and the beaver cap on my head, I probably looked like a giant wounded beaver." The crowd tittered at the image.

"It was a rusty-yellow bear." The crowd moaned. Pasqually explained to a puzzled Mac. "They are part of the Black Bear clan, but for some reason, they are the meanest, maybe because they are so ugly." He whacked his neighbour on his shoulder, a handsome young man with large startling grey eyes and thick wavy hair, "Like Alexander here." The teen grinned shyly.

Pasqually took a quick sip of his tea before continuing. "He jumped me without a sound or warning. The first thing I saw was his claws swiping the knife from my hand. The power of it knocked me flat on my back and he went right for my throat. I could smell his stinkin' dog's breath." He paused, "I think he had fish for lunch, rotten ones too." The crowd smirked then quickly fell silent.

Pasqually looked into his teacup, swirling its contents, "When we were kids back in St. Boniface, my father shot a sow bear and brought her cub home for us to play with as a pet. We had a lot of fun with him, that little bear cub. He loved to wrestle. But when he got mad, ten kids sitting on him couldn't hold him down. He'd hiss like a cat and send us flying in every direction. The one thing that really made him mad was if we accidentally kicked him between his hind legs. He'd bawl with rage, spin and bite at whatever was behind him. Eventually, we had to shoot him, he just got too mean."

He set his cup down and took out his pipe. He tamped it with slightly unsteady fingers. "I remembered this somehow when that cinnamon bear started chewing on my shoulder. I could hear the skin popping." The crowed winced and Mac's gut twisted.

"So I kicked the bastard right in his castors!" The group cheered in approval.

"That old bear, he spun like a top, shadow boxing with thin air. I rolled away, trying to get to my feet. But no, he whirled back and hit me with both front paws." Pasqually raised his arms to demonstrate, his right high, his left low. "He whipped them across his body like two giant slaps. One hit my shoulder and the other hit my knee on the opposite side. He flipped me end for end, that *muskwa*. I did about three cartwheels in midair before slamming into a tree trunk. Every time I got up, he'd flip me again. Finally he knocked the wind right out of me. Through the stars, I saw his teeth coming for my face and I punched him hard as I could in the nose. That was the other thing we learned from the cub. Bears have a tender nose.

"That cinnamon bear, he backed away, shaking his head. It gave me time to grab my rifle off my shoulder but before I could aim, he was on me again. I rammed the stock into his mouth and he ground it into chunks, leaving gouges on the barrel too. He broke the trigger right off.

"Luckily my sash protected my stomach though he tried hard to bite through it. Then he attacked my thigh. I could feel him ripping out tendons and muscle like he was picking maple sugar candy off the snow. I kicked him between the legs with my other foot and he spun away. All I had left was a small knife in my pocket." The crowd moaned.

"I kicked him again and again to get some relief. He flipped me end for end a couple more times before I could unfold the knife with my teeth."

"When he came for my face, I stabbed his nose. He sprayed blood and snot all over me. I could barely see with no time to wipe my face. When he gnawed on my leg again, I stabbed him in the head. The knife blade caught him in the eye, sinking to the hilt. That stopped him. He bawled and backed away, still snorting blood out his nose. But I hung on and he lifted me half off the ground. He swiped his face trying to clear away what blinded him."

Pasqually stared into the fire for a moment, "Thirteen times he charged me; thirteen times I fought him off. This time . . . the bear walked away."

The crowd murmured in awe.

"Polou heard me yelling and the bear snarling. He came stumbling and falling back across the beaver dam. He ran so fast, his shoes fell off." Pasqually graciously waited for the crowd to settle down. "When he saw me and all the blood, he started to gag. His hands shook so bad, he couldn't shoot.

"I yelled, 'Give me the gun! I'll kill that hard-headed son of Satan!' I grabbed the gun and fired at the devil, but he ran into the trees. I saw fur fly so I knew I'd hit him. But neither one of us wanted to chase him." Pasqually's wry comment drew gusts of relieved laughter as people relaxed and drew deep breaths.

"How did you stop the bleeding?" Mac leaned forward, shaken by the sheer horror of the story. Bears terrified him more than any other animal of the plains.

"Polou used his knife to strip willow leaves, bark and last year's seeds. He shoved so much in his mouth he choked. All I could see was the whites of his eyes and his big cheeks bulging like gopher pockets as he chewed. He spat gobs of the stuff on the holes in my shoulder. Next time, he thought to give me some to chew on too. When we pulled my leggings off, they were full of blood. He picked some *Usnea spp*, grey mossy hair hanging from pine branches. We packed them right into the wound on my leg along with the willow mush and some muskeg leaves. They all stop heavy bleeding. I could see white bone through the blood and torn chunks of skin. But the bone wasn't broken. Once the bleeding stopped, Polou gathered some spruce gum to draw off the infection and packed that in too. Then we plastered my leg and shoulder with heavy swamp mud and wrapped them with soft, soaked birch bark. Polou, he killed the poor tree, ripping the whole trunk off to get enough bark to cover my 'holes'."

The group grunted.

Pasqually smiled wryly. "He tied sticks to my leg outside the bark and made a sling for my shoulder with his sash. Then we started walking. I don't remember much of the twenty mile walk back to our cabins. What I do remember is cussing all the deadfall I had to back up to and swing my stiff leg over. I think I passed out a few times but Poulou kept talking to me and half carrying me until we made it home. I was laid up all winter but Celesta saved my leg."

All eyes turned to Alexis' wife, Celesta, a short, slim woman in her late thirties who was the group's medicine woman. She tilted her head; a slight smiled playing across her full lips. "Ehe! I saw lots of Pasqually that year." Everyone chuckled at her double meaning.

Narcisse took up his story, "De nex' spring, I was hout in de same harea wit' my wife, Chi Marie. A big cinnamon bear, he growl at us from de bank above our heads. Chi Marie, she scream, 'Dere's a bear up dere!' So I tell her, 'Trow him a stick. Maybe he ron away!' So Chi Marie, she trow 'im a stick. But de bear, he not ron away. So I tell her, 'trow to him a bigger stick.' But de bear, he growl. Den he take a ron at my Chi Marie." Narcisse leered mischievously, "Nobody take a ron at my Chi Marie! So I shoot him."

The circle of listeners howled.

When Narcisse, still grinning, continued, "Dat bear, he fall over dead at my feet". The listeners gasped at how close the bear was. "When I turn him over, I see 'e 'ave a gunshot 'ole in his shoulder dat still not heal. And 'e 'ave only one eye dat work; his nose, she is cut completely in two."

In the stunned silence, Mac studied Pasqually, the flickering firelight revealing jagged white scars running down the side of his neck and beneath his jacket. The shoulder drooped slightly lower than the other, but Pasqually appeared to have full use of his arm. "And your leg? It healed properly?"

Pasqually leapt to his feet, unbuckling his belt. He froze at the grinning women around him. "Come on Pasqually, show us what you got!" They teased. The younger girls tittered shyly, hiding their mouths behind their hands.

"Ehe!" Leered the men, "Show dem what dey are not missing!"

With a mischievous glitter in his eyes, Pasqually grabbed the sides of his long fringed jacket and dramatically crossed them over his stomach and groin. The crowd hooted and giggled at his blatant modesty. Then, with a little wiggle and tap dance, his pants slid out beneath and dropped to his ankles. Women and girls screamed. Some hid behind shawls or tucked their heads behind the shoulders of their laughing men. Others clapped hands, their tilting eyes half-moon slits of laughter as they took in the scene.

What they saw made them gasp in shock, while their men murmured in a mix of French, English and Cree, "Mon Dieu! Jesu! Hiyee!" Thick, twisting ropes of stitched scars covered Pasqually's entire upper right thigh to well below his knee. Mangled craters, the size of a man's fist remained where smooth flesh had once grown. The bear had not only bitten but also ate part of his leg! A collective groan arose from the onlookers as they grasped this horror.

In spite of it all, the leg had mended. Celesta's stitches had obviously reattached severed tendons, mutilated muscles and torn skin while her healing medicines had saved the limb. For Pasqually, with a flip of his buckle, pulled his pants up and danced a light-footed jig around the fire midst the cheers and clapping of his comrades . . . .

*   *   *

A tiny breeze waffling under the open sides of the tipi woke Mac to the morning's sun. The two wolf Powakans had drifted through his dreams . . . silently watching him . . . waiting for something with a sleepy eyed intensity. Mac inhaled the now familiar scent of smoked hides and musky buffalo hair overlaid with fragrant sage leaves that wrapped him. He'd learned the sweet, pungent leaves stowed in the bedding kept the bugs away. Across the dead campfire from him and B.A., their host, Alexis, yawned and slowly sat up, lightly swiping his wife on her hip.

"Up *Iskwew*, (Woman)! I am so 'ungry I could chew my moccasin!"

Celesta sat up, yawning and rubbing her smooth, unlined face. Mac marvelled at how little these people seemed to age. Celesta looked but a few years older than her pretty teenage daughter, Eliza. The young girl slept on undisturbed at her parents' feet while their son, the teenaged handsome Alexander, slept at Mac's head. B.A. had explained to him how the smaller children were left behind in the Metis villages with their grandparents. Only those old enough to help were allowed to join the hunt.

Celesta began winding her long braid into a coil on top of her head. "Mah! You ate the whole pot of Boulet last night!" She scolded Alexis, "You keep eating like that and Sewaw will throw you off for hurting his back!"

A sleepy Broken Arrow entered the fray, "You should give that miserable horse to the Blackfoot." Then he chortled, "But they'd probably bring him back! Or shoot him!"

"*Cha*!" Alexis argued, "He is my frien'! You'll see. Dat horse, he will ride de buffalo into de groun' today."

"Just as long as he doesn't take you in too!" B.A. had the last word as he cleared the tipi doorway cover, letting in a blinding spear of brilliant sunshine. Mac quickly joined him. Twas was a fine day to hunt!

Celesta had spent much of the previous evening handing out herbs and roots to people seeking cures for their ailments. Antoine complained of stomach pains and spat brown blood like tobacco. She'd made him a hot drink from the Marsh Valerian root. Old Mrs. Gledu received a small pouch of dried yarrow for her arthritis.

To sickly Mrs. Laboucan or Lubicon, who needed a break from having more children, Celesta gave oil pressed from a tiny white flower. The tired woman refused the bitter root drunk in a tea, which would stop her fertility forever. Life was so sacred, even Celesta was not taught its name or its whereabouts until she was a full-fledged medicine woman. Cousin Lalouise needed some rat root to chew for her toothache. Vain Hilare, her husband, paid for a gooey tonic of ground sweet grass and boiled hooves to stop his hair from thinning. When the last sick person had wandered away clutching his or her medicine, Celesta had wearily sought her buffalo robes. Today might not be easy. Always there were injuries from a hunt.

After a hasty breakfast of coffee made from fried barley; cold bannock with soaked and mashed Saskatoon berries along with dried deer meat, the group readied the wagons. The men reloaded their skinning tools and harnessed the oxen. They tied the extra emptied carts together, one behind the other, freeing horses for the hunt. Some of the women saddled up, checked their guns and rode with the men. Like their Native ancestors, women could join the hunt if they chose. Celesta often hunted too but chose to remain behind this year. She and her tall slim daughter, Eliza, along with the rest of the women, drove the carts, forming two lines behind the hunters.

"Ho, *Sewaw*, my Sweet, Sour and Salty frien'!" Alexis addressed his horse as he climbed aboard. "*Nea!* Allez! We Go!" The horse's pale beige hide and black mane proved as contrary as his nature. Ears back in fury, he kicked a cart beside him, worked to spit his bit, tried to rub his rider off against a cart then reared in disgust when Alexis merely lifted his leg. Furious, the horse crow hopped around camp midst the cheers and catcalls from other hunters. Some trotted away from the bawling, uncaring stallion. Alexis clung like a burr, unperturbed by his temperamental horse or the crude advice from his companions. Eventually Sewaw slowed, chuffed a couple times, shook himself in irritation then settled into his master's command position at the head of the cavalcade.

Mac was enthralled with the military order of the men. At the head of each group, a Captain carried his flag, its crimson surface flapping cheerfully in the light breeze. Behind him, ten riders rode abreast. Behind them came the next Captain with his ten hunters. Instead of the rigid silence of disciplined troops, however, these riders sat at ease, laughing and teasing one another mercilessly. Fringes on their tawny moose hide jackets swung in unison; beaded patterns across the men's backs sparkled in the early morning sunshine. Many of the hunters wore dark striped Canadian tweed or serge pants tucked into the tops of their buckskin leggings. Some preferred knee-high leather boots while others sported flexible moccasins that wrapped their ankles and lower calves. A few hunters rode bareback but most had beautifully beaded buckskin flat saddles stuffed with buffalo hair and hanging stirrups made of shaganappi like Broken Arrow's. Every hunter packed a muzzle loader or single barrel flintlock, a buffalo horn full of black powder, plus two pockets filled with powder plugs and lead balls.

"Allors! (Now then!) Broken Arrow!" Alexander, Alexis' son called out from down the row of ten riders behind his father. "You bring dat fas' horse of yours, Brownfoot? My Flash, he will leave you in his dust!"

"Bring 'im along, Alexander. You always lied a lot anyway!" Broken Arrow turned, his eyes following the young Metis with a mix of pride and humour. He had taught his cousin how to break the colt last summer when he spent more than a month with the Cardinal family, relatives of his mother. The teenager was obviously anxious to show off his new buffalo runner.

Mac rode beside Broken Arrow, in line behind Alexis and hoped he had the guts to see this through without disgracing himself or his friend. He had heard of these hunts but never thought he'd participate. He swallowed convulsively then grinned. Aye, twould be an adventure to tell for the rest of his life. Should he survive it! Fleetingly, he wondered if this is what the Powakan wolves watched and waited for. Was this another test for him?

Looking down, he admired his new leggings. They were actually quite comfortable, like regular trousers from ankle to groin. From the crotch they cut away to a small strip along the hip which tied to his belt. Cowboys must have copied these Indian leggings when they designed their chaps he mused. Last night, Mac had made the mistake of admiring Narcisse's newly tanned leggings with their row of purple crocuses beaded from knee to ankle. The cheerful Metis had immediately removed them and presented them to Mac as a gift. Red-faced and embarrassed, Mac had politely accepted. He had forgotten B.A.'s warning of this traditional Cree protocol, which proved their scorn in hoarding and their joy in sharing. Mac had hurried to his pack, removed his favourite green brocade vest with its burnished brass buttons and presented it to Narcisse. The older man accepted with delighted surprise. During the exchange, Mac caught B.A.'s slight smile of satisfaction. The Irishman's shoulder muscles had relaxed; he'd done the right thing.

Glancing over his shoulder, Mac noted Narcisse proudly sporting his new green vest beneath his fringed jacket—a sign of honour for the gift and the giver.

They crested a small knoll, downwind from the massive herd spread out beneath them, a thousand and more like a billowing black lake on the prairie, peacefully grazing the tall grass. From the distance, Mac caught his breath at the majestic size of the beasts, their great hairy heads and shoulders making them look overbalanced and slow. The ones lying down still looked like miniature mountains dotting the prairie! Small red-gold calves gambolled about, chasing one another or playfully butting heads. One gigantic bull, a tip of one thick horn broken, raised his enormous head and sniffed the air. His hairy bell beneath his chin, easily the size of man's head, swung angrily as he turned to challenge the riders, his back to the herd behind him. A large hoof pawed the prairie, sending a spray of grass and dirt high into the air.

All speech stopped. Captains' flags cautiously lowered, passing authority to Alexis. Every hunter dismounted and knelt on one knee, removing his or her hat. Alexis said a hushed prayer, half Latin and half French, in gratitude for the large herd and for the safety of each rider. Then he quietly instructed each captain to position his group of ten at strategic points, about a quarter mile out, in a great circle around the herd. Keeping their distance, several groups slid behind small hillocks, cautiously walking their horses out of sight from the curious herd, careful not to startle them.

Once in position, all the hunters filled their mouths with lead balls and waited.

Mac's throat closed in fear. He struggled to work some saliva around the bitter iron balls in his mouth, praying he wouldn't swallow the damn things. Earlier, he had tied the reins across Willy's neck, loose enough the grey could bob his head and lower it should he stumble. Mac's hands tightened on the barrel of his gun, hoping his Irish hoss would keep his feet and his head for Mac would have little time to steer him! The Metis horses around him were well trained to do both.

The silent women sat in their carts on a small knoll much further away from the herd. Celesta quietly organized her medicines beside a small fire she had built in a little Coulee out of sight from the herd. Even smoke could spook a wary herd.

Alexis raised his arm, paused, and then slammed it down shouting, "Allez!!! Go!"

Every rider exploded into full gallop, darting towards the startled herd, whooping as wildly as their Native ancestors. Buffalo cows leapt to their feet racing towards their calves. Amazingly, even the tiniest calf could keep up with his mother, running swift as a deer at her side. Gigantic bulls roared their surprise and anger. The herd streamed into a seething mass of heaving brown bodies, the air thick with their deep bellows and swirling prairie dust. Faster and faster they ran while the hunters pushed their horses shoulder to shoulder with them, stretching the herd out.

In one fluid motion, a hunter would pull his gun down and fire into the neck of the labouring animal at his knee. If it went down, the hunter dropped a cloth with a special mark on it – proof of his personal kill. While his horse raced on, the hunter poured powder into the muzzle of his gun, plugged it with a wad, spat a lead ball in behind, tamped it down with a whack of the gun stock against his thigh, spun the barrel and fired once again.

Mac hung on by his knees and thighs, riding the galloping grey while his hands frantically worked the gun, its barrel heating up from his repeated shots. He plugged in the cap, spat out a ball and lost two before one hit the barrel. He spun the barrel, tamped it on his thigh and fired point blank into a labouring animal's musky shoulder so close it rubbed his stirrup. The animal groaned and collapsed, tumbling head over heels, his flying feet almost ripping Mac's gun away. Mac immediately dropped one of his markers beside the animal. He blinked rapidly, struggling to see in the churning dust smelling of rank animal sweat, blood . . . and fear. With no more time to think, Mac righted the barrel, cracked it open and clumsily poured in the gunpowder, spilling some over his legs and praying he didn't blow himself to smithereens with the next blast. Through the billowing clouds ahead, he caught occasional glimpses of Broken Arrow's shoulders and flying hair, his gun crackling at regular intervals. Obviously the Cree had done this before!

Across the herd from Mac, a man's horse rolled end over end in the whirling dust. Another rider behind him swooped down, yanking his friend to safety behind him just as the stampeding herd trampled the downed horse, stilling its terrified screams. Now Mac understood why the men hunted in close groups.

"Alexander!" From the row of carts, Celesta shrieked in horror as she saw her eldest son thrown to the ground by the panicking Flash when a buffalo cow charged him. Helplessly she watched the teen struggle to his feet, then fall back. In a flash of pale gold, Sewaw was there, Alexis leaning far down to the right, Broken Arrow to his left, scooping the fallen youth by his armpits, suspended between the two flying horses and riders as they spun away to the open prairie. The rider-less Flash ran on with the herd, his tail up and mane rippling in the wind.

Celesta sobbed in relief as the men raced towards them, still holding Alexander like a long-legged puppet between them. They stopped to set him down, but he crumpled to ground with a cry of pain, grabbing his leg. Scooping him up again, they galloped to the carts.

Celesta snatched up two birch bark rolls and poplar sticks. By the time she reached her son's side, Alexis had reassured himself his son was okay. He raced away to re-join the hunt, his duties too pressing to dally. Broken Arrow knelt by a pale and sweating Alexander.

"That Flash may be fast, but he has very poor manners! You must have trained him all by yourself after I left! That old cow was ready to teach you both some respect."

Alexander winced leaning back on his hands, trying to move his leg into a more comfortable position. He closed his grey eyes from the agony. "Mah! You're just jealous 'cause you're so ugly she didn't want you!" The gathering women laughed along with his mother and big cousin.

Celesta asked one of the women to hold the bark over the fire, softening its texture for easier moulding. Broken Arrow seated himself behind a pale and sweating Alexander. Grimly he reached around his cousin; his big hands providing tension on the youth's upper thigh while Celesta braced her feet against his. Holding her son's knee, she slowly, gently pulled on the ankle to reset the broken bone in his leg. With a bellow of pain-filled rage, Alexander passed out, collapsing into Broken Arrow's arms. Relaxing now her son felt no pain; Celesta gently washed Alexander's leg with warm water and applied a layer of bear grease to keep his skin from flaking as the bones healed. B.A. wrinkled his nose at the rancid smell then smiled to himself. Poor Alexander, he would have to endure the smell for many days, along with a great deal of teasing. Celesta tossed flakes of wild ginger and spikenard into another kettle of boiled water. Dipping a cotton cloth in it, she made a warm poultice to wrap the leg. The herbs would draw the pain and ease the swelling. When the poultice became too dry, she would renew it, or if his leg was still too tender, she would moisten the poultice with warmed water and leave it a bit longer. Working carefully, she wrapped the leg with the curled piece of warmed birch bark. Splinted by wood sticks on either side and bound into place, the bark would harden to a cast-like shape around the broken leg, supporting the bone lightly but firmly until it healed. B.A. broke several long fringes from Alexander's buckskin jacket and offered them to her for bindings. Although decorative, the fringes shed the rain from clothing but also acted as quick ties when needed.

Below them, hunters continued firing into the solid heaving mass of dark, sweaty bodies. They choose the prime young bulls, two to five years old. In the fall hunt, they would go for the bigger cows that now had small calves. Passing through the herd, the men would wheel and "run" the herd again, shooting, reloading and shooting again. Finally, there were enough dead animals for all. At Alexis' command, captains signalled their men the hunt was over. The remaining herd thundered away across the flat prairie.

Before the dust had settled, the hunters were claiming the animals with their personal markers, shooting the wounded ones before leaping down to slit their throats and 'bleed' them. Too much blood left in the meat tainted it with a bitter, unsavoury taste. Captains recorded the tally for each man's animals. Broken Arrow's and Mac's animals would be presented to families left behind in LeBret—families with men too injured or sick to hunt for themselves. Like the Cree, the Metis allowed none of their people to starve.

Narcisse came trotting back with the errant Flash in tow. The young buffalo runner appeared no worse for his run.

Now the women rode in with the carts, helping their men skin, gut and de-bone the carcasses. Using a very sharp knife, they carefully shaved the meat into long, paper-thin strips before hanging them on wooden racks they set up on the land. The bigger bones were tossed into the fire. Once cooked, they were cracked open and drained of their nutritious bone marrow oil. Eliza helped the other girls gather dry buffalo dung, green grass, sage and twigs, making small, smoking fires around the racks to smoke the meat for three days yet keep the flies away. Towards evening, everyone rubbed pungent sage leaves over their skin to stop the hordes of vicious mosquitoes from biting.

While the meat cured, the women scraped all fat and flesh from the inner side of the hides before smoking them also. These preserved hides could be sold to the trading posts as winter lap robes for open carriages and buggies across Upper and Lower Canada and Europe. Much of the dried meat would be sold to trading post employees, their families, the voyageurs in canoes and the Red River cart brigades who travelled back and forth from Fort Garry to Fort Qu'Appelle, Fort Carleton and on to Fort Edmonton on the North Saskatchewan.

That evening, everyone was in a good mood. It was a successful hunt with no major injuries beyond Alexander's leg; just a few cuts and gun powder burns. One hunter had his leg gored by a razor-sharp buffalo horn but it wasn't a deep wound.

Several fiddles appeared amongst the group, familiar strains of 'Mom and Dad's waltz' and 'Whiskey before Breakfast' filled the night air. Mac closed his eyes and let the old Celtic melodies, songs from his childhood fill his head and heart. How his grandfather would have loved this music! Mac remembered watching the old man lift his beloved violin to his chin, close his eyes and play the sweet, sweet music. Black Velvet Band had been his favourite song. On this warm summer evening, Mac felt like he'd come home, at last, surrounded by the music he loved and the people who welcomed him unconditionally. When B.A. took out his flute, Mac pulled out his tin whistle and joined the fray, encouraged by the whoops of delighted laughter around them. Alexis slapped Mac's back in open camaraderie.

A couple leapt to their feet. Side-by side, not touching, they matched their steps in a toe-heel jig, originating from Scottish and Irish reels combined with the intricate footwork of the Plains Indian dances. Mac had never seen lighter, faster steps even amongst his people's legendary Irish jigs. Other couples lined up behind the dancing duo, politely waiting their turn in the wavering firelight. Two by two, a couple danced until out of breath then gracefully yielded the floor to the next couple. Gradually, the music warmed and the beat changed, faster and faster from a one-step, two-step to a fox trot, jig. From the familiar 'Drops of Brandy', the makeshift band swung into swifter versions of eight and four-handed reels and jigs: the Duck Dance, Reel of Eight, Strip the Willow, Rabbit Chase, Tucker's Circle and finally, the ultimate symbol of the Metis people's roots, their beloved Red River Jig. Two brothers, with a cup of water perched on their heads, gracefully danced a light-footed jig without spilling a drop. Grinning couples stepped it up into single, double then triple beats, their moccasin feet or boots a blur of motion and poetry, rhythmic and sensual. On and on they played and danced until Mac's mouth and fingers turned numb and his lungs heaved. Sweat poured down the faces of musicians and dancers alike and still they played on, their cheering whistles and laughing faces flickering in the fire-lit night.

The following days passed in idle bowl games, knife throwing contests and horse races for the men while the women made pemmican. Mac spent a fascinating day with Narcisse pouring molten lead into shot molds for new ammunition. After three days of smoking the meat, the women left it in the hot sun to dry. When the rain came, they covered the meat with the smoked hides. Five days later, Eliza joined Celesta and the other women in the bone jarring 'lub-dub, lub-dub' beat—the song of the prairies—pounding dried meat strips into shredded, flaky pulp. To every fifty pounds of shredded meat, they added the melted bone marrow oil and dried saskatoons, cranberries or ground chokecherries picked the previous fall, crushed into small cakes and sun dried. No salt was added to the pemmican. It only made people thirsty. Pepper was unheard of on the prairies and would remain so for many more years.

The women used dried buffalo sinew to sew ninety pound chunks of pemmican into the cured buffalo robes. Hair on the outside kept the meat in good condition regardless the weather. Celesta and Alexis cut off chunks of the pemmican, eating it raw, while others preferred to boil it first. The couple offered a full bag to B.A. and Mac but they chose only half, knowing they could supplement it with fresh meat along the way. One pound of the concentrated pemmican was equivalent to four pounds of fresh meat. It kept indefinitely and was less bulky to carry though it usually took two men to load the lumpy bundles into the carts. The rest of the dried buffalo hides were placed on top as the group broke camp to return home.

After many hugs and handshakes, Mac and Broken Arrow turned their horses north towards the Quill Lake Salt Plains, while the Metis climbed atop their laden carts, picking up their French song, 'Le Braconnier' as they rolled back eastward in their caterwauling wagons.

*   *   *

Fifteen years later, in 1878, the last remaining buffalo herds crossed south into Montana. They never returned, slaughtered mercilessly to extinction by buffalo hunters who left their carcasses rotting in the hot sun. Some say it was a diabolical plan to starve the Indians into submission.

21.

SACRED AND SILLY

The next morning, Mac slowly stirred cornmeal mush, flavouring it with a small chunk of the maple sugar Celesta had given him. "Why do they call you Chillay?"

They were camped at the foot of the Touchwood Hills facing the Great Salt Plains. Mist-filled and blurred without trees or bushes upon their surface, the white salted land fled away to the oblivion of grey sky. From Wolverine Creek on the West, to where the Red Deer River of Lake Winnipegosis bends to the Pasqua Hills, they stretched their eerie length, offering neither shelter, nor food or water.

B.A. snorted. "Those Metis. They think they're a good looking lot with their father's French curls and their mother's beautiful Cree face. It is a standing joke amongst them to call each other 'ugly'. Me? I'm full Cree, so I'm just a little bit ugly. That's what Chillay means."

"So Chi Marie means 'little bit Mary or tiny Mary?'" Mac snickered, remembering the ample proportions of the older lady. The Metis took great delight in understatements. "Then what about Pasqually? He was more than a little ugly."

B.A. grinned, "The English and Cree half-breeds don't fare as well as the French and Cree mix. They take too much from their ugly English fathers"

Something else bothered Mac but he wasn't sure how to say it without offending.

Broken Arrow unerringly voiced it, "I noticed you cringed when people joked about what they do under the buffalo robes."

"Aye!" Mac's cheeks reddened. "Tis between them and a taboo topic not for public discussion."

"Why?"

"Well and sure tis nobody's business but their own. Fornication is the wages of sin according to Father Reilly and not to be bandied about in idle conversation—certainly not in mixed gatherings of men, women and least of all, with teenagers!"

B.A.'s eyebrows went up, "Why not? Our people laugh about it all the time. It brings a great deal of joy to a gathering, talking about coupling with all its pleasures."

"Tis crass, crude, to bring up such a topic! Ye embarrass people with such unconventional talk."

"Uncon . . . ventional?" B.A. stumbled over the word, frowning.

"Aye! Not common or normal." Mac felt cornered and struggled on. "To enjoy the act of coupling was a sin. It should be done only for the purpose of making children. Tis evil and dirty, this passion, passed down from the sinful Eve. For centuries, women were not allowed to attend church because their very presence might sully the sanctity of the hallowed ground. Later, they allowed a woman in. But if she just had a child, she was not allowed to enter a church for at least six months after birth."

"Cha!" Broken spat in disgust. "Why would a woman dirty a church after such a sacred act as giving birth? We honour our women with gifts after their hard labour!"

Now Mac snorted in disgust. "One priest instructed my mother to cut a hole in her nightgown for the act, but never remove her gown. She must close her eyes and pray for Ireland during the entire process."

"Mah!" B.A.'s eyes widened, his mouth open, "And miss all the pleasures? All the fun in teasing and joking and wrestling? Coupling is a chance to remember our spiritual selves, our spiritual Creator and his power of sharing, giving, taking and creating. Why would something that brings us the understanding and joining for creation be so wrong?"

Mac's cheeks reddened, "'Tis what we are taught in church."

Broken Arrow considered this in silence. To him, coupling and all the pleasures surrounding it were as normal as breathing, eating and sleeping. It was part of the cycle of birth and death. How could something all the plants or animals did, be a sin?

After a while, he explained, "In our clans, the greatest sin was pride: to forget we are part of the great Creation, like blades of grass in this land. So we tease, reminding each other to be humble and grateful for this life. We keep a twinkle in our eyes and joy in our hearts and we learn gratitude for every blessing in life. Our elders show true humility by being able to laugh and tell jokes about themselves. Yet they also remind us to keep our humour gentle so we do not interfere too much in one another's life."

Mac considered this. Narcisse and Baptist's raw humour made a little more sense.

B.A. struggled on, his dark face sincere and contemplative. "The old people have a way of teaching with their humour. Sometimes it's a story to make people think. Other times it was a medicine to help people heal and forgive one another. Sometime they tricked people into figuring something out rather than giving them the answers. When people finally got the joke, they laughed themselves silly. It taught them choices, that nothing is beyond repair."

B.A. leaned back, wrapping one knee with a negligent arm. "The old people's humour is so powerful. Their wit is much appreciated in our clans when life becomes too hard or serious. Their Wesakechak stories remind us to laugh at ourselves and one another because living is about joy. We call him Wesakechak or Trickster because he could appear as a man or any animal he chose. Often he appears as Coyote, the greatest trickster of them all. Anyone who has tracked a coyote will find his trail doubles back on itself many times. Coyote can fool the most experienced tracker, making him totally befuddled and confused. When an angry hunter is sitting in the middle of the prairie with coyote tracks going out in every direction from him, he suddenly learns a very good contrary lesson about how foolish he looks. He is tricked into laughing at himself and seeing what is really important in his life. Tracking coyote isn't! No bird or animal in this land will eat a coyote. And there is a lesson in that too."

"Teasing and joking is a gift we share with one another. Our wit is creative and joyful, making us live in the moment. When we laugh, joke and tease, we do not live in the past or the future; instead, we simply enjoy the moment. It is a way of playing. It matters not what we laugh about as long as we laugh together."

B.A. squatted by the fire, stirring his bowl of cornmeal mush. He paused, thought for a while and then nodded. "When we laugh, we throw back our shoulders, lift our chins and laugh from way down inside ourselves. It spreads a warm feeling between all who hear and share the joke." His dark eyes sought Mac's, "It is truly a form of survival."

Mac's head came up in surprise.

"In our legends, if the Children of the Earth forget to laugh at themselves, they will die from the actions they take when seriousness strangles their sense of play and laughter. The Human tribe can use humour to break down even the most painful or destructive situations. The best medicine we have, no matter the problem, is laughter. If we can laugh so hard it brings our tipis down, that is good medicine.

"If we forget how to balance honour, respect and love with all that is not, the joy of living will be lost."

Mac finally caught on, "You mean humour helps balance the good with the bad?"

B.A. chuckled, "Tapwe. We have reached a union or balance of opposites when we learn to celebrate more than we mourn, to be good as well as bad, in a way that harms no one. And our old people can be very bad! They use humour to tease one another constantly. Rather than complain about their aches and pains, they play a game of joy. The old men brag and the old ladies poke great holes in their pride. Then they'd laugh together."

He swallowed a few mouthfuls of tea then laughed outright. "I remember Pipestem, Tall Man's old friend. He outlived several wives and now he lives alone. On this day, he bragged about going to Lac Ste. Anne, out of Fort Edmonton. That is the healing lake I told you about before."

Mac nodded, hunkering down by the fire, enjoying his hot cereal while his friend continued.

"Pipestem said he was going to wade in those waters right up past his waist. When he came out, he would be like a young man, ready to bother the women again." B.A. chortled, "But Mitsue shot him down.

"She said, 'Mah! Old man! Those healing waters are for the sick not the dead!'"

Both men sniggered.

"But why do they joke so much about sex?" Mac's cheeks reddened in frustration and embarrassment. "I am no' comfortable with it at all."

"It's about balance. All of Indian Medicine is about balance. If you can joke about sex, see the funny side of such actions then you can also recognize the sacredness of coupling."

Mac stiffened but held his counsel as B.A. continued, remembering what his grandmothers had taught him during his manhood ceremonies. "The act of coupling was a prayer to the Creator. A man joins a woman who is the pathway to the spirit and the Creator. She is the one who keeps the family together. She connects them to Great Spirit through her intuition, her inner knowing, her dreams and her Earth Mother wisdom.

"Coupling, when it is done with honesty and love is a sacred act of Creation. Still, it is a funny thing to do. We find ourselves in awkward, often silly positions, doing crazy things to get there. So we joke about its truth. We balance the holiness of the act with our humour of being silly humans. We balance the silly with the sacred."

Broken Arrow sighed, "I know the Black Robes hate this act, especially with their vows of celibacy, which prevents them from taking part. I think they are angry because they fear a woman's temptation may break their vows. So they hate the act, call it dirty. When human beings are taught to be ashamed of their coupling, it creates all kinds of damaging results in the body, mind, heart and spirit. This lack of respect also damages the woman and her purpose in life. This is what my grandmothers taught me."

Mac snorted. "Good thing our women don't receive those kind of instructions!"

"Tapwe," B.A. agreed, "and your people are the poorer for it."

22.

ALORAH AND SALVIA

One morning, after cresting the summit of the Manitchinass Hills, they rode down a hillside covered in brilliant wildflowers. In their midst, a ribboned, broad-brimmed straw hat slowly lifted to reveal two dark eyes, an oval face and a slim, very feminine body. The two men sat upon their horses in open wonder at the young woman crouched below them, her wide skirts spread upon the grass, a bouquet of sunny flowers clutched in her hand. She stared back with equal intensity. A gleam of twilight lit the dark hair pinned beneath her hat. Sunlit radiance graced her tanned cheeks.

Mac cleared his throat and eased his horse closer, "Top of the mornin' Miss. Forgive our bad manners, but we are more than surprised to be seein' a lady like you in this vast land."

The woman stood up, an apricot-hued silhouette in the morning sunshine. She raised her hand to shade her midnight eyes, an unnecessary gesture with her wide hat. Silent and alone, she watched them, her rigid stance the only clue to her fright.

Mac judged her to be in her early twenties, a beautiful woman with luxuriant black hair looping behind her ears. Slim brows, long slanted eyes and a patrician nose gave her an exotic elegance. Yet her skin was a darker hue than most Europeans. He wondered what nationality she was: not Indian but maybe Far East?

B.A. slid off his horse and led him quietly down the small hill. "Are you lost? Can we help you in some way?" He used a careful, easy walk, his hands relaxed on the reins.

The woman's heavy-lidded eyes wandered from his naked shoulders to the peaceful twinkle in his eyes as he drew nearer. Her face relaxed somewhat, as she lowered her hand to her skirt. "You can if you know how to make two stubborn oxen pull a wagon from the mud." Her voice was soft, rich and warm, with no trace of accent. She gestured towards a covered wagon below them near a cluster of willows.

The wagon stood mired axle-deep in a muddy creek bed. Another woman, her wet cotton skirts held up in one hand, moved restlessly back and forth beside the stranded wagon. She slapped a whip against her skirt in agitation. Two oxen, belly-deep in the water and hitched to the wagon, totally ignored her. One, a deep roan, had its muzzle buried in the waters; the other, a sturdy white-haired beast with a crooked horn, wrenched clumps of grass from the shoreline and calmly munched them into oblivion.

Mac dismounted and the two led their horses towards the creek. The dark-haired woman slid gracefully along beside them over the uneven clumps of grass. "Salvia!" She called, "I have found someone to help us!"

The other woman, as young as her companion, spun around, hastily dropping blue skirts over her crinolines as the men approached. When she saw the Cree, she paled, "Alorah," her lips barely moved, "what have you done?" Her knuckles whitened around the handle of a whip she held.

Mac yanked his hat off, crumpling it in his hands before him, "I see ye're havin' problems with your oxen. Maybe if we hitched our horse to them we could get you out . . . ma'am!" He added the last in reaction to her shocked face and backward steps.

He strove for a civilized tone, "This is my good Cree friend, Broken Arrow, and I am John MacCarthay, a harmless Irishman. I have a mother and two older sisters back east who would brain me for sure'n they found out I did not assist two ladies in need. Tis my good fortune to be finding two such lovely ones as yourselves. We are dusty travellers on our way to Fort Edmonton but are more than honoured to help you any way we can."

The second woman slowly tucked a blonde curl behind her ear, her wide blue eyes never leaving Mac's who found her as fair and comely as her darker companion. She switched the whip to her left hand, holding out a cautious right, "I am Salvia Brennan and this is my best friend, Alorah Durham. And yes *gentlemen*." Both men picked up her subtle emphasis. "We could use some help."

Mac took her hand, pumped it gently then quickly released it, searching about him. "D'ye not have menfolk to help ye lass?" When the two women exchanged wary glances, he knew he had blundered once again.

When Alorah blinked at her with a small nod, Salvia's shoulders eased slightly as she turned back to the men. "We were travelling with my father but he passed away three days ago. We are on our way to my brother's home in Fort Carleton, on the North Saskatchewan."

Mac bobbed his head, "We are sorry for your loss, maam."

"You're probably about three to four days away." B.A. rubbed his horse's muzzle but made no other move midst these very tense women.

Salvia's eyes narrowed as she turned towards him, "Are you a friend of the Sioux?"

B.A. smiled and indicated Mac's big grey, "We stole this horse from a couple of sleepy Sioux warriors. I doubt they would call us 'friend'."

A tiny smile mobilized her mouth, "Then I shall thank the Good Lord for your presence in our lives." She gestured towards the mired wagon, "Gentlemen, assist away. Mayhap you can make these stubborn oxen move." She and Mac fell into step while Alorah waited for Broken Arrow.

As they walked together, she nodded towards Salvia and explained in soft undertones. "She hates the Sioux. They attacked the farm she and her father had in Minnesota during the Minnesota Massacre. She hid in the woods and watched it all, unable to help. Her father was badly wounded in the fight and lived in horrible pain from then on. Though hard to admit, it was a relief for everyone when his suffering ended."

B.A. made no comment so she continued, "My parents died in a flu epidemic three years ago. I was at Ft. Ridgely, helping a woman in labour when the Sioux hit. At least the soldiers protected me." She said it so bitterly, he wondered at her meaning. She blew air through her nose in soft disgust, "One of them protected me so well, he thought I owed him. When he decided I could pay him back by becoming his wife, *I* decided to come west with Salvia and her father. The prospect of this land looked . . . more charming." She tipped her head, her dancing eyes meeting his.

They kindled in reply, "I've never heard it called so before."

She clasped her hands behind her as she walked, "Maybe the mosquitoes, the cactus, or the wind make people blind. Then again, maybe the emptiness of this land makes them miss its beauty." She gazed at the wildflowers in her hand.

His face hardened, "It is not empty. My people have always lived here. Only the White Man chooses to believe it is empty and therefore his for the taking." He lengthened his strides to reach the mired wagon, his broad back angling away from her as he bent to study the submerged wheels. She remained on shore, watching his rigid shoulders in confusion.

B.A. went to his pack and pulled out a long, thickly braided shaganappi he'd made from a fresh buffalo hide after the Metis Hunt. He tossed one end to Mac, "Double it and tie it to the wagon tongue." Mac made a quick wrap around the wagon tongue, securing it with a slip knot.

Meanwhile, B.A. backed Spense into position in front of the oxen. He twisted the shaganappi into a double loop around the big Percheron's tail and tied it tight.

Mac scratched his head, "Ye're tying it to his tail! I never heard of such a thing! What cross-grained nincompoop would make a horse pull with his tail? Jaysus, ye'll yank it off!"

"Watch the oxen!" B.A. growled.

Salvia had climbed to the wagon seat but her eyes darted anxiously between the irritated men.

B.A. straightened from his task and grabbed Spence's reins. "Now," he spoke quietly to Salvia, "Back your oxen a little, and when I tell you, command them."

She picked up the harness lines snapped to rings in the oxen's noses and threaded through a loop on the sides of their heavy leather collars. Pulling hard she shouted, "Back! Back!"

Using small willow branches, Mac and Alorah whacked the bawling oxen's noses, making them rapidly blink their watery eyes and swing their heads away. Their backing legs rattled the chains on the doubletrees attached to the collars around their necks which connected to the wagon tongue. Bony haunches pushed at the wagon box which barely moved in the deep mud.

"Go!" yelled B.A. and he leaned back, hauling on Spence's reins. The Percheron bowed his great neck and lunged forward. Salvia yelled "Hiyyap!!" while Alorah slapped the oxen's gaunt rumps and Mac leaned into a wagon spoke, pushing hard. Stiff-legged and stubborn, the oxen fought the big horse but found themselves drug along in his wake. With bellowing complaints, they finally leaned into their traces and heaved. With oozing suction, the wagon wheels groaned, moved and lurched from the thick mud. Slowly the group rolled up the embankment and halted on dry land. Spence released a loud disgusted snort and rested on quivering legs, his tail intact. He ignored the bellowing oxen as something beneath his notice and not worth his time.

Mac checked out his horse before sliding his hat back on his head, "Well I be . . . daa . . ." he quickly remembered himself, "darned, how did ya know?"

B.A. whistled a robin's territorial call. Some distance away, Brownfoot's head came up with a snort. He trotted immediately towards B.A. "What a horse cannot pull in harness, he can pull with his tail."

Later, the two men argued as they rode to the creek to water their horses. Mac was so furious his arms reeled out like a windmill as he slid from his horse, "What d'ye mean, ye won't go with them?!!"

B.A. remained silent, his face set and remote, refusing to get off his horse.

"Are ye daft? And I'll no' accept your blank Indian face, damn ye to hell and back! Don't be givin' me that sugar-wouldn't-melt-in-your-mouth, polite bullcrap! Talk to me! God a'Frighty, you know we can't leave these wee girleens out here alone!"

"They are not part of my plans. They have survived this far. If Creator wants them to reach Fort Carleton they will."

"Sure'n what condition would they be arrivin' in? Sweet Christ! Ye saw some of the slick badach's we've run into so far. Lord knows I wouldn't be wantin' my sisters or mother to tangle with any of them. I tell ye we have to stay with them until they reach the Fort. Then they're on their own." Mac's square jaw knotted with determination.

"You take them in. I have no wish to travel North with them. Our paths end here."

"No! Be damned if I'll let you go. You and I aren't through! Not when I'm just beginning to learn from you and you from me. Never! Ye stubborn Cree! We'll travel together! I am just starting to understand about Earth Mother and her crystal at the centre of the earth and by damned ye're goin' to teach me the rest if I have to hog-tie ye and drag ye along with me!" Mac threw his hat to the ground, wanting to stomp it like his friend's face. Never had he wanted so badly to hit someone.

In the next instant he reached up, grabbed a startled B.A. by his vest, toppled him from his horse, flung him to the ground and followed him down. They rolled about in the rocks and dirt, grunting furiously. Each tried for a handhold, braced a foot or knee, tumbled again, gritted his teeth and swung wildly. They knew each other too well and easily blocked the other's fist. Over they rolled, closer and closer to the creek.

A quiet voice entered the fray, "We call her Shekinah."

The two combatants froze, blinking through the dust to see Alorah Durham seated calmly on a big rock about fifteen feet away. Hat in hand, she studied the clouds above, her face turned slightly away. Both men cringed. She must have heard their every word.

"Who the Sam Hill is Shekinah?" Mac shoved B.A. away and sat up, trying to calm his wild frizz into some kind of manly control.

"I am Jewish," She continued calmly.

Mac grunted and B.A. looked askance at them both.

Mac swiped at his face, and dusted off his clothes, "This woman is one of God's 'Chosen Ones', privileged owners of His Holy Law." His outright sneer increased B.A.'s frown.

Alorah ignored Mac, meeting Broken Arrow's dark eyes, "Just like you are Cree from this land, I am from the Jewish Kabbalists in south western France. In our ancient text called the 'Zohar', Shekinah was the female part of God upon earth. She is the feminine half of his soul, his mind, his energy, his creativity and . . . his wife. In our rabbinic literature, she even scolds God for his vengefulness. It said she is the Divine Spirit, the light at the centre, the heart of the earth, mayhap the crystal you talk about."

Mac moved closer in spite of himself, "Jaysus, sometimes I think I've travelled into another world. What d'ye know about this Mother Earth stuff?"

"Shekinah was the feminine face of God. In our stories called, "The Voice of the Turtle", Shekinah brings together heaven and earth, the divine and human. It is a sacred marriage of the Father and Mother, who become one in continuous creation—Creator and Creation."

The simplicity and the blasphemy of it stole Mac's breath away. "God is not married! And certainly not to an Earth Spirit! How could you get it so mixed up? He rules alone, Creator of all!"

She peered up at him, blinking from the blinding sun at his back, "The Song of Songs in your bible was the text most used by the kabbalists to understand this loving, divine union. The Kabbalists describe the feminine image of the godhead as Mother, Daughter, Sister, beloved Bride and Holy Spirit, giving woman what she lacked in your Judeo-Christian culture—an image of the Divine Feminine in the godhead. The Shekinah is the Divine Motherhood, Mother of all Living things. Women can know themselves in their role as mothers, in their care and concern for their loved ones—for women are the symbolic custodians of Shekinah's creation.

"In your Christian bible, Shekinah, the wife of Jehovah, was rewritten as God's 'Glory', the 'Holy Spirit' but just a spirit with no feminine image." She sniffed in disdain, "At least they kept the symbol of Wisdom—her feminine wisdom, by the way. According to Jewish records, she lived in the temple of Jerusalem until it was destroyed some five hundred years before Christ was born. She left and never returned, leaving Jehovah to rule alone. The mystics claim he can never rule properly without his bride who was the source of his wisdom. Jewish people have always sought the return of this lost bride, a matron who could plead or mediate with Jehovah on their behalf."

"There is no lost bride! Gods rules alone! He needs no woman to tell him what to do! Even Christ was celibate! Just like our priests and bishops!" Mac's hands were on his hips, his legs spread wide, his feet planted.

She leaned back, her hands planted firmly on the rock, keeping determined eyes on Mac's narrowed ones. "Why did your ancient artists always paint Mary Magdalene in a red gown with a black or dark blue cape?"

"She was a harlot! A prostitute! The scarlet woman in red! How else would they paint her?" Mac ground it out, legs braced.

Alorah bent her head bent, shaking it sadly, "The word harlot comes from a Greek word, *hierodulai,* meaning 'sacred women'. Only the high priestesses in our Jewish temples were entitled to wear red. They were the writers of the tomes, the historians, the learned record keepers under our chief scribes. The initiates wore the maiden white, the nuns or sisters wore black and the high priestesses wore red. The Roman Catholics stole our high-ranking colours for their bishops, cardinals and priests then denounced the priestesses as whores. And it began with Mary Magdalene, our honoured High Priestess. She was the Head Sister of the Order of Marys, her position equivalent to a senior bishop. Even Christ's mother, the so-called Virgin Mary, was part of the same order. Mary Magdalene was no whore! She came from a wealthy family that sponsored Christ and his disciples' pilgrimages!"

She glared at Mac, "And Christ *was* married! As a descendent of King David and King Solomon, under Jewish law he *had* to produce at least two sons. Our records say Mary Magdalene not only accompanied him on his travels, *she was his wife!*" Alorah's voice rose in anger. "The earliest Christian texts, before the bible was ever written describe her as 'The Woman Who Knew All', 'the one Christ loved more than all the disciples'. In your bible, Mary Magdalene's anointing his feet was actually part of their Jewish Wedding ceremony! The sacred oil she used was part of her wealthy dowry! As an educated High Priestess, she was a source of great wisdom to Jesus and he honoured her advice, despite bitter complaints by his Apostle, Peter, who hated all women. After his crucifixion, Jesus's friends hid her away in Egypt. There, she had Christ's third child, a son, having already birthed first a daughter then a son. He too was called Jesus."

Mac's face paled, his mouth opening in argument, but Alorah rushed on, "Some say Mary Magdalene's body was the true Holy Grail, because she carried Christ's blood! When she moved to southern France, she was worshipped as the 'Black Madonna', a widow in mourning, part of the original Earth Mother goddesses. She was honoured by the Cistercians, Dominicans and Franciscan monks! The Knight Templars, the great architects of the world dedicated all their Notre Dame (Our Lady) Cathedrals in Europe not to Jesus' mother Mary, as your Catholic literature would have you believe, but to our real Lady, Mary Magdalene!"

Tears filled Alorah's eyes, "And for that the Roman Catholic Bishops had the Knight Templars tortured and burned at the stake for heresy." She lifted her chin as Mac's frown furrowed. "Your Christian Crusades put a descendant of Christ's on the very Throne of Israel! Mary Magdalene was still worshipped as the feminine side of God for centuries despite the Spanish Inquisition. The high kings did not want Christ's lineage known either. His was the true fisher king line, a joining of the Jewish priesthood from his mother, Mary, and Kingship lines of David, Solomon and Abraham from his father, Joseph. Your so-called righteous kings and priests wanted the power, the control to appoint their own choices not the rightful lineage of Christ's descendants! So your pious Christian kings and their holy Catholic priests tried to destroy any trace of Mary and Jesus' children. They called her whore, harlot, scarlet woman. In France they attacked her followers and burned their villages, killing men, women and children! Those were my people, my ancestors in southern France!" She spat the words at him through curled lips. "And we do not forget!"

Mac backed away in horror, "Blasphemy! Right from the black hell of your Jewish souls. Never will I believe such lies! Blasted Jews, the Romans should have fed the lot of you to the lions." He wheeled about and stomped back up through the willows to the wagon on the hillside.

For a time, nobody spoke. Alorah looked down at her feet, and scuffed a couple of rocks, her face sad and weary. "The Romans tried to kill us for centuries and their churches continued our persecution because we knew the truth, Broken Arrow. The real Messianic lineage of Jesus should have passed through his descendants, not the man-made ones the Roman Catholic Church created through Peter, the headstrong Apostle who hated women, especially Mary Magdalene."

She raised haunted eyes to B.A., her dark hair a shining aura around her head. "We aren't so different Cree Man. We both know the cruelty of prejudice and disgust. I know it as a woman and as a Jew. My people have been persecuted for thousands of years because of our beliefs and way of living."

B.A. hunkered down in front of her. "I thought you white people were all alike, but you fight over your beliefs about the same God. Yet what you fight about is not the God so much as the people connected to him. That is man-made history is it not? In spite of our differences, our tribes never fight over the Great Spirit. Nobody can fully understand it anyway. Yet I do not agree with the Black Robes either. It is good to know others disagree with the way they treat women."

Alorah's dark tilted eyes locked into his. "In the Albigensian Crusades of 1208 A.D. the Cathars of the County of Languedoc, my family's home in southern France, followed the traditions of Lazarus, Simon Zelotes and Mary Magdalene. They upheld the equality of the sexes. Girls and boys were both taught literature, philosophy, mathematics and the wisdom of the Cabbala, Jehovah's laws."

B.A's forehead pleated in confusion. "Why are you hated if you own the Creator's laws?"

"Because the bible was supposed to have been a message from God. Yet the Roman Catholic bishops rewrote it to exclude the feminine side of God. They believed it weakened their male dominating power. As the mother of true kings and priests, Mary Magdalene posed the greatest threat to a fearful Church who wanted their man-made succession from a mere Apostle of Jesus. And people still follow this bible blindly. The Catholics hate us for our truths." She chuckled sadly, "At least that is my view of the problem."

B.A. took up a small stick and dug in the sand, "We come from different areas, each with our own views of what is truth. My elders tell me the White Man must learn to live on this land with all the races of the world. But I am beginning to see how these differences, part of who we are, keep us apart, not united. How can my people convince anyone we are related, all one?"

When he lifted his head, the sun caught his eyes. Alorah noted instead of black, they were a rich, dark brown. She placed the back of her hand next to his bent knee. "Look at our skin Broken Arrow." Her slim hand was a mere shade lighter than his golden skin. "My mother was part Egyptian, my father a French Jew. Perhaps our ancestors were related at one time. They say there was a tribe of Abraham's lost in the desert for many years, which eventually travelled east. Mayhap they travelled to this land and kept their memory of the traditional stories, which in my faith they call "The Voice of the Turtle.""

B.A.'s head came up, his brown eyes searching hers of deep hazel. "My people have legends of travelling east to the lands of the Rising Sun and spreading out across this land. We do have many stories about turtle. We call this land Turtle Island because it is shaped like a turtle according to our medicine men that fly above it in their dreams and visions."

She studied his fitted buckskin vest with its fringes tied with copper and brass beads and sea shells. Someone had carefully designed the front and back with trails of beaded roses, graceful leaves and swirling vines. The brass and copper beads on his necklace matched perfectly. In the warm sunlight, his body had a reddish cast beneath deep golden skin, which appeared beautifully smooth and silken. No hair graced his face or chest, similar to her less hairy Egyptian relatives.

"Why won't you travel with us?" More than anything, she simply wanted to keep him talking. His lips were fuller than most men's yet they shaped his words in fascinating detail.

His head ducked, covering his lean face with flowing hair. "I have no place in my life for women right now." He pried a small stone loose and flipped it away into the creek with a strong flick of his wrist.

She smiled slightly, wanting to touch his thick hair, curious about its texture. The wind sent her a faint scent of some herb from his hair, fresh and clean. "What was her name? This woman that made you hate all women?"

"Not all!" He glared at her peaceful countenance. To his surprise he blurted, "Her name was Melissande. She's white too. She was supposed to be my wife but she chose my friend instead." His chest rose with the fury of his thoughts.

"Ah, we women cannot control where our hearts lead us. That too is a woman's gift – to choose for herself. Could she not love you as well? Maybe . . . just differently? Maybe the choice broke her heart, because she loved you both, just differently." She reached out to touch his forearm and felt him flinch, though he did not remove her quiet hand.

He drew a long breath and looked away. "I couldn't stay and watch their happiness." He glared at her, waiting for the shock to appear on her face. "I wanted to kill them both in their marriage bed as they lay together."

The lines around her eyes deepened from the sorrow reflected in his eyes. "But you loved them both enough to leave." She squeezed his arm for emphasis.

He turned his head away, watching the creek waters wind slowly past. He pushed her hand away.

She waited a while. When he remained silent, she repeated her question, "Please won't you come with us? We need your help. I am afraid . . . ." She squeaked in fright as he leapt at her, pushed her off the rock and pinned her to the rough stones, his knife at her throat.

"What are you afraid of Jew Woman?" He snarled into her face, his knife point digging into her throat.

She struggled, twisting against a hard rock beneath her head, trying to shove the knife point away, "Don't! Don't hurt me! Please!"

When her long black hair tumbled free, his knife slackened and his gut clenched. He suddenly felt like he held one of his own clan. Then he gripped the handle furiously, his teeth gritting. "Are you ready to die?"

She blinked away tears, pounded his shoulders, "Die? No! Stop! What did I . . . ?"

He locked onto her flailing fists with one big hand. "Are you ready to die? Is this a good day for you to die? If you are one of God's chosen people, why are you so afraid to die?"

She gasped for breath, blinking rapidly, trying to get her terrified mind to work, "I . . . No! I don't want to die. I want to live! Please! Don't do this! I'm too young to die!"

"Is that the only reason you fear death? You're too young? Where did you get the idea age matters? People die any time, any age. You think you control when you die?" He shoved the point a little harder and she wondered frantically if she could still swallow without drawing blood.

She watched his fierce eyes and gulped. No blood ran. She breathed in, gathering her scattered horror. "I . . . I can't. No, I can't!" She exhaled shakily, breathing in deep sobs, her chest lifting and falling frantically, her heart pounding in her ears. He never moved. She felt his hair tickling her cheeks, the warm musk of his breath drifting over her. She struggled again but he held her easily, her wrists secured over her head, clenched in one massive fist. His solid weight immobilized her. Still he waited, though his eyes eased their fury somehow.

"I can't stop you." Her chin lifted. "If you wanted to kill me, you could. Right now!" Her defiant eyes locked with his.

"You could scream." he whispered.

She froze, searched his eyes, which did seem softer now, waiting, yet challenging her too. She made no sound, suddenly unafraid. The thought shocked her, locked her breath in her throat, her wide eyes never leaving his. Salvia would fight for her. Would the angry Mac?

"The Creator chooses our time of death, not us." He released her hands and eased back on his knees, his knife still clenched in a fist on his thigh.

She sat up warily, never taking her eyes from him or the knife. When he made no move, she pulled her legs beneath her. "You scared me deliberately!" her eyes darkened, hurt and accusing as she scuttled backwards away from him.

He returned his knife to its sheath, letting her work it out.

She cleared her throat, smoothing her wild hair with trembling fingers, "You . . . You're saying we have no control over dying. That God can save us or allow us to die any time."

"My people say any day is a good day to die."

"A good day to die. What's so good about dying?"

"Dying, living . . . same thing." He gave a Gaelic shrug much like one of Mac's.

"No it's not! When you die, your life ends! It's is all over. What's so good about that?!" She didn't want his relaxed indifference, her fear rode too high.

He knew he owed her an explanation. "Our people believe in an afterlife, that the Creator made everything in the form of a circle. The circle is unending. So is life. Our medicine people, who are respected for their wisdom, conduct ceremonies which reach into 'the Beyond', the Spirit World. Their ability to looking into the beyond convinces us our spirit does not end. So we say to live fully, you must accept your death fully."

She stumbled through the words, her frantic mind slowing. "Then . . . you go into each day and just live it . . . fully, in case it is your last?"

"Life does not end; it goes on forever, just at a different level, in a different place. Why fear something that has no end?" His palm lifted in a slow, graceful flow. "You live on anyway."

She licked dry lips, trying to calm her racing heart, "I thought you would kill me . . . I was so scared. I realized I could die and there was nothing I could do about it."

"Fear is a failure to live in peace with your self, accepting what is . . . as is."

"You don't live in harmony with anyone in this land! I know how you war amongst yourselves, let alone against the white people!" She wanted to poke holes in his calm, though she wondered at her actions, given his violent reprisal.

He shook his head, his face quiet, "Fighting is more about courage, facing down fear. You can still feel peaceful if you are not afraid to live, or die. That's why we paint our faces before we go into battle, so the Creator may find us if we die."

She gazed at him in wonder, "I've seen mice stand up to my cat like that. Rather than run away, they'd rise up on their hind feet and challenge the cat. They showed no fear. I thought it was courage . . . maybe it was acceptance? Then maybe it was 'do your worst! I am ready to die!'" She grinned then shook her head at her own silliness.

He allowed a small smile to lift his mouth. "Your power ends where your fear begins. When you get beyond the fear, you are ready, not lost in endless possibilities of what might happen. Instead, you watch, you listen, you pay attention to the warning signs of danger and you choose how to deal with it the best way you can. But beyond that, you will survive, or you will die. It's Creator's choice, not ours. We are just blades of grass in his land."

"Humbling thought. Our life is not precious, just a blade of grass that can be crushed or eaten at any time. So you enjoy each day." She scrambled back onto the rock she'd perched on earlier, shaking the sand from her skirt. She peeked over at him, her lower lip full and curling, "You could have been kinder in the teaching!"

He snuffled a small grin, lifting one knee to loop an arm around it, "Only when you face your fear can you make it go away."

Muscles in Alorah's back relaxed, making her seat a little more comfortable. Her gaze lifted to the creek before her while she sifted through the words of this strange man, his ideas like none she had ever encountered. "It makes me look at this trip differently. Since Mr Brennan died, I have been terrified, unable to sleep at night. Every squeak or scrape had my heart pounding. I could scarcely breathe at times from the fear. I've been so fearful I couldn't enjoy the days at all. Perhaps my time would have been more enjoyable had I kept my gun handy, a knife under my pillow and just stayed vigilant, accepting whatever happens." She smiled shyly at him. "Nothing has changed my situation except how I chose to look at it."

Then her face pinked. "A woman alone is still alone. She can suffer a fate worse than death."

He stuck a grass stem into his mouth, "Our people never raped our enemies' women. We might take them in battle, use them as slaves for a while, but they were usually adopted into our clan. Many remained with us for the rest of their lives. The choice to come to our bed was theirs to make. The most severe punishments handed out in our clans were sex crimes against a family or a woman—especially if it was against her consent. It is part of what our elders taught us about honouring ourselves."

He slanted a frown towards her uplifted face, "Like the union of your male and female Gods. Union of a couple is a sacred act. If done with honour it becomes part of the connection with the Great Mystery of life. In our medicine pipe, the bowl is feminine, the stem masculine. When joined, they become one, whole, in balance and in harmony."

She cocked her head to one side, "I never knew that. We just assumed women were all raped by Indian men, because it's what a lot of our men would do. Well . . . not all, but many." She took a deep breath, clasping her hands, thinking about all the other assumptions she had about his people. How many were actually true? "You see, Broken Arrow, we too have our prejudices about strangers."

She frowned, shading her eyes suddenly, looking towards his still crouched silhouette, seeing the sun dance off his broad, gleaming shoulders. Then her eyes sharpened, "You've talked a lot about facing fear. So . . . when are you going to get over your fear of women?"

He leapt to his feet, angry again. Leaning forward, he grabbed her shoulders and stamped her mouth with a fierce kiss. Abruptly he straightened. "I don't need them!" he gritted and strode away.

She watched him go, her face sad, "Ah . . . but will you live joyfully?"

23.

MELISSANDE

Broken Arrow's long strides carried him into the canopy of trees and beyond to the open prairie, out of sight of the wagon and the others. He climbed onto an outcropping of rocks and seated himself on the largest, flattest one. His gaze swung to the far horizon, his gut clenching in self-loathing. It wasn't a good thing, what he'd done to the Jew woman. Mitsue would have scolded him in fury, probably slapped his ear with her sewing. He could almost hear her words:

"Each man his own way. You don't interfere! They must find their own path and you can not influence that! You are not to judge how they live their lives. Pay attention to your own and learn from your own mistakes!"

B.A. sighed, closing his eyes. He definitely had lots to learn about interference. A muscle in his jaw worked furiously. But the Jew Woman pushed too hard and dug too deep with her nosy questions. His heart cringed from the terror he'd created in her eyes. He hadn't told her the full truth. His people also believed they were accountable in the Spirit World for all they had said and done in this life. He drew another deep breath, letting it go, out into the heavy, warm air of morning sunshine. It was time. When he had reached early manhood, his vision quest had taught him the necessity of digging deeper inside to find his truth, beyond his anger, beyond the fear. Anything less would be cowardly. He owed the woman that, especially when he'd forced her to face her own fears.

Melissande.

The young girl of golden hair, like ripened prairie grass and sage green eyes. He was nine summers old when Mitsue traded a surly Iroquois warrior a copper kettle and several pieces of her winter beadwork for the silent eight-year old with her strange sad eyes.

Melissande.

She had been taken in a raid out east somewhere when she was small and had no idea how to find her way home nor even what her family name was.

Melissande.

Both she and Broken Arrow were raised by Tall Man and his sister Mitsue.

B.A. silently chuckled. He had been so jealous of Melissande at first. He was used to all the attention from his grandparents, aunties and uncles. As a young orphaned child, they had let him do and say whatever he wanted. He liked all the pats and hugs and stories and didn't want to share them with this washed out Iskwesis. But his uncles had bounced him on their knees and teased him until he was okay with it. They had become very close, he and Melissande. She'd taught him proper English from the white captive woman who had raised her and he'd helped her with her Cree.

B.A. sat in silence, his mind echoing with her laughter, with the memories of their midnight raids on the Crow. Like the time Melissande got into trouble, attacked by three warriors at once. She'd mudded her hair, darkening it to the colour of night, but they'd found her as she raced towards her horse. Once they'd discovered she was a woman, the rules had changed. Before he could reach her, their hands were all over her. He'd killed all three, in a red blotched rage. His first kill. Never would he forget the nauseous combination of blood, urine and faeces coating his body like paint. She'd held his head while he gagged over and over. Neither mentioned it again. At the following Council gathering, she spoke long and eloquently about his strength and courage. He'd won his first white eagle feather for it, dipped in red, for the first blood he had spilled and three dots on it, one for each enemy killed. Absently, he stroked his fingers down the feather tied in his hair, from its topknot to the silken tips of the shaft . . . and tried to block out the pain arrowing through his soul.

Behind closed lids, he allowed more memories to sweep him, finally accepting the emotional winds they brought. He remembered them laughing together one morning. His life-long friend, Red Arrow, had thrown his head back, his strong throat vibrating in the sheer joy of living after the dark night of their raid. And Melissande, her bright braids shining in the early sun, green eyes sparkling from the fear, excitement and success. They pushed a full score of horses before them. It had been a good raid. Nobody was hurt. All three had counted coup, creeping close enough to touch the Crow warriors as they slept unawares. And the bounty of horses they'd taken from the sleeping camp would help ease the burden of Mitsue and Tall Man's families when they broke camp for their winter shelter in the forest during Indian summer, the last warm spell between frosts before winter snows covered the land. They rode home eagerly, waiting for their relatives to spot them and start singing the Thanksgiving songs, happily organizing an evening dance to honour their coup.

Broken Arrow let the high spirits of that day fill him, chasing out the shadows his anger had occupied for so long. He drew another heavy breath, releasing his thoughts in exhale, letting them flow through him, picking up the vibration of his feelings as they blew away in the wind. Anger? He'd had a bellyful of it ever since he'd left his tribe that morning. All night after Melissande and Red Arrow's wedding ceremony, he'd paced, circling the silent camp, over and over, while bitterness ate his gut. Anger had him packed and leaving at dawn. Anger made him pass their silent tepee, made him ignore their rush outside and their calls to him as he rode away He was so sick inside he'd wanted to destroy everything in his path as he rode away.

He'd wanted to kill that red headed *Moniyaw* he spied limping across the prairie a few hours later. He'd wanted to attack and pound and rip with his wild, bare hands. But something in his gut wouldn't let him strike from behind. Tall Man had taught him his quarry must always see him first before he killed; it must have a fighting chance. But oh how he'd wanted to kill! Mitsue always insisted he listen to the quiet voice of inner truth and it refused to allow him to kill without warning. He must be close enough to see the man's eyes – and be seen. So he'd angrily stalked the White Man all morning, staying out of sight, getting closer with each bend of the river.

But as time passed, he began to know the red-haired man, to understand his bellowing delight in running full tilt into the cool river and splashing about in the deeper pools, a welcome relief from the sweltering sun. He'd hid in the shadows of the leaves and watched the man squirt water in long spouts out of his mouth and laughed silently when some of it ran back into his nose, making him snort and shake his woolly head like a wallowing buffalo. He'd even felt a twinge of sympathy when the man's wet shoes dried and shrank, causing him to limp. He noted the man's courage to stubbornly continue and not turn back.

Then he'd closed in for the kill. But seeing Mac's eyes, those pale green eyes, Melissande's eyes, the colour of new ferns in the spring, had undone him. Something died within him, making his arm weak and useless. Instead, he'd wanted to throw up. Then he found himself laughing silently at Mac's cactus holes, clumsy confusion and silly words. He surprised himself further by offering his best moccasins and salve for the White Man's blistered feet. The loneliness he'd sensed in the White Man felt like an echo of his own. Now he felt grateful for Mac's friendship and all he had learned from him. Creator had a much bigger plan than a man's puny anger.

For the first time, Broken Arrow allowed the faces of his two childhood friends to come closer instead of shoving them away. For the first time, he thought about what his leaving must have done to them. He'd spent so much time on his anger, he'd never moved past the final memory of them standing outside their tepee calling to him and watching him leave. After witnessing their marriage ceremony he'd stood alone, helpless and furious as they giggled, shyly entering their new home, hand in hand. A place he could not follow.

Pride.

How it stung. He gritted his teeth and bowed his head in acceptance of the pain billowing up from his stomach. Pride dug deep. Pride because she chose Red Arrow over himself. But what had it cost her? Was the Jew Woman right? Melissande's smiling face and gentle eyes filled his thoughts. She *had* loved him. He found it now in the memories of her laughing eyes, the gifts she made for him and the thoughts she had shared. Had she cried when he left? Maybe she grieved his absence in her life as much as he did hers. Maybe just differently, like the Jew woman said. He felt water burn his eyes. Pulling his legs towards him, he wrapped his knees with deadened arms and rested his forehead on their crossed support. His breath drew ragged and raw. For the first time since he'd left, he allowed his pain to ripple through him, from the top of his head to the bottom of his feet. He planted them squarely upon the rock. Let Mother share his sorrow. She always had, without complaint. He let the sadness drift through him feeling it flow into tears sliding down his cheeks, dripping into the dust beneath him. His face crumbled in agony as the pain intensified, choking him, making him cough out its power . . . .

He'd lost.

And it reduced him, embarrassed him—pride, just pride. What the elders said to guard against at all times. And still it ruled him. He was the outcast, the one left out, to suffer alone. They at least had each other.

His ragged breath quivered and stilled. On his cheek a single teardrop caught the sun's ray while truth speared him.

Jealousy.

How had he missed it? Jealousy, from the one left behind, severed from a friendship bond. They went where he could never follow.

Their relationship with him could never be the same. He realized his grief stemmed not only from pride, but from loss. He'd lost something with his two friends that could not be, any more. And the pain burned deeper . . . .

Red Arrow.

How he'd hated this friend, had wanted to kill him for his betrayal. But Red Arrow only followed his heart. He had loved Melissande as much as Broken Arrow. Who could fault him for that? And at what cost to his soul? Red Arrow probably knew, just as Broken Arrow now realized, the cost to his best friend who wanted and loved the same woman. Was that so bad? She was worthy of their love. She had not dishonoured one or the other. She had chosen which one she wanted to live with, have children with. For the first time, B.A. wondered what her choice had cost her in pain. What of Red Arrow's choice, knowing he'd destroyed his friend's dreams? What price to both when they realized they could have each other only by breaking ties with Broken Arrow? The agony ripped him apart, blurred his vision, and clogged his throat until he gagged. His breath whistled back and forth, painful, jagged and raw. He lost himself in the water of his eyes . . . .

Sometime later he sniffed a couple of times and stared into the horizon. Choices. Tall Man often told him life was choices and they always came with consequences. B.A. swiped his face and closed his eyes in despair. What was the point of asking why this choice? Why did the sun rise? Why did people feel so strongly about one person and not the other? Why were they forced to choose one over another? No answers came. Nothing could undo this day, nor change this moment back to the happy ones they once shared. Nothing changed this life that still found him alone, staring out into the prairie haze of a ripening day, far from his family, friends and home.

For the first time, he considered what he had left behind. If he'd stayed, would his anger and bitterness have destroyed the new bond between his two friends? It certainly would have hurt them, likely filling them with guilt, perhaps making them ashamed of the pain they inflicted upon him. His mouth tightened. He didn't need their pity. Still, they deserved the chance to build a life together, without his influence.

He drew a full breath, suddenly pleased he had left. He felt selfishly vindicated too. His leaving must have hurt them. They had loved him. No lies masked the honesty of their open affection to him in the past. And no marriage could wipe out all the laughter they'd shared. His staying would have hurt them all. Perhaps leaving was the best marriage gift he could have given them, hiding his pain until he could deal with it himself, without spreading it further. He had made a good choice, the right choice, for all of them. The thought changed the deep grief inside, broke it apart and released it. He felt it sliding down through his feet and back into Mother, from where it came, where all energies were born. He blew the rest out, off his chest, using long gusty exhalations, freeing it, clearing it away until only peace remained.

Emptied from all emotion, he worked a few more deep breaths while his heart calmed and his face dried. "Blades of grass," Tall Man had told him, "We are nothing but blades of grass upon this prairie. We bend with the winds and storms; we feel the sun and moon on our faces and we give thanks for the life Creator gave us. Life is a gift of feeling and thinking all things. As we grow older, we track the seasons of our lives, developing, sleeping for a while, then reawakening, to another spring, another renewal." It was Mitsue who reminded him, "Like the rain falling to renew the land, tears are the pledge of our renewal. They move us into a better place of understanding."

From the shadow of the immense trees above him B.A. stared out into the thickening heat waves of late morning. To the north-east, the purple contours of the Birch Hills merged into a pale blue cloudless sky. The air was still, as if Mother held her breath. He had never felt so alone. Tall Man had a saying, 'How puny is the strength of man'. A blade of grass was such a tiny piece of the power surrounding him. It made Broken Arrow feel small, vulnerable to Mother's storms, like the one he had just worked through. He stared at his hands and felt their futility against the power of change surrounding him. For the first time, he understood the occasional glimmer of fear in Mac's eyes as he gazed upon this great, silent land. Why would the women feel any less fear? Was the real lesson in the grass's ability to simply bend and move and dance through the storms, to live beyond them and grow again in the storm's quiet aftermath of gentle sunlight? He felt the emptiness beyond this simple purpose called life. Still, he breathed on. Perhaps each blade found comfort in the other blades growing around it, clumped together in similar experiences.

"Wisdom," the elders said. "Life was about learning and it would always be hard, always create suffering and always be a struggle." He used to wonder why they'd shake their heads and sigh. Now, he snorted and smiled.

"Ye gonna sit there like a damn statue forever or ride with us?" Mac stood over him, his fisted hands riding his hips in furious, yet wary defiance.

B.A. tilted his head and looked into those light green, angry eyes. Now, he understood the pain behind them, sensed the loneliness of his friend. He held up his palm, open and relaxed.

Mac stared at it, searched the calm, slightly reddened eyes that slowly sparked once again. He allowed a small grin to play upon his lips as he clasped his friend's hand and hauled him to his feet.

As they walked to the wagon, B.A. remembered Mitsue's parting words before he'd ridden away that morning. She had shaded her eyes with trembling fingers, her broad face a quivering mass of sorrow, "When you learn to forgive grandson, then you will find renewal." He wasn't sure he understood her, even now. Maybe he'd found forgiveness today, but renewal? What was that?

24.

COYOTE DICK

As the two men walked towards the wagon, Salvia met them with a small tray of biscuits. "Gentlemen, help yourselves. "We have gooseberry jam to go with them."

Alorah came forward grimly offering them a spoon to dig the deep purple sweet from the pint jar in her hands. With her continued silence, Mac knew she had not forgiven him. He was surprised to see B.A. also turn his head away from the small treat.

Mac took one biscuit, spread it and thrust it into his friend's hands, determined to not upset these ladies any more. He wanted to smack B.A. for his rudeness. Quickly he popped the second biscuit into his own mouth.

Closing his eyes, he savoured the light crust as it melted slowly upon his tongue, his jaw aching with the tart bite of the bitter purple berry. He chose loquaciousness to cover B.A.'s silent stiffness. "'Tis the most delicious morsel I've had in months, my ladies. Why, a poor Irishman like meself could perish waiting for another such delight in the dry years ahead. Perhaps we need a wee bit more to stave off that endless starvation." He quickly plastered two with jam, shoved one into B.A's hand and popped the other into his mouth. He broke more apart, coated them in jam and made tiny sandwiches, stuffing them into his pockets—"for a later treat". Closing his eyes he savoured the flavours,

"Never have I tasted such ambrosia! Tis indeed a soft day when I taste the wonders of a woman's home cookin'. Me poor mouth cries out in awe. Thank ye! Thank ye my ladies! Me heart thanks ye and so does me beggarly stomach. Truly I have found heavenly food today!"

The two women laughed at his shameless flattery as they walked away with an empty tray.

B.A. gave him a sideways sardonic glance, still holding the biscuits. "Feeling itchy?"

Mac frowned at him but chose discretion over curiosity. He turned away, assisting first Alorah and then Salvia as they climbed to their high wagon seat. Salvia slapped the reins across the backs of her lazy oxen until they bowed their heads and hauled the wagon forward. The two men rode on ahead, staying out of the dust from laden steel wheels.

"So what is this about itchy?" Mac looked back to make sure the oxen gave the women no further trouble. They were also out of earshot.

B.A. grinned at him, took a bite then chuckled, pure mischief dancing in his eyes as he swallowed. "It's an old story I overhead Mitsue telling Moya one day. It's about Coyote Dick."

Mac frowned then found himself smiling back, still relieved the Cree rode with them. "I have a feeling I'll no' be likin' this tale but tell on."

"Stories about coyote or Wesakechak are very much a part of our grandparent's memories. He is often called 'The Trickster' because just when you think you have him figured out, he'll pull something on you to make you laugh even more at yourself. When coyote comes calling, you know you're in for a good lesson. Coyote stories have many meanings. They seem like a simple story, but thinking about them brings deeper understanding of a message or a warning."

"And Mitsue told this story?"

"Yes, but I don't think I was supposed to hear it – not as a little boy anyway. The grandmothers were very careful about which stories children were told."

B.A. laughed outright. "Those two old women were always teasing each other. This was another time I stalked them. They were out gathering moss. They would dry it over willows then use it to scrub their pots and spoons. They'd pad their bed of spruce boughs or chink their tipis with it to keep out the cold in winter. Mitsue's daughters also used it to line the moss bags they laced their babies into. That fall day, Mitsue and Moya were stuffing it into buffalo paunches they carried on their backs. Moya was swatting at flies and accidentally whacked Mitsue across the chest with her bag:

"Mah! You hit my eyes!" Mitsue scolded, rubbing her chest.

Moya looked closer and snorted, "You're eyes aren't on your chest old woman!"

Mitsue swayed back and forth, arching her back. "Ehe! I can see through these." She rubbed her chest suggestively.

Moya giggled, her mouth wide, "You crazy old woman! What do you see?"

Mitsue strutted with an easy stride, her ample hips swaying out then up with each step. Her large eyes closed then opened slyly, "I can see when old Pipestem watches me with those itchy eyes of his."

"Itchy?" Moya looked totally bewildered, "there's nothing wrong with his eyes!"

Mitsue swung her braids over her chest, sliding her hands down their twined strands. She swished one greying tip back and forth across her lips. "You ever hear about Coyote Dick?"

Moya dumped her bundle of moss on an embankment and plunked her lean butt down beside it. "No."

Mitsue sauntered slowly back and forth in front of her, swinging her wide body. She swatted Moya on the shoulder with a playful braid. "I'm talking about his *mitakisiy*."

Moya gurgled deep within her belly, letting out a small mischievous snort. "Uuunh! . . . His mitakisiy, that little chunk of skin between his legs he's so proud of!"

"Ehe!" Mitsue continued, her big hips swaying to the toed-in shuffle of her moccasins. "Old Coyote got tired one day so he lay under some willows and fell asleep. But his mitakisiy wasn't tired. It got so bored waiting for him, it decided to go wandering about on its own. It broke away from Coyote and ran off down the road. Of course it had to hop . . . having only one leg." She peered at her friend over a wide shoulder and arched her brow.

Moya snickered, her narrow shoulders shaking.

"Well old Mitakisiy was having lots of fun on his own, hopping about, poking into all kinds of places he shouldn't be." Mitsue turned a bland, innocent face towards her seated friend who snorted then giggled when she caught on.

"Then he thought he saw something he might like over a little hill and he hopped off the trail, taking a shortcut. He landed right in a big patch of stinging nettles. "Ouch!" he cried, "Ow, ow, ow!" He screamed. "Help! Help! Help!"

Moya clapped her hands together, covering the lower half of her narrow, grinning face as she following her old friend's every move.

Mitsue continued her saunter, caressing her beaded necklace while her other wrinkled hand rested on a gargantuan hip. "All that crying finally woke Coyote up. When he reached down to start his heart with the usual pull. It was gone!"

Moya grunted as she leaned forward, elbows on her thighs.

"So he ran down the road, holding himself between his legs, sniffing everywhere, trying to find his mitakisiy. Finally he found it crying in the nettles. He dug it out, licked it clean, petted it and stuck it back where it belonged." Mitsue sighed dramatically.

Moya clapped a hand over her chest, stifling gut-deep gurgles. Lines around her eyes and cheeks deepened and lengthened.

Mitsue stopped, turned to her friend, her face serious and thoughtful. "And you know, even though Coyote got away from them, those nettles made his mitakisiy itch like crazy forever after." She leaned down, rubbing a rounded shoulder against Moya's bony one. "That's why men are always sliding up to women, rubbing up against them with that 'I'm so itchy' look in their eyes. Their dicks have been itching ever since that first one ran away."

Moya shrieked, falling over backwards as she howled with laughter and pounded her heels in the mud. Mitsue's cackles joined in, her huge belly and breasts shaking with every gust. They laughed until tears ran, each setting off the other when she stopped to catch her breath. They laughed until they had no muscle to stand or even sit, collapsing upon the bank, their heads thrown back and their mouths wide open, screaming at the sky."

*   *   *

Mac ducked, yanking his hat low over dark red cheeks while Broken Arrow's shout of laughter pierced the air.

25.

FORGIVENESS

"I'm sorry."

Alorah turned in surprise. A penitent Mac stood nearby in the darkness, crushing his hat between his hands. She returned to kneading the bread she had mixed at noon. For the rest of the day, it had bounced around in the back of their wagon, raising and falling with the rough land and its many bumps.

Mac watched her small knuckles gently punch the bread. Small air bubbles popped beneath her kneading fingers as she rolled it into a large ball. With a deft whack of a big meat cleaver, she cut the dough in two. He winced, thinking of other possible things sliced in two. Alorah chose one doughy lump and again flattened it with her fists. With small, deft flicks of her fingers, she rolled the flattened edges towards the middle until they formed another ball that she turned over, smooth side up. She greased the top with a small rag dipped from a nearby pot of warmed bacon fat. Picking up the dough, she walked to the campfire and lifted the lid of a huge cast iron Dutch oven resting near the coals. Swiping the interior of the tall pot with her rag, she gently dropped the dough in, greased side up and replaced the lid. The dough would have to rise once more before she placed it on the edge of the dying embers to bake slowly. She returned to work the remaining lump of dough.

Mac's sombre eyes followed her quiet grace. He sighed with her silence, "Tis beggin' your pardon I am. I should not have attacked your beliefs. They are ancient and probably wise beyond my understanding. As a Catholic, I must respect your faith, though I canno' agree with it." His sense of fairness made him add, "I remember reading about our Druidic high priestesses of Avalon who also wore a scarlet dress and black cape – just like Mary Magdalene's."

One of Alorah's eyebrows lifted as she worked the bread. It was an apology of sorts. The best she was likely to get from this stubborn man. His quiet voice in contrast to his cheerful talkativeness all day bespoke a heartfelt sincerity.

She turned to him, wiping a stray strand of hair from her face, inadvertently leaving a streak of flour in its wake. It was time for some ownership. "And I should not have jumped on you about my beliefs either. Perhaps it was the fear of watching you two fight that made me react so strongly." She smiled at him, "Or perhaps I thought it time you learned some new truths."

His shoulders eased as he grinned back, "Aye, between you and B.A. I'll soon be a newly educated man."

He gestured towards the bread. "D'ye suppose you'll be forgivin' me enough to sample some more of your excellent fare before nightfall?" He swallowed at the thought of warm bread and jam rolling over his tongue.

She sliced off a small chunk and rolled it between her fingers on the bread board until it formed a long, cylindrical strip. She held it out to him. "Wrap it around a green poplar stick and roast it over the fire. Mayhap I'll give you some more gooseberry jam afterwards, provided you don't eat the entire jar."

Mac's jaw ached from the promise of this treat. Reverently he drew the thin dough towards him, swallowing in delight. "Thank you! Thank you my lady. I am ever at your service . . ." His curly head dipped while his emerald eyes sparked again with mischief in the flickering firelight, "More so should you decide to depart with another piece."

She watched him walk away, carefully holding the dough like a little boy with an unexpected treat. In spite of herself, she grinned, shaking her head at his retreating back. The man was a handsome charmer despite his temper.

As she returned to her work, she sensed rather than saw him. Only when she sought the shadows did she find his outline. A man who walked in shadows. Was it symbolic of his life? Somehow she knew him too determined to stay there for any length of time. She wondered what it was about this man that drew her curiosity so strongly. Whatever it was, it came from deep within her, deeper than her heart. The thought surprised her. What was deeper than that?

She chose the defensive. "I suppose you want some dough too?"

He drifted towards her, his eyes following her quick movements as she used her rolling pin to flatten the dough, cut it into pie-shaped pieces, place them on a plate and carry them to the campfire. Taking up a small green twig, she stuck it into a fry pan of lard heating over fiery coals. When tiny bubbles appeared around the stick, she knew the fat was hot enough. Using two fingers, she punctured a couple holes into one triangle of bread then gently slid it into the sputtering fat. Immediately, brown grease foamed about the bread, sizzling merrily. She added two more triangles of dough then picked up an iron lifter to flip the first over. A rich golden brown coated the smooth dough. Liquid lard surged around the holes and around the pieces, setting off a mouth-watering aroma of yeasty bread. She preferred this bread to the unleavened of her people's.

B.A. swallowed in spite of himself. He moved closer, fascinated by the cooking bread. He realized he missed his family and all the wonderful fry breads Mitsue had cooked for him and their family. Now another sizzled in front of him. A renewal of sorts? The remaining sadness he'd felt earlier lifted, wafting heavenward with the grey smoke from the campfire. He drew a long breath, shifting into this moment.

"It smells good." He hoped she forgave him enough to share it. Words never came easily to him like they did for Mac. How could he explain his earlier reactions when he struggled to understand them himself? Yet the sunny morning's peacefulness remained with him, leaving him with no desire to upset her further. He wiped his hands down his leggings, glad he had just washed them in the small slough they were camped beside for the night. White women, he remembered were fussy about clean hands around food. At least the nuns at the mission were.

Wordlessly, Alorah lifted the first cooked piece from the pan, setting it back upon the nearby plate. She reached into their wooden grub box and pulled out a pint of her carefully hoarded Saskatoon jam. When she held it out to him along with a butter knife, he took them, his eyes meeting hers as he broke the jar's seal. Scooping out a generous portion, he spread it over the hot bread, yanking burning fingers back from its steaming sides. Cautiously picking up the dough, he tossed it lightly from hand to hand, biting off a generous chunk, sucking in air to cool his sensitive tongue from the burning grease. He closed his eyes, savouring the fragrant bread and sweet berries.

The expression on his face was enough thanks for Alorah. She watched with a silent pride in her work as he slowly chewed his way through the triangle, his powerful throat working with each swallow. Finally, she shook off her bemusement. Returning to her simmering scones, she quickly flipped them over just before they blackened.

A hard thumb on her cheek had her jumping back, startled.

His eyes smiled down at her in the gathering darkness. "You have flour on your face."

She picked up a corner of her apron and industriously scrubbed the spot before laughing up at him, "My war paint in case I die today."

His head bobbed back slightly as he took the hit, feeling his shoulders ease with her humour.

Alorah removed the golden scones, added the last three to her pan then lifted hopeful eyes to the silent man at her side. "Tell me some more about your people. I would like to know them if I am to live with them in this land."

He studied her, gauging her sincerity. "What do you want to know?"

She shrugged, her eyes returning to the sizzling pan, "Anything you want to tell me."

He reached into his beaded fire bag and held out his fist, palm uncurling to reveal a stone tied with a strip of leather. "I give this to you."

She wiped her hands on her apron before lifting it from his hand. It was a circular stone, smoothly polished, with a hole through which a tanned hide strand was looped to make a necklace. In the firelight, the stone turned semi-transparent, a rich, green texture of light shade and shadow – like this man. She flipped the scones, let them cook then sat them on the plate to cool before removing the empty pan from the coals.

He explained, "A stone with a natural hole worn through it like this one brings the wearer good luck. Rarely is a stone perfectly rounded. This one so shaped by Mother Earth's water and air, doubles its power of protection. I bring it to you as a gift, to ask your forgiveness for my actions today."

She turned to him in surprise, amazed at the quiet sincerity in his words and the kindness in his eyes. Never had she thought such a proud man would apologize, yet he did it with such dignity. Holding his gaze, she lifted the thong over her head and settled the stone on her chest, her fingers gently caressing its glossy texture. "It is beautiful. Thank you."

He looked away, eyes restless. "What I never told you about dying was we also believe we are accountable for our actions in this world. When we harm another, we must offer some form of compensation, a gift, an apology, or whatever it takes to restore the harmony between us. How we advance our souls depends upon how well we treat our fellow man. This means treating people with respect and friendliness, using kind words to uplift a person's spirit, to keep them growing in a good way. It means being helpful and generous." He tilted his head down to her, his eyes narrowing with laughter. "When we offer a gift, we are really asking for forgiveness. It is the most honest form of love the offended person can return. Forgiveness releases the anger and hurt, restoring harmony."

Her eyebrow lifted at the challenge in his eyes, "So I'm to forgive you for scaring me half to death with your knife today, for forcing me to face my fears? And now I must let go of my anger too? In exchange I get a necklace? Is it truly a fair exchange?" Her chin tilted her face serious while her eyes danced.

One corner of his mouth lifted, "If not, I could kiss you again."

She laughed and moved away to the wagon, returning with a pot holder to check the rising bread in the Dutch oven. "I'll accept your necklace Broken Arrow but I'll hold off on the other offer."

His head gave an infinitesimal nod. She had not totally forgiven him but it was enough – for now.

As she raked the coals into a bed of glowing embers, and set the heavy Dutch oven amongst them to cook her bread loaf, Alorah considered what he had said. Forgiveness – the world had so little of it. Revenge seemed more important: an eye for an eye. Where was the love in that? It only destroyed another eye and another and another.

Her eyes narrowed as she straightened and turned back to him. "What about your feud with the Blackfoot and Crow? Where is your forgiveness with them?" She wanted honesty from him, not ideals.

His shoulders tensed. This woman gave no quarter, her mind too quick. "Revenge is still strong with our warriors. Yet the greatest test of our men is to make peace not war. The highest honour amongst our warriors and chiefs is to walk unarmed into an enemy's camp, knowing you could be killed on sight, and negotiate a peace agreement."

"Peace." She scorned the word as she washed her utensils. "Look at your friend Mac and the Irish feud with the British, forever re-enacted, forever stubbornly replayed, never forgiven, the people just pawns in a war always taken to the next generation." She swung her spatula for emphasis, "Look at the suffering of the Jews. This world has no use for forgiveness. Too many battles, too little resolution for peace is more the truth."

He seated himself on the wagon tongue, hands on muscular thighs. "Our women are better at this than we men, especially our grandmothers who are keepers of the next generation. They teach fierce love is the centre of a woman's power, to protect and nurture against all odds. This caring is what our women must teach our men. We are not born with this gift our women have. Only a woman holds this power and becomes powerful when creating cooperation and harmony, and therefore health, at all levels . . . from themselves, outward to their family, their clan and to Mother Earth. Without it, all becomes chaos, hostility and death. So our women wield great power."

Intrigued, Alorah came to sit beside him on the long wooden tongue, idle hands resting in her lap, her head gracefully tilted as she listened to his story.

"Our women, because of this power, they survive, they care, teach, nurse, bear children and feed us all. They laugh, love and stick with us, no matter what. Some of our women elders have the power to convince our warriors not to fight. They plead on behalf of the families to stop a war before it begins. Many times they succeed and our warriors stay home."

He bent forward, arms on his knees, "There is something you should know about that Minnesota Massacre. Mac and I met a party of Wahpeton Sioux, a branch of the Santees, fleeing north from that battle. Their elder told us his side of the story.

"Many of the Oglala and Brule Sioux crossed the Missouri over a hundred years ago to get away from the settlers moving in from the east. Those of the Santees, another Sioux tribe, remained behind. They were gradually crowded out by settlers buying up their land. The Indians were forced to depend more and more upon the government for food they could no longer hunt or gather. Crooked traders let the Santees run up false debts, more than they could ever repay at the trading posts. When government rations for the Indians came in, the traders and Indian Agents, who were hired to support the Indians, sold the rations to settlers for what the Indians supposedly owed them and pocketed the money, leaving the Indians hungry.

"This loss of land and food made the warriors restless. They were young men who had never fought but were the sons and grandsons of men who had. They demanded change. A year ago, in 1862, Little Crow became their leader. He was a fiery man with great energy and determination. His vision was to take over the entire state of Minnesota, driving out all the white men. The elders saw how useless his dream was. There were too many people, too many large towns and too many soldiers. Still, they wanted a leader who would stand up for their people and fight if necessary.

"The treaty the Santees signed with the American government said they would be given food in exchange for sharing the land with the settlers. The food came but it was held in the storage room by the Indian agent who refused to give any to the Santees. Little Crow and a group of warriors met with him, explaining how their old people and children were sick and starving. The men could not hunt on their traditional lands and the women could not gather their herbs and medicines because the settlers lived there. Their hide clothing became tattered and worn, with no way to replace them. Little Crow warned if the warriors were not given food, they would take it. The agent, Thomas Galbraith, was a hard, cruel man with no respect for the Indian people. He was often drunk, making deals with the crooked traders. Surprised at this demand from Indians who were usually quiet and peaceful, Galbraith turned to one of these traders, Andrew Myrick and asked what he should do.

Myrick sneered, "If they are hungry, let them eat grass."

The next day at dawn, a late summer day in August, Little Crow's warriors attacked the warehouses of Lower Agency. They took the supplies from the storage room. In their anger and despair, they killed many settlers. Myrick's body was later found with his mouth stuffed with grass.

"Other warriors attacked the Upper Agency about twenty miles away on the Minnesota River. Two hundred settlers were killed the first day and over two hundred women and children captured. Three hundred others fled to Ft. Ridgely. It was a grouping of buildings rather than a real fort. The government sent more soldiers from Ft. Snelling. Their cannons and barricades held off Little Crow and his four hundred warriors."

Alorah nodded, adding what she knew, "They say Little Crow gathered eight hundred men and invaded New Ulm which had been attacked three days earlier by a hundred of his warriors. The town had only three days to organize two hundred and fifty fighting men under Judge Charles E. Flandrau. Sixty settlers were wounded, twenty-six died. But the town held."

B.A.'s lip curled, "The old elder said there were only a few hundred warriors in that battle; the warriors spread out to fight other places. The government always exaggerates to justify their position."

Alorah's chin came up, "Our Governor Ramsey asked Henry Sibley, a militia captain to develop a state-wide military movement to put down the uprising. Even with most men off fighting the Civil War he gathered 1400 soldiers and eventually routed Little Crow in September."

Alorah turned the Dutch oven on the bed of hot coals to ensure the bread baked evenly. "We left Fort Ridgley soon after with a train of settlers running west, afraid of more battles. But we soon left them and drove north. Salvia's brother from Fort Carlton said the Indians were friendlier in Rupert's Land, this territory."

B.A. took up the story. "The old elder said the American Army set up a prison camp for the warrior's women and families on the banks of the Minnesota River, just below Fort Snelling. The military wanted to hold the women hostage at least a day's journey from the men to make sure the warriors behaved themselves. The army was afraid the women might strike back and somehow make their men fight again.

"Four hundred Santees were brought to trial; three hundred and three sentenced to hang. Little Crow and many of the leaders escaped to Devil's Lake in the Dakotas. A Bishop Whipple had worked with the Santees for four years. He knew about the cheating, thieving agents and traders so he travelled to Washington to plead with President Abraham Lincoln on behalf of the Santee. Lincoln studied the trial for many days then reduced the number to thirty-eight warriors, those most involved.

The men marching to Mankato and the women dragging their children to Fort Snelling had to pass through many small Minnesota town where the townspeople lined up to form a gauntlet of hate. Many of the Santee women were badly hurt from these attacks. One of the settlers snatched a baby from its mother and smashed its head against a rock. 1600 elders, women and children, in tepees, were forced to make this place their home for one year. After that, many fled north to this country. When we met them, they were thin, ragged, exhausted and hungry. Mac and I gave their elder an antelope we had just killed." His eyes sparked for a moment, "At least it kept the warriors from killing us and stealing our horses."

He drew a deep breath, returning to his story and the point he wanted to make. "Thirty eight warriors were hanged on a large gallows at Mankato by the government of Abraham Lincoln, on the day after Christmas in 1862. He declared it the largest mass execution in North American History. The warriors' families, parents, wives and children were forced to watch."

Alorah gasped, covering her mouth in silent horror at the graven images etched upon her mind.

B.A. held her eyes in the twilight. "It was a warning to all warriors. If they gave the US government any trouble fighting the White Man's lies, they would die. What better way to control a people than to kill those who would defend them."

She shook her head, nauseous with shock, "I never knew why they attacked. None of us knew they were starving. They were so quiet, almost shy whenever we saw them around the fort. Maybe they were ashamed because they had to beg for food."

B.A. rubbed his hands together, studying his palms. "Mankato, where the Minnesota and Mississippi rivers meet, is where the ancestors of the Dakota Sioux first rose up from Ina, their mother the Earth. Mankato marked the sacred place where human life was created. Death of the hanged Santee destroyed the harmony of that area."

He watched her face in the flickering firelight. Would she understand? "The Sioux elder we talked with had a vision. He said eventually their women would dance at Mankato, holding forgiveness ceremonies there each year in remembrance. On this sacred land, scarred by war, they would seek to restore the harmony, restore balance to the land and reconcile its history of pain. They would dance to bring peace to the people who died there. They would dance to bring peace amongst themselves and the white people. They would dance to make peace with Ina, the Earth Mother, whose act of creation at this place had been abused and defiled by the terrible things committed upon it."

B.A.'s eyes narrowed in frustration, "The White Man has learned much about fighting from our warriors, but he knows nothing about our elders' lessons for making peace."

Alorah's hands clasped the beautiful stone around her neck, her eyes slowly filling with tears, "Such a beautiful way to deal with all that hate and anger. If only we could all forgive so graciously. Your elders must be very wise. Truly it is a woman's lot to forgive. And maybe your women have the right of it, teaching their men the same. Most men don't seem to realize this on their own."

Her hands twisted in her lap as she contemplated the darkness surrounding her. "I have learned so much from you today. You taught me about fear and how to face it; about living joyfully in the moment because it's all we have anyway. And now you teach me a powerful lesson about forgiving. It is true. We can never live joyfully in the moment if we cling to our fear, our anger or revenge. I never knew the Santee's pain, never saw them starving while we had plenty to eat, some of it probably their rations! I never got past my position, my anger and my need for revenge against them."

Alorah sighed, watching her warm breath drift into the cool moistness of the night. "More than anything else, you have restored my faith in a woman's position. She is truly needed in this world. Forgiveness is 'for' 'giving' really." Her lips twisted, "We women are good at giving. We're raised to it from the cradle. And you are right. It is a form of love from the offended, surrendering to a higher cause, for peace, beyond the wars and petty anger. Maybe this anger is rooted in our fear of the unknown. When we know, when we understand each other, then it is easier to forgive. Even my Jewish people need lessons about forgiveness."

She reached out to touch his arm, "I shall not forget." She chuckled, "And I will forgive you. To do less is too petty after your story." Her fingers slid gently over the stone, her forehead creased in thought for a long time. He sat beside her patiently waiting for her continue.

Finally she explained. "I feel like this forgiveness is changing me inside, like something restored somehow. The stone comforts me and eases my feelings, like a sigh released; maybe it does bring inner harmony because it is from this land that we all must live upon, together"

He nodded abruptly, "Together." And he smiled.

26.

BATOCHE

The next morning, they slowly rode down a steeply inclined river crossing on the south branch of the South Saskatchewan River and into the town of Batoche. It was about fifteen miles from the forks where the South Saskatchewan River joined the North Saskatchewan before wending eastward and emptying into Lake Winnipeg. Batoche consisted of wooden framed houses, painted in brilliant hues and assorted logs cabins, dark stained and mud daubed for insulation. The town was named after a Mr. Batoche. B.A. pointed out his house, a pale green dwelling with many windows, perched atop a rise overlooking the river. A small cluster of buildings near the river crossing: a blacksmith shop, livery stable, post office and hotel, made up the local business centre. Some of the owners came out when they heard the wagon. The travellers, however, merely waved and drove on.

They camped for dinner upon a terrace just above the gliding river, overhung with poplar and a few clusters of sweet smelling pines. Across the river, about two hundred yards away, a rough-hewn sign on a cabin proudly announced 'Cameron's Store'. Around it sprawled more log cabins with their inevitable outhouses or toilets, built at various levels on the rolling bluffs above the river. Behind many houses, crooked fences lazed at various angles, enclosing grazing cattle and horses. Somewhere, a rooster crowed and a dog barked.

When B.A. stuck his thumb and forefinger in his mouth and whistled several times, a man came out of the store and waved. He and another man soon climbed into a small flat-bottomed ferry tied to a rope cable stretching across the river. Their industrious hand-over-hand pulling on the rope cable brought their boat quickly across. The cable, attached to the ferry through steel slats prevented the boat from slipping downstream in the fast current. The broad raft, with railings on either side, had hinged inclines at both ends for wagons to drive on one side and disembark from the other. The raftsman, a stocky Metis in his thirties, sported a heavy red mustache though his hair grew long and black. His broad face lit with delight when he spied Broken Arrow.

"Broken Arrow! Tan'si! You back for anodder dip? Ehe?" His smooth cheeks dented into mischievous dimples. His cheerful garb consisted of a scarlet fichu tied over a neat white shirt, a brightly beaded golden vest and well pressed suit coat. Atop his shining boots, in brilliant silken splendour, he wore lavender trousers. A wide brimmed black hat sporting a perky peacock feather topped his eye-stopping outfit.

The shorter man, just as swarthy but rounder, displaying a slightly tattered mustache, had features similar enough but not as attractive, to be a close relative. Like an opposing force, he wore a dull grey shirt tucked into brown corduroys pants and a navy wool jacket, none of which had rubbed against an iron or water for some time. His rounded crown hat, drooping in odd ripples and dips, merely sported a bedraggled green ribbon. With a toothy grin beneath his heavy black mustache, he slapped Broken Arrow on the back, "You ready to teach us some more of dem swimming lessons. Oui? Yes?" He chuckled, his round face a wreath of open delight.

Broken Arrow shook his head in laughing disgust. These Cameron brothers never let him forget four years ago when he was training Brownfoot. He'd made the mistake of turning his back on the young horse while visiting with the two ferrymen as they pulled the raft across. The spooked yearling had suddenly leapt over the raft's railing. With the reins wrapping his wrist, Broken Arrow immediately flew backwards, head first into the freezing water. He'd surfaced and swam for shore, still clinging to the reins and fighting to stay away from the terrified colt's flailing hooves. The two brothers had fallen to their knees with laughter, totally useless.

"Ah Zamari!" he addressed the shorter brother, "Anytime you want a bath, I'll take you in." B.A. grinned at the rumpled Metis while his resplendent brother hooted, "Dat's a good idea. Oui?" He turned to Mac and the girls, "Ma'am'selles and Monsieur, may I introduce my brodder, Zamari Cameron et moi, me, I am Isidore. I caution you, don' stan' too close to my brodder. He live by de wadder but he don' go in!" He slapped his leg and guffawed at his own joke.

The red-faced Zamari brushed a negligent hand over greasy trousers and bowed elegantly, "Bonjour, ma petites. I am not'ing but a poor bachelor man, moi. Dis ugly person, my brodder, ignore him. He is married and therefore ver' stupid. He forget his manners around pretty girls. You wish to come aboard. Ehe?"

Mac introduced the girls and himself. Then he escorted them to the edge of the river, away from harm. With Zamari's help, he cautiously drove the oxen and wagon onto the raft. Zamari thrust blocks of wood beside two wheels to hold the wagon in place.

Isidore pulled B.A. aside. "What's dis? You gonna marry one of dese ladies. Eh? De dark one, she too pretty for your ugly mug! She need a good looking man to make 'er 'appy." He adjusted his hat to a cocky angle.

B.A. slanted him a wry look. "Forget it Isidore. You already have three wives who hate you. Why make another one miserable?"

The handsome Metis howled with laughter, "My ladies, dey fight over who gets to climb under my buffalo robes. Ah l'amour. C'est ci bon! Who can fight it? Moi? I am just too weak." He kissed his fingers and blew the kiss across the river where two slender women in long skirts and bright shawls watched from the veranda of the store. Another slim woman soon joined them.

Broken Arrow regarded the women, his eyes crinkling, "Isidore, if you don't fight, soon you'll be too tired to dip your oar."

"Nevare!" vowed the irrepressible ferryman, "I am evare ready!"

The Cree slapped his back and the two led the horses on behind the wagon. Zamari unhooked the rope which anchored the scow and cranked up the raft's back approach. The oxen bawled, shifting their feet restlessly when the raft swung into the current. Alorah and Salvia hung onto their bonnets and the railing. Lifting excited faces to the wind, they enjoyed the free floating rhythm of a rocking boat in the dizzying swift current. Brownfoot snorted and stamped a foot, sidling close to the older Blackfoot who dropped his head in sleepy acceptance. With Zamari pulling on the rope cable, Isidore too busy chatting to help, the scow floated easily towards the opposite side. The loose cable snaked through the water before whistling out with a taunt snap as the cable took on the full weight of the load. The river ran higher than normal and even B.A. thought they were coming onto the landing too fast. Suddenly the raft ran aground, bounced over boulders and slammed headlong into the wooden wharf. The girls screamed and grabbed the railing to keep from flying overboard. The wagon rocked precariously, sliding sideways. Oxen bawled in fright, struggling to maintain their footing on the slanting raft. Brownfoot screamed and reared, his eyes wild and white. Broken Arrow hung on to his mane, talking softly to him until the paint quieted, muscles shivering under his hide.

Isidore rearranged his skewed hat and pulled himself off his knees. "Zounds Zamari! As always you are too rough! Slow down! Keep dem eyeballs in your head, not on de ladies and mind your speed, eh! Nex' time, you smash our boat!!"

"And what of you!" His brother snarled, "Too busy talking to help. As usual! You think the work gets done all by itself?!" The hard-working Zamari looped a heavy rope around the post to anchor the scow and slowly cranked the exit ramp down. He took off his hat and whacked his lazy brother with it. His sibling whacked him back with a glove and both cursed each other in rapid fire French.

Mac drove the wagon off the ramp while the oxen bawled in gratitude when their broad hooves hit solid ground. The women shakily followed, lifting their skirts to step off the raft onto the wooden slats winding to the store above them. The young Metis women walked down to meet them, smiling and shaking hands in welcome. All five disappeared into the store's shadowy interior, talking animatedly.

Isidore shook his as he looked up at Mac, "I 'ope you have lots of money my frien'. Dos women, dey sure can spend it."

Mac locked the brake and jumped off the wagon, taking the reins of his horses from the stocky Metis. "They're not our problem Isidore. We're just a couple of dusty travellers who found them stuck in a mud hole a few days ago. We offered to escort them to Fort Carleton. One has a brother there." He lifted speculative eyes to the doorway. One day he might come back and court the fair Salvia. But he wanted to see Fort Edmonton first.

Isidore lit a pipe, his merry eyes studying Broken Arrow's stillness as he watched the women leave. The Cree noted the man's mischievous perusal and quickly turned away. Women had no place in his life. Not yet. And he wasn't in the mood to joke about it.

27.

FORT CARLTON

Just before sunset, the group stopped for one final camp before reaching the fort. They chose Duck Lake, a body of water about seven miles long in a willow-fringed hollow backed by bluffs of birch and poplar. The men picketed the oxen and horses in the high, abundant grass while the girls built a fire and prepared a tasty meal of boiled potatoes and fried ham. They feasted that night on fresh bannock and thick butter washed down with cups of hot tea laden with heavy cream and sugar, all purchased from Isidore's wives.

That evening, Broken Arrow showed them how to rub juniper berries on their skin. The oil from the crushed berries kept the hordes of mosquitoes from biting. As they savoured their final cups of tea in peace, the women marvelled at Isidore's family. "Is that common amongst the Cree" Salvia inquired, "to have more than one wife?"

B.A. nodded, "Often the wives are sisters, like Isidore's. If one loses her husband, she has a hard time on her own, especially if she has children. So she marries into her sister's family for protection and survival." He stared into the fire then grinned. "If the man isn't good to her, she can move on and try another man. It is her choice. An unhappy wife can also return to her parents. If her husband wants her back, he must again pay the bride price to her father. Some men have paid it several times to bring their women home. To us, a joining should be joyful and honourable. If a man abuses his wife, her entire family might tell him to pack his gear and budge." He chuckled, a flash of strong white teeth in his tanned face, "If he's smart, he'll move quickly before the women make sure he does. I've seen sisters use sticks and tomahawks to assist his leaving!"

Mac sipped his tea. "The Celts had broad-minded views about marriage too. Though it was generally the custom to have only one wife, a man could have a chief wife and a second wife. If a couple did not suit each other, they could get a divorce without difficulty. Some couples stayed married for just one year."

Alorah nodded, "Jewish men could divorce their wives if they did not give them a son." She smiled in mischief, "That's why I'm in no hurry to marry. I want to be appreciated for being more than a brood mare!"

B.A.'s eyes narrowed, "At Fort Carleton you will see what happens to our women and children with no husband or father. Many are cast aside, scorned as 'Country wives' and 'Turned off' or left behind when their white husbands bring their white wives across the ocean. Many men just disappear and never return. If the women have no one to marry, they are forced to sell themselves to any man who offers a few pennies."

Alorah moaned, covering her mouth in dismay. Salvia hugged her in comfort, "You know you will always have a home with us."

Broken Arrow slanted a sidelong glance at the young blonde woman. "Isidore told me there is a large Sioux encampment around Fort Carleton, runaways from the Minnesota Massacre. Are you ready to face them in peace?"

Salvia paled, her face shifting in fear and anger in the firelight. Turning to Alorah who watched her carefully, she remembered what her friend had told her about the plight of the Santee . . . and forgiveness. Was she ready? She didn't think so. Not yet, not with the death of her father still raw in her heart. She shook her head silently and stared into her cup, vowing to avoid the Sioux as much as possible. Surely Fort Carleton wasn't that small.

Suddenly Broken Arrow rose to his feet, leapt atop Brownfoot and rode into the night. The others watched him in confusion. The women looked at Mac who shrugged and returned to his tea. The tall Cree never returned before they sought their beds. When they arose in the morning, the girls from the wagon and Mac from beneath it, B.A. was untying the carcass of a young buck from one of the trees. From the blood below it, he had obviously killed it the previous night, gutting it before hanging it up. Wordlessly, he tied it, skin intact, behind his saddle, offering no one so much as a slice for their morning meal.

The two young women went about their chores, making coffee, setting out the bannock and frying up the final pieces of ham. To this they added fresh boiled eggs from the Cameron store. Mac had offered to pay for some of the food but they'd refused saying the men's protection was payment enough. Alorah continued casting curious glances at Broken Arrow but he ignored her completely.

Mac watched in frustration, not understanding his friend's withdrawal but too polite to bring it up before the women. He did what he could to help them break camp while Broken Arrow busied himself with packing the horses. It was a sombre group that rode out, everyone affected by Broken Arrow's continued silence.

Heavy clouds rolled in, grey and sullen as the people beneath it. Thunder rumbled and ineffective lightening flickered around them. A deluge of cold rain dumped its weary load upon their heads. Mac pulled out a slicker while the women moved back beneath the covering of their wagon. Only Broken Arrow seemed oblivious to the rain pouring over his head. His buckskin shirt and leggings easily repelled the water, which dripped off their fringes. If he was uncomfortable or cold, he gave no indication, looking straight ahead and riding easily on his beaded saddle.

Damned stoic, Mac raged inwardly. What the Sam Hill was the matter with the man? He hadn't wanted to go to Fort Carlton, but eventually agreed. Now he acted like he wanted nothing to do with the lot of them, totally withdrawing from them. Was he offended by

Salvia's hatred of the Sioux? Mac sat up, studying the Cree. Or did it go deeper than that? When B.A. became this quiet, something bothered him. And he would think it through without saying a word until he was damned good and ready. Mac sighed in disgust, tamping down his frustration.

When they crested a hill, the winding road fell away beneath them to Fort Carlton. The town rested on a flat, open space near the south side of the North Saskatchewan. Across the river, banks rose onto gently rounded hills, lush meadows and heavy forests of spruce, pine and poplar. In the marshlands, tamarack trees rose just as tall and green, the swamp evergreen. As the group rattled down the steep road, the oxen were forced into a clumsy trot, pushed by the heavy wagon behind them. Salvia occasionally stood on the brake stick to slow the wagon down. To the west, women and children worked in nearby fields and a huge garden plot. Many stopped their labours to wave to the newcomers. Salvia and Alorah excitedly returned their welcome, busily identifying crops of barley, oats, potatoes, peas, beans, carrots, parsnips, radishes, lettuce, cucumbers and cabbage. Maple trees nearby spouted wooden funnels tapping their sugar. Wagons with carcasses of deer, moose and elk entered the fort ahead of the group. Still other people fished peacefully along the rivers, some checking their nets and filleting great boxes of jackfish, perch, pickerel and sturgeon. Women and men alike hung slabs of the various coloured fish on big racks to smoke and dry. This fort ate well indeed!

Mac studied the enclosure, noting its design resembled the ancient fortresses and Roman villas built in Britain from AD. 43 to 410. It was a quadrangle area defended by wooden instead of the Roman stone walls. Headquarters for the executive and administrative staffs occupied the inner buildings. Barracks nearby housed the labourers while the inner centre revealed an open courtyard, just like the ancient Roman villas. At the corners and gates, high watchtowers held lookouts for the enemy. Mac suppresses a chuckle, for the 'enemy' was permanently camped outside the walls in clusters of brightly painted tipis. From B.A., he'd learned earlier how the local Cree, Assiniboine and Sioux lived together quite peacefully with the white men.

Fort Carleton was a bustling trade centre, strategically situated near the forks of the North and South Saskatchewan. Freighters in Red River carts and wagons went in every direction from the fort. Birch bark canoes and the bigger flat bottomed York boats with their gigantic sails floated up and down the river. Some rested at the docks while workers swarmed about them, loading or unloading their cargoes. In the spring, incoming furs of muskrat, black bear, beavers, along with buffalo robes were stacked into screw and leaver fur presses to flatten them into compact bails for easier shipping eastward and across the ocean. In the fall, the returning York boat cargo of blankets, beads, ribbon, knives, pots, pans, kettles, gunpowder and pemmican were repacked for northern and western trading posts. Warehouses stacked to the roof with the ninety-pound pemmican bundles gradually emptied, used by the hungry fort employees, canoers, voyageurs, sailors and freighters.

Mac knew from his geography that the two great rivers of the Saskatchewan originated in the Rocky Mountains. The South branch moved through the heartland of the Blackfoot, connecting with waterways from the American Frontier. The North Saskatchewan flowed past Fort Edmonton parklands, connecting to the North's Athabasca River with its towns at the Athabasca River Landing and north to Fort Chipewyan before emptying into the massive three hundred mile long, Lake Athabasca. From there, the voyageurs portaged west onto the Peace River and Jasper House in the Rockies. North of Fort Carleton, people brought their furs by canoes and dog sled from Ile-a-la-Crosse, a French name for Lake of the Cross. To the east, the joined Saskatchewan Rivers linked Hudson Bay trading posts of Cumberland House, Moose Lac and Grand Rapids on the north end of Lake Winnipeg then on to Norway House and the great Churchill River system. From the south, Red River Carts brought goods from Fort Qu'Appelle and Fort Garry south of Lake Winnipeg.

When they rode into the fort and introduced themselves, Chief Factor Pruden immediately dispatched a youth to find Salvia's brother, Daniel, who built York boats down at the wharf. In no time at all, a tall young man with broad shoulders and a heavily muscled frame pounded into the fort. When he drew close, he snatched off his hat revealing identical blond curls to his sister's.

She cried out, running into his arms. He lifted her high, swinging her around in delight, hugging her close. Their chattering voices echoed back in snatches to the others:

"How did you get . . . ?"

"We came . . . ."

"Why didn't you write . . . ?"

"Didn't you get my letter?"

He shook his head, bits of sawdust flying everywhere. The young man looked excitedly about him. "Where's father? Is he . . . . !"

Salvia explained in soft tones, her eyes welling with tears. Her brother pulled her close once again, lost in his own silent grief. The wind wrapped them in gentle isolation from the bustling activity around them.

Wiping her eyes, Salvia took his hand and pulled him to meet Alorah who had stood back, politely waiting. Neither of the watching men missed the young man's immediate stillness and admiring smile when introduced to the exotic Alorah. B.A.'s eyes narrowed, his face intense as he studied the brawny blonde man. After a few minutes, the Cree turned his back and untied the still packed Blackfoot from a hitching post. He leapt upon Brownfoot once again, and waited, rigid and still. A muscle worked in his jaw.

Salvia introduced Mac and B.A. to her brother. The Cree took his hand and nodded, remaining silent. Mac found Daniel's handshake strong and effusive; his gratitude for his sister's protection, open and honest. Mac liked the man's sincerity and his warm affection towards Salvia whom he kept closely tucked under his arm. Daniel smiled down at her, "Wait 'til you see the grand home I have built.

There is room for us all." His exuberant joy encompassed Alorah as well, "And I am so sick of my own poor cooking!"

Alorah turned to Broken Arrow and held out her hand. He leaned down and clasped it briefly. She shielded her anxious eyes from the sun, trying to gauge his thoughts. "Thank you for escorting us here, Broken Arrow and Mac." She turned to acknowledge the Irishman, and then spun back. "Will I see you again before you leave?"

Broken Arrow looked up and away, his eyes pensive and distant. With a silent shake of his head he bent towards her. "Maybe in a few months, maybe next year."

He watched her clasp the necklace he had given her. Suddenly his mouth quirked and his eyes sparked, his soft words for her ears only, "Don't forget to scream."

Her lips tilted up, "I promise. And I won't forget." She placed her hand on his leggings for a brief moment before he turned his horses away and rode out of the compound without looking back. Unmoving, Alorah watched him go, her face thoughtful and sad.

With a wave to Salvia who called a cheerful "Thank you again!!" to his "I'll see you later!" Mac followed the Cree.

28.

OTANESHA

Broken Arrow rode directly for the encampment of tipis outside Fort Carleton. Some people called to him but he merely nodded, too intent upon his mission. He pulled up beside a tipi painted dark blue on the bottom, shading into turquoise at the top. As he dismounted a wiry, bearded man stumbled out of the tipi, tucking in a wrinkled shirt and doing up his belt. Without a glance at B.A., he picked up an axe lying nearby and wended his way towards a group of men cutting firewood for the fort. When the dishevelled worker shuffled by Mac, he caught a whiff of rank sweat and sour whiskey mingled with the fresh aroma of cut spruce.

Broken Arrow dismounted and untied the deer carcass from his saddle. As he hoisted it to his shoulder, someone called to him from the interior of the tipi. He answered in Cree, abrupt and short. Before he reached the opening, an obese native woman stumbled out, barefoot and rumpled. She caught herself from headlong flight by clinging to the buffalo skin frame. The entire tipi shuddered with the force of her movement. When she raised her head, Mac sucked in his breath. A huge bruise covered the entire left side of her face. Her eye, what could be seen of it, was blood red and swollen to twice its size. Grey hair hung in filthy strings from her head, missing chunks revealing patches of gleaming scalp. She growled something as Broken Arrow placed the deer at her feet.

When he lifted his head, her broad face softened in the warm sunlight. For a brief moment, Mac saw in her tanned features the tattered remnants of a once mystical beauty. It disappeared when her battered lips moved into a twisted smile, revealing dark gaps between tobacco-stained teeth. A filthy, trembling hand reached out to touch Broken Arrow's smooth shoulder. Tears formed in her eyes and slid down the deep lines in her cheeks as she continued to speak to him. He listened unmoving; his head down, shoulders slumped. Finally, he raised his head and gently cradled her battered face. When he spoke in Cree, she laughed then coughed. And coughed some more, until spasms doubled her over, forcing her to lean on her knees, thick fingers spreading across her shabby, badly stained buckskin dress. She spat towards the side of her tipi. Mac saw crimson spittle glistening in the sunshine. Broken Arrow continued talking, quietly pleading but she shook her head. She gave him a quick hug then pushed him away. Grabbing the deer, she dragged it to her tipi. Without looking back, she bent and entered, disappearing into the shadows with her bloody cache.

Broken Arrow turned away. When he saw Mac, he froze, red and white blotches appearing on his cheeks. Then his face closed down. He stalked past Mac in tight-lipped silence and bounded aboard Brownfoot. Spinning his horses, he wound his way through the other tipis. He glanced back only once, his broad face lined with grief.

Mac trotted up beside him. "Well and now, you obviously know that squaw."

B.A. rounded on him, his face fierce. "*Iskwew!* The word is *Iskwew*, White Man! And it means 'woman'! Nothing more!" His eyes were black with pain.

Mac apologized immediately, "I'm sorry. I did not mean to offend you or her."

They rode together, Broken Arrow visibly fighting to control his tears. He swiped angrily at them and blinked rapidly, sniffing loudly.

Mac left him alone. The intensity of his friend's pain radiated from him in waves.

Eventually, B.A. pinched his nostrils, rubbed his mouth, drew a harsh breath and released it in a long sigh. "She is my auntie, my father's youngest sister, Otanesha. I remember her when she was with our band. She was so slim and pretty, with thick, shining hair well past her waist. I used to stare at her, thinking she was the most beautiful woman I had ever seen. She and her husband, Blue Owl, were good people, kind and generous. They loved to tease and joke with everyone. Their son, Asiniy was my cousin and best friend. One day, when he and I were about sixteen summers, I challenged him to a race across the prairie. His mare fell in a gopher hole and tossed Asiniy over her head. He landed badly." Broken Arrow drew a long shaky breath, "It broke his neck. He died in my arms. I had to slit his horse's throat; her left leg and shoulder were totally shattered."

B.A. swiped at his eyes again. "Otanesha and Blue Owl never got over it. Asiniy was their only child. When Tall Man moved his band to Portage La Prairie, they stayed behind in Fort Carlton. And they started to drink."

Mac winced, rubbing his neck.

The tall Cree swallowed, releasing a ragged breath. "When I was back through here four years ago, I learned Blue Owl had died several years before. Otanesha said he drowned in his own whiskey vomit. Now she gets her whiskey the only way she knows how."

Mac shook his head and sighed. "What does Asiniy mean?"

"Stone"

Their rock. Mac breathed deep, releasing it slowly, "And Otanesha?"

B.A. sniffed loudly and swallowed. "Tall Man gave her that name when she was a tiny baby. It is what you call a 'nickname', a loving form of *Nitanis*, my daughter."

Must have broken the old man's heart to see her like this, Mac mused.

Broken Arrow read his thoughts, "Tall Man doesn't know. He's never been back this way. I told him Blue Owl drowned and Otanesha still worked at the fort, that she was doing well." His voice cracked.

"You saw the blood." Mac gently reminded him, "She's dying."

Broken Arrow turned to him, his eyes welling once again. "She died when I told her about Asiniy." He turned his head away, undone by his pain.

Guilt. Twas a terrible thing, Mac knew. He could tell the man it wasn't his fault the boy died but he'd never believe it. "Why doesn't she go home to Tall Man's band?"

The grieving Cree shook his head, "I plead with her to do so every time I see her but she refuses. She is too ashamed. She says she will never show her face amongst her family again."

"What did you say to her to make her laugh?"

Broken Arrow closed his eyes, his mouth twisting downward, "I told her I remembered when she was much uglier." He drew a ragged breath, tears seeping from beneath crumpled eyelids.

Mac cringed, absorbing his friend's anguish, imagining how he'd feel if she was his aunt. He studied B.A, thinking deeply. "You didn't want to see her again did ye? No' like that. Who would? That's why ye didn't want to come to Fort Carlton." He pieced it together, "Yet ye brought her a deer."

"She is clan!" Broken Arrow snapped.

And that, Mac concluded, said it all.

29.

And So She Waits . . . .

The next night, a day's ride out of Fort Carleton, the two men sat quietly drinking their tea around their campfire. Broken Arrow picked up a small piece of mud and rolled it in his fingers.

"Do you know why the White Man has prostitutes?"

Mac's stomach was full, his body tired and relaxed from the day's ride. His eyebrow lifted, "'Tis the oldest profession in the world."

Broken Arrow shook his head, his mood still dark and brooding. "It is because of his fear and his pride."

That gained Mac's attention. "Fear? Hell, tis more like lust!"

Broken held to his thoughts, "It's his fear of Mud Woman and his pride in himself. I will tell you what Mitsue taught me." He leaned back using his saddle as a backrest.

"Instead of accepting Mud Woman's gift of coupling and creating new life, the White man scorns it and uses women to spend his seed. Black Robes call the act dirty, an evil temptation and a sin. In his pride, the Black Robe blames woman for seducing him away from his goal of being celibate, an independent man, an island of his own isolation and perfection. He thinks to create a better world without women's interference so he curses all women, out of his own fear of sinning and possible failure. He takes all his worst qualities and dumps them on women, judging, condemning and blaming them for all the wrongs and failures in life. His attitude and hatred convinces white men to blame women for all that is wrong in their lives too. With the blessing of the Black Robes, the White Man can hit a woman, hurt her, blame her, call her whore and feel justified he is living a good live, securely in control.

"Our elders say we have both a male and female side. When a man and woman couple, she balances him and he balances her. It is a meditative prayer parallel to Earth Mother joining with the Creator. A woman, like Mud Woman, the spirit of feminine earth energy, is the pathway to this sacred joining. It is our responsibility, as a person to develop both our male and female sides equally. Mud Woman still waits for the White Man to accept the female side of himself, the deepest, swampiest part, the half that knows compassion, the half ruthless as the coldest winter wind and enduring as the inevitable spring. She waits for the part of him which knows how to nurture the smallest seed and create the largest tree. When he finds this part of himself, he becomes a creator, a spirit of creativity, as magical and as wonderful as she. What the White Man cannot see, is he has lost half of his spirit in his pride and his control of woman and what she represents. When his pride rules, he becomes not a creator, but a destroyer, out of cycle, out of balance, out of harmony with himself and all creation. His pride truly becomes a sin because he denies all that he is. If a man denies his own body, his inner feminine truth, then his dark side will rule him. Instead of loving, he learns to hate."

The folds around Broken Arrow's eyes deepened into sorrow, "That is why he calls for his squaws and his prostitutes. He holds no reverence, no honour for the energy cycle that would flow through him and all women. He wants only the selfish easing of his body. He uses women like he uses Mud Woman, the feminine spirit of this Earth, taking everything she has to offer for his personal gain and greed."

B.A. studied the ball of mud in his fingers, watching it coat them. "The White Man will never understand Mud Woman. Not until he realizes he is Mud Woman too, part of her Earthly creation. In our clans, when a man used his sexual powers in a bad way, our healers covered him in mud and prayed over him. They prayed his sexual wisdom from the Earth would return and he would again use his body in honourable ways. They asked Mud Woman to heal him and return him to his honourable self." Broken Arrow gently patted the ball into the ground.

"In the days which are coming, Mitsue said the priests, the Black Robes, will tell mankind what is good and what it evil; what to think; what to pray; what to believe. She warned me to never trust the Black Robes with my soul. They have an unbalanced religion which denies woman, the female half of all creation. The Black Robes, like White Men, have lost half of themselves and do not know Mud Woman still waits for them, patiently keeping their souls in trust, until they come back to her and ask for them."

For a while, only the fire's crackling logs filled the quiet night air.

"You know," Mac rubbed a bristly cheek, "The druids believed the human body was made of clay: mud and water. They believed man is a Shepard of clay, a representative of an unknown world which wanted him to express it in new forms through what he did with his life. Like your idea of man's creation I guess. They believed we are all ancient brothers and sisters made from one clay. Sort of like your Mud Woman. I remember reading how churches in England built as late as the 1500's still had carvings of heads with hair made of green leaves, twigs and grass. Plato, one of our philosophers believed man and woman are merely halves of humanity, each requiring the qualities of the other in order to reach the highest personal development—like your balancing idea.

"And . . . Pythagoras, one of our great mathematicians in the sixth century, believed the Earth was a living, intelligent being. He also believed in the kinship of all things and a recycling of the life force. An ancient Greek orator or spokesman called Cicero once proclaimed, "The world is an intelligent being and indeed, also a wise being." Mac shook his head, "Yet our bible, even the Roman Catholic religion which came after these great men, never mentions the Earth

Mother and her teachings. Women are viewed as holy and chaste like the blue and white Virgin Mary or crude and sluttish like the black and red Mary Magdalene. The bible says women come from the rib of man, his chattel to do with as he chooses. Today, women are still controlled and yes, abused sometimes by their men."

"Why did your people allow it?" Broken Arrow was confused and angry with it. "Why did they cut woman off from the very purpose she is born to? Warrior woman, healer, leader, wise woman and loving mother—she is the female power of wisdom and spiritual vision, sensitive to the vibrations, cycles and heartbeat of the Great Mother and through her, the Creator! The Black Robes with their vows of celibacy cut themselves off from the very half that offers true spiritual enlightenment, our female side. She is the half connecting us to our spirit, our soul and therefore, to Earth Mother and the Creator. Out of his fear and pride, the White Man has developed only his masculine side, cutting out the feminine until he is so unbalanced; he creates unbalance in the world around him."

Mac snorted, "Cut them off? Hell man, we burned women at the stake as witches, practitioners of evil, spells and destruction. We hunted them down like animals, judged them, sentenced them and killed them, by the thousands across Britain and Europe, less than four hundred years ago. And still today, a woman is often viewed by men as something less than human, a chattel to be argued over like two dogs over a bone."

B.A. sighed, "Your missionaries claim to have divine reason for how they treat women, but so far, all I see is a refusal to accept responsibility or guilt for their cruel actions. They create an explanation in their religion, but is it truly the Creator's? The higher power my people experience daily? Yet we are judged as heathens, pagans."

"Pagan simply means country people—no' such a bad thing." Mac grinned at his companion then became serious and thoughtful once again. "I think I would like to meet your Mud Woman one day."

Broken Arrow went still, "When you are ready, she will come. Not before, Irish Man."

30.

THE BLACK KNIGHT

Mac whipped through the door of the Battleford trading post and stomped across the courtyard. From astride Brownfoot, B.A. watched him come, studying his rigid shoulders and stiff stride. Wild red hair stood out in every direction. Mac, his face scrunched with fury, looked ready to explode.

"That mulichen, mash-faced badach!" Mac slammed his hat against a nearby post sending up a cloud of dust that would have gagged him, had he noticed. "That trading post bastard, Morton, says Spense is his and I have to give him back. Claims he was stolen a month ago. Now he's back, he's Morton's again. Who the hell does he think he is! Tis my horse. I found 'im and I own 'im! Devil take the surly, horse thievin' shyster. Why . . . !" he stopped in mid-sentence as B.A.'s intent face moved into a small smile.

Mac spun away, his face slowly turning red. After a few moments of calming silence and deep breaths, he turned back to his waiting friend. "Aye . . . you're right. And who is the biggest thief of them all? I should have known sooner or later I'd pay for me sins. Father O'Reilly would be laughin' his head off about now. He always said I would come to no good and here I am, a thievin' pot callin' the kettle blacker than me."

B.A. frowned, "You stole a horse. Someone wants it back. Get another. My people do it all the time."

Mac shook his head and sighed, "Ye pay for your sins. Never are ye allowed to sin without punishment."

B.A. swung his head, his lips pointing towards the compound of horses beside him. "Pick another and we'll ride."

In spite of himself Mac swung an idle glance over the horses in the nearby corral. "Sure'n you'll have me hung for horse thievin' before the year is out." Suddenly, he leapt to the rail and gave a piercing whistle. In the milling herd, a horse answered. Through the dust, a tall red bay trotted towards the men. With a soft nicker like a gentle chuckle of delight, the horse thrust its black nose into Mac's chest. Mac hooted, climbed the top rail and threw his arms around the horse's neck. He buried his face into the tall horse's mane and squeezed mightily. "Tis Jim! Jim!" he yelled, "My horse from back home!" He patted a red shoulder, slapped the arched neck and tugged on the horse's ears, clearly delighted as the dancing horse in front of him who nudged him back, measure for measure. "Ah, ye old softie, sure'n I thought I'd never see ye again. Aye, tis like a breath of fresh air from home to be findin' ye again." He bent to check the horse over, happy to see no scars or new marks on his sleek coat. "Looks like ye faired well me Boyo!"

"That's my horse your petting mister."

Mac whirled around, almost losing his stance on the top railing. A young man with a broad-brimmed black hat and carrying a new pitchfork stomped towards them. As he lifted his head, his thin face twisted in fierce challenge. "That's my horse. I just bought him from Factor Morton to haul my wagon home."

Mac's face tightened, his fists clenching, but Broken Arrow saw the new clothes and the slim, unscarred hands of this newcomer. He had the slender, graceful hands of a cleric not a farm boy. The tall Cree leaned confidentially down from his horse towards the youth. "We were looking at the cinch gauls on his belly. He's sickle-hocked and hip-shot too, making him rough-gaited to ride because he'll stumble a lot. When that happens to a horse, his bowed tendons never completely heal."

The man's forehead crinkled, "You think he might not be able to pull?"

"Well my grandfather was a horse trader, not me," B.A. tugged at an ear, looking innocent, "But he always said, those with weak fetlocks almost always hurt themselves on a heavy pull. Sooner or later, they come up lame. Some of these horses are just too inbred." He ignored Mac's growl of outrage, "Makes them weak in the bloodlines and they pass it to their offspring."

The farmer took off his hat, scratched his head, smoothed his slicked-down hair and replaced the hat. "Well I had planned on breedin' him to my mare and making some money off her spring colts."

B.A. waited, giving the steaming Mac a calm glance. Mac looked away towards the horizon and gritted his teeth.

The farmer squinted up at B.A. still seated quietly on his horse. "Ye got any suggestions?" He stuck his hands into his new suspenders and casually rocked back on his new balmoral boots.

Mac remembered those boots being manufactured in Ontario just two years previous, a front-lacing shoe introduced by Queen Victoria at Balmoral, Scotland. This young man was a definitely an Easterner. Mac shrugged and made himself the picture of boredom.

B.A. pointed to Mac's big grey, Spence. "That is a true pulling horse. They're Percherons, according to my grandfather. He said they used to carry the big knights into battle. Is that your warriors?" He swung a querying glace to the farmer, who looked surprised then nodded wisely. "So they have been bred to carry or pull heavy loads. We saw this one put two oxen to shame when it came to hauling a covered wagon. I know the factor owns this one too. Maybe he'll do another trade with you. This one's healthy, not spavined like some cart horses get. It's all in the bones, you see."

The farmer looked from B.A. to Mac who now watched the proceedings with glittering eyes. "What do you think Mister?"

Mac spat on the ground to buy some time, "Well, my friend here knows more about horses than me. But I know quality when I see it. Being just a poor Irishman, I certainly couldn't afford the bloodlines that big old grey steamer comes from."

B.A.'s eyes sparked at the 'old' comment but his face remained smooth and innocent.

"Well," the young farmer squinted at the sun, "Me and my wife, we're just buildin' our homestead but it makes sense to start out with good stock, for breedin' and workin' purposes. I think that grey might throw some mighty strong colts."

"I heard the factor say something about gelding this big bay just to calm his temper down a little." Mac refused to meet the farmer's eyes as he crawled off the fence, ignoring Jim's whickering protest.

"Maybe I'll just go have a long talk with that man, trying to sell me such poor stock. With me and my wife about to have our first child, we don't need crippled wild horses!" The farmer whirled about and stomped across the compound towards the factor's headquarters, his pitchfork a battle-ready lance in his clenched fist.

As soon as he was out of sight, Mac undid the corral gate, snapped a bridle onto Jim, cinched on his saddle and swung aboard, gathering up the halter to Willy his Irish Gray saddle horse. B.A. was already calmly walking his horses out the fort gates. As they neared the gates, one of the workers squinted at Mac's horse. "You swop hosses young man?"

Mac waved a vague hand in the direction of the fort. "Aye, we traded that young farmer for me grey. He's settlin' up with factor Morton right now."

The worker nodded and went about his duties, leaving the men free to leave.

They walked their horses around the corner of the post and out of the clearing. As soon as they hit the trees, they raced headlong down the trail. After a few miles they slowed their labouring horses to an easy walk, hooting and howling.

"Whooeee!" Mac grinned in open-faced glee. "Did ye see that young fool's face? Ole factor Morton's gonna get an ear-full. Bet he'll do some fast talkin' once he figures he can sell the grey for free."

B.A. chuckled, "I thought you were going to swing at me when I talked about your Bay's weak points."

"He's fine Irish stock and here you are layin' it on like he's a useless mess. Your grandfather taught you well, ye old hoss trader!" Mac went off again, howling out his delight as he patted his horse's shoulders and withers, beside himself to be reunited once again with his old friend. And he wasn't about to tell B.A. about how deep that first contact had felt inside him. Old Jim definitely had a soul. This time Mac sensed it right down to his toes when he'd wrapped his arms around the big bay. But a niggling ache sobered him. He frowned at B.A., his eyes worried and dark.

"There's a story about a White Knight who rode a white horse." Mac leaned to give Jim another loving pat on his neck. "In our legends, the white knight always stood for good deeds. He was honest, trustworthy, brave, strong and kind. The Black Knight, however, always stood for the opposites: bad behaviour, dishonesty, cowardliness, weakness and cruelty. So in this story, the White Knight set out to destroy the Black Knight. He followed him across the countryside, finding burned fields, empty gardens and the women he had raped. The White knight vowed to kill the Black Knight and stop his destruction. For weeks, months he followed, but he couldn't quite catch the Black Knight, no matter how hard he tried. Finally the white knight grew tired and hungry. He thought, "I'll just help myself to these gardens. The people won't mind because I am the White Knight, I fight for justice. I will stop the Black Knight's raping and pillaging. I vow to kill the Black Knight." So he rode on. When he became tired, he slept in a farmer's barn and used his hay to feed his horse. He thought, "I'll just help myself to the hay. The farmer won't mind because I am the White Knight, I fight for justice and to stop the Black Knight's pillaging. I vow to kill the Black Knight.

"But he couldn't catch the Black Knight who stayed just ahead of him. He stopped to ask some young girls if they had seen the Black Knight, for he was the White Knight who had vowed to kill him. The girls were so impressed with his courage that he dallied and played with them for a few days. He thought, "I deserve this rest for I am the White Knight. I fight for justice and will stop the Black Knight's raping and pillaging. I vow to kill the Black Knight!" So he rode on. And still he couldn't catch the Black knight. So he helped himself to more food from nearby gardens, cut hay from farmers' fields for his horse and took the maidens wherever he stopped to rest.

One day he saw a rider coming towards him. As it came closer, he realized it was another knight, a very young knight dressed in white armour, flying a red flag of dragons. The older White Knight rode out to meet him, thinking, "Finally! Someone is brave enough to join me in killing the Black Knight!"

As he rode to meet him, the young knight yanked down his visor, pulled out his sword and yelled, "I am the White Knight! I fight for justice and vow to stop the Black Knight's raping and pillaging. Prepare to die Black Knight!" And he attacked.

Broken Arrow studied the blue horizon for a time, thinking deeply.

Mac looked out at him, a fine line appearing between his brows, "I fear I'm becoming the Black Knight, my friend. It gets too easy to tell a lie and to steal."

"And what will happen to you then?"

Mac threw up his arms, "Purgatory! Eternal damnation for my soul and its sins upon this earth! If you steal, you get punished for eternity! That's why we go to confession: to confess our sins and be forgiven. Though I prefer to live my life as I please and repent at my leisure in my old age, I may not get the chance in this wild land."

"And so you must lead the life of the White Knight? You set yourself up to fail."

"What d'ye mean? There's good and there's bad. It's quite simple! Stealin' is no' good!"

"He's your horse."

Mac raised a palm in mid-air, "Oh aye. Tis my horse, but stealin' and lyin' to get him back is no' the way to do it. We become thieves in the process like the Black Knight."

"We got your horse back; shared the grey with the young farmer. He's happy"

Mac broke it down, "Sharin' is good! Thievin' is bad!"

Broken Arrow looked totally confused; he waved his arm back towards the fort, "You want to share your horse with that young farmer?"

Mac sighed in disgust, "Nooo! Tis the principle of good and bad, black knight or white. One is wrong, one is right! And you pay for doing the wrong things!"

"Pay who?"

"God! Who sits in judgement of our sins, who sees every move we make. With every sin, we chance the eternal damnation of purgatory, the burning flames of hell!"

Broken Arrow's eyes narrowed. "I think you make too much of getting your horse back. Black, white, good, bad. How can you be one without the other? Our elders say for every good thought we have, a bad one follows. We are both all. Good and bad! It is not for us to sit in judgement of the two halves of ourselves. It will rip us apart. We just are. Both are who we are."

"Then repent ye sinner! For the fires of hell await you!"

B.A.'s lips curled, "You white men are so swift to judge, to condemn without forgiveness. We are all human, we make mistakes, do things we shouldn't but we learn from them and we go on. That is part of life and wisdom. The Creator made us imperfect, with the will to make our own choices. How can he punish us for making us what we are? And we are both all—good and bad!"

Mac threw up his hands and refused to speak anymore.

Broken Arrow pushed his horse forward, his face tight-lipped, eyes glaring straight ahead. "You White Men have such split thinking! Either your women are virtuous mothers or dirty prostitutes; saints or sinners—and they are punished forever if they make a mistake! Nobody is that perfect. Never will I think like you fearful white men! Your Black Robes preach forgiveness and they practice none. I prefer my elders' teachings who speak of forgiveness within ourselves and with those around us. We are all just learning. And making mistakes is something we do all the time."

"This wasn't a mistake!" Mac couldn't hold back, too inflamed, "We chose to lie! We chose to steal that grey horse and now Jim. You want choices? What do we do now Indian Man?" He sneered, raising an upward palm, "Forgive our souls for being thieves?"

"Hiyii!! Life is a game, a dream of wit and thought." B.A. growled. "He's just a horse! Everything we own comes and goes in our lives. As warriors, we are taught to scorn all possessions. We give away our most prized items, our best blankets, moccasins, anything we own. At our feasts, we pass around our best blankets for people to wipe their greasy fingers on. It teaches us the importance of sharing, not hoarding or valuing possessions. They are nothing! All the possessions in this land will never advance your soul!"

B.A.'s mouth tightened, "I harmed no one. The young man got a good horse for his family. You got your horse back. Even the greedy trader made money." He rode ahead, showing Mac his stiffly held shoulders. "Take your horse back. But I won't ride double with you anymore!"

Mac's troubled eyes followed his friend, sensing the rift and unsure how to deal with it. "Well and now . . . I don't want to give Jim up after just findin' him."

"Then it seems you have made your choice White Man." B.A. taunted over his shoulder, "Can you forgive yourself or will you burn in hell now?"

Mac spurred Jim forward, "Ye don't have to be making fun of my beliefs, just because they're different from yours. I will go to confession with the next priest I see."

B.A. speculated how that made it right for this man. Could he then steal again? It seems these Moniyows just made up rules to suit themselves and it didn't go any further than the next confession to their priest. How could one man, a Black Robe at that, be responsible for removing everyone's sins and mistakes? Surely the Creator required more restitution than a couple of prayers? Perhaps there was this burning hell, but his elders had never spoken of such, saying only that people are answerable for their life after death. If restitutions were not paid in this life, then they will surely be paid in the next. It made him wonder what he had done in previous lives to be stuck in such confusion now.

31.

THE BLACK ROBES

"Why is Man always bad? The Black Robes say he is full of sin from the time he is born. Why?" B.A. looked across the campfire that evening to Mac seated on a log. They were munching on the small bulbs found at the turn of a bulrush root.

Mac enjoyed the raw crunch and sweet taste while he scratched an ear, "Well, I suppose it goes back to the Original sin. The first sin he, or rather she, committed."

"A woman did it? She made all men bad? How?"

"Well, ye must know the story of the Garden of Eden where the first man, Adam, and his wife, Eve, lived on the land? It was a paradise of fruit and plants and all they needed."

"Ehe! I heard this story from the Black Robes at the mission I went to as a young boy, but I did not know enough English to make sense of it."

"Well, Eve was tempted to eat the fruit, an apple from the Tree of Conscience. God forbade them to eat it, telling them its fruit would open their eyes, make them aware of right and wrong, good and bad. He told them if they ate this fruit, they would be doomed to die rather than live eternally."

Broken Arrow's eyes rounded in astonishment, "Why would the Creator forbid them from being wise. It's our purpose in life: to learn and grow old in wisdom!"

Mac pushed his hat back, contemplating the flames. "Sure'n that's your ways but the bible says God told them not to eat it and Eve did. She disobeyed God."

B.A. sniffed, "Smart woman." He took another bite and chewed thoughtfully.

Mac shook his head, "And she tempted Adam to eat it too. The first thing they realized was they were naked and embarrassed by it. When God came, they hid in fear and shame. For the sin of eating the forbidden fruit, they were thrown out of the Garden of Eden. Eve was punished by having to bear children in intense pain and suffering, yet must welcome her husband's affections and he would be her master. Adam was made to toil and constantly struggle to make a living from the soil.

"The Church believes it is woman's proper business to be married and bear children. Women had to be especially careful to do the will of God because it was through a woman that mankind fell into Original Sin and every woman must beware. It was her work to atone, to make amends, make good for the Original Sin in Eden. No woman could ever be really good except for Virgin Mary, the Mother of Christ."

B.A. could not understand. "How can any woman remain a virgin and still become a mother? You set your women up for impossible standards. This Eve, with her original sin, why did all the women who came after her have to pay, be judged, scorned and hated for something they had no control over and never did themselves anyway? It seems like no matter what they do, they are wrong and blamed for it."

Mac parroted what he had learned in his catechisms. "All other women were evil; they never had any chance to be anything but evil. L'abbe' Provencher from St. Boniface, out of Fort Garry preached how women are inferior and therefore dependent upon the male, *'le chef de famille'*, or head of the family. He referred to women as "*la sexe*" implying their tainted sexual role. This was their punishment for being like Eve, sinful, filled with rage and rebellion against the will of God."

"So a vengeful woman rebelled against God? Why? If her life was a paradise, why was she so angry?"

Mac shrugged, "Tis what the bible says."

"This Adam, did Eve hold him at knife point? Force him to eat the fruit?"

Mac blinked, "Ah no. The bible says she gave it to him and convinced him to eat it. So he did."

"Did she force him to swallow it by beating him?"

"No . . ."

"Then why is the woman at fault?" B.A. shook his head in disgust, "Mah! He could have said, 'No!'"

Mac started grinning, if it were only that simple.

B.A. watched him in total confusion. "So the woman got smart and realized they needed clothes. Then they both were really stupid before eating the fruit."

Mac chuckled at his logic. "But they had the perfect life before they disobeyed God and became sinful forever. It was a paradise. They needed nothing more to live."

B.A. shook his head, "The woman had the right of it. How can any man have a good life if he is not wise? How did this Adam convince Eve wisdom is a sin? Did he tell her that so he could blame her for his own choices and actions?"

Mac choked. He blinked, frowned, turned red. "Here and Now! Don't be sayin' words I do no' mean!" He scrambled to his feet, his fists clenching. "We could have had eternal life—never die!"

Broken Arrow looked up, keeping his seat, "We have that anyway. Why is it a sin to be wise? To know right from wrong, good from bad? How else would we know when we, or someone else is doing wrong?"

Mac was in turmoil. His anger goaded him, put him on the defensive, yet he felt locked in by the man's simple logic. As he opened his mouth to argue, B.A. frowned.

"Then who profits from the punishment?"

"Whaat?!!" Mac had a sudden wild image of himself skipping sideways on one foot, trying to catch his balance.

B.A. struggled to explain, "No man profits from being stupid. So who would benefit by making him think he is better off stupid?"

"Well, our priests say . . ."

"*Ekosi*! So that's it!" Broken Arrow was filled with admiration.

"What's that supposed to be mean?" Mac wanted to throw his hat at him in pure frustration.

"Your priests benefit." B.A.'s face beamed at his discovery, "Of course! Because then, as messengers of your God, they can appear wiser than their foolish followers. The priests can tell them what is good and what it evil, what to think, what to pray, what to believe. The original sin was if the White Man became too smart, he would not listen to the Black Robes' lies."

"Devil take ye! They're no' lies! They're the word of God!"

"Written down by men in your bible. How do you know they are truth? Have you asked yourself? Does it feel like the truth inside you where all truth lies?" B.A. stubbornly held out. "From what I know the Black Robes change truth to suit their purpose. Under this sin of ignorance, they can beat little children for not understanding English words. Where is the good in that? Where is the wisdom in thrashing a young girl who speaks to her little cousin in their own tongue so he may understand the Black Robe's English words?"

Mac stared into his narrowed eyes, stunned at the bleakness in their dark depths.

B.A. looked down, unwilling to keep the contact. "When I was six summers, the Black Robes came and took away all the children in our camp. They shaved our heads, cut off our braids. They ignored our belief that our badge of honour lies in our hair and how we take care of it. They told us we were lousy and filthy. Us! My people bathe every day, summer and winter. This is how we purify ourselves for our Creator. Then the Black Robes forced us to burn our clothes and made us wear clothes with stripes on them, like the uniforms people in jail wear. We were told we were no good. Savages! Heathens! They beat us for speaking our language, made us ashamed of being Indian. Boys were not allowed to talk to the girls lest they fornicate with them. The priest beat us for talking to our sisters and cousins. My older cousin was chained outside on the stairway for one night in her nightgown and bare feet. There was frost on the ground. She had made the mistake of talking to me, a little boy! Where is the kindness in such cruelty to children?"

Broken Arrow's face tightened, his eyes narrowing "Where is the goodness in forcing small children to wear their soiled undergarments on their heads as punishment for wetting their lonely beds? Where is the goodness in starving little children and then beating them for stealing a crust of bread?" His voice dropped to a whisper, "And what about a young boy who polishes his hard shoes just to please the Black Robe. Where is the goodness in a Black Robe who spends his seed inside a small defenceless boy? Why is it not wrong to spill a little boy's blood down his legs and upon his newly polished shoes?"

Tears filled B.A.'s eyes. His broad shoulders heaved as he drew a breath, "Where is God's goodness and wisdom in these shameful actions that no one must ever speak of?"

Mac froze, barely breathing, his eyes never leaving his friend's shattered face. His hand lifted and dropped uselessly. The pain he saw filled his chest and closed his throat.

B.A. looked away, lifting his face to the stars, tracks of glistening silver on his cheeks. "To question right from wrong, good from bad is not a sin!" He turned back to Mac, his face accusing and hard, "What is sinful about thinking? What is sinful about using our minds to decide for ourselves what is right and what is wrong? How can it be a sin when you are forced to believe another's lies? I ran away from the Black Robes in the middle of the night, in the middle of the winter. I almost froze to death but I never went back. Never again will I believe anything a Black Robe says. Never!" He shouted into Mac's face, shoved past him and spun away to the silver moonscape.

Mac's legs gave way, he fell to his knees, body hunched, his head shaking back and forth uselessly as he pounded his fist against the unyielding soil.

32.

KISTIN

B.A. got up from the campfire, fidgeted with his horse's saddle and hackamore, returned, sat, then rose and walked around the camp, searched the hazy sky, sat breifly, stood and walked to the river. They were still following the North Saskatchewan, several days' ride out of Fort Pitt.

Finally Mac had enough.

"*De tha cearr ort?* What is wrong with you? You're jumpy as a cricket on a hot stove! What ails ye? Ye got rats in your attic?" Mac was in a foul mood. It had rained and rained, each and every day for the past seven. He was heartily sick of being wet, sticky and muddy. He was fed up with sputtering campfires and dried food, damp bedding and endless, endless cold. The sweet anise flavour of B.A.'s hyssop tea eased the chill but not his misery. Mac felt trapped and frustrated with the unending hardship and discomfort. Faith, he could sell his soul for a warm bed, dry clothes and a dish of his mother's Colcannon. His mouth ached for the steamy combination of cabbage, bacon, potatoes, onions, cream and sweet, sweet butter.

B.A. studied the shallow, sweeping valleys before him and the hazy purple hills marking the distant Battleford Rivers. The sky had softened to a blue-grey mist in the hot, humid afternoon sunshine. Something was wrong. Blackfoot felt it too. The older horse constantly bobbed his head, pawed the ground and tugged on his tether. Yet B.A. found neither sign nor sound to clarify his unease. It was so quiet and calm, no grasshoppers moved, no birds sang.

No birds sang!

With one more glance at the sky, Broken Arrow whirled to Blackfoot and yanked the backpack straps away, stripping the hackamore from his horse at the same time. Then he set to work unsaddling Brownfoot, his hands a blur of motion.

Mac yelled, "Here and now! What the Sam Hill are ye doin'? I thought we were leaving?" He rushed to B.A.

"Unload your horses, set them free." He unhooked Brownfoot's bridle.

"Whaat?!!! Set them free? Are ye daft? We're several days from Victoria and Fort Edmonton, how the Sam Hill . . ."

B.A. whirled to him, "There's a storm coming. Free your horses! They'll know where they must go to survive."

"Well why can't we go with them?" This made absolutely no sense to Mac.

"Because they will listen to their foolish riders and not their inner wisdom. Then we all die."

A stunned Mac searched the sky above through its grey humid haze. "There's nary a cloud to be seen. Ye're acting like a half gutted mackerel! What have ye been eatin' now?" He tilted his hat back and found no answers in the peaceful countryside.

B.A. finished stripping his animals and set them free. He whispered something in the older paint's ear then sent him away with a swat on his rump. Blackfoot flew across the prairie, his feet a blur of pounding motion. The younger Brownfoot paced him without complaint.

B.A. met Mac's puzzled look. "I told him to return when it was safe. Your horses will follow them if you free them now."

Mac threw up his hands and reluctantly unsaddled Jim and removed the bridle. He undid the straps on Willy's backpack and pulled off his hackamore. With a slap on the rumps of both horses, he sent them galloping off to join the two paints. "Jaysus, sometimes I think I'm getting as daft as you. Tis the land what does it to a man." He folded his arms and glared across at B.A. "So now we're footloose and fancy free. Just how do we go on from here?"

"We don't. We dig!"

The big Cree searched through the grass and came up with a broad moose antler. He thrust it at a stunned Mac then rummaged his pack for his hatchet. Striding to a soft embankment along the river, he began hacking at protruding roots. Mac followed more slowly, nonplussed and suddenly afraid. He searched the sky again, but found its grey innocence unnerving in the face of his friend's bizarre behaviour. Confused, arms hanging, he watched his friend wrench roots out and fling them aside.

He decided to try logic, "Is there something under the bank we can eat?"

"No." B.A. grabbed the antler from Mac's unnerved grasp and gouged large clumps of sand and dirt out of the embankment.

"Did you leave something here a long time ago?"

"No." A mound of dirt grew between B.A.'s feet as he continued widening the hole.

Mac threw his hands in the air and spun in a circle. "For the love of heaven! Will ye leave off long enough to talk to me?!! Tell me what the Sam Hill ye're doin' before ye drive me mad with yer silence!!!"

"There is a storm coming. A bad one. The only way we survive is to dig a hole in this bank and crawl inside until it passes."

"A bad storm." Mac searched the hazy horizon. "I see only a few dark clouds."

"No birds sing. They leave an area a coming storm will damage."

Mac was totally lost now. He looked around and realized how silent the land had become. No birds called or flitted about. Even the crickets were silent. This grey calm frightened him more than downtown traffic in Toronto at closing time. He found a broad stick and joined his friend, shoving the tip deep into the soil and yanking chunks out.

"Just how bad do storms get in this land?"

"You ever heard of *Kistin*, the Big Wind?"

"Aye, I know the wind."

"Loud Spinning Wind?" B.A. straightened, arching his back for momentary relief.

Mac paled, searching his friend's eyes, "Jaysus! Are ye talkin' tornado?"

When B.A. nodded, Mac dug faster and harder. "Sweet Jaysus, Mary and Joseph! How much time do we have?"

B.A. pointed to two clouds one to his right, the other to his left above the horizon and moving closer. They increased in size and volume, looming larger, blacker and heavier. The one on the left had an ugly green cast in its shadows. "When those two meet, it begins."

Mac swallowed, fell to his knees and pawed with both hands, showering dirt in every direction. Bent from the waist, they thrust their heads inside the hole and dug harder, pulling out the dirt, covering themselves in their haste. Finally B.A. crawled in, digging out the back while Mac pushed and kicked at the growing heap of loosened soil at his feet. Cold sweat beaded his brow and ran unheeded down his cheeks. His shirt dampened from the unusually humid, silent air around him. He grunted and gasped, then dug harder, ignoring the aching burn of muscles across his shoulders and back.

"Enough!" panted B.A. He crawled out and strode to his saddle and packs. Heaving them onto his back, he quickly retraced his steps and flung them to the back of the large hole. Mac copied him, tossing in his gear while gauging the sizeable miniature cave they had dug. He straightened and looked up, losing his breath as he did so.

The two clouds, silent and ominous, sped directly into each other's path. The sky had darkened as they worked. Now the surrounding hush of the land raised hairs on Mac's arms. Soundlessly the two clouds merged. Geysers of white and grey water shot from the bottom straight up like a waterfall in reverse. The muscles in Mac's back clenched in disbelief at water surging *upward*, gushing over the top of the cloud and disappearing inside the seething, bile green cloudbank.

"And now . . . ." B.A. breathed it out. A small grey wisp fell out the bottom of the looming behemoth above them. So close. So damn close. Rain gently misted their faces as they watched the wisp grow, like a tiny serpent hanging down, lifting and dropping, again and again, cautiously tasting the earth with an inquisitive tongue. A whirling dervish of dust from the earth rose up to meet it, like a tiny teacup with a spinning saucer beneath.

Mac stood spellbound. Hair lifted on his head, gently wafted about then subsided. He felt surrounded by silence, suspended in a void of gentle calm, an untouchable peace, mesmerized by the swaying, innocent coil growing thicker, darker, . . . closer.

At the edge of their campsite, a dead poplar tree toppled quietly away to their left. Another joined it, pushed by a silent, invisible force. And still the calm held.

Beneath the snake of spinning cloud, grass bent their blades towards them, bowing to embrace the earth in ever-widening circles. The silence moved in rippling waves forward, slamming grass and shrub to the ground, mangling them to green blobs, ever closer and closer. Mac waited, seduced by the deafening hush, mesmerized by the snake dance, intrigued and beguiled by its silent query.

B.A. grabbed Mac's shoulder and flung him head first into the hole. Mac tumbled and rolled, feeling B.A.'s head slam his thigh as he scrambled to the right, leaving space for the Cree.

And the world exploded outside, sucking air away in a bellowing "Fwoomm!" The men wriggled to the entrance, shoulder to shoulder, gaping at hundred-foot trees, compelled by an invisible, gigantic hand to bend at unimaginable angles and whip the ground in wild frenzy. Willows, shrubs and grass slashed one another, their branches stretched like pleading fingers across a blackened plain. Pieces of grass, twigs and rocks flung themselves into the grey murk. Wind howled in agony, piercing their ears, depressurizing the cave until the men's ears popped. Dizzy and disoriented, they were attacked by a shrill whistling screech spinning around them in rage, spraying their faces with dirt, sand and water, enclosing them in a cacophony of black violence. Through red blinking eyelids, the men glimpsed terrifying rainwater outside their burrow. Braided and rolled into four inch ropes of grey, the water spun parallel to the ground, twisted into coils of writhing agony. It shredded to eight strands and whirled up to ten feet off the ground in endless dirty coils. And still the wind rose higher, louder than a train, louder than detonating dynamite, louder than their ears could stand. Numb from the horrendous uproar, Mac felt like he sat in the centre of a top, a whistling dervish of chaos, confusing and terrifying, its very magnificence spellbinding. Such power blasted him to his soul. He wanted to both watch and close his eyes in horrified denial of a world gone mad.

The buckle from his bridle slammed into his head from behind. He snatched it from mid-air. B.A. captured his own flying hackamore and scrabbled back from the entrance, dodging his chokecherry wooden bow. Arrows flew by, flint-tipped and razor sharp. The men ducked, feeling tiny pricks as some hit home before being sucked outside. "Sit on your packs!" B.A. yelled over the deafening roar.

They flung themselves away from the entrance, fighting the sucking air pulling greedily with strong angry fingers at their clothes and hair. It tugged on their shoes as they rammed their bodies against the deepest part of their hole. They snatched at bits and pieces of their packs suspended in the airless vacuum. A cup and plate were enticed away, seduced into the screaming black tempest beyond the hole. And still the wind shrieked louder, a screaming wind tunnel that numbed the mind in horror, until the men couldn't think, couldn't talk, their hands gouging into the earth to anchor their bodies and belongings. B.A.'s moccasins were plucked away, loose fringes and beads from his vest went next. Mac threw his hat beneath his body, wrapped his arms around his saddle horn and hung on with every ounce of strength he had. He could barely catch his breath in the black miasma of flying dirt. Mud rolled in a thick heavy stream through their entrance, enclosing their scrabbling feet in smothering grey ripples. Soon they'd be buried alive!

They kicked frantically at the mud until some of it spilled back outside, dropping out of sight below. Grass and sand and dirt pelted them, choking them into coughing fits. Gravel clogged their eyes. They spat and fought to breathe through their nostrils alone. Mac wiped his face on his shoulder, still hanging onto his pack and saddle. His hat wriggled from beneath and flew upward. Frantically, he snatched it from mid-air and stuffed it down the front of his pants. He rolled to his stomach, clinging to his gear, kicking at the mud, constantly fighting to stay away from the leeching hole. It was totally black inside and out; so dark he could not see beyond the dim curtain of water, dirt, straw and grass and rocks rushing past. From overhead he heard loud thumping, a heavy vibration he felt through his fingers. B.A. yelled above the screaming wind, "Mud Woman walks the earth with Stone People today!"

Mac flinched in horror as a huge rock, thick as his body slowly rolled down from above and sank into the mud at their entrance. He half expected it to talk! But it remained, motionless and silent, partially blocking their entrance, leaving a narrow foot of space to see beyond it. More rocks followed, some flew away while others rolled down and stayed, anchored in the oozing mud. As the two men watched helplessly, their sanctuary's opening slowly filled with rocks, all sizes and shapes, leaving a smaller and smaller hole. At least it blocked the wind so they could breath.

They coughed and caught their breath. B.A. slid forward, kicking at the rocks with muddy toes. Some rolled away, others refused. Mac joined him, jamming his slippery boots onto the higher rocks, shoving the smaller ones out and away. Gradually their hole increased in size again.

B.A. stopped moving, "Listen! The wind is leaving."

They held their breath and sensed more than heard by infinitesimal amounts, the wind decreasing. Both waited, every muscle tensed. Would it begin again? Louder than before? Was it the eye of the storm? Or the calm aftermath? They drew shaky breaths and waited. Gradually, in phases so slight they couldn't pinpoint the change, noise eased. Time gave them truth. The wind was leaving. Eventually it calmed until it soothed their ears and they could relax and think once again. The whistle waned to a soft moan. Raindrops gently washed their pile of rocks. The mud ceased moving. A soft gust of wind swirled about them, cool, fresh and damp.

Together, they renewed their efforts to clear the mud and rocks away, enough for B.A. to squeeze past. He tossed others aside as he crawled out. Mac was on his heels, anxious to be free of what could have been their coffin. He stood up, stretched cramped muscles and retrieved his battered hat. Then he froze.

Where once a tall canopy of trees stood, jagged stumps remained, naked and white, skinned of all bark, branches and leaves. Every tree was snapped off or totally removed. Gigantic, gaping holes marked where once majestic trees had stood. A few pale roots, mangled and stripped clean, clung to the barren earth. Grass, wet and muddy, lay in shattered clumps, broken and mangled. Amongst their tangled blades, once bright flowers lay shredded to a bruised pulp. Grey and brown gravel, rain-washed smooth, lay bared to misty wind. Nothing over a foot high remained standing. The only sign left of their campfire was a blackened stain upon the smooth gravel. Not a speck of its wood or bark or ash remained.

"Jaysus!" Mac whistled as he contemplated the silent, dripping land. "No wonder this damned country is flat and barren." He stumbled awkwardly as he turned slowly, unable to grasp the carnage. He shook his head, bewildered eyes unable to leave or believe the silent destruction about him. Oblivious to his filthy clothes and coated boots, he rubbed his face with shaking hands, smearing mud further.

Broken Arrow bent and pulled his pack from the hole. He crossed to the river, washed his feet and slipped on his last pair of moccasins. Mac knelt beside him, dipping his hands and finally his face in the murky water. He found himself wondering how many of the rocks in this river had just relocated themselves.

His lips formed an ancient hymn of the druids, or older than that, perhaps from the lands that lie beneath the sea. For twas said the ancestors of the druids were the priests from Atlantis who washed upon the shore of Wales after the great land sank:

> "For lo, all the days of man are as a leaf that is fallen and
> as the grass that withered.
> Thou too shalt be forgotten, like the flower that falleth
> on the grass,
> Like the wind poured out and soaked into the earth.
> And yet even as the spring returns, so blooms the land
> and so blooms life which will come again."

In the middle of the night, the horses returned: their eyes wild and white rimmed; their nostrils blowing at every sound; their feet restless and stomping; their trembling bodies . . . undamaged and sound.

33.

OUT OF THE MUD

In the clear morning sunshine the following day, with life restored to somewhat normal, Mac wanted answers. "Why did you say Mud Woman walked the earth yesterday?"

Broken Arrow sat cross-legged, stripping bark from a Saskatoon sapling to make new arrows. Later, he would search for goose feathers and split them to balance the shaft's direction. "I will share with you what Mitsue told me when I was a young man of thirteen summers:

"Mitsue reached her fingers down into the earth and lifted a handful of mud, leaves and small roots, holding them out to me.

'See this? White man calls it dirt, something that makes him filthy and disgusted, coating his life and belongings – black and ugly, like sin. And the Black Robes put women into this same category."

"Why?" B.A. remembered the Black Robed priests of the mission school. Tiny frissons of alarm rolled up his spine. He had spent one winter in their schools before running away back to Mitsue and his grandfather Tall Man. Something in his defiant face had made them never question his refusal to return. Whenever the mission riders came searching for children to teach in the schools, he hid until they left. Though he never spoke of it again, Mitsue and Tall Man were often awakened by the young boys screams and they must have wondered . . . .

'Because they are afraid.' Mitsue replied.

Broken Arrow's brow wrinkled in confusion. During all the cruelty the Black Robes meted out, fear never crossed their faces.

Mitsue nodded, her dark eyes dulled with sadness. 'They are right to be afraid. They have no understanding of Mud Woman. She has the power to destroy everything puny man builds. Nothing he makes can withstand her anger or destruction. He is totally helpless to his fate.'

The old woman filtered the mud gently through her fingers, watching chunks of it return to the earth. She spoke with the eloquence of a master in her descriptive Cree language. Her complex, majestic words spun rich, colourful details and panoramic images. 'Mother Earth is the essence of all life. Where there is mud, there is new beginnings, new life. Mud is where everything begins, in the swamps, the river bottoms, lake shores and rain puddles. Mud nurtures all life forms and sets them out into the world, from small grains of sand, to hardened rocks and cliffs, to seeds, to plants, to animals, to food for all life. Woman also brings forth new life, nurtures it and sets it out into the world. Mud Woman is a part of her spirit. She teaches us all lessons. Without Mud Woman, we do not, cannot survive. Her lessons are often hard, very ancient, yet loving as she teaches us how to survive, how to feed and care for ourselves and each other. If we allow it, she will come into our dreams, take our hands and walk us deep in the swamp. There, she reminds us of our connection to all creatures of the swamp—something we can never lose sight of. There she will sit us in the mud and talk to us until we understand.'

'Understand what?' Broken Arrow contemplated a heavy swamp on his left.

'Sit!' Mitsue ordered sternly, pointing a sturdy finger at a nearby mud puddle on the edge of the swamp.

Broken Arrow rose slowly, peered at his grandmother, frowned at the puddle. When she said nothing more, he walked to the puddle, lifted his breechcloth and cautiously lowered his youthful haunches into the mud, feeling it ooze around his bottom and thighs. He winced at the coldness on tender parts but soon felt oddly warmed.

Mitsue regarded him solemnly.

'What do you feel?' With a heavy fist, she thumped her abdomen, beneath her diaphragm. 'Here, inside, where your spirit dwells. Some people call it gut reaction but it is your spirit, connected to your sacred soul.'

Broken Arrow closed his eyes. For a long time, he breathed deeply, exhaled slowly. He focused on the mud, its wetness confining and surging around him.

Surged? Yes, a tingling energy encompassed him, swelled in waves, slowly at first, rising up his right foot, making his leg tingle, past his butt to the centre of his being, billowing up his torso and arms then out the top of his head. It pulsed, tingled, cold, then warm, strengthening until his body swelled with its flow, like a heartbeat, like his own but separate and far more powerful. Energy poured back down through his left side all the way to the mud beneath him. He tingled in delight, consumed with joy until he could not tell where it left off and he began. Instead, he became part of it until his heart beat with its rhythm, in unison, in endless harmony. He crowed with pleasure, his lips lifting in a broad smile.

Mitsue hummed softly and swayed in gentle rhythm. "We all come from her, man and woman" she whispered, "and we return to her. In between, we borrow her energy to keep us going, to nurture ourselves. For women, the energy surges up through our left side, the feminine side, where our heart dwells. We draw our strength directly from Mother Earth and it flows off the top of our heads towards Creator. His energy flows back down our right side, the masculine side, to Mother Earth. For men, it is the opposite. They feel Mother's energy rise up their right side, their masculine side.

It surges up to Creator while his energy flows back down their left side, grounding them in their feminine side. The energy creates a circle inside of us, connecting us to both Creator and Earth Mother. Its flow through men and women creates another circle of harmony when they join together with respect and honour.

'Male and female, we create the circle of life, the cycle of endless energy. We are her children, the children of Mud Woman, Swamp Mother, a spirit of Earth Mother. We are her, just as she is a part of us in here, where our spirit dwells." Mitsue patted her rounded stomach, just beneath her pendulous breasts.

'Why does the White man fear this?" Broken Arrow didn't want to move, enjoying the energy flowing so lovingly through him.

Mitsue scooped a chunk of mud, grass and twigs and held it with both hands. "He sees only mud, not the endless life cycles it creates. He sees only dirt, something filthy and bad, something he must wash from beneath his fingernails and his body. He thinks he controls his life, clean and clear if he is free of all contact with dirt and mud. Instead, he creates chaos inside himself. He denies the flow of energy from Creator and Mud Woman and isolates himself from it. His denial creates a blockage, a barrier to its natural flow. It makes him sick inside but he does not know why. So he is afraid without knowing why.

'To be a strong man, he thinks, is to be alone, dependent upon no one. But to be alone on this Earth is to know fear. So the White Man seeks to control his fear by controlling everything around him. He fights for control amongst his people and amongst other races. He thinks if he is better, richer, stronger than others, then somehow he is closer to perfect independence. He thinks this is his reason for living—being in total control of his life. Yet Mud Woman can never be controlled. She is Earth in all her storms, beauty, power and serenity. And she lets no man forget this. So the white man hates her because she is stronger than he. In his anger and his fear, he takes everything he can from her: food, forest, furs, even the gold rocks and he gives nothing in return, nothing in gratitude, nothing to restore the emptiness left by his taking.'

As Mitsue rubbed her hands together in a rapid circular motion, bits of mud, dirt, leaves and twigs flew in all directions. She sadly contemplated her empty mud-stained hands. 'The White Man is afraid because he feels so alone. So he fights, he struggles to control this vast world, to make it his, in his image of what he wants. He loses himself to the pride of his wants not his needs. He plays a game of power, falsely believing it will put him where he wants to be: on top, in God's favour, respected by those beneath him. On top, he believes he comes closest to the Creator, closest to the perfect god-like image.

Mitsue sighed, 'But he is still a man, still living on this earth, playing out his life, learning lessons only Spirit can teach far beyond the yellow gold, the furs, the food to survive and beyond his hopes and wishes for the lessons his soul must learn. Man can never be more than a worshipper of life, living it out, moment by moment. That is soul development. That is truth given to him through his passion and experience.'

Mitsue shook her head, her forehead wrinkling in pain. 'The White Man has no dream or even a vision of his spiritual path. He seeks not his soul but success, material wealth, even fame. He believes these will fill the hole where his soul should be growing. But they mean nothing! He leaves his passion unfulfilled, his dream dying of emptiness. He searches in the wrong place for what he is missing: the piece of himself beyond the fear, all the way to hope.

'This happens when man fails to dream, fails to see his creativity as special gifts beyond his race. From the continual creation of Earth Mother and God who made us in their image, so too can we create. This is co-creation at its best. We deny our own gifts when we seek something outside of ourselves. Outside, we search for fulfilment instead of finding our gifts inside. When we finally come home to our gift, we can develop them for the entire world to treasure.'

Mitsue leaned towards her grandson, 'Think this through, find your own answers, and find your own choices in your own truth. What is truth to you? What is passion to you? There your gifts will be found. Look within! Always within! As Mud Woman creates, so you create – from within! This is the truth missing from the ages, beyond man's mind controlling lies of doing too much for others; always wanting more; seeking answers and following others with their man-made rules instead hearing the quiet inner voice of truth within our soul.

'This is what can destroy the White Man. What he fails to understand is that what Earth is, so is he!

'His pride will lose to her power. If he chooses not to listen, not to hear her in ceremony or honour her, he loses her wisdom to find his soul. His denial of her cycles will only make them stronger. In the end, if he chooses not to listen, not to enter her ceremony, he stands to lose a great deal more than wisdom. He loses when he denies her a rightful voice in spiritual leadership. She holds the answer to his search for soul.'"

*   *   *

Mac twirled a mangled grass blade between his fingers, his back bowed with the heaviness he felt in his chest. "Ye know the druids felt each blade of grass had the possibility of becoming a soul. That all things alive were the same, separated only by a difference of accumulated experiences—that all humans have been simpler things at some point in their past.

"They also believed the knowledge gained from these earlier states were necessary for present or future growth. They studied nature as a divine imitation of God. A flower, a pebble, a snowflake, the path a salmon takes in the water were all reflections of the Great Cosmic Order, glimpses into the mind of God and therefore worthy of great study and respect. They also believed it gave them insight into what the Afterlife would be like, even reincarnation."

Mac glanced up at B.A., his eyes pensive, "I remember my oldest sister Shannon sitting in her garden. How she loved that miserable plot of land so stingy with its produce. She would sit for hours, with a handful of soil, sifting it slowly through her fingers, a faraway look in her eyes. I never asked her what she felt or thought."

He sighed, "We have truly lost the faith of the mud and Earth Mother somewhere along the way. Aye and we are the poorer for it."

34.

MUD WOMAN

Mac dreamed of her that night and held his breath in rigid fear. Out of the swamp she rose, her head a mud-woven hummock, her eyes, two golden oak leaves blazing with light, her hands, gnarled roots of ancient trees and her skirt a drifting sea of dried grass. Danu. Mud Woman.

When she took his hands, he knelt before her, raised her twisted fingers and kissed them reverently as a knight.

When he lifted his head, she held a red rose. Her voice whispered about him, more in thought than words, "A Rose is first a rosebud, then full blown becomes the rose-hip berry, full and round and crimson, pulsing with the tart life of the rose." As he watched, it shrank, withered and lay dried in her hand. "A flower, then fruit is only the beginning. In the seeds lie the life and the future. So much of your future work lies hidden, as the rose is hidden within the seed."

"Come," she husked, "there is much to learn. The earth has many soul lessons for your tonight."

He followed her or rather floated beside her, bemused and beguiled with his ability to do so with ease. They drifted over deep, gentle valleys and high, savage mountains. "Here are the heights, depths and breadths of all that we are and can experience in life."

They flew over the sea. "Water always represents spirit. So a journey into the waters is always a journey inside ourselves, into our soul, with all its depth, mystery, magic and wonder. The deeper we go, the more danger involved, and the more truth we find—full glory, full fear, full anger, risk and whimsy. It may feel disorienting, but it is still who we are completely."

They drifted to the shore and danced atop the tiny waves. "Here is our playful gentleness which can change to storm-lashed, pounding fury. So too are we all: from the tempest to the calm; from the violence to the delight. And still, that is not all."

They journeyed to the heart of Earth and the molten lava boiling through her veins. "Here is the hot searing pain of our hidden wounds: suffering, churning and violent, remaining inside until that cataclysmic moment, when it erupts, exploding in all directions, a volley of melting rocks, like our memories, fire and agony and furious vengeance. It changes everything and everyone around us—forever. In its aftermath, we seek healing, driven by remorse, by fear and pain and finally . . . the acceptance and forgiveness of all that we were and are. Then we can look to the sky once again."

She raised her arms of writhing roots, uplifted in reverence. "Again, to the sky, the freedom to fly is your choice—our gift to you. It is yours to use as you will. Beyond suffering comes healing and the challenge to grow through all known dimensions and to touch new heights, depths and breadths of the galaxies beyond. That is your destiny, your life's work. As in nature, so in yourself—what 'All My Relations' means. All that we are and can be is mirrored in nature, in Earth Mother and her dwelling place in the universe. She guides us, offering comfort while she encourages us to go on.

"She confirms your existence and your journey through her soul lessons. In your dreams, she sends you spirit creatures, like the wolf and me, to beguile, to tempt, to teach and to confront you. Always her message is, 'learn and think it through' for yourself. Always, the choice is yours. Always your actions are the direct result of your will. The wisdom is there, inside, should you take the time to listen.

When you tap this wisdom, it is a warm wash in your gut, a vibration of knowing the rightness and truth. You think it a heritage of being the seventh son of a seventh son. And true, your memories allow you the freedom to move into this wisdom quicker than others. But everyone has it. They only need listen—inside."

Mud Woman turned to Mac, her eyes a blazing gold radiance, as they floated back towards the earth. "I have spoken so you may learn the truth about yourself and others. I see the people around you, burnt people, burned by their pride and lack of understanding. They confuse you. But they too can heal when they search, once again, for their soul, inside. And they must find it themselves, they must find where their strength lies, beyond the fear to all they are and can become."

Her golden leaf eyes glowed softly, "As in nature, so in yourself. All you are and can be is found in nature. And it is good." She rested her hands together and bowed her head. "Learn the truth about yourself and others. Do not be caught up in your judgement of others. Forgive: as in you, so too in others."

When they drifted back to his campfire, she stopped him with a gentle touch on his arm, "Travel in peace and alone with your spirit. Treasure and honour the ancients who guide you in your dreams, they will help you keep your path." She disappeared into the mists before he could ask her more.

Mac opened his eyes and sat up, finding himself still wrapped in his blankets. Dawn approached in twilight shadows. "As in nature, so in ourselves." He said it aloud, struggling to understand the dream. He surveyed the quiet scene around him and the solid ground beneath him. Mud Woman was a spirit of Mother Nature, Earth Mother. A connection blossomed in his gut, a straight line of understanding filled him, surrounded him and blended him in with the air above, the earth below and life itself, until he felt part of it, with no defined boundaries between it and his body: all one, all—as is—One. He felt the rightness of it, inside, in his gut: this moment, this land and himself in it. And it filled him, made him part of the dirt, filled with the same elements, same energy, part of the All. He felt totally connected to this land at last, with no fear. This time it stayed with him instead of fading back into the mists. He knew he would never feel alone or isolated again. Nothing to be judged or even feared he realized, only experienced—as it was, in this moment . . . .

"All My Relations." He mouthed it in understanding . . . then in reverence.

35.

NAGUAL

Broken Arrow also travelled into the earth that night. He too found the familiar crystal with its dark purple-brown colour and jewel-cut facets. Shards of the crystal were clustered together like a stack of giant sceptres, the hand-held transformers all the ancient gods had carried. Mac had told him about them, drawing a picture in the sand one day. One of the crystals rounded into a ball at the end with a ring of gold at its base. Was it placed by a massive hand and forgotten? Or was it merely waiting until the right moment for the return of its creator? When B.A. looked closer, he saw swirls of red, blue and green inside the mass, alive and moving, vibrating into a gentle hum that he felt rather than heard. The powerful crystals towered over his head, reaching for the top of the cavern in silent splendour. Overhead, a giant portal opened to the midnight blue of galaxies beyond. Through a blue mist, he saw distant stars.

She glided towards him, over the cave's stone floor, her dry grass skirt rustling in the dim light filtering from the crystal. Somehow, he knew her skirt covered no legs; she needed none. Instead, she merely floated on the ends of dried grass, her body a mud-woven hummock of ancient thought, space and time. She smelled of swamp, dampness and wind along with the subtle freshness of wild mint. Hands of gnarled and ancient roots reached out and clasped his. "Come," was all she said as she drifted away, drawing him with her until he floated beside her, uncaring about his feet, willing to follow wherever she led.

"Mitsue taught you about the mud, now it is time to teach you about the sky."

Then they were in the portal and flying up into the night, carried by gigantic wings. For the first time, he saw the bird's enormous golden head, something his dreams had never given him before. Was he ready now? What had changed in him that they welcomed him now? Somewhere between a loon and an eagle's, the totem bird's head sported a crest of softly tufted, multi-shaded feathers, like a neat little bouquet, dancing merrily in the wind. Its whimsical irreverence seemed in balance with the powerful bird's ancient wisdom. Crackling with lightening, his enormous wings boomed with thunder, echoing down through the massive thunderstorm beneath them, flashing wildly spectacular lights in the dark night's wind.

They flew, lifting like the giant Phoenix of Mac's tales, away from the earth, into the stars of the heavens, to the bird's faraway land. Later, Broken Arrow would remember only its warm rocks, hills and cliffs, a land of gold and brown and white, like the thunderbird's feathers, which swirled into magnificent, intricate patterns across its back in a thousand shades of brown.

They landed in a vast swamp; a gilded place of hummocks, small willows and endless dried grasslands, which appeared as dead as the strands upon Mud Woman's mounded head. A sweet, dry smell of slough grass wafted about him.

Her amber eyes turned to him. "This is where the real swamp is. This is Nagual, the opposing alter of Earth. Nagual, or Shadow. It is where the Powakan, the gods, live as human beings. They are either medicine animals or a group of entities representing the forces of nature. They are part human and communicate telepathically. Once in ancient times, the Powakan were able to speak directly to humans in dreams and visions. Fewer and fewer people remember how to communicate with them now."

"Another land in the stars?" Birds with a thousand different cries called and sang around him, unseen, yet there. Occasionally he caught brilliant flashes of coloured wings. He recalled Mac's druid bards with their cloaks of many coloured feathers and the Tuatha De Danann's king called Nuadha. Now he understood their ancient message: to remember this land from whence they came so long ago.

He stared in astonishment as green grass sprung up around his feet. His very presence altered the world around him—a testament of the power of his free will. He *had* wondered if the grass was dead.

"This is where everything is in balance, where all the seasons and cycles are known and honoured. This is a place of balance and harmony, all things considered as part of the whole. Your earth was a dream played out."

"A dream?" He echoed her words, unable to grasp it all as he numbly gazed about the land. And still the grass grew taller, almost to his knees.

"It was a chance to see what happened when free will was allowed to disrupt the harmony. Earth was a place to grow our swamp and see what happened when all thoughts, good and evil, from love to hate, giving to stealing, helping to harming, emptiness and abundance were allowed to grow, without interference. We wanted to observe the effects of such disharmony."

She shook her head in sorrow. "The results shocked us all. Your world could reach a point where there is no return. What we learned is what Mother tried to teach us all along. We cannot remain out of balance for long periods of time without self-destructing. She creates disharmony as the first phase in growth. Growth is needed, but only to restore the harmony. Your world does not see this. It seeks perfection not balance. Since perfection can never exist, disharmony results—continuously.

"People think if they seek forgiveness then they are back in harmony with themselves and their world. Their blindness is the result of living hard, believing too many falsehoods and thinking only work, money and materials keep them from happiness. They believe they can live a flawless life, find it somewhere out there, in some thing, some word or action or deed or service. They deny the wealth of wisdom within. They never seek the beautiful crystal inside themselves whose truth will always guide them back to themselves and their true purpose."

He turned to her in surprise. "We all have this crystal? I thought only Earth Mother possessed it."

Her hair rustled gently as she shook her massive head. "She is the crystal. We all have a piece for we are her children. We house it deep within ourselves, within the cavern of our soul. It is a gift from Mother, to ground us in her wisdom, to connect us to our Powakan at will. This is the ancient wisdom stored in the crystal cave, which she holds to guide us always."

She sighed and it was the wind moaning through barren trees. "Yet the cave is what people fear the most. To them, it represents all their fears. They think if they leave it alone, they will be fine. Some try to fill it with food, religion, alcohol or other addictive behaviours. Yet it houses their very soul—the crystal of infinite potential. Their cavern connects to Mother Earth's gigantic crystal and from there to here and to God the Creator. Yes, Mother Earth holds their souls in trust in her crystal. But who has come to claim them? Certainly not those who hide in fear behind their vices and addictions! Not those who seek perfection! And never those who think themselves perfect already because they are wealthy, or serve others or belong to some group or religion, upholding themselves in righteousness!"

She growled in disgust, "Man's eternal quest: to long for something with no faith in where to find it."

Her skirts settled about her as she drifted to an ancient rock, "I know the reason for their lack of faith in the Earth Mother. They think they can get along without her, without the feminine, the 'Evil Eve' as their religions remind them. It started with Ishtar in Babylon. She stole the virgin princesses of Zion in Israel and set up rituals of procreation—the fertile creative side of the Goddess. The full role of the masculine and feminine is creation, through love and passion and honour.

"But it was misunderstood by the warrior societies of Rome and Greece, even the Jews and their priests who saw it as fornication, an abomination of their vows of celibacy. So they destroyed the feminine in their righteous anger. Instead of love, they hated; instead of understanding, they condemned. Out of fear, they controlled and destroyed, instead of loving, sharing and creating together."

She used her crooked finger to draw a circle in the mud. "These actions twisted the circle of male and female unity and spun it into a figure eight, creating a 'cross-over'." She emphasized the cross now created in the middle of the two halves. "This is the 'cross' both male and female have born for thousands of years—two halves, eternally separated. With their vows of celibacy, the men suffered their own loss of connection to love, passion and healthy sexuality. It created a duality, an eternal conflict inside them. And the women have been punished for their temptations, punished by their leaders, fathers, husbands and sons for being wrong, sinful, lustful and dangerous.

"Earth became totally unbalanced with the masculine need to fight and control. Men's strength and ability to do, their drive, ambition, logic, wit, passion and energy is needed, true. But if not balanced with the feminine compassion, mercy, understanding, feelings and intuitive wisdom, without her enduring love, the masculine becomes too aggressive, violent and destructive, creating endless wars. Many women follow this same path of destruction, refusing to listen to their internal truth, refusing to share their own wisdom with the young women following in their footsteps. All the ancient teachings have become twisted, the mentoring of our youth lost, lost to her wisdom awaiting them in the crystal cave. Now, there are no checks, therefore no balance and no harmony within each person or between the world's races.

"When the males destroyed the feminine act of creation and love, they also destroyed her passion and intuitive connection with the Goddess and through her, with God. She is the irresistible feminine power who can destroy old forms and bring new ones into being. She is the cycle.

She is death, rebirth and growth. She endures all things. She is the one who loves and creates with passion, the other half of the Godhead.

"She is our intuitive wisdom within, our gut feeling of insight we all possess, man or woman. Through the feminine we find love-in-action, the heartbeat of all our feelings. Through the heart, our passions and emotions, we find the path to our spirit, and eventually, to our soul. Our soul is the total of our body with its male and female sides plus our mind, heart and spirit. So, our feminine side is the pathway to spirit, to the crystal of our soul and Earth Mother's cavern. She is the wisdom, the spiritual wisdom, the enlightenment connecting man with his soul and therefore to the souls of all races, all parts of Earth Mother and through her, to all the galaxies of the Creator.

"The feminine takes the masculine to heaven when they couple or join. When we create in any form, with love, we are in an act of god-like behaviour and it creates its own joy and ecstasy and rapture. It lifts us to a higher level of understanding and spiritual consciousness and connection. Sexuality is the key if it is done with honour, respect and love. But man never got it right and it has twisted his thinking ever since. Sex for the sake of sex, makes a shallow mockery of all man can do and create. Calling a woman saint or sinner ignores who she really is, denying her soul purpose. Yet, without her, man is unable to find his path to harmony within.

"This path is so needed to transform a world radically out of touch with its soul. The Earth Mother is this unseen cavern of soul to which we are all connected through our instincts and dreams, our feelings, and the longing imagination of our hearts."

She looked about her, "See this? This is the shadow world. Is it any less beautiful than its twin on earth?"

He narrowed his eyes, seeing no difference from his homeland. He shook his head.

"Ignoring the shadow, the dark side gives it far too much power over people. It controls them but they don't realize it. Until they see the shadow within themselves, they cannot grow, nor can they take it to the next step to understand the *need* for dark and light in their world. Their Dark defines their light, creating balance. Light illuminates the darkness, revealing its truth. The thunderbird reminds us of this power revealed in the thunderstorm of dark and light in perfect balance."

She swung twig-like arm outwards, "It is good, some of the things people on Earth do. What needs to change is their awareness of their part in it. For every darkness they create, they must also bring in the light. For all they take, they must also give back. This is balance, away from the disharmony. It creates endless possibilities of what can be held as solid upon Earth."

"People believe all they need is the logic of their minds. They think they can control their world, if they just pray and be good citizens or even hoard all the power and material things they can. But they never grow in this stationary life of mindless, repetitive and therefore, meaningless words and actions. They never see beyond to the ownership of their own truth. They *are* full of faults and goodness: the dark and the light and they are *deliberately* made this way! Yet they choose to see only the light, ignoring or condemning the dark as if it were an evil to be cut away or hidden."

She grew angry. "You don't understand! Do you? You own the light but you must also own the dark! All those good, bad, terrible, awful things we do to ourselves and others must be owned, accepted and loved or changed. It's key here! You can never grow beyond selfish worship of the light, that foolish search for non-existing perfection, if you cannot appreciate the dark! It defines you, makes you human, vulnerable, humble, needful of harmony! This is not illusion! Your world is the illusion, created out of your own blindness of what you think is perfection and thus right! There can never be just right or wrong, only balance! And it will never be achieved so long as man thinks he can create his world out of prideful judgement not humility from what he really is.

"This is not a test! This is not about being strong or the best! This is what Mother is trying to tell you! Balance comes at the cost of disharmony. That is its price! We must walk in the fullness of what we are, accepting our inner disharmony, before we can ever begin to understand the complexity of Mother Earth. She creates both chaos and harmony. Both are needed. Both create the cycles: Destruction and Creation; Death and Birth. Both are needed! The entire range from the deepest valley to the highest peak of our experiences and emotions are needed! From the ocean floor to the dancing waves all are there for us to explore and learn from. We . . . are . . . ALL of her!!!" Her voice echoed through the canyons in the distant and rained down through the blue misted winds. It crackled with age, dried and rusted from a long silence.

It wrapped him in prickling barbs of awareness, swirled through his head, down through his heart and back into the earth at his feet. And still the grass grew around him, unfolding green spikes of truth and renewal. Now he understood: forgiveness truly meant renewal; it meant accepting all he had done and said in the past. Oh how he had judged the white men, judged Mac, Red Arrow and Melissande, Salvia and even the dark-haired Alorah. He had placed himself as somehow different than they. Now he ached with the painful humility of his mistakes. He gazed down in sorrow, because they all were just blades of grass, learning and sharing together—no different—all composed of the same height and depth and breadth of feelings and spirit—like all humanity, like all his relations, like all of the Earth and the galaxies beyond. Because *he* wanted greenery, unwilling to accept the beautiful shades of brown surrounding him, he'd created it around his feet. His very power to do so, to change this land with his will alone, humbled him and in truth, frightened him. Tall Man had always said, "With great power comes great responsibility."

His eyes lifted once more to the sky and the gigantic thunderbird hovering there. His heart ached with the painful lessons before him and still the bird patiently waited.

Her voice crept up from behind, "And man believes if he can just shut out her winds, her cold, her storms, her fury, then he will have a perfect world. He cannot see the need for what she brings, creating the circle, the cycle of life: birth, death and rebirth—living life to the fullest—nothing held back, nothing controlled, suppressed, subverted and narrowed—neither repetitive prayers nor celibacy nor feelings nor truth! Man has never found the courage to admit his faults, to stay in his awareness of them and how they influence his life every day! He never honours how they made him what he is. If he did, then he could accept them all, grow to love them all and use them to build himself into all he can be, the best he can be. Like the crystal, with its rainbow of colours from dark to light, each are needed for his inner harmony – his full gift from Earth Mother and Creator!

"To be aware of our human faults is to find peace and joy once again. For when we know all our faults and strengths, then we can choose to be ourselves, choose to take the good, accept the bad and create something worthwhile for the world. We learn to live within our own body, without hating it for its shape or colour or hating others for the same. When we no longer judge, we can let go of the hatred, the sorrow and the grief of what we are. We can let go of our expectations of what life should be like and just create our own. We can live joyously, in a static type of harmony of all we are—both the good and the bad. When man can accept both his good and bad, then he is both all. Then he finds balance. He finds peace! This is awareness. This is living in the moment, with passion and love!

"But man cannot find his soul, the other part of himself, until he can walk down into the darkened cave of himself, the seat of his soul and face honestly, truthfully and squarely, whatever creeps, scuttles or launches itself at him from every nook and cranny. That is his quest. And it must happen within him, not based on what any other man or religion decrees he should do."

She pointed her blackened finger roots at him, "You can learn from the White Man, but be aware of his faults because he cannot always see them. His pride denies their existence." Her voice softened, "Your quarrel was never with the Creator but with His foolish and narrow priests who mistook their own narrowness as His. It became part of religious doctrine for thousands of years and people followed it unquestioningly. That is man's blindness and your folly should you not recognize it. This is what will cause all the horrors yet to come on Earth."

She brought him back to the prairies of the Earth. As he looked at the withered grasslands and gently mounding hills, he truly found no difference from the shadowed planet they had just left. She stood at his side, her dried skirts rustling in the wind, wafting the dusty aroma of wild mint around him. "This is Sacred Land. You know that. Your people hold it in trust while we do this experiment. Soon there will be a council meeting of all the races. They will decree who shall come to this land to learn, to observe, to hear the sacred messages and then decide, as they all must, what to do about the darkness that will shroud this land in helpless agony in the years to come. Your people will suffer along with the white, yellow and black people." Her golden eyes dulled for a moment, "And it will not change until the people of the Earth change, until they understand their connection to Her, the feminine side of every man and woman, until they find Earth Mother once again and through Her, the connection to the one who created them, until they understand they and all their relations, are part of the Creation and the Creator. That they are also part of the Godhead. No less, no more."

He looked about him, filled with turmoil. "And I Grandmother? Will I be here to see it happen?"

Her skirts rustled through the silence. "That is your choice grandson. The final result is found in seven generations ahead. This you already know."

Tears filled his eyes and slipped unheeded down his high cheeks. "I must stay to watch this destruction? I must live through it too? Even though you have already shown me what is to come? What more can I learn but pain? Am I to send my children's children into this horror? How do I live with their hatred and anger towards the blind White Man who is now my friend? Do not ask me to change that Grandmother. I have no heart to kill him anymore. He is my brother."

"Yes, a brother. And that too will be forgotten in the generations ahead. None will remember this simple truth."

He sank to his knees, rubbing the earth with his palms, "Why will we forget Her?"

Her voice cracked in pain, "Because man truly believes he is right to destroy and defile Her and he will convince others the same."

"What about our Elders? Grandmother surely they will remember Her and all Her teachings!" B.A. wanted to believe, to hang on.

She shook her head, "For the next hundred years, they will be raised in schools built by the Black Robes. They will never learn the teachings of their parents and grandparents, only the shame of their ways. They will be separated and live alone in the dark schools of pride and control and anger. When the next generations of children go to these elderly damaged children, in the time of rebirth these old ones will be blind, have no ears, their mouths sewn shut; their brains washed with White Man beliefs. Your people's struggle back to the Mother must be done in despair and suffering, the path of true humility. From the heart crystal's pain, they will be connected back to their spirit and the Mother who holds their souls in trust. These damaged elders will need their spirits to re-connect with the Powakan who will return from the shadow world, Nagual, to teach them once again. That is the only truth they can rely on. At the end of the next seven generations, nothing left on this Earth will be worth listening to. Only the messages from Earth Mother and her spirits, the Powakan will hold truth. Only the feminine, the intuitive inner voice of us all will once again connect to the Powakan whose truth will bring us back to wisdom and harmony.

"Look about you grandson. Already it begins: the prejudice, the lies, the greed and the destruction. This sacred land will know nothing but disharmony in a world too blind to see its fate.

"Disharmony!" She shouted, her dry hair rustling about her head, her skirts quivering in agitation. "Harmony is an internal calm. What you have on Earth is the opposite! This is truth and truth creates its own chaos while people struggle to accept it and change before it is too late.

"This is not a time to sit back on your haunches and contemplate your hands! Your people are entering a period of great stress and it cannot be taken lightly as something that will pass into oblivion. This is your heritage! This is your soul journey to find *your* answers. You have been chosen for your wisdom and the ancient heritage you carry in the memories passed down to you from your ancestors and the thunderbirds. This is what comes from drinking freely of the waters of history and the future. You become charged with the responsibility of owning the task yet to come. You have not been forsaken, you have been foretold. This is part of your heritage and when the time comes, you will know how to end it. Remember, you have not been forsaken. We are with you. You will see the way soon enough." A rising wind swirled grey mists about her, enveloping her, only her. When they lifted, he was alone and terrified.

Broken Arrow awoke with a start, flinging himself upright, reaching for his knife. Across from him, Mac slept on peacefully, his face glowing slightly in the dying embers of the fire. For long moments Broken Arrow stared at this White Man, half in wonder at his presence in his life, half in despair at what his coming meant.

36.

SOUL SONG

Mac dreamt of a melody, haunting and vivid, ancient and wise. As it played, a tree materialized in front of him. A tree like none he had seen before. It had a thousand leaves, each made of clay. Upon each leaf, a single symbol of Ogham, the ancient language of the Celts, lay in relief. When he rubbed each leaf with his fingertips, he could read the symbol and follow the story, from one leaf to the next. As he read, music flowed through him, until he ached with it, wanted to memorize it, play it on his flute, move into it until it became a part of him and he it; until there were no boundaries between them, only one, united. Now, he constantly yearned for this elusive unity.

He awoke, reached for his flute and began to play. The song poured out of him in endless, flowing waves. It moved him with its energy, until he climbed to his feet and swept into its sound. He could no more have stopped playing than stopped his breath. So he played the song only his soul knew. The melody filled the campground and rolled out across the sleepy prairie, further and further away until it faded into distant trees and echoed down the silent skies, before returning faintly on the wind.

As he played, he felt it, for the first time. He *felt* it! Felt its vibrations become one with his, a rippling, swirling energy that encompassed and expanded around him, loving and warm and wise. And it was *his*! For the first time he knew a piece of what he could give back to this land

– a part of himself, his soul in song . . . a soul song. It pleased him even as he felt the connection, felt a part of this land through his song. It centred him even as he filled the land with the song from his soul: All One.

Tears came then, seeping through his closed lids, sliding down his cheeks and dripping upon the land, her land. She danced with him. He could see her, just behind his closed lids, her ancient skirts rippling in the rhythm of his song, her twisted fingers following the melody, lifting and falling, flowing to his overture and dipping with his heart's painful delight. Beside her, gambolled the big black wolf and his grey mate, their tongue lolling, feet gracefully keeping the rhythm, their golden eyes glowing.

She grew larger and larger, her grey-green dress expanding with the fullness and heaviness of her massive breasts. Her giant hand lifted him and drew him upward. He honoured her strength, her power to destroy. Though he felt no more than a blade of grass in her hand, he was not afraid, feeling only her gentleness, her kindness and her delight as she moved and swayed to his song. And so they danced, as friends, as soul dancers, united in the sound, united unto one . . . at last.

B.A. sensed the profound depth of his friend's soul unity. He lay in his bed, unmoving yet moved beyond words by the melody surrounding him. He watched the tears tracking down Mac's face as he swayed in the music – Soul Music. The grieving Cree recognized the haunting creation as a song just for his friend, from the Creator and Mud Woman. His people fasted and prayed many moons and seasons for just such a song that his friend now played. Elders needed four to become full medicine people. The song's beauty flowed through both men. Broken Arrow also sensed her nearby, dancing and moving to Mac's song, his overture, his seduction and hers . . . as one. Mac had finally found what he never knew he searched for. It was indeed the Mother of them all, the Mother of this land. Finally, through her, Mac would find not only his soul but the one who had created it. At last he would understand oneness. B.A. sighed and closed his eyes. Now he understood why the old people came to truly love the soil.

His work was done. And the thought filled his heart with sorrow.

37.

STONE MANSION

Broken Arrow had a vision several nights later when they camped
near Victoria, about seventy miles downriver from Fort Edmonton.
Long after Mac sought his bed, B.A. sat before the fire, staring into
its flames, filled with a melancholy he could neither name nor release,
Mud Woman's teachings played endlessly through his mind. What
was he to do now? He put it out to his Powakan and waited for
answers. Where did he fit? What was his purpose now? The flames
danced and flickered before him, green, blue, red and yellow until his
vision blurred with their dance. He moved deeper into the trance,
beyond the flames to an image which slowly took shape in his mind:

*A lone man picked up the elaborate brass door knocker on a grey stone
mansion and dropped it. He waited, peering over his shoulder at the
shadowy trees lined like sentries along the field stone wall stretching away
from him. He trembled, gathering his black woollen cloak around him. He
struggled to find an inner silence, a peace missing now for months. Instead,
his unease intensified, gut-deep and aching. It weighed upon him, heavier
than his damp cloak. He sighed. In this ungodly humid climate, even winter
brought no solace, only icy indifference. The bitter damp made him shiver,
creeping into his hands and bringing on the pains that had troubled him
since he'd left here two years ago. It was over now . . . almost.*

*The door opened quietly, a sober, bespectacled butler peered down through
heavy lids at the visitor.*

"I have an appointment with the master."

"Your name?" the butler asked coldly, his nose rising in a disgusted quiver at the man's damp, woolen odour.

The stranger sagged slightly, his wide brimmed hat dipping to cover his distressed features. For a fleeting moment, the butler wondered if he beheld a young man or an aging one. And how could a man change from one to the other before his eyes?

"Tell him Jacob, his missionary, is back."

The butler closed the door in his face.

Once again the visitor turned to the immaculate greenery around him. Such perfection, each flower in its place, juxtaposed with shrubs for balance and aesthetic pleasure. How different from the wild, free-flowing land he had just left.

"He'll see you now." The butler opened the door wider, stepping aside for the man to enter. The stranger had few lines on his face, yet his hair was white, his eyes old and weary. The butler felt an unfamiliar twinge of pity for this odd young-old man.

As the stranger followed the butler down a hallway, a door suddenly opened ahead of them. A dark haired woman in her thirties, her head down, rushed out in a swirl of green taffeta skirts. Over her shoulder, the stranger glimpsed a shattered room of overturned chairs, tilting tables and broken lamps. As the woman raised her heavily ringed hands to straighten a jewelled barrette in her neat chignon, she spied the men. With a gasp of horror she quickly averted her face, backed into the room and slammed the door. The stranger froze, the shock of her swollen, bruised cheek and bloodshot, black eye flashing through his mind, rendering him helpless and ill.

The butler whirled angrily, glaring at the visitor, "Not a word! Not one word of this or I shall know exactly where it came from! Do you understand?!!"

The stranger raised a gloved hand in tired supplication, bowing slightly in silent promise.

So the rumours were true. He breathed deeply, inhaling warm air laden with stale cigar smoke, spilt rum and ancient mildew. The aroma of decadence. Or was it power?

He was led into a dark, heavily curtained drawing room, where the hot air writhed with a blue haze of cigar smoke. A tall, gaunt man leaned carelessly against a marble fireplace. Above him, from a massive gilded portrait, Queen Victoria observed the stranger with cold disdain.

As he moved closer, the visitor noted the taller man's rumpled white neckcloth with its faint yellow streaks. Beneath it, an opulent gold broadcloth vest hung over a lean stomach. No wig hid the man's wildly mussed hair, its strands thin and greying, over-long on the sides. No photographer was available to retouch the portrait of sagging jowls, pouch-lined eyes and thin lips twisted into a sneer of dissatisfaction. The newspapers wrote much about this man's bulbous nose. They claimed it rendered his character an air at once mocking and artless. Flickering flames heated the room's rancid reek of old tobacco and raw rum to a suffocating stench.

The stranger's fingers tightened on his cloak as he felt the butler tug at it from behind. Nothing could be left behind.

The lean man glanced at the waiting butler, "Nobody disturbs us." His soft voice held a touch of hoarseness, perhaps the result of too many years of public speaking or, according to the newspapers, too much rum and tobacco.

The silent visitor watched the butler close the door behind him as he left.

"Drink?" The man plucked a half-full glass from the fireplace, toasted the stranger then tossed it back in one swallow.

The man in black reached out to the fire, shivering again, but not from the cold. "No thank you, Sir."

The taller man snorted, "What's this Jacob? Have you been wearing that damn pious white collar for so long you believe the drivel attached to it? You could match me drink for drink before you left for that godforsaken Rupert's Land. I thought it might make a man out of you, but a priest? Hell man, if I'd even considered such a result I never would have sent you!" He kicked a nearby chair in sullen violence. "Sit down."

The stranger stubbornly chose a red velvet chair across the hearth, pulling his cloak from his shoulders and spreading it carefully across the back, a fastidious gesture that enraged the watching leader.

"I see you're as precise as ever Jacob. No doubt you were damn believable as a bloody missionary, fake though you are. You know, I wonder if God Almighty ever created a man as honest as you look Jacob. Your prissy manners would have fit right in with the rest of those worthless bible punchers."

"I have done as you asked, sir."

The haggard man snorted, "Alright, let's get to it. What did you find out about the damned heathens in these past two years of travelling the West?"

"They are a strong and healthy race sir, oddly happy with their lot. They are like no other people I have ever met. Somehow we—as the superior white race we claim—have never found the elusive happiness these people live with every day. Perhaps we like our melancholy overmuch . . . it gives us a certain sense of . . . justification for our fears."

"Yes, yes. Never mind the loquacious philosophizing. Damn me but I always hated that about you Jacob!" He poured another tall shot of rum and downed half in one toss of his head. "What did you find out that I can use?"

"They have a strong sense of family ties. It is the foundation of everything they do. They love their children so much they will not lay a hand on them, letting them run freely like the miniature savages they are. Yet I could not help but admire the spirit of the young imps, so mischievous, yet touchingly sweet and innocent."

"You're getting soft Jacob. What else?"

"They fear nothing. Not even death itself. They paint their faces in preparation for war only so their God will find them in death. They believe life is always a struggle and what comes next is the true world to live in."

"And?" It came in a surly sneer

"And they are fully independent, living off the land as they have done for hundreds, indeed thousands of years, if you listen to the stories their elders tell. They need nothing from us. Oh they like the iron tools and guns, but their arrows and bows they value just as much because it proves their courage to use them. The buffalo, the plants and the waters bring them everything they need, from food to medicines."

The stranger leaned forward eagerly, "You really should travel the west and see for yourself sir."

The lean man snarled, "I have never been west of Bruce Peninsula near the Great Lakes; few of the ministers have. I have no desire to ever set foot in the lawless lands of the West. As Minister of the Interior all these years, I represent what they should have, not as they are, the bloody savages. What of their leaders Jacob? How do I deal with them?"

"Their leaders change with whim and need. A chief of many men can be the leader of none the following day should he make foolish choices. The warriors follow whomever they want. The old, wise elders give counsel, but they can be ignored too, though few warriors will gainsay them."

"And their women? Do the men at least have control over them?"

"Oddly enough, sir, I would have to say 'No." The man in black stretched his legs towards the fire and rubbed his face in thought. "The women own their households, as we would call them, make choices as to who travels in their bands, have much say in raising the children and even run their own councils and ceremonies. The women are as much the decision-makers as their men and heaven help the silly fools who forget

this. I have seen some men beaten over the head by their irate wives for making choices without their counsel."

"Idiots! Women should never control anything! They cause nothing but trouble with their whining outside of the bed chambers." The Minister studied a skinned knuckle, sniffed and downed the rest of his rum. He wiped his mouth on a lacy cuff. "Anything else?

"A word of caution, if I may sir. I hesitate to tell you, but feel I must. I have come to respect these people. Far from pretending to bring them religion, I have struggled to understand theirs. It is as complex and rich as our own Christianity. You may be able to change some things but their faith is too different, too strong for even your power and wealth. It will not break."

"You fool! Do you really think this is some omnipotent race we speak of? They are nothing but a bunch of filthy savages who deserve to be hunted down like the dogs they are. How dare you question what I can or cannot do! Do you think I arrived at this place with such snivelling cowardly ways? I have accomplished this position by my own hand and by God, not only will I maintain it, I will expand it sea to sea!" His mottled face reddened as he raised a fist in spitting fury. "And no goddamn redskin will stand in my way! I'll kill the whole bloody works of them if that's what it takes. Religion! Pah! A pox on the lot of you black-robed whining curs! Think I need you?!"

He paced, in small furious loops before the fireplace, rubbing thorny whiskers scattered in grey clusters on a sagging jawline. "I will use what you have given me Jacob to get back into power and build this country. The French will always be French." He shrugged a bony shoulder, "and the English, an over washed lot . . . utterly ignorant of the country and full of crochets but I can bring them around. But those bloody Indians will never amount to a pinch of snuff. Make no mistake. I will have this country. A united Canada is the only way to defend us from those southern bastards. I'll make it work!! If family ties hold the damned Indians together, I will cut them. If they value their children, I will make damn sure they never see them again. If they fear nothing, by God I'll find something they'll fear for the rest of their lives. If they live off the land, I will give them land that offers them nothing. And if they fear no death, I will give them a life that will make them wish they were dead. I'll even help them along. They are nothing but useless spawn. I will rid the land of them and fill it with my people, God-fearing people, who understand true leadership. And I will rule! I will rule this land, no doubt about it. I will be its King from Atlantic to Pacific if I have to step on stinking redskin bodies all the way across this goddamned land!" Spittle foamed at the corners of his mouth, "Do you hear me? I will . . . be . . . King!!!"

The man in black stared in horror at this slobbering, ranting maniac quivering like a shrivelled cadaver," You are mad! You cannot kill an entire nation of thousands, including women and children!"

The tall, gaunt man bent over him, his breath as fetid as his mind. "Who will stop me? They will never know where the orders come from. I have men who will follow them to the letter and never question why. Nothing written, nothing proven I say." He flipped at the stunned man's nose and walked away. "As far as I'm concerned, this conversation never took place."

He spun to watch the frozen figure in black, "You may go Jacob. And do find a suitable bath sirrah. You stink of the West!"

Sickened to the point of nausea, the man groped his way from the room, staggering down the hall until he slammed into the front door. He fell outside, into the crisp air, pulling it into his lungs, seeking something clean, fresh, anything to absolve the creeping blackness almost driving him to his knees. Visions of laughing brown faces, gilded by warm firelight, reeled through his stunned mind. "What have I done? Dear God what have I done?!"

Behind him, in the grey stone mansion, the man who for almost half a century would be the major parliamentary representative of the North-West Territories or Rupert's land, all the way to the Pacific Ocean; the man they would call 'Old Tomorrow' because of his endless procrastination in the face of an Indian nation's dire need; the man who would be knighted, honoured as the Father of Confederation and elected

Canada's first Prime Minister, John Alexander Macdonald, calmly poured another shot of rum and downed it in one swallow . . . .

Only the night owl perched high above in the giant poplar heard the ragged sobs of Broken Arrow's crumpled figure beside the dying flames. After listening for a long time, it answered . . . once.

38.

SLAN AGAT

'Mud Woman!" Broken Arrow closed his eyes in agony.

"Why?" He cried out to the blackened heavens, tears filling his eyes. "Why must we go through this? Why such pain? Why can we not go directly to the peace? Why was I born as witness? Why must I learn all this only to be held to it? Locked into it? I cannot! Do not ask it of me. I cannot! I cannot bear to watch the agony of my people or my children yet to come. I cannot stand and helplessly wait for their destruction. Mud Woman! Where are you!!! Why can you not visit them all? Why me?"

Only the wind in his ears answered.

He whispered into it, "Is this my answer? Because nobody listens to the wind anymore so it must grow loud enough to be heard once again?" His head bowed. "I cannot change it, can I? This was written long ago and now must play out. From pain comes all learning." Back hunched, he fell forward on his knees, tears slipping down his cheeks.

"What am I? What am I against this force? I am nothing! Whipping uselessly in the winds of change coming to this land. Where can I go? When all the land is divided into little squares for the White Man, where can my people go? Where can we pitch our tipis? Create our circles? Where will we pray?"

He cried out to the heavens. "This is my only land! I cannot immigrate to another place of hope. I am here and there is nothing left in this life I want to see anymore. Nothing! *Nothing!* Do not ask it of me! Creator! Do not ask." His great shoulders shook with the power of his grief as he sank face first to the dirt, sobbing in shattered reality.

Finally, spent of all emotion, drained of all energy and thought, purified to the most powerful point of humility, he heard her speak, her voice a dusty rasp of dead grass:

"Pride is something your people have to lose to be teachers of humility. Their strength will be born from their suffering. Truth will be delivered up out of all the lies they will be told and experience. The infinite dignity of their soul will lift them out of their despair. And the spirituality of the world will be reborn out of the hypocrisy of a man-made religion, the unbalanced view of those who have lost touch with their feminine side and Earth Mother. It will be born and it will grow.

One day man, the son, will realize he is from all of Him – the Creator, and all of Her – the Creation. The trinity will return as it once was. We are the children of the Father and the Holy Spirit Mother. When people understand the crystal at the centre of the earth is their connection to Her; when they reach inside themselves, beyond their granite wall of unchanging judgements, beyond their congested physical, mental, emotional and spiritual perceptions, beyond the fear of the pit, they will find Her energy, Her wisdom. Then they will enter the loving flow of the river of life. Their awakening is the eternal wearing away of their rigid, granite containment in the heavy concentration of the mind, flowing into the lessons of their heart and spirit, away from all that won't move into the free fall flow of Her truths, the free fall flow of their ability to live in the moment, all moments, to think, experience and *live* each second to fullness. It is life, the miracle of life, which is the greatest gift of all, from birth till death and beyond. Beyond to more than the Godhead, more than anyone ever considered, ever thought possible, all the way to their intentions, their will of what it should be, beyond the earth, the stars and the galaxies, to unlimited space, unlimited creation. That is man's heritage, his birth right, his free will to create, using Her wisdom and compassion and spirit for the betterment of all his relations."

She began to chant:

> All you feel is yours.
> All you wish to be is yours.
> All you hope, dream, desire and drive towards is
>   yours
> for the asking and the deliverance.
> What you intend, so will it be.
> This is the promise of men's free will in freedom
>   flight, ecstasy, joy and tears.
>
> So **Will** it out."

Wiping his face, he lifted to a cross-legged position and closed his eyes.

*   *   *

The next morning, Broken Arrow announced, "I will die today!"

Mac whipped his head up and almost dropped the bone needle and sinew he was using to repair Jim's bridle. "Ye're daft! You have no choice about things like that!"

B.A.'s eyes narrowed, "Have you learned nothing from me about choices? Our whole life is choices and I shall make mine. It can go no further. I see no purpose in continuing this hated life. I have listened to you and what happened to your people. It will happen again to my people because the White Man has not learned his lessons. I see the destruction of this land through the greed and power of the White Man who lost his soul and doesn't even know it. I see the way our women are already treated and it will not change, only worsen. I see no future, at least not in this generation, for my people who will be fenced in like dogs. They will be lied to, cheated on, and then scorned for their failure to agree with an empty life. Yet it will be their lack of agreement which will save the foolish White Man in the end. But it will not be now, not in this lifetime, not for me or my people. And I will not stay to watch it! I choose death and the next lifetime, when the rebirth of my people will come again.

"I will tell you a prophecy my elders have shared for many generations." Broken Arrow squatted by the smouldering fire, stoking embers until it flamed once more. Mac moved his gear to the fire and joined him, sighing gustily as he hunkered down for another story.

"The Europeans who came to Turtle Island had a choice: Come into loving harmony and gain the knowledge of this land, which would bring them into balance with Creation. By sharing with our people who were already on this Turtle Island, they could blend their knowledge and their power with ours and all the races of the world who will come here. According to our elders, if the Europeans didn't do this, the Indians would lie upon the face of the Earth as if dead in the dust for a hundred years or more. Then the power would come back to us. At the end of the one hundred years, we would stand up once again. We would be alive as if we were Earth spirits newly reborn. We'd stand up and have our power again. We would be able to call in the forces: thunder, lightning and storms, bringing back the thunderbirds of old. We would once again speak with the Powakan, remembering their powers as part of our ancient knowledge. We would remember our past lives and the wisdom we gathered throughout them all. These are gifts we will bring to teach others about spirit so we could all return to the sacred path.

"At that time, our sons and daughters would again come to us and ask about the sacred ways. And the sons and daughters of people from across the Great Waters would also come, asking for teachings to stop the destruction of the earth."

He shared his dream with Mac and what Mud Woman had told him about the terrible imbalance of man and what his free will would create on earth.

Mac rubbed his curls uneasily, struggling to follow the powerful message he now accepted as true. He searched for logic from his ancestors. "The druids taught this same idea of Imbalance: 'From the Point of Greatest Imbalance, Comes the Point of Greatest Stability'. They believed the spirit of a man needs opposition—imbalance in his life to promote growth. He must See all, Study all and Suffer all, to reach the cycles governing rebirth. Suffering is the result of imbalance in man's life; growth the result of his attempts to stop the suffering and return to balance. Druids reasoned that perfectly balanced forces result in the net movement of zero. There can be no growth without movement. So . . . imbalance results in movement or change in the direction of the weakness, where it is most needed."

B.A. listened closely. Mud Woman's final words made more sense now. The coming pain would force every man to face his greatest weakness and change it. His head dropped. *Ekosesa.* And so it was . . . .

Mac took his time, thinking it through, pulling both cultures' thoughts together, before speaking, "Your elders say the imbalance we create will force us to move in the direction of our greatest weakness: our loss of soul. We need to do this and will learn our most powerful lessons of the soul from your people." He nodded smiling as he peered into his friend's face. "The Good Lord knows I have learned so much from you already, my *Anam Cara*."

B.A. stilled, "What is that?"

Mac's face softened, his smile turning whimsical, "Soul Friend, one who listens from the heart, without judgement—though I beg to differ occasionally," he offered slyly. "A soul friend guides and counsels and appreciates the soul of another, even as he travels beside him, sharing life. He or she takes pleasure in empowering the other. In the Celtic tradition, our wise women were masters at this. But good men have this ability too if they have the self-confidence to listen to others and accept them as equals, without feeling threatened or needful to prove anything." He tilted his head, watching his friend closely to see if he would accept.

B.A. thought for a time then nodded abruptly. "We have been that together. Anam Cara." He tested the words on his tongue, holding Mac's anxious eyes. "But now I have no place to go. You say your Irish people came here to escape persecution. Where can my people go to escape the same? The White Man is everywhere and more are coming. They refuse to blend our knowledge with theirs. They scorn our very presence, shoving their prejudice and hatred before them. They feel too badly about themselves to ever encourage us."

Mac shook his head and sighed, "Aye, I canno' wish the war on ye like the one we still wage with the British. Never would I want to see all that blood, anger and hate in this fair land, generation after generation. Tis a terrible way to live, miserable and empty – a war with no end where the constant cry for revenge splits the family and destroys all ties."

He watched his friend, "Could ye no' try to be more like us? Maybe take the best we can offer?"

"I can never forget I am Indian. The White Man will never allow it, just like he never allows the Irish or Jews to forget." Pain dulled B.A.'s dark eyes, "I have no red hair or green eyes. I am as I am. If I cut my hair and wear your clothes do you think the White Man will let me forget I am Indian. I think not. I will not do it. I will not live this life any longer. I chose to die."

Mac's eyes filled with horror, "Blasphemy! You face persecution forever if you take your own life! You will burn in the black halls of hell for such rejection of God's gift of life. You cannot, you canno' do this!"

B.A.'s eyes darkened. "Always you think with your anger first!"

Mac gritted his teeth and shoved his fist into the dark face. "I could knock you out with one punch. Maybe when you wake, ye'll see how stupid ye sound!"

Broken Arrow remained seated, his eyes narrowing, "Your fists change nothing!"

"Sure'n I never took ye for a coward either!" Mac snarled.

"Stop thinking with your mind, you foolish White Man!" Broken Arrow's temper rose.

"Better than me arse!" Mac was spoiling for it. He lunged to his feet, hands fisted and ready, his jaw like granite.

"Listen! Listen to me!" Broken Arrow's fury exploded from deep within his gut as he arose and faced the Irishman. "This is not about the mind, or the heart! This is not about your thoughts or your anger! This is soul truth! And it will . . . not . . . change!" His fist slammed his ribs, beneath his heart, the centre of his soul. "Listen to me!"

Mac waited, his teeth clenched. He lowered his fists a few inches. "Then stop talkin' like an idjit!"

B.A.'s eyes sparked once more, "You have the conscience of your people and your religion. But they are not mine. Have you forgotten my lesson already? You are not my keeper!"

Mac's face tightened, "Aye, but I will no' stand back and watch ye kill yerself either! I'll knock some brains into yer thick head first!" He danced around in front of his friend, shoulders hunched, fists cocked.

Broken Arrow smiled sadly, "You bring no honour to me by telling me how to live my life. Nobody can change what is to be in this land."

"And how d'ye know this will all come to pass? Ye have only legends and dreams to rely on!" Mac sneered, frustrated with an enemy he could neither see nor destroy.

Broken Arrow sighed, "You are one White Man of many in the *Kistin*, Big Wind sweeping the land. You have travelled with me long enough to understand much more than many whites will ever know. And from you, I have learned all I want to know about the White Man."

Mac glared in disbelief. "And this is your answer? Tuck your tail between your legs and run to your death? Where's the honour in that?" He threw the Cree's words back in his face.

B.A. closed his eyes and sank into the Earth, his breath shaken with the power of his faith. He opened bleak eyes to meet the flashing green above him. "I will tell you something I have never told another. I am Thunderbird, clan of the stars. I have known since my birth I was different but Mud Woman told me the truth in a dream last night. Thunderbirds were a race that came to Earth a long time ago, because they were attracted to the humans who knew a love like no other. From the humans, the thunderbirds learned the many forms of love found in relationships between a man and woman, their children, their family, their friends and even for the land they walked upon. The humans taught them the love in grief, in laughter, forgiveness and making peace with one another. In return, the Thunderbirds taught the humans the wisdom of the stars, how their bodies are part of the heavens and the power that created them. They taught the humans to create with great love, through thought alone. They taught the humans the power of their greatness."

Mac blew a gusty sigh of frustration, unclenched his fists and hunkered down once again beside the big man who continued, "But the human race was not ready for this wisdom. Some used it with hate, to destroy, to control and manipulate others. Selfishly hoarding the power for themselves, they created creatures to kill the thunderbirds, who they now resented. So the thunderbirds left in distress, removing the wisdom to the mists of time."

Mac's head came up, "The mists? Blue mists?"

Broken Arrow's eyes crinkled, "Aye," he teased, waiting.

Mac's eyes widened, "But I saw the mists! I walked them in my dreams! I was there!"

B.A. nodded, easing his friend into this one. "In your land, the thunderbirds were called dragons."

Mac paled as he searched the black eyes before him, seeking weakness but finding none.

He leapt to his feet, strode away in agitation, running his hands through his hair, thinking. He spun to the waiting Cree. "But they are only mythical creatures in our legends . . . ! They weren't real, just creatures of the mists, flying through man's dreams."

Broken Arrow stilled. "You told me once your druids wore blue robes. How their flower symbol was a blue rose. Have you not wondered why they were blue? Could they not have worn blue to remind them of the truth hidden in the blue mists?"

Mac rubbed his jaw, his face tense, "Jaysus, I never considered a connection. Many of our ancient leaders wore blue robes—even Mary Magdalene and Christ. And there are so many stories about killing the dragons . . ." He frowned, "This canno' be! The dragons were evil, destructive! We have many tales of them stealing the maidens, hiding them in their caves."

Broken Arrow nodded, "They protected the feminine, the crystal cave and all it represented. Even your Christ and Mary Magdalene believed what the dragons believed. Mud Woman said that's why your knights painted dragons on their shields."

Mac shook his head rapidly, quivering with the intensity of his revulsion. "Twas only the bravest of knights what sought the dragons and killed them. The Christian knight, Saint George was said to slay the last dragon on earth."

B.A.'s eyes narrowed in fury, "After all I have told you, you still believe everything the Black Robes say and write? Would you reconsider if I told you dragons represent freedom? To slay a dragon was to slay the feminine, to lose your right of free will, to choose and think for yourself—just like your first Adam lost his? It means giving your power to others, to a society, a religion or a cause. Death of the dragons meant losing the power of your human birthright!"

"Jaysus! Ye scare me!" Mac reeled away, making furrows in his wild hair. "Ye make me head spin with all this!" He whirled back, "How d'ye know? How d'ye know this be true?"

Broken Arrow shook his head in sorrow. "White Man, if you cannot see your bondage, how can you possibly be ready to fly?"

"Arrgh!" Mac roared his fury, his fists clenched, his body rigid with frustrated confusion.

B.A. went on, "Would it help if I told you the Thunderbirds or dragons were visionaries who understood the true nature of life, of this Earth and man's own magical heritage he must grow into as his wisdom expanded. That is why they loved him; for All that he was capable of. If you saw the mists, then you can find the truth within them."

Mac swung his head like a hunted animal, his back coming up against the unrelenting tree behind him. "And what *will* I find?" His breath came heavy and ragged, his throat fighting the dryness within.

The Cree watched him, nodding, "Yes, the legends say when man has his back firmly up against a wall, only then will he willingly consider that maybe, just maybe, there is a different way of thinking, feeling and doing things. Only then, when he is charged with enough emotion, will he start fighting for what he believes in and what he longs for."

"Which is?" Mac wanted it all. Now!

"A desire for change, away from the power and control and destruction; a deep wish for peace; an intense search for abundance in all four levels of his life and most of all, a growing desire for the spirit knowledge, the wisdom that will help him reclaim his individual power and lead the impeccable life of a balanced, spirit warrior. The Thunderbirds, the Dragon spirits, will return to help him."

Mac shook his head, his mouth thin and unyielding. "Ye're lost in ideals, not reality!"

"The dragons were destroyed because they *knew* man was a magical being, able to both *create* and destroy—part of his true role within the greater universe. To know the dragons is to accept the immense power we have. But the power is so great; it can only be used with love! And man is not ready yet!"

Mac continued shaking his head, "Ye have gone way over the edge with this one my friend. Never can I follow ye there."

Broken Arrow nodded in quiet acceptance. "So I will go and you will stay." When Mac opened his mouth, B.A. quickly continued, "I am Thunderbird spirit and I will follow my soul's truth. Have you not wondered why we met? And why we spent so much time learning from each other?"

Mac spread his hands in confusion. "Tis the way all friends get to know one another."

B.A. shook his head in and sighed with exasperation, "Our paths joined for our own growth! What will you do with what I have taught you? I honour you as a special gift from Creator. Will you go on in your life and teach our ways to the whites you would meet? Will you teach them, as I have done with you, the lessons that will one day save their souls?

Mac's eyes slowly filled with tears he refused to blink away as he stared into his friend's eyes. "How can I do that? How? It took me so many months to learn from you, to understand what your words meant, from all the levels that you spoke in. How can I in turn teach such hidden meanings to others who have no concept, no dream or vision to begin with?"

B.A. smiled slowly, "You are Wolf. You are teacher. Your wolf Powakan know the teachings of Mother Earth wisdom. Your memories of your heritage recognize the truth in mine. The lessons were always there in your mind, in your memories passed down from your ancestors. This land and Mud Woman awakened them and they became yours, once again, just as she became part of you. In your dreams, she will lead you further and further into the blue mists of truth. You can never go backwards, my friend. That too, is truth. All humans have these memories within. They only need awakening. Your job is to trigger them in others; their Powakan will do the rest. Then they can experience what they really are. Their souls already know the answers they need to hear. And when it is time, they will go out to meet the returning Thunderbird and dragon spirits, speaking with them in their dreams and visions. This is the future, when all races, all creeds, all relations will unite once again. The Creator wished for this, he designed it in his great Plan of Destiny. And it will take seven generations for man to remember all that he is. It already begins; Mud Woman already prepares the land and plants the seeds."

Broken Arrow thought of the bright flash of feathers he saw behind Mud Woman in Nagual. Yes, he was not alone in his visions. Many others would see what he had seen and would also plant seeds for the seven generations yet to come. Giving the pioneer woman his eagle feather now made perfect sense—she too would plant seeds for her children and those yet to come. The Plan moved on, as it was meant, as it was designed. He need go no further here.

B.A.'s mouth tightened, "We quarrel, my friend, because we are too different; our people teach such opposing views. Now I see why it will take many generations of uniting the races before we will truly understand one another. And my heart cries out to the people's pain in their confusion and their judgements based on so little truth. I cannot stay to watch, I choose to go beyond. I have walked the warrior path for the last time.

"When it comes again, it will be a very different path. The strength, honour and courage of the warrior, his drive, his energy and his passion will be mixed with Her wisdom, the spirit of Her powers of Creation and inner knowing. The warrior of tomorrow will be content with the full range of all that he is. He will feel comfortable enough within himself to listen to her, his feminine half and love all she brings to his life: endurance, compassion, along with the strength to destroy lies and create truth. He will live and be all: the emotions of the heart, the drive of the body, the power of the mind and the spirit of Mud Woman. He will hear her in the wind, in the inner knowing of his soul again at last. And he will be free to be himself, no longer chained by the granite thoughts of convention and judgement, but in full flight awe and magical wonder of all he can be: his gifts developed and shared with the world's growth.

"And the warrior women will be the same—Both All—containing the masculine power of energetic drive, wisdom, protector and truth blended and balanced with the feminine ability to receive and share, her intuition, her creativity, compassion and nourishment. These new warriors will be filled with Earth Mother's wisdom, unashamed, undaunted, understanding and celebrating all sides, both sacred and unholy—Both All—experiencing and enjoying the possibilities and abilities of the feminine and masculine combined. This far generation of warriors will *live* the flight to freedom's passage.

"When women stand in the truth of whom they are, their loving presence allows their men to do the same. They will blend their voices together, in the care, protection and development of this Earth.

"Mud Woman's voice will join with theirs, bringing harmony after the chaos. The feminine will return and rule with the masculine in peace, joy and awe of the miracle of each moment of life and its continual creation. It is too powerful to be denied any longer, too needed after the full extent of human suffering yet to come. Endurance will be something we all require.

"She will come. It is written in the wind and only the women will hear her at first. She will come to restore what has been missing far too long on this earth: Her wisdom; soft, full blown ecstasy of passion; pride; energy; power and truth. Each person will become a whole bodied, whole minded, whole-hearted, whole spirited soul, all sides developing simultaneously, all growing in the moment to moment existence of life, all appreciated, created, energized by Her, the Creation of all. Every person will be accountable for each choice he or she makes. The feminine half must return. And she will. It is needed and full met.

"But not yet, not in this changing world. I have seen enough so I choose to return to Spirit World. Perhaps there, I may do more good, provide more guidance to people than I ever could here in this land. I cannot stay to watch it destruct. The pain in my soul is too great to bear and it will not change anything. My sorrow is too deep. My heart lies broken with my people's pain still to come. Never think I can stay." Broken Arrow's face twisted with grief and distress.

Mac leapt to his feet, his fists clenching once again. "I canno' let ye leave! Don't do this! I could no' live with yer death on my conscience. As yer friend, do not be asking it of me!" His face twisted with horror and distress.

B.A.'s dark eyes sparked once more, "You have travelled with me long enough to understand much more than most Whites will ever know. And from you, I have learned all I want to know about the White Man. I honour you as a special gift from Creator.

"If you want a reason to accept my choice, then go on in your life and teach our ways to the whites you would meet. Teach them, as I have done with you, the lessons that will one day save their souls. I cannot do it. They will not listen to a red man who looks too foreign, too frightening and too different for them to reach out to. So go my Anam Cara and do not look back. You need no forgiveness from me who has loved you like a brother, a very special brother. And I thank you for your presence in my life.

"I give you Brownfoot, who will carry you easily across this land." He held out the reins of his paint, already packed for travel. "The Creator wished for this, he designed it in his great Plan of Destiny. My elders say it always takes seven generations to heal rifts between people."

"And how many years is one generation." Mac wanted him to keep talking, his mind still reeling.

B.A. grinned, "With our busy people, about twenty to twenty-five years."

Mac calculated it easily, "So if this is 1863, then you say it will be one hundred years into the future plus the 40 odd years of the seventh generation prophecy . . . ." His eyes widened, "It will be the new millennium, the twenty first century."

B.A. closed his eyes and nodded peacefully, "And so it is written in the stars already. The prophecy tells first of the return of the elders, wise and gentle people, born as babies with all their spirit powers and memories intact, to bring unity and peace to this land. They will be called the Crystal Children, knowing about the Crystal Cave and what it holds. They will be born in legendary numbers when the White Buffalo Calf is born, marking the future Time of Woman."

He grinned openly, "Maybe then we will both come back and be friends once again! Maybe next time we will be women warriors." He laughed outright at the horror on his friend's face.

"I canno' do it!! Mac roared. "Who will believe this? You have so much wisdom to share with those who need it." Mac wanted to fall on his knees and beg. Only his pride kept him upright. He had begged this man to stay with him once before. He would not do so again though his breath grew ragged with suppressed pain.

B.A. remained unmoving. "I have brought you within a day's ride of Fort Edmonton." He pointed with his lips to the heavily rutted tracks nearby. "You can follow the cart trails easily."

Mac grew desperate. "We never finished our twistin'! Ye can no' go without squaring it between us."

B.A. leapt to the back of Blackfoot. "It will never be a contest. You are right handed. I am left." Looking down, he sadly contemplated his friend, "Even our strengths lie on opposing sides."

"Off hand?" Mac bellowed, "Ye wrestled me off hand and I still could no' take ye?!" His mouth dropped open in disgust.

B.A flashed a white-toothed grin, "With a little help from my Powakan."

Mac growled and threw his hands in the air. Helplessly, he stared at the determined set of B.A.'s shoulders and realized there was nothing he could say or do to stop him. Aye, and according to the damned badach, he had no right to do so anyway! Gritting his teeth, he walked to Blackfoot's side. His throat closed, his chest filled, smothering his breath. He blinked in fury at the tears filling his eyes and held out his hand to his friend, his best friend in the entire world. As they met, so would they part: a circle completed. "*Slan agat,* tis Gaelic for 'final farewell'. But I will no' stand and watch you do this! I leave!"

B.A. nodded and clasped the outstretched hand without shaking it. "There is no word in our Cree language for good-bye. We believe we will always meet again, if not here, then in the Spirit World. Go now. And do not look back." He spun his trusted paint towards the cliffs along the river.

Mouth rigid and tight, Mac tied Brownfoot's hackamore to his own packhorse, climbed to his saddle and rode away, his back stiff, his jaw rock hard, determined to never look back. Some distance away, in spite of himself, in spite of his friend's request, he turned, his face wet and twisted with grief.

The image burned in his mind for the rest of his life, part of the endless story he would tell to all who would listen even those who scorned him for it.

Broken Arrow sat on his paint above the red and grey granite cliffs of the North Saskatchewan, a warrior at the end of his trail. Far below him, the river flowed on in silent splendour through magnificently treed gullies and warmly rounded grassy hilltops. Broken Arrow's head bowed, his back bent in sadness, his shoulders slumped, laden with the weight of seven generations yet to come. Blackfoot bowed his head too, his tail drifting gently through the warm winds wrapping them.

A loud crack of thunder rent the air and lightening blasted down upon the pair, surrounding them in golden light, flashing around them in jagged, ragged shards until their faces and bodies shone white and warm, until the bolt pierced their bodies and lit their skeletons from the inside out.

Fhhoom!! Thunder boomed again and death touched their faces with macabre shadows.

Lightening exploded, brightening, whitening their images, restoring them to full-fleshed, spiritual glory, bathing their bodies in soft golden light. In the aftermath of the flash, the pair rode west, between the rocks and out into space. Through the wind and smoke, Mac saw B.A. smile, looking stronger, more powerful in spirit than he ever had in physical life. For a brief moment rider and horse remained outlined in blue spirit mists then both vanished into the wind.

Tears slid down Mac's face, his body vibrating in the aftershock of what he witnessed. Through his stunned mind drifted an ancient druid poem. A long time later, he would remember its name:

The Mathnawi

I died as a mineral and became a plant,
I died as a plant and rose to animal.
I died as an animal and I was man.
Why should I fear death?
When was I ever less by dying?
Yet once more I shall die as man
To soar in the Blessed Realm but
Even from the Godhead
I must pass on . . . .

Author's Notes

Native Elders say Canada is sacred, a land reserved for peace. No blood should be shed between the races on this Clean Land, their *Canata*. To the Aboriginal leaders, signing treaty meant an agreement to share the land, as part of their prophecy. They knew the four races had much to learn and share, and many generations would pass before people discovered the wisdom waiting for them amongst the Aboriginal people. The Elders knew this and they kept the faith.

Sexual abuse in the residential schools of Canada was a legacy of hundreds of years of similar abuse in European orphanages and halls of learning. It took the Aboriginal people of North America to stop it and teach the wounded how to heal. It truly is a long road back to Spirit, back to the fundamental belief in the missing feminine counterpart of the Creator. Today, Elders say, "The Time of Woman is here. The White Buffalo Calf has been born." Miracle, the first of several white buffalo calves, was born in Wisconsin, USA, at the beginning of the millennium. And her father died soon afterwards—also part of the prophecy handed down through generations of Elders. Perhaps it symbolizes the death of the unbalanced masculine power.

Also prophesied, Thunderbird spirits and dragons of the Powakan will return. Indeed, many people are now seeing them in their dreams. People from all four races are intermarrying, creating the prophesied Rainbow Clan which will blend all races and the wisdom carried to Canada by their ancestors, quietly building a bridge for all nations to walk together, side by side. As Canadians and Aboriginals, we offer the lessons of peace, kindness, gentleness, and hope—the ingredients for true harmony on our Mother Earth. I see this happening with our troupes' peace keeping missions in the Middle East, teaching once again, the respect for the feminine. Love is the only antidote to fear and every person should have the freedom to choose a good life for themselves.

In 1999, I attended a 100 year celebration of the signing of Treaty Eight between the Aboriginal people and the government of Canada. This agreement encompasses Northern British Columbia plus most of Alberta and Saskatchewan—one of the largest treaties ever signed in Canada. As I sat and listened to a Cree Elder speak about the above prophecy, I was stunned to find myself in a dream-like vision, watching hundreds of massive thunderbirds drop from the sky and fly over the bandstand where the old man spoke. Their wingspans covered the entire grandstand. Elders say they cloak themselves in black for protection, only showing their true colours in sacred ceremonies.

Later, I wrote this poem:

Thunderbirds
By
Esther Supernault

Flashing light and thunderous reply,
They're coming cloaked in black,
They're singing and rejoicing, calling out to the bold,
Returning truth and justice to this sacred land of old.
Yes, the thunderbirds are coming to this land.

They're flying down in legions from on high,
blasting out the drumbeat created from a sigh.
They're marking off the dreamers of their kindred spirit clan.
In clamouring calls of promise, they make their presence known
For the thunderbirds are coming to this land.

By the honour that they keep, from a love the world will reap,
they gather wounded children and elders who still weep,
whose broken, beaten souls are scarred so very deep.
Yes the thunderbirds are coming, on wings from on high.
Bringing the gift of healing, God's answer to our cry.

From the shadows that once filled us,
from the fear that almost killed us,
they will heal this wounded earth
as they dance upon her hearth.
For the thunderbirds are coming to this land.

We will dance again together, a nation strong and free.
Together we stand on guard for She and He.
And we'll sing our songs from a kindred soul's decree.
Yes! We hear them drumming, hear their wing beats on the sand
For the thunderbirds . . . are coming to this land!

· ·

When my book was finally finished, my Irish grandfather returned in
another dream. He wrapped me in his arms and we waltzed together
in celebration and perfect harmony.

ABOUT THE AUTHOR

Esther (Sewell) Supernault loves Canadian history because she lived it. Her parents were the last of the pioneers in northern British Columbia (near Mile '0' of the Alaska Highway). Esther recalls sleeping in log cabins, racing horses bareback; riding wagons and snow cutters; splitting wood for heat: taking meals to her father's big threshing crews and getting her education in a three-room schoolhouse. She grew up on Irish music played by the Sewell family band which her grandfather led with his fiddle.

Esther started out as a bookkeeper, became a nurse in her twenties and then completed her Bachelor's Degree in psychology in her forties. Married for over forty years (fun-filled for her—according to him), Esther and her Cree Metis husband, Cliff, have two children and five grandchildren.

They live on a sunny hillside acreage in the middle of Alberta, Canada.